BENEATH THE FALLEN CITY

THE OMNI TOWERS SERIES BOOK 1

JAMIE A. WATERS

Beneath the Fallen City © 2018 by Jamie A. Waters

Cover Art by Deranged Doctor Designs
Editor: Beyond DEF Lit

ISBN: 978-0-9996647-0-4 (Paperback Edition)
ISBN: 978-0-9996647-4-2 (eBook Edition)

Library of Congress Control Number: 2018906545
Second Edition *September 2018

THE OMNI TOWERS SERIES

Beneath the Fallen City

Beneath the Fallen City
Shadow of the Coalition
Tremors of the Past
Drop of Hope
Flames of Redemption
Spirit of the Towers

AUTHOR'S NOTE

The original story of *Beneath the Fallen City* was published in 2014 under the title *The Two Towers*. Like many authors, every time I read the book over (and I read it many times), I recognized places where rewriting would make it better. After several years, the publisher finally allowed the rights to revert back to me, and at that point I decided to revise the book. What you hold in your hand is the satisfying result.

CHAPTER ONE

KAYLA KNEW she was in trouble the moment her foot touched the ground. Feeling the floor give way beneath her boots, she tucked in her arms, forcing her body to relax in order to minimize the impact. She crashed through the floor, bringing building debris with her. Landing hard on a lower level of the ruins with a loud *thump*, a cloud of dust obscured her vision.

A rough voice sounded from the earpiece attached to her helmet. "What the hell's going on down there? I'll kick your ass if you damaged any artifacts."

Kayla shifted slightly. Thankfully, this level appeared stable. She moved her limbs to gauge the extent of her injuries. *Nothing broken, just my pride.* She'd have plenty of bruises tomorrow, and she was sure she'd never hear the end of it.

"Floor collapse in Sector Twelve. I'm fine, Leo. Thanks for asking." She rolled her eyes at his lack of concern.

There was a moment of static before the angry voice came back over the frequency. "You're supposed to be in Sector Four. Sector Twelve is still being mapped."

Kayla recognized her spotter's calmer tone when he interrupted Leo's impending tirade. "Leo, this is Veridian. We detected Carl's team on another frequency. It sounded like they were headed toward Sector Four. We thought it best to avoid them."

"Dammit," Leo swore. "They weren't supposed to be back in that area for another few days. We're working off bad information. Get out of that hole and get your asses back to camp. I don't have time for this shit."

"Understood," Veridian replied. "Kayla, are you secure?"

She grimaced and glanced around the room, her helmet light shining through the dust as it settled. "Not yet. Let me get into position. You'll need to lower the cable and harness about five meters." Kayla paused, and then added, "I hope you've got some hydrating packs. I'm parched."

She flipped open her wristband and switched channels on her commlink. Trusting Veridian would remember the code phrase indicating she wanted to speak with him on an unmonitored channel, she said, "Tell Leo the gear is jammed. I need at least ten minutes. If Carl's crew is working this area again, I don't know when we'll be able to come back. Let me see what I can scavenge."

Veridian huffed in exasperation, but he agreed. "Try to make it five, Kayla. Your vitals are out of sync, and Leo's monitoring from camp. He sounds pissed."

"That's nothing new," Kayla muttered and switched back to the main channel before flipping her wristband unit closed. She rolled over and got into a crawling position, wincing from the pain. Once she was confident the floor would support her, she stood and took a better look around the room.

The abandoned apartment building was several hundred years old. Neglect and the elements had taken their toll. Faded wallpaper peeled from the walls, and a thick layer of dust coated the floor. Most of the furniture had either been scavenged or had rotted over the years. It was easy to get disoriented in the ruins with the sloping floors, partially collapsed walls, and extensive structural damage. One of the tricks she'd learned over the years was to reconcile the current scene with the echoes of the past.

Kayla closed her eyes for a moment and visualized the way the room used to be. In her mind, she saw a large bedroom with an ornate bed against the wall in front of her. A low bookcase sat on the far wall with two overstuffed chairs. A strange painting hung over the bookcase and seemed to beckon her. On the opposite side of the room was a dresser with a large mirror where she imagined a woman modeling a silly-looking hat.

She shook her head to clear the realistic image from her mind. *Keep it together, Kayla. It's only your imagination.* Even so, she trusted her instincts. Veridian often joked that the ruins spoke to her. In a sense, she guessed it was true. Her instincts never let her down.

Moving across the room, she focused on the dilapidated painting hanging over the bookcase. The painting was unsalvageable, rotted and covered with mildew. Something about it had drawn her attention though. Kayla pulled the painting off the wall and set it on the floor.

With gloved hands, she ran her fingers over the surface vacated by the painting and bit back a grin as she felt a niche in the wall. Pulling open the false wall, she stared at an old metal safe. It was tempting and probably faster to force it open or even pull it out of its resting place, but there was no way she'd risk damaging the structural elements further. The whole building was little better than a death trap. Fortunately, she'd been trained by one of the best.

Kayla opened her backpack and withdrew a long, wand-like instrument that also doubled as a handheld drill. With her other hand, she pressed her frequency detector against the door to the safe. Drilling a small hole, she then jimmied the cylinder inside the locking mechanism. Watching the detector's display, she moved the wand until she heard a click. Tucking the tools back into her toolkit, she opened the door.

Ignoring the worthless stocks, bonds, and other papers piled in the safe, she pulled out a small box tucked in the back.

Kayla flipped open the lid of the box. A ruby necklace and a pair of earrings, along with several other valuable pieces of jewelry, winked at her under the light from her helmet. Not bad. On occasion, she'd found weapons or ammunition. Those that could be salvaged were more usable to her camp, but jewelry could be traded for other supplies.

She stuffed the box into her backpack before turning back to the safe. Rifling through the papers, Kayla discovered a small cloth pouch. She opened it and shook the contents out into her gloved palm.

A small green sculpture of a strange-looking creature with a long snout and a pair of wings sat in the palm of her hand. It was slightly larger than the length of her thumb, carved from a mineral she didn't recognize. She shook her head in resignation. *You people should have paid more attention to survival rather than collecting stupid trinkets.*

Veridian spoke over her headset again, an undertone of urgency in his voice. "Kayla, time's up. We've got company. I've got three bikes incoming on the radar. They've got trader camp signatures. ETA is about three minutes. Get up here now."

"Dammit," Kayla swore as she unscrewed the false bottom of her frequency detector. She'd never make it to the surface in time, but she wasn't about to walk away empty-handed either. She pushed the small carving inside, snatched the jewelry box from her backpack, and dumped out the contents. Shoving most of the jewelry inside the secret compartment, she closed the opening. She unzipped her jacket and stuffed the ruby necklace into her shirt before tossing the empty box in a pile of debris in the corner.

Kayla zipped up her jacket and made her way back to where she had crashed through the floor. Climbing into the harness, she hit the indicator button to let Veridian know she was secure. "Ready, V. Pull me up."

The engine came to life, and the cable harness slowly lifted her out of the ruins, giving her a chance to evaluate the depth of the building. Kayla had been scavenging several levels down, and she suspected there were at least a few more levels below her. *Something big is down here. I can feel it.*

A hand reached out to help her the moment she passed through the roof of the building. She gripped the offered hand and pulled herself the rest of the way out of the ruins. When she saw the owner of the hand and realized it wasn't Veridian, she yanked hers back as if burned.

"You lousy, blood-sucking, rat-dicked bastard," she spat as she pulled off her helmet. Tossing back her dark hair, she glared at the man standing in front of her. Veridian was standing a short distance away, and he shrugged as though to say there wasn't much he could do. She should have come up to the surface sooner.

"Ah, Kayla, still as charming as ever," Carl replied, his voice smooth. "We intercepted your transmission earlier. I'm sure you can imagine my surprise when I heard you and Veridian were in Sector Twelve. I thought it might be a good idea to take a short trip to see what you've been up to."

Kayla scowled at the man. Easily over six feet in height, he towered over her much shorter frame. If she had to guess, she'd estimate his age to be several years older than her, maybe somewhere in his mid-twenties. His shoulders were broad, and his muscles were well defined in tribute to the time he spent navigating the ruins. His long, dark hair was pulled back into a ponytail and accentuated his incredible face. Dark, penetrating brown eyes focused on her, and his lips twitched into a teasing smirk.

Like Kayla, he wore the special UV-protective pants and jacket to shield himself from the harsh sun. The world had changed since the last war, and the environmental conditions were deadly without several protective measures. Even now, they stood under a portable UV guard that encompassed the area where Kayla and Veridian had been scavenging.

As good-looking as he was, Carl was a pain in the ass. It didn't help that she'd mistakenly thought he was a ruin rat when they first met. Of course, he hadn't been in a hurry to clear up the misconception either. If Kayla had clubbed him over the head with her wrench instead of flirting with him, she would have saved herself months of irritation. Instead, he kept showing up at different scavenging sites as an unwelcome reminder of their first meeting. Never mind that he seemed to get an almost perverse pleasure at cutting into their earnings. *Yeah, if he weren't so damn pretty, I would have clocked him months ago.*

The thought was still tempting. Determination in her movements, Kayla dropped her pack on the ground and unhooked the harness. She might not have her wrench handy, but her fists would do well enough. When she yanked off her gloves and started to take a step toward him, Veridian made a small, pained noise. His look of warning stopped her in her tracks.

She pursed her lips and let out a long exhale. Okay, so maybe wiping the smug expression off the trader's face wasn't the best way to handle the situation. As though sensing her thoughts, Veridian gave her a slight nod of approval before packing up the metal cabling and the rest of the equipment. In an effort to calm herself, Kayla reached for a hydrating pack and took a long drink before turning back to the uninvited guests.

As usual, Carl wasn't alone. He had brought two of his lackeys with him, Cruncher and Elyot. Cruncher was a short, stocky character with a knack for electronics. Kayla had admired his skill on more than one occasion when he'd dropped off deliveries to their camp. He was a former ruin rat himself, which was why she'd thought Carl had been the same. She never believed a trader would sully himself enough to visit a ruin rat camp.

Elyot was fairly new to Carl's crew, and she didn't know much about him. He had sandy-blond hair and a wiry build, leading her to believe he was one of Carl's scavengers. It didn't matter. She didn't have much interest in traders or their crews. They were a necessary evil. Nothing more.

Kayla wiped her mouth with the back of her hand. "Nothing better to do than listen in on other people's conversations?"

Carl smiled. "I have to protect my interests, don't I? You two are scavenging in a claimed sector."

"You must be mistaken. We came here to tour some ruins and see the sights."

"I see."

He gestured to Cruncher, and the large man picked up Kayla's discarded pack. He pulled out her frequency detector and other tools, giving them a cursory glance before putting them aside. Cruncher shook his head to indicate it was empty. "It's only her equipment, Boss."

"Like I said," Kayla said sweetly, "we were touring the ruins."

Carl raised an eyebrow. "With a frequency detector and hand drill? Take off the jacket, Kayla."

Veridian, normally serene in comparison to Kayla's more fiery nature, stood up. His long, light-brown hair fell in disarray around his face. He stood a foot taller than Kayla but met Carl's eyes evenly.

Kayla often thought Veridian had been born during the wrong century. He seemed to lack the ruthlessness and cunning necessary for survival during these harsh times. But there was no questioning his loyalty or the sense of protectiveness he felt for Kayla. They'd been raised together, and Kayla would do almost anything for him. As far as she was concerned, she could be manipulative and deceitful enough for both of them.

"That's not necessary, Carl," Veridian said, jumping to her defense. "We'll get out of your sector. Just leave her alone."

"Stay out of this, V," Kayla warned. Veridian frowned at her but didn't raise any further objections. She didn't want him getting involved in any altercation with Carl. Confident she'd receive more leeway if she played him right, Kayla shrugged out of her jacket and tossed it to Cruncher.

He grabbed it with one hand and began searching her pockets. She turned back to Carl, who was gazing at her with new appreciation.

Her short red tank top left her midsection bare. Dark, UV-protective pants hung low on her waist and clung to her curves.

"Jacket's clean, Boss," Cruncher informed him.

Kayla put her hands on her hips. "Are we done now?"

Carl grinned slyly and walked over to her. He wrapped one of his arms around her waist and pulled her against him. Kayla gasped in surprise.

Veridian made a lunge for Carl, but Cruncher grabbed him and held him back.

Carl leaned down and whispered into Kayla's ear, "You can either hand over what you've taken, or I can go searching for it. The second would suit me fine."

With a look of disgust, she pushed against his chest. He

grinned and took a step back as she reached into her shirt to pull out the necklace. She tossed it to him. "Take it. It's not worth having your hands on me."

Carl caught the necklace and held it up to admire it. "I'm impressed, Kayla. You were down there for how long? Twenty minutes?"

"Twelve," she retorted, crossing her arms over her chest.

He lowered the necklace and rubbed his chin in thought. "I have a proposition."

"Forget it," Veridian interrupted. "We're not interested in anything you have to offer."

Carl ignored Veridian and kept his focus solely on Kayla. He held out the necklace to her. "You gave this up way too easily. I doubt this was all you took. But I'll allow you to keep this and whatever else you smuggled out today as a gesture of goodwill. In exchange, I want a small favor."

Kayla considered him. Between the necklace, the rest of the jewelry, and the carving, she estimated Leo could probably bring in around two thousand credits. That amount would pay the camp expenses for at least a week and she'd have enough left over to finish fixing their auxiliary cooling system. It was tempting, but her past experiences with traders had taught her to be wary. "What favor?"

"I want a few hours of your time, Kayla. Nothing more. Come to my base tomorrow."

Her eyes narrowed. "Why?"

"Because your talents are wasted on Leo," Carl said. "He doesn't have the resources or connections we do. Why waste your time as a ruin rat when there are other possibilities? Let me show you our operation. You can meet some of the crew."

"So she can scavenge for you, Carl?" Veridian asked coolly. "You traders are all the same. You'll screw over anyone and everything so long as it benefits your bottom line. Kayla's part of our family. She can't be bought."

Carl spared the briefest glance at Veridian. "I appreciate the fact that your *friend* is trying to look out for you. Feel free to bring him along if it makes you more comfortable. It's just a few hours of your time, and who knows? We might surprise you. I'm not asking for a commitment, only a chance to show you what we're about."

Kayla weighed her limited options. They were outnumbered and outgunned. If she refused and Carl found the jewelry, there was no telling how he'd react. It would be far too easy for her and Veridian to take an "accidental" dive into the ruins without a harness. The other alternative would be to give up the items and walk away empty-handed.

It was a possibility, but she'd already burned up a lot of Leo's remaining goodwill. If she returned to camp without anything to sell, it wasn't just her and Veridian who would suffer. The camp only had another two or three days of food supplies left. She had no choice. Leaning forward, she took the offered necklace. "Done. I'll stop by tomorrow. Send the coordinates to my commlink."

Veridian's mouth formed a thin line, but he remained silent. Kayla didn't miss the disapproving look on his face before he turned away to finish packing up their equipment. She quelled her initial impulse to reassure him she knew what she was doing. Instead, she focused on keeping her head in the game as long as Carl and his crew were still around. Traders would pounce on any sign of weakness.

Cruncher winked at Kayla as he handed her jacket back to her. "Notorious ruin rat considering going legit?"

She gave him a smug smile as she slipped her jacket on and stuffed the necklace into her pocket. "Hardly. But I've never been one to turn a blind eye to a profitable deal. A few hours of my time to get the grand tour and I keep my loot. It's not my problem if your boss has a brain that fits in a gnat's ass and still has room to rattle."

Carl raised his eyebrows while Cruncher let out a loud laugh. "How much are you walking away with, Kayla?"

Kayla smiled cryptically. "I don't know what you're talking about. But I believe we might have some items we need to get prices on. I'll see about bringing them with me tomorrow. Oh, and stay off our channels, Carl," she warned as she recalled his earlier mention of intercepting their transmission. "Or you may end up hearing things you don't like. I'd hate for your delicate trader ears to be forever scarred."

Carl chuckled. "I doubt there's much you could say that I haven't heard before."

"You might be surprised," Kayla muttered. She picked up her helmet and walked over to her speeder. The other men followed her example and mounted their bikes.

Veridian hit the button to disengage the UV guard attached to his bike. A loud beep signaled the one-minute warning. Kayla put on her helmet and activated her bike.

Carl and his crew waited on their speeders, making it clear they didn't trust her and Veridian to leave the scavenge site without their presence. She couldn't help but smile at their lack of trust. It went both ways. Veridian held up his hand to let her know he was ready.

With a nod, she threw the bike into gear and took off over the desolate landscape. The war that had occurred over one hundred and fifty years ago had left much of the world a wasteland. Ruined buildings crumbled over onto themselves. Once lush areas had become barren.

Biological, chemical, and nuclear weapons had taken their toll, and a large portion of the planet was rendered uninhabitable. People lived differently in some places, either in areas less hard-hit or locked up in shelters that had been outfitted in preparation for the attacks.

Twin white towers stood in the distance, a constant reminder of the changes. A company called OmniLab had built them before the war. Kayla wasn't sure how they'd managed to stay intact when much of the surrounding area was a wasteland. All she knew was based on what little information they'd found over the years and stories told by other ruin rats. Even the traders were tight-lipped when it came to the towers. Supposedly, entry into the fully self-sustaining towers had been permitted to several thousand individuals who met specific criteria, but if the rumors were true, the price tag for entry had been steep.

But even those self-sustaining towers had their weaknesses. The inhabitants craved the lost memorabilia that had once been commonplace in their society. These relics were considered luxury items, and people like Carl were appointed by OmniLab to obtain artifacts from the ruins. In exchange for the items, traders provided necessary equipment, food, and other supplies critical for survival outside of the towers. If it weren't for this bartering system, Kayla wasn't sure how long her camp could continue to exist. Everything on her person right now—from her commlink to her clothing—was purchased with the artifacts they'd scavenged in the ruins.

The Omnis, as they were called, had little to do with the outsiders. Carl and a few others were the only ones permitted to trade directly with the elusive Omnis. This trading relationship granted them exclusive rights to certain ruined areas. Only once the traders abandoned an area were the ruin rats permitted to scavenge and sell any additional findings to the traders. If a ruin rat scavenged in an area actively controlled by an Omni trader, the trader could essentially blacklist them from selling their findings. More than one ruin rat camp had disbanded or died out from being blacklisted. The threat of blacklisting was every ruin rat's bogeyman.

Leo and other ruin rats had tried to approach the Omnis directly over the years, but they refused to acknowledge them. As a result, the ruin rat camps were forced to work with an intermediary, usually Carl or another trader named Henkel. These traders usually took a cut off the top for negotiating with the Omnis, which could be significant depending on the item.

Leo was going to be furious when he found out about the incident with Carl. He was already ticked off that they'd been in a different sector, but Kayla knew he'd fly through the roof when he found out Carl had caught them.

Needing a distraction, she shifted into a higher gear and felt a slight thrill as the bike tore across the landscape. Veridian's voice came over her headset. "Are you trying to kill us? Slow it down a bit before you fry another solar cell."

With a disappointed sigh, she downshifted. Veridian was right. Her bike was going to need another overhaul soon. The tires were both growing worn, and a few of the solar cells weren't working as well. Besides, they were approaching their base and she didn't need to set Leo off any more than she already had.

As they pulled up, Kayla slowed the speeder until it came to a stop. She shut off the engine and went over to Veridian's bike to help him unload the gear. They carried the equipment into the temporary base they'd set up a few weeks earlier.

Their lifestyle required them to move around periodically to locate new areas to scavenge. Usually, they stayed in a place for several months or even a year before they needed to move. The farther they were able to travel, the more they were able to scavenge without interference from the OmniLab traders, but they wouldn't be able to trade for supplies as often. It was a delicate balance.

Kayla pulled off her helmet as Leo approached them. He was a tall, thin, balding man in his early forties and had been leading the camp for the past ten years. He was cantankerous, and his mouth seemed to be permanently fixed in a frown. The years hadn't been kind to him, but Kayla supposed he hadn't been kind to them either. He wasn't a bad man. They just had different styles, and Kayla preferred her independence.

"Where the hell do you two get off scavenging in an unmapped sector? If you know Carl's crew is headed to the planned sector, you pull out and contact me. You don't just decide to do whatever the hell you want."

She shrugged off her jacket, reminding herself Leo's tirade was only temporary. Once he got a good look at their daily take, he'd be salivating. "Maybe you should wait to see what we found before jumping down our throats."

Veridian put down a box of equipment with more force than necessary.

"You mean, what Carl let us keep," he reminded her.

Kayla elbowed Veridian in the ribs, earning her a grunt in response. Leo looked back and forth between them. "What do you mean? Did something happen with Carl?"

She didn't bother to reply. Instead, she pulled out her frequency detector, unscrewed the base, and dumped the contents onto a nearby table. Leo's eyes widened at the sight of the jewelry and the carving.

"Mmmm," he murmured as he examined some of the pieces more closely. "These are excellent."

Pleased with his praise, she pulled the ruby necklace from her pocket and put it on the table with the rest of the jewelry. Leo frowned when he realized she had kept that piece separate from the stash.

"Why the diversion piece? What happened?"

She waved a dismissive hand. "Carl showed up. But the situation was handled."

"Handled how? Dammit, we can't afford any problems with him."

Veridian folded his arms across his chest. "He's trying to recruit her. She agreed to meet him at his base tomorrow to hear his offer in exchange for keeping what she scavenged today."

Leo's eyes narrowed on her.

"What's the harm?" Kayla asked with a shrug, feigning nonchalance. "I go, pretend to listen, nod my head at the right times, and leave. I think we ended up ahead in this arrangement."

Leo threw up his hands. "What's the harm? Everything! Kayla, you know how these traders work. They'll screw over every single one of us to get what they want. We're trash to them. I don't like it, and I don't trust him."

"I don't either, but I already agreed to meet with him. Do you want me to break a deal with a trader?" Kayla gestured toward the back of the camp. "The auxiliary cooler is shot and needs to be repaired. If our main one goes down, we're in trouble. Our food supply is low, and Mack said one of the computers crapped out again. You're down one scavenger already from Johnny's accident last week. We need the credits and you know it."

"Fine," Leo relented with a scowl. "At least take Veridian with you. Hopefully, he can keep you out of trouble."

"That'll be a first," Veridian muttered, staring up at the ceiling as though seeking divine intervention.

Kayla gave him a playful shove. "I was planning on taking V anyway. But this visit isn't anything to worry about. I can handle Carl. I'm more concerned he's somehow managed to put a sniffer on our communication system."

Leo scratched his head. "I thought you said your comms were clean."

"Mine are," Kayla insisted. "I can't say the same for yours though. He keeps showing up in places he shouldn't. No one's luck is that good. I'm heading to the tech room now to run a scan."

Leo grunted an affirmative answer and turned back to

fully inventory the items Kayla had scavenged. She smiled inwardly at his eagerness. *One crisis averted.* Motioning to Veridian, the two of them headed back toward the tech room.

The tech room was a small room filled with computers, both working and non-working. Machines disassembled for parts were pushed up against the walls. Kayla pulled up a crate to use as a makeshift chair and took a seat in front of the communication system's interface.

Veridian stood over her shoulder while she started the system scan. "Kristin ran a scan yesterday after she adjusted the antenna on the roof. She didn't notice anything unusual."

Kayla didn't look away from the data flashing on the screen in front of her. "She would have only checked the transmission range for our commlinks and done some basic maintenance. She probably wouldn't have thought to look for a sniffer."

Veridian leaned forward to study the screen. "How could Carl have gotten one on this system? We have it locked down pretty tight. He would have had to manually install something."

"I'm not sure," she admitted, tapping in a few commands. A new set of data appeared on the screen. She scrolled through it, trying to find anything out of the ordinary.

"Wait a second!" Kayla grabbed Veridian's arm and pulled him down next to her. "Here we go. Gotcha, you bastard. Sneaky son of a bitch."

"You found something?"

Kayla nodded, drumming her fingers on the side console. "I think so. Some of these readings don't add up. I may have to rethink my earlier assessment of him. The guy is an absolute genius, or he's got geniuses working with him."

She pointed at the screen. "Check it out. You were right. This couldn't have been done remotely. We would have picked up on it otherwise. That jerk managed to get one of his crew close enough to our physical system to install this. From the look of it, he's been monitoring Leo's comm system for weeks. I'm betting they did it during one of their deliveries. No wonder Cruncher's been so helpful lately."

Veridian swore. "Can you remove it from here?"

"I don't think I want to remove it," she said with a wicked smile. "I think we should leave it alone, with one little exception. I'm going to reroute the sniffer to link with another file."

Veridian cocked his head. "What file?"

Kayla's eyes glinted mischievously. "If they want to eavesdrop on our comms, we'll give them something to listen to. Remember that clip we snagged last week of Leo singing?"

Veridian laughed and bumped fists with her. "Brilliant. If that doesn't get them to stop listening to our comms, there's not much hope."

She grinned and fell silent for a few minutes while she finished redirecting the file. It was a start, but they needed to be more proactive. Kayla turned back to him. "I have another idea, if you're up for it."

He eyed her warily and ran his hand through his hair, a nervous trait he seemed to use when he was worried. "Uh oh. I know that look. This isn't going to be good, is it?"

"I want to turn his idea back on him," Kayla began. "If we put together a bug or two to plant in Carl's base tomorrow, we could get a jump on him and know which areas to avoid."

Veridian frowned. "That's pretty risky. You got lucky today, but it won't go well if he catches us."

"Then we won't get caught," she declared, standing up to sort through some of the boxes of old equipment. "I think we have what we need to put something together. I'll need your help though. You're better at building devices than me."

Veridian hesitated for a moment, as though debating whether she would go through with it even if he refused. He finally shrugged in resignation. "Fine, I'll help. But planting a bug in his base is going to be difficult. He'll probably suspect something like this."

"Don't worry about that. I'll make sure Carl will be watching me most of the time. He doesn't trust me. I doubt he'll be expecting you to do anything though. You've got that wholesome, innocent thing going on," she explained, pulling out an old circuit board and inspecting it for damage. "I'll distract him while you plant a bug near his communications room. If I get a chance, I'll plant another one in his office. Even if we only get one planted, that's better than nothing."

Veridian picked up the soldering gun and magnification goggles. He pulled the goggles over his eyes and took the circuit board from her. "I hope you know what you're doing."

Kayla grinned. "What's life without a little excitement?"

CHAPTER TWO

THE COORDINATE NAVIGATION system flashed on Kayla's bike monitor to indicate they were nearing their destination. She let Veridian know of their approach through her headset and slowed down.

Carl's facility was substantially larger than the largest ruin rat camp. It was also a permanent fixture, built with specially treated building materials designed to withstand the climate's effects. More than half a dozen bikes were parked at the front overhang. Kayla had a moment of speeder-envy, eyeing the bike closest to her. Both its wheels had the new bionic skin to automatically adapt its traction based on the traveling surface. Even the mounted solar cells were shiny, polished to a gleam and sparkling in the sunlight.

She wrinkled her nose and patted her bike affectionately. Sure, the other speeders were more than a little pretty, but they probably couldn't keep up with her retrofitted transport. Hell, who was she kidding? She was tempted to steal those tires on her way out the door. With a sigh, Kayla disengaged her engine and climbed off, careful not to damage any of the scavenged items stored in her backpack.

Veridian pulled up beside her, hesitating before dismounting. He'd been upset about this visit, even going so far as to suggest they consider canceling. It had taken her a while to bring him around, but he still wasn't fully on board. Hoping to lighten the mood, she gestured to the size of the base.

"Think he's compensating for something?"

Veridian groaned and shook his head. "Kayla, that's awful."

Pleased she had cut through some of his nervousness, she grinned and stepped through the UV guard at the front entry. The sight of Carl and Cruncher waiting made it obvious Carl's crew had been tracking them since they approached the facility. Unsurprised, Kayla pulled off her helmet and jacket and hung them on the rack by the entry. Veridian followed her lead.

"Glad you decided to join us," Carl said, extending his hand in greeting.

"Yeah, yeah," Veridian muttered but took the proffered hand.

Kayla stepped forward, placing her hands on her hips. "Let's get this moving. I'm a busy girl. Business first, or the tour?"

Carl's mouth curved into a slight smile. "And that's one of the many things I like about you. You get right to it. Let's go to my office. You can show me what you've brought to sell."

"Suit yourself," she replied and followed Carl down a long hallway. She noticed Cruncher followed a few steps behind her and Veridian, careful to make sure they didn't stray. She'd have to find an opportune moment to distract them so Veridian could plant the bug. The other bug rested in her pocket. Although it was smaller than her fingernail, her awareness of it made it feel more like a large speeder.

Electronic dividers with the capability of blocking out light and sound surrounded Carl's office. The costly technology gave the occupants a large measure of privacy. Despite herself, Kayla was impressed with the extravagance and interested to see what other gadgets they had in their camp.

Carl stepped over to his desk and waited while she opened her backpack. She spread out the jewelry and carving on the desk.

Cruncher let out a low whistle. "Holy shit, girl. Did you smuggle all of that out of Sector Twelve yesterday?"

She sat on the corner of the desk and feigned innocence. "I don't know what you're talking about, Cruncher. These trinkets have been in my family for generations. I told you I was just taking in the sights yesterday."

Carl gave Kayla a hard look before turning to assess the merchandise. He studied each piece carefully before moving on to the next one.

"I may have underestimated you," Carl admitted. He pointed to the collection. "I'll give you twenty-five hundred for the lot. That's a final offer. There's no negotiation on this one."

"Done." Kayla smiled sweetly. "I wouldn't dream of trying to take advantage of your generosity."

"Hmm." Carl turned on his commlink and initiated the instructions to wire the credits to her camp's account. When the transaction was complete, he scooped up the jewelry and put it in a lockbox behind his desk.

Kayla verified the transaction was final and hopped off the desk. At least something positive had come out of this trip. "Are we still on for the tour? Or have I worn out my welcome?"

Carl's mouth twitched as though he were suppressing a smile. "You're not getting out of here so easily. You just cost me a few thousand credits, and I intend to make sure you hold up your end of the deal."

He pressed his hand against the small of her back to lead

her out of the office. She stiffened slightly at the gesture but allowed the contact. Veridian frowned at her but remained silent when she shook her head. There was a fine line to walk when dealing with a trader. So far, Carl had kept his word. She'd give him some leeway, at least to a point. Besides, there were far worse things than having a gorgeous man's hands on her.

As they exited the room, Kayla caught a glimpse of Cruncher still trailing behind them. Planting the bugs was going to be more than a little challenging if they kept watching this closely. Carl escorted them into a large, open room they used as a common area. A dozen chairs surrounded an elongated, conference-style table. Cabinets covered most of one wall with an expansive countertop. A state-of-the-art food preparation and storage machine sat in the corner.

Two people turned toward them when they entered. She recognized Elyot from yesterday, but the young woman was unfamiliar.

"Kayla and Veridian," Carl began, introducing them to the new people. "This is Elyot and Lisia. He's one of our scavengers, and Lisia's one of our crew techs."

Elyot smiled warmly. "Nice to see you guys again. I've heard quite a few stories about you, Kayla. You've impressed the hell out of some of us."

Lisia, a tall, thin girl with a mass of blond curls on top of her head, looked at Carl and Kayla with open hostility. "I've got stuff to do," she announced, pushing away from the table. "I'll catch you later, Elyot."

Without another glance, she headed out of the room. Surprised by the rude departure, Kayla peeked up at Carl for an explanation. His jaw was set, and he stared at the door where the young woman had disappeared. Elyot cleared his throat and offered weakly, "Uh, Lisia's somewhat temperamental. Ignore her."

"She's a good tech, but Elyot's right," Carl elaborated on an exhale, rubbing the back of his neck. "She'll warm up once you get to know her."

Kayla shrugged. She wasn't there to make friends or get caught up in camp drama. Leo's camp had more than enough to keep her busy. Carl continued the tour by saying, "Through here we have the crew's quarters and the tech room."

The crew's quarters consisted of a large room separated into individual personal areas with modular constructs. Each personal area had a cot, a small desk, and a storage locker. It was different than the setup at Leo's camp, where the bunks were sandwiched together in an open room.

Kayla ran her fingers along the wall, admiring the privacy dividers installed in this area. They were reinforced to block out sounds and light from the outside, although someone could always leave the door open if they weren't in the mood for privacy. She wondered what it would be like to have a place of her own, where she could shut out the world. The only place she ever felt a few moments of peace was down in the ruins. If nothing else, she had to give Carl credit for providing his people with some rather expensive comforts.

They moved to the tech room next. Carl paused outside the door, an expectant look on his face. "I think you'll enjoy this room."

Puzzled, Kayla moved past him and stepped inside. Realization dawned, and her eyes grew wide in excitement as she stared at the equipment Carl had recently acquired from OmniLab.

"No fucking way." Forgetting her plan to act nonchalant, she moved across the room to pick up one of the underground sensors designed to identify rare metals. She ran her fingers across it with reverence, recalling what she'd read about it. Not only was it one of the prototypes unavailable to ruin rats but it was also capable of locating specific rare metals housed within other metals. It had the potential to detect artifacts hidden miles below the surface.

She looked up at Carl in disbelief. A knowing smile flitted across his face. "I picked it up a few days ago. There are some other prototypes in there too. OmniLab developed a new chemical monitoring kit and some other UV-protective gear. We were asked to test it out."

"Oh man. I read about these, but to actually see them..." Her voice trailed off as she rifled through some of the other equipment, incredulous at the playground of toys around her. Veridian crossed the room to study some monitors mapping the topography of the area.

"This is amazing." He gestured to the monitors. "You're able to track all of this from here?"

Carl nodded and pointed to one of the screens. "That's the IM-XL system. It uses our current geographical location to generate some basic topographic maps of the underground ruins. It uses the old-world maps as a basis for comparison and updates to provide new potential high-artifact ruin locations."

Veridian whistled in appreciation and watched the screen. Kayla barely spared them a glance, clutching the sensor in one hand and digging through some of the other boxes with the other. It'd be interesting to find out how difficult it would be to smuggle the sensor out of Carl's camp.

Carl cleared his throat to get Kayla's attention. "If you can manage to put the sensor down, we picked up some new lock-cracking tools too. I've got Zane trying them out in the testing lab. I've heard you have an interest in locks. You're welcome to take a look."

Kayla jerked her head up, trying to decide if the man was serious or toying with her emotions. It would be an evil prank if it were the latter. "Really?"

Carl chuckled and nodded. It broke her heart a little, but

she carefully replaced the sensor. Trailing her fingers over it in farewell, she gave it one last, longing look. "You've definitely got some cool toys in here."

There was no mistaking the pleased look on his face at the compliment. Motioning for them to follow, Carl led them past what appeared to be the communications room and into the testing lab. Remembering their purpose, Kayla shot a meaningful look at Veridian. He returned a barely discernible nod.

The testing lab was only slightly smaller than the tech room and had a wide variety of different locking mechanisms set up like an obstacle course. Kayla recognized most of them from her scavenging expeditions.

There were two men in the room. One had rich caramel-colored skin with short, dark hair and eyes. He lounged against the wall and flashed a smile when they entered. Kayla had met him several months earlier when he'd helped Cruncher make a delivery to Leo's camp.

Kayla didn't know the other man sitting on the floor working with one of the locks. He possessed an average build and fair skin. His blond hair was pulled back in a ponytail, and he seemed to work the locks with an intimate familiarity Kayla recognized.

Carl cleared his throat, and the man on the floor looked up expectantly. "Xantham and Zane, I'd like you to meet Kayla and Veridian. Xantham is in communications, and Zane is another one of our scavengers and master locksmith."

Kayla narrowed her eyes at Xantham. If he was a communications expert, he was likely the one responsible for planting the sniffer on their system.

As though guessing her thoughts, Xantham winked at her. "We've already met, Carl. Besides, I feel like we're already intimately acquainted, given how often you've asked me to intercept her communications."

Kayla crossed her arms and gave Carl a dark look. He offered her a sly smile in response. "I protect my interests, Kayla. You've caused a significant dent in my revenue over the past year."

"Ah, sad but true," Xantham lamented.

Zane stood and wiped his hands on his pants before offering his hand to Kayla in greeting. "Nice to meet you. I've heard a lot about you. Cruncher says you've got a knack for locks?"

Kayla shrugged, deciding the change in subject was a welcome one. It probably wasn't a great idea to keep reminding Carl she'd been stealing from under his nose for months. She studied the lock Zane abandoned. "I've been called more than fair. That's an 8600, right?"

Zane nodded. "Yeah. We brought it up a few days ago to let the others practice on it. It's one of the most difficult in the series. I figure if they can crack this one, they should be good on most of the others in the line."

"No one's been able to beat Zane's time yet. With the new equipment, he's running at one minute fifty-four seconds," Cruncher added.

"One minute forty-six seconds," Zane corrected proudly.

Kayla cocked her head and said casually, "Is that so? Well, how about a friendly wager? I'd be willing to give it a shot."

Zane looked interested. "Sure. How much are we talking?"

"A token. How about twenty credits?"

Zane nodded at the amount. Carl rubbed his chin and considered Kayla for a moment. "If you don't mind, I'll sweeten the pot. One hundred credits for the best time."

Surprise crossed Kayla's face, but she shrugged in response. It wasn't an exorbitant amount, but it wasn't chump change either. "Your money. V, would you mind grabbing my equipment for me?"

Veridian nodded and headed back out the way he came.

Carl studied Kayla carefully for a minute and then motioned for Cruncher to follow him. Kayla flashed a charming smile at Carl, inwardly cursing his intuitiveness. "I'm sure your equipment is nice, but for a hundred credits, I prefer to handle something I know can get me where I'm going."

Carl smirked. "There's no doubt in my mind my equipment can take you well and beyond where you want to go."

She arched a brow, scanning him up and down to assess his "equipment". He might be right, but she damn well wouldn't admit it. "We'll see about that."

When he grinned, she turned away to hide her smile and pretended to look over the equipment in the room. Veridian and Cruncher returned a few minutes later. Judging from Veridian's demeanor, Kayla knew he had planted the listening device. He handed her the equipment, and she walked over to the lock, confidence in each of her steps.

"Start the timer, boys, and I'll show you how it's done." Kayla knelt and placed her frequency detector on the safe. With practiced motions, she slid her lock-picking tool into the lock and easily worked through the combinations.

With a flourish, she pulled the handle and the door swung open.

"One minute fourteen seconds," Cruncher said in amazement.

Xantham chuckled in amusement while Zane stared at her in disbelief. "I've never seen anyone work a lock that fast."

Kayla sauntered over to Carl, holding out her hand and rubbing her fingers together. "I believe that's another hundred credits you owe me?"

"Apparently so." His eyes skimmed up and down the length of her body as though assessing and considering her in a new light. "If you'll join me in my office, I'll transfer the credits now." He turned to Zane. "I'll do your transfer as well. I believe you owe her twenty?"

Zane nodded sheepishly. "Mind if I take a look at your equipment, Kayla?"

She hesitated for a moment before handing her equipment to Zane. Motioning for Veridian to stay behind and retrieve the device when Zane had finished trying it out, she followed Carl back toward his office.

"Protective of your equipment, are you?"

"I like to keep my toys clean. Nasty things happen when they leave my sight."

"But you left them with Veridian," Carl pointed out.

"Yes, I did. They're safer with him than they are anywhere."

"You have that much trust in him?"

Kayla frowned, becoming uncomfortable with the personal direction of the conversation. "You ask a lot of questions, Carl. But, yeah, I do. Veridian is... I guess you could say he's like a brother to me."

"A brother then," Carl mused. He nodded as though that cleared up some question in his mind. "He mentioned family yesterday. Is that important to you?"

Kayla shrugged. "Only Veridian. Most other people are a waste of perfectly good oxygen."

"I see," he observed, stepping back into his office. Kayla hopped back on the edge of the desk and watched while Carl initiated the credit transfer. So far, the day was turning out to be more profitable than she'd expected. When the transfer was complete, she verified the transaction.

He put down his commlink and leaned across the desk to study her. "Now that we have that settled, I'd like to talk to you about the reason I asked you to come here."

Kayla tucked her hair behind her ear and cocked her head.

"Is this the part where you try to turn me into a legitimate scavenger?"

Carl smiled. "Something like that. You've met most of my crew, except for Jinx. She's out mapping some sectors right now. I asked the crew to stick around today so you could meet them. But we usually try to do two separate shifts. One group is on one day and the other on the next. It seems to work out well for us."

Kayla nodded. Most crews scavenged that way. She was scheduled to be back underground tomorrow.

"I know what most ruin rats think of us, but we're not bad people. In fact, the majority of trader crews are made up of former ruin rats."

"Yeah." Kayla blew out a breath. "Ruin rats who decided they'd rather sell themselves and live under OmniLab's thumb."

"It's not that bad, Kayla," Carl insisted. "The benefits far outweigh the negatives. I'm prepared to offer you a salary with an added percentage of whatever you scavenge. This percentage would be directly from an OmniLab trader with no negotiation fees attached. It would be far more than you've ever seen working with Leo."

"How much?" Kayla wasn't really interested but was trying to hurry the conversation along.

Carl walked around the desk to stand next to her. "Five hundred credits a month with a twenty percent bonus to whatever you bring in. I'll pay for all of your equipment and living expenses, and you can spend your credits on whatever you want. Send it back to Leo, for all I care. I want you, Kayla."

Kayla was momentarily taken aback. She hadn't been expecting such a generous offer. But either way, there was no way she'd accept the offer of a trader. The thought of working for OmniLab left a bitter taste in her mouth.

"No, thanks. I wouldn't ever leave Veridian."

Carl studied her for a long moment. "If you want him, you can have him too. He'll have a salary of two hundred fifty a month. No bonus, though, since he doesn't scavenge."

Kayla's eyes widened, her fingers gripping the edge of the desk to prevent her from falling off. She hadn't expected Carl to want both of them. Veridian was skilled, but he wasn't a scavenger. Most trader crews had plenty of techs, but there was a high demand for people who were actually willing to navigate the ruins. "Holy shit. Um, wow. Uh, I guess I'll think about it and get back to you."

"Of course," Carl said easily with a trace of a smile on his face. He tapped a few instructions into the keyboard on the desk and pulled up a contract. "I'd appreciate it if you could read through this. I've outlined the salary, bonus percentage, and other benefits. The contract is for a year. At the end of the year, we can renew it for the same terms or renegotiate. Veridian will have a separate contract."

Kayla sighed as she glanced at the lengthy document. "You want me to read through this now?"

At Carl's nod, her shoulders slumped in dejection. Resigned to her task, she pulled her hair into a ponytail to get it out of her face.

Carl froze, studying the side of her neck. "Is that from yesterday?"

"Huh? Is what from yesterday?"

"You've got a particularly nasty bruise back there." Carl frowned, his gaze fixed on her neck. She reached up to touch the area in question and winced when her fingers brushed against a painful bruise that crept up from her shirt.

"Yeah. Guess so," she said with a shrug. "It happens when you fall through the floor."

"I heard about that. I've got something that can help." He moved around the desk. "You should take a couple of days off to heal. Your muscles won't be relaxed, and you could injure yourself even more if you try scavenging too soon."

Kayla scoffed at his statement. "Some of us don't have the luxury to take days off. I'm amazed people aren't lining up at the door if you treat all recruits like this."

"Not all," Carl admitted and reached into a drawer to pull out a bottle of dark-colored liquid and two glasses. "Just the promising ones." He opened the bottle and poured a small amount into each glass.

She accepted the offered beverage, sniffed it apprehensively, and grimaced. "You want me to drink that?"

Carl didn't reply. Instead, he lifted his drink and took a long sip, savoring it before putting his glass back on the desk. Kayla looked at his beverage and then considered her own. It seemed harmless enough. Raising it to her lips, she took a drink, making a face at the unfamiliar taste. Her eyes watered from the burn in her throat.

"Hell's balls. What is that?"

He chuckled at her reaction. "It's an old-world drink OmniLab recreated called scotch. It helps relax the muscles."

"Hmm." She licked her lips. "It's not too bad once you get past the burn."

She reached over to confiscate the bottle, poured herself a slightly larger amount, and took another drink. This time, it went down a little easier. She examined the bottle while Carl watched her in amusement.

"Be careful," he warned. "It packs a hell of a punch, especially if you're not used to drinking it."

Carl reached into the desk drawer and pulled out a small tube of cream. Kayla recognized the OmniLab medicinal cream used to promote healing. It was extremely expensive and, in Kayla's experience, should only be used in dire emergencies.

He tried handing it to her, but she pushed it back toward

him with a look that clearly let him know she thought he was nuts. "It's a bruise, not a gaping wound."

"Use it. You ruin rats don't take care of yourselves and wait until someone's near death before trying to fix the problem. If you use it, you'll heal faster and it could help prevent further injury."

"If you say so," Kayla huffed. She put a tiny amount of cream on her finger and rubbed it half-heartedly on her neck before handing the tube back to him.

Carl sighed at her lackluster display. "Well, there's not much point if you're going to do it that way."

He flipped open the cap and squeezed a generous amount of the cream onto his fingers. When he touched her neck with the cream, she yelped.

"Hey! That's cold."

"Shh. Don't be such a baby."

She scowled but kept silent. Gentler than she thought he'd be, Carl massaged the cream into the back of her neck and shoulder. She relaxed against him and closed her eyes as his fingers caressed her skin.

He pulled his hands away far too soon and closed the cap on the cream. Kayla opened her eyes in disappointment and watched as he dropped it back into the drawer.

"That's much better. You looked like you were falling asleep. I can't let that happen when you've got important reading to do."

"Yeah, right," she grumbled and turned back to the detailed document. She was relatively quiet for several minutes while she skimmed the monotonous legalese, making occasional, colorful mutters about boring contracts. When she finished, Kayla pushed the tablet away and hopped off the desk. She pulled out her ponytail and shook out her hair.

"All done. Is that it?"

Carl nodded and crossed the desk to stand in front of her.

"For now." He looked down into her eyes, and a tingling feeling crept into the pit of her stomach.

Yep, I should have clocked him yesterday when I had the chance. He's too damn pretty for his own good.

"Ah, looks like I missed some," he added when he spotted a tiny bit of cream still on her shoulder. He ran his hand along her shoulder and gently massaged it into her skin.

Yeah, too damn pretty, and I'm a sucker—a sucker with a bug to plant. Kayla placed her hand on Carl's chest, curling her fingers into his shirt. With her other hand, she discreetly slipped the listening device out of her pocket and attached it to the underside of his desk.

Leaning closer to him, she closed her eyes and tilted her head back. That was all the invitation he needed.

Carl lowered his mouth to hers, capturing her lips with his. He tasted like the scotch—warm, spicy, and surprisingly soft.

Damn, the man can kiss. Might as well enjoy this.

He wrapped his arms around her and pulled her against him. This time, she didn't resist and pressed her body against his, winding her arms around his neck. Kayla let out a soft moan, and he deepened the kiss in response. His mouth moved against hers, nipping and teasing and she clutched him tighter, wanting more.

A loud beep interrupted them.

"Damn," he swore as he broke away from her.

She wasn't sure if she was talking about the kiss or the noise. Kayla blinked in confusion, trying to get her head around what happened. He pulled back slightly but didn't release her. Running his thumb along her swollen bottom lip, he gave her a long, heated look. Kayla swallowed and managed, "What was that?"

Carl smiled, looking amused and smug by her flustered

state. "It's probably Cruncher and Veridian. Your friend is probably worried about you."

"Oh, right." Kayla slipped out of his grasp, casually straightening her shirt. She glanced up to see Carl still watching her. She flushed and nodded toward the door to remind him about the visitors. He sighed in resignation and hit the button to open the door.

Cruncher and Veridian stepped inside. Veridian was grinning and held up Kayla's equipment. "Zane wasn't able to beat your time even using OmniLab's fancy equipment. I think he got frustrated and gave up. He wants to watch you again at some point."

Cruncher took a quick glance around the room, his eyes moving to the bottle of scotch on the desk and then settled on Carl's annoyed expression and Kayla's mussed hair. His mouth twitched in a grin.

"How goes the recruitment, Boss? Convince her to switch sides yet?"

Carl frowned, giving Cruncher a dark look. "It *was* progressing nicely. I think I covered most of the major points. Did you have any other questions, Kayla?"

She shook her head, shoving her hands in her back pockets. "Nope, I think you covered everything."

The door beeped again and slid open. Xantham stepped through the door and tsked at Kayla like she was a naughty child. She narrowed her eyes at him. He held up a small metal device no bigger than his thumb. "Hey, Boss, you know how you mentioned you wanted me to do a sweep to make sure Kayla and Veridian didn't accidentally leave anything behind? Well, I found this little bug in the comm room. It must have gotten away from them."

Xantham slid the listening device across the desk. Carl picked it up and examined it closely. He tossed it back down on the desk and looked at Kayla expectantly.

She looked down at the bug and then back up at Carl, giving him her best innocent look. "Gee. Looks like you've got bug problems here too. Nasty little things. You know, we had that same problem up until last night. Seems like there's something going around."

"Imagine that," Carl replied in a dry voice. He turned to Xantham. "Start scanning my office."

He leaned across the desk toward Kayla. "I can only guess what we're going to find in here too. Although, I can't say I didn't enjoy your little distraction."

Kayla bit down on her bottom lip, still feeling the effect of the kiss. With a small shrug, she said, "It's always nice to take pleasure in one's work."

He raised an eyebrow at her. "You're going to be more trouble than I expected, aren't you?"

Veridian snorted. "Leo tells her that all the time. You might want to reconsider whatever offer you made."

Carl gave Kayla a long, lingering look and then shook his head. "No, I don't think so. The offer still stands. I enjoy a challenge."

"Glad to hear it," she replied easily and winked at him. "I'll enjoy giving you one."

She took her equipment from Veridian and turned to look at Carl one last time before heading out. "Thanks again for the tour. It was enlightening. Good luck with your bug problem."

CHAPTER THREE

KAYLA WOKE up in a bad mood. Her commlink had somehow been turned off during the night, and she was running late. She'd stayed up too late last night trying to get the defunct computer terminal back up and running. Her brand of creative engineering wouldn't keep that piece of shit working for long. They would have to replace it soon. It was just one more thing that was going wrong. She'd planned to be down in the ruins first thing in the morning, and it was already approaching noon. On top of that, Veridian wasn't in camp. She didn't have a clue where he could be.

I have to go chase his ass down now too.

She hurriedly pulled on her jacket and yanked on her boots before throwing the backpack containing her tools over her shoulder. If she found him soon, they might still get some scavenging done before calling it a day. As she neared the exit, Leo came around the corner and stopped her.

"Where the hell do you think you're going?"

Kayla frowned, wondering what could have agitated Leo this early. He usually saved his tirades for the end of the day. Part of her wondered if he spent the whole day thinking up new colorful insults to try to best her in their verbal sparring matches. One of these days, she was going to retaliate by giving him a hug or maybe a kiss just to throw him off balance.

Glancing around, she half hoped someone else would show up so he could yell at them instead. When no one else magically appeared, she resigned herself to her fate.

Better to get it over with and get on with my day.

"I'm going back to Sector Twelve if I can find my damn spotter. My piece-of-shit commlink got shut off and I'm running late. I doubt Carl will expect us back there so soon after they caught us." She leaned closer to him and lowered her voice. "I've got a feeling about that sector, Leo. I'm never wrong about this. Something big is down there. I'm going back."

His eyes lit up greedily, but then he shook his head.

"No. You're above ground for the next several days until you fully heal from that fall. You're not to go into the ruins until I give the word."

Kayla stared at him blankly and laughed at his outrageous demand. *That's a new one.* With one of his scavengers injured and another ruin rat camp near their territory, there was no way he would keep her out of the ruins. They could barely make ends meet and keep the camp functioning.

She pulled her helmet off the rack. "Right, Leo. That's cute. Now leave me alone and let me do my damn job."

Leo grabbed the helmet out of her hands and said more forcefully, "Dammit, girl, I said no. Veridian's been temporarily assigned to another scavenger. You're above ground until I say so."

Kayla's eyes widened and then narrowed, her heart pounding in her chest. V was hers. How dare he reassign him and threaten to take away the one constant in her life? When everything seemed to crumble around her, Veridian had been the person to help keep everything together. She couldn't lose him.

Her nails dug into her palms, the pain a reminder that fear was a weakness, an exploitable emotion. She forced herself to push aside her panic and focus on her anger, unwilling to show Leo how much the thought of losing Veridian scared her. Instead, she reached for an emotion she could wield and lashed out, going on the offensive.

"Where the hell do you get off breaking up my team? Veridian is *my* damn partner. I'm perfectly fine to go underground. I've taken worse falls before and you've never given me shit about it. I'm not some precious artifact that can't handle a few scrapes and bumps."

"It's your own damn fault," Leo snapped. "You had to get involved in Carl's business, and now he's paying me to keep you above ground. He says you were hurt the other day and if I don't keep you off schedule until he says so, he's threatened to increase his cut in future trades. You stay up here for a week and I collect a thousand credits. You go below ground, I lose much more than that."

Kayla froze as his words registered. She'd kill that manipulative bastard. The idea of a trader trying to control her was anathema to her. Fury made her reckless, and she slammed her hand against the wall in frustration.

"If brains were explosive, yours couldn't make a ripple in a teaspoon full of piss," Kayla spat. "He's playing you, you idiot. He's trying to control your operation and push me into accepting his offer. That's what these traders do. Tell him you kept me above ground and collect your damn credits, but I'm going down."

Leo's face turned red at her words. Kayla knew she had overstepped herself, but she was too angry to care about the consequences.

"If you go, you're out!" he shouted. "Don't you dare drag

Veridian down with you either. Just two days ago, Carl had our comm system bugged. He's got the resources to find out if you drop below. I cross him and we're out of the game, Kayla. You've already screwed up two trade relationships for me. As good as you are, even *you* aren't worth this. I've got a dozen other people who need to eat."

Kayla snatched her helmet from him. She couldn't stay, not like this. Her emotions were clambering inside her, and she was close to her breaking point. "Fine. If you don't have the balls to handle this, I will. I'll deal with Carl myself."

She yanked on her helmet and headed to her bike, ignoring Leo's shouting behind her. Flipping on the engine, she backed up quickly, spraying dirt against the wall. He'd be pissed, but she didn't care. She was furious and needed to let off some steam.

Throwing the bike into full gear, Kayla sped toward Carl's camp. The landscape flew past her as she pushed the bike forward.

There's no way in hell I'm going to let that insufferable, pompous ass coerce me into doing anything.

Kayla made the trip in record time and shut down the bike's engine before climbing off. The ride had done little to cool her temper. When she recognized Carl's speeder leaning against the wall, she kicked at it. Keep her above ground, will he?

Cruncher cut her off at the entrance, curtailing any attempt at storming the fortress. He scratched his head, looking puzzled by her appearance. "Hey, Kayla, I thought it was you. I don't think Carl's expecting you today. Did you decide to sign up after all?"

Kayla yanked off her helmet and tossed it on the ground. Fury lit her eyes. "Get your worthless, slimy, piece-of-shit boss out here so I can see how far my boot'll go up his ass."

Cruncher stared at Kayla, taken aback by her temper.

"Uh, I guess that's a no. I sent him a message when I saw you on the radar, but he's on a commlink call right now."

"Do I look like I give a shit? Get him out here by the count of ten, or I'll find him myself and it won't be pretty."

Cruncher held up his hand and began, "Kayla, I'm sure he'll—"

"*One...*" Kayla narrowed her eyes. "*Two...*"

"Uh, I'll go check and see if he's done." Cruncher turned to go find Carl.

"That's not necessary," Carl spoke from behind him. "I finished my call."

Carl walked toward the entrance, his brown eyes warming when he saw Kayla. He wore a loose, green shirt and a dark pair of UV pants. He looked as though he had just returned from being in the field, which pissed Kayla off even more. If he was determined to keep her above ground, he had no business going into the ruins himself.

She strode over to him, clenched her fist, and took a swing. Her fist connected squarely with his jaw. Shock flashed across his face as he stepped back, his expression now wary.

"Where the hell do you get off meddling in my affairs? You had no right to pay off Leo to keep me above ground."

Cruncher's eyes widened at her declaration. His jaw dropped, and he gaped at Carl. "Oh shit, Boss. You didn't, did you?"

Carl gingerly rubbed his jaw but kept his expression neutral except for a slight tightening around his eyes. "If you'd like to discuss this, Kayla, maybe we could do so privately in my office?"

"Fine," she snarled and stormed off down the hall toward his office.

"That woman packs a hell of a punch," Carl muttered behind her.

Still fuming, she leaned against his desk and crossed her

arms over her chest. She glared at Carl when he entered and closed the door, calmly engaging the privacy fields behind him. Kayla wasn't sure if she should be impressed with his cool façade or kick him in the shins to get more of a reaction out of him. She shouldn't be the only one who was having a shitty day.

"I'm sure I probably deserved the punch back there, but I'm hoping you'll give me a chance to explain."

He took her stony silence as consent and began. "I contacted Leo out of concern for your welfare and suggested you take a few days off to fully recover. He said he couldn't afford to have one of his best scavengers lying around for a few days. I simply offered to cover the costs associated with that."

"Bullshit," she accused, pushing away from the desk. "Leo said you were going to cut into future trades if he didn't agree."

"Ahhh, well, yes, I might have indicated something to that effect." He gave her a sheepish look and held out his hands in a placating gesture. "Leo, as well as yourself, can be difficult sometimes. You're both stubborn, and I had to be a little firm with my request."

Kayla put her hands on her hips. "You have absolutely no right to make any such requests. Call it off. *Now*."

Now it was Carl's turn to be stubborn. "Forget it. I view you as a potential asset and a pain in my ass. Either way, it benefits me exponentially to have you above ground for the next several days. If you come to work for me, I need you healthy. If you decide not to join me, a few days out of the ruins will only help my bottom line."

"You're nothing but a scum-sucking, OmniLab bootlicker who couldn't hack it in the pits. I'll be damned if I'm going to let you control whether or not I go underground."

"Watch it, Kayla," Carl warned, his eyes hardening. "You

can only throw insults at me for so long before you cross the line."

Kayla moved to stand directly in front of him, challenging him with her eyes. "You don't intimidate me, Carl. You may have your crew and the rest of the ruin rats wrapped around your little finger, but I won't be one of them."

Carl held her gaze for a long moment. Suddenly, he grabbed her and yanked her to him. He lowered his head to hers, almost punishing her with his lips. His kiss wasn't gentle but was entirely consuming.

If this was what it felt like to be plundered, she would gladly surrender. His tongue invaded her mouth, questing and demanding a response. Kayla whimpered, and her body melted against his. Unable to resist him, she returned his kiss with equal fervor.

She vaguely registered his hands moving to unzip her jacket and tug it off. When he began kissing and teasing the sensitive areas of her neck and shoulder, she could barely think beyond the sensations she was feeling.

Kayla purred in his ear and nipped at his neck as he lifted her and put her on the edge of the desk. She wrapped her legs around him, pulling him close to her. Her fingers worked their way down his muscular chest and up under his shirt to touch his bare skin.

Carl groaned in response. Pressing his lips against her throat, he inhaled deeply and murmured her name as his lips reclaimed her mouth. "You're driving me crazy."

His words brought her back to reality. Kayla broke the kiss and stared up at him. "What the hell am I doing? I'm a complete idiot." She pushed him away. "Okay, stop. If you keep putting your hands on me and kissing me, I'm going to forget why I came here."

"From my point of view, that wouldn't be a bad thing," he said huskily and pulled her closer to nuzzle her neck.

Kayla shook her head, trying to clear it, and pushed him away firmly this time. "Get back. I can't think straight when you're close. You're too damn pretty." She slipped off the desk and out of his grasp.

Carl stared at her and then burst into laughter. "Pretty? I don't think I've ever been called that before. I'm not sure men qualify as pretty."

"Yeah, well, you're not seeing yourself from where I'm standing." She shoved her hands in her pockets and took another step away from him. If she stayed any closer, she'd be all over him again.

"And you're absolutely breathtaking."

Her stomach fluttered as he gazed at her, desire clearly etched on his face. Her eyes widened. "Oh man, V's gonna kill me. A freaking OmniLab trader. What the hell am I thinking? I'm beyond stupid. I've gotta get out of here." She grabbed her jacket and headed for the door.

Carl caught her hand and stopped her. "Kayla, wait. What will it take to get you to join my crew?"

She turned to peer up at him. "I'm not joining your crew, Carl. What happened just now has nothing to do with your offer."

His mouth twisted into a teasing grin. "Should I scan for another listening device?"

She gave him an exasperated look. "Oh, like you wouldn't suspect that. Give me some credit, will you? I was just returning the favor. But no, I'm not joining your crew. It's not that part of me isn't tempted. But this life? For me? Not in a million years."

"Why not?"

Something in his voice made her pause, and she turned to study him. He seemed to be sincere in not understanding why she would reject his offer. "Do you really not get it? You're an OmniLab trader. From what I've seen, all you traders seem to do is try to run our lives. We're constantly held under your thumb and have to tiptoe around you. If we piss off the great trader, we're screwed. Our lives mean nothing to you. I mean, look at what you did earlier today. You threatened Leo, took away my freedom, and split up my team. Now you think I should join you? So I can give you and OmniLab more control over me?"

Carl blew out a long breath and released her hand. "I see." He lowered his gaze for a moment and rubbed the back of his neck. When he looked up, she saw the frustration and disappointment in his eyes. It wasn't what she expected from a trader, and she wasn't sure what to think about it.

"It's obvious you have some pretty strong feelings about the matter. But not all traders are the same, Kayla. I'm not sure what you've been told or what you've experienced, but each of us has different styles. I try to guide my crew, but I wouldn't say I control them. I trust them and rely on them."

It was a nice story, but everything she'd experienced led her to believe otherwise. Kayla knew firsthand how cruel and manipulative traders could be in their dealings with ruin rats. Even though he seemed to be more trustworthy than others, it might be a ploy to manipulate her further. She wasn't willing to take that leap of faith.

"I find that hard to believe. Your actions earlier were classic trader. Do you handle all your crew members the way you handled me? Do you decide you know best and order them around?"

Carl sighed. "No, I don't. But then again, most of my team is much more sensible and cautious than you seem to be. From everything I've seen over the past several months and from what I've heard, you consistently push the limits. You're talented, Kayla. You're probably the best scavenger I've ever seen, but you're also the most reckless." When she didn't reply, he took a step toward her. "I don't want to control you.

I respect your talent. I just don't want to see your potential go to waste either from recklessness or an idiot like Leo who doesn't know how to utilize your skills."

Kayla glared at him and crossed her arms over her chest. "Leo may have napped on the wrong side of the ion shield a few too many times, but he doesn't try to control me. He may yell, scream, and threaten, but up until today, he's always let me go my own way. You changed that, and it pissed me off."

She wasn't sure what Carl saw in her expression, but his eyes softened. He was silent for a long moment as though choosing his next words carefully.

"You're right. I admit it wasn't the best approach. I didn't understand how important your independence is to you."

His admission surprised her. Just when she was convinced he would react in a certain way, he would do or say something unexpected. She bit her lip, unsure how to handle this situation. The man kept throwing her off balance. The intense chemistry between them didn't help matters either.

As though sensing her turmoil, he took her hand in his again. "Kayla, I want you on my crew. I'll try to give you the freedom you seem to want. I can offer you things and opportunities you'd never experience as a ruin rat. If you decide this isn't the life for you, you can always leave. You have nothing to lose."

Kayla shook her head and pulled her hand away. It was too much—his touch, him, the whole OmniLab trader thing. "I can't. Look, I appreciate the offer, but I won't ever join a trader's crew."

A loud beep at the door interrupted them. Carl cursed and pressed the button to open the door.

Veridian entered the room, panic on his face when he saw Kayla and Carl together. He looked anxiously back and forth between them. "I came as fast as I could. Are you okay?"

Carl raised an eyebrow. "She's fine. Why wouldn't she be?"

Veridian shook his head. "Not her. *You*. Leo called me and told me Kayla was pissed off and headed here. I was worried she was going to come over here and try to kick your ass."

"One punch is hardly an ass kicking," Carl admitted.

Veridian's eyes flew open. Whirling around to face Kayla, he threw up his hands in exasperation. "Are you crazy, Kayla? You hit him? You hit a trader?"

Kayla gave a small shrug. "I didn't get to finish a full ass kicking. Give me a few more minutes and I'll see what I can do."

Cruncher stuck his head through the open door. "Sorry to interrupt, Boss. Ramiro and Vex just pulled up. You want me to bring them in here?"

Kayla jerked her head up to look at Carl. "Uh, would that be Trader Ramiro and his trusty sidekick?"

Surprise crossed Carl's face. "You've met them?"

"Oh, shit," Veridian swore, running his hands through his hair in agitation.

"What is it?"

Kayla shifted uncomfortably, not liking the turn of events. "Yeah, Ramiro and I go way back, and not in a good way. So, if you've got a back door, it might be a good idea to show us to it."

"Oh?" Carl leaned against the desk, waiting for an explanation.

"Shit, shit, shit." Veridian paced the floor. He spun around and pointed at Kayla. "Dammit, Kayla, this is what happens when we get involved with traders."

Kayla gave Veridian an annoyed look and then turned to Carl. "Ramiro and I had a misunderstanding about a year ago."

Veridian shook his head. "It was a lot more than a misunderstanding."

"Keep them in the entrance for a minute, Cruncher," Carl

instructed. The moment Cruncher disappeared, he turned back to Kayla, "You'd better tell me fast."

Kayla crossed her arms over her chest. "It was his own damn fault. I found that data cube. That pig-headed sack of shit stole it from me, so I stole it back."

Veridian nodded, his shoulders slumping. "Not to mention she slapped him down in front of his crew when he made a pass at her. By the time he realized it was missing, she had already sold it to Warig."

Carl gaped at Kayla. "The Aurelia Data Cube? That was you?"

"Well, you don't see anyone else claiming credit for it," she retorted, annoyed that he seemed surprised. "Besides, don't you traders talk to each other?"

Carl took a deep breath. "Yes, but Ramiro was pretty tight-lipped about that one. Cruncher heard about it from some of Ramiro's crew. It's a low blow to a trader when an artifact like that disappears. They lose a lot of respect. He tried to keep it quiet as best he could."

Carl's commlink beeped, and he glanced at it. "Cruncher just met them at the entrance." He pointed to Kayla. "Stay here. You're a potential recruit, and I'm going to resolve this one way or another."

Veridian gaped at Carl. "You're crazy if you think Ramiro's going to listen to anything you say when it comes to her."

"He's right. I tend to piss Ramiro off simply by existing. I appreciate the gesture, but you might want to show us a back door."

Carl headed for the door, ending the discussion. "Forget it. You're staying here. I'll take care of this."

Kayla grimaced and leaned against the corner of the desk, trying to mentally prepare for the inevitable showdown. She caught Veridian's worried look and tried to give him a reassuring smile. There wasn't much she could do to extricate the two of them from the situation. They'd have to roll with it.

She heard the voices in the hall and recognized Ramiro and his right-hand man, Vex. In Kayla's opinion, they were both creeps.

The door slid open, and Carl and Ramiro entered, followed by Cruncher and Vex. A look of confusion crossed Ramiro's face when he saw Kayla standing in Carl's office.

Ramiro stood a few inches shorter than Carl but was considerably wider. He wasn't overweight, but simply massive. His dark hair was cropped extremely close to his head, and his arms were covered with intricate tattoos. He reminded her of some pictures she'd seen of tanks from the pre-war era, both in stature and personality.

Vex was a bit taller and thinner than Ramiro, but his brown hair was slicked back away from his face, rather than cut short. His dark eyes narrowed dangerously when he saw Kayla. Neither one of them had much love for her.

"Heya, Ramiro," she said cheerfully, giving him a little finger wave. "It's been a while, hasn't it?"

"You little whore," Ramiro sneered, his face twisted in rage.

Before anyone could react, he leapt across the room, grabbed Kayla's arm, and yanked her off the desk.

"Get your slimy, ass-grabbing hands off me!" she shrieked and kicked him. He backhanded her across the face.

Pain lanced through her cheek as she stumbled backward, falling to the ground. Carl and Veridian both tackled Ramiro and wrestled with him. Cruncher grabbed Vex and held him back.

Kayla scrambled to her feet and rubbed her throbbing cheek. Veridian and Carl both managed to subdue a raging Ramiro. He glared at her with venomous hatred. She considered blowing him a kiss to piss him off more but then decided that might be akin to suicide.

Carl gripped Ramiro's arm and said, "We'll let you go if you can keep your hands off her."

Ramiro pulled away from Carl and Veridian. "Why are you protecting this little bitch, Carl? If you think you can trust her, you're a fool."

"She's a potential recruit."

"Bullshit," Ramiro declared. "She's screwing with you."

Carl pulled up her contract on his monitor and pushed it toward Ramiro. "I've already made her an offer. See for yourself."

Ramiro stared at the screen and his eyes narrowed. "She hasn't accepted, and this doesn't change anything. She owes me. I intend to collect."

"I don't owe you a thing. The Aurelia Data Cube was mine!"

"You stole it from my sector," he snarled.

"Your crew cleared those tunnels!" she shouted, clenching her fists. "If they can't figure out their asses are on fire with a flashlight and three-way mirror, that's not my problem."

"Wait a second," Carl interrupted. "You cleared the tunnels, Ramiro?"

Ramiro crossed his arms. "You're a trader, Carl. You understand how things work. Maybe my crew had already finished in that sector, but that was *my* sector. I offered her a generous finder's fee for the data cube. She refused and then walked into my base and stole it."

"You lying sack of shit," Kayla spat. "Your 'generous offer' was five hundred credits and me flat on my back while you tried to figure out how to pilot my speeder."

Carl's eyes narrowed. "Is that true, Ramiro? If you said those tunnels were clear, you know she was damn well within her rights. As painful as it may have been, the data cube was hers."

Ramiro turned to Carl in disgust. "You would take her side over another trader? She's nothing but a piece of ass."

Carl's face hardened. Understanding crossed Ramiro's face.

"Ahh, I see now," he sneered. "You're hoping to get a piece of her. So how much are you offering to pay her?"

Carl's fist shot out, and he punched the man square in the face. There was an audible crunch, and blood gushed from Ramiro's nose.

"You bastard! You'll pay for that!" Ramiro yelled, grasping at his nose.

"Get the hell out of my camp," Carl growled.

Cruncher pushed Vex toward the door and yelled for Xantham and Zane, who appeared a moment later. Along with Veridian, the four men forcibly escorted Ramiro and Vex out of the camp.

As soon as they were gone, Carl turned to look at Kayla. She gaped at him, incredulous that he had defended her against another trader. The side of her face was beginning to swell, but it was insignificant compared to the emotions coursing through her. She swallowed, deciding it might be best to make light of the situation.

"Well, shit, Carl."

"What?"

"I wanted to be the one to hit him."

Carl stared at her for a moment. He shook his head in disbelief and laughed. "Are you okay? It looked like he hit you pretty hard."

"He hits like a girl," she replied, gesturing to her swollen cheek.

"As I recall from earlier, some girls can hit pretty hard."

Kayla considered that for a minute and then admitted, "Well, I guess he hits like a pissed-off girl, then."

He chuckled and reached out to touch her cheek. Although his touch was gentle, she winced. "You need an ice pack on that cheek. Come with me and we'll get you fixed up."

"Do I get more of that scotch?"

"Against my better judgment, but sure," he agreed, grabbing the bottle from the drawer. He took her hand and led her out to the common room. Plopping herself down in one of the seats, she poured herself a glass of the liquor while Carl put together an ice pack for her.

Elyot came into the room followed by a tall, fair-skinned, willowy redhead with hazel eyes. The girl's gaze swept over everyone before settling on Kayla. "We heard the commotion. What's going on?"

Carl handed Kayla the ice pack and introduced her to Jinx, a former ruin rat. "We had an incident with Ramiro."

Jinx sat next to Kayla, studying her cheek. "Wow, the bastard hit you? I knew I never liked that guy." Kayla pressed the ice against her cheek and winced. That made two of them.

Kayla looked up at the sound of excited voices to see Xantham, Cruncher, Zane, and Veridian enter the room.

Xantham walked over to inspect her cheek. "Holy shit balls! What the hell happened?"

Cruncher shook his head and stared at Kayla in amazement. "Unbelievable. You were the one who stole the Aurelia Data Cube?"

Xantham's eyes grew huge. "No freaking way! That was *you*?"

Kayla looked around in exasperation, lowering the ice pack from her cheek. "I don't know why everyone seems to have a hard time believing that. And it's not entirely accurate.

I stole it back. That pustulant zit on the ass of humanity stole it from me first."

Xantham climbed over the chair and sat down. "I've gotta hear this story. You better start talking, girl."

Carl nodded. "I'm curious too."

The crew gathered around while Kayla pressed the ice pack against her face and took a sip of her drink. She didn't usually subscribe to the practice of swapping personal tales with trader crews, but she figured she owed them an explanation. Carl hadn't thrown her out on her butt after hitting him, and then he'd stood up for her against another trader. She gave him a long look, once again contemplating the sincerity of his earlier words.

Carl leaned against the wall, arms crossed over his chest like some sort of ancient warrior standing sentinel over his troops. His gaze, along with the rest of the crew, focused on her, and she resisted the urge to squirm under the scrutiny of an entire trader camp. She spared a quick glance at Veridian and he gave her a nod of encouragement. Somewhat reassured by her friend's presence, she took a deep, steadying breath and began.

"Veridian and I were scavenging in a sector Ramiro's crew had cleared the week before. I didn't expect to find much since it looked like some sort of office building and was pretty picked over. I ended up locating a false wall that hadn't collapsed. The room behind it had mostly trash in it, but I found a safe in the floor."

She twirled the scotch in the glass and took a sip before continuing. "The data cube was in there, along with a bunch of journals that looked like lab records. I took the cube and the journals and went back above ground."

Veridian nodded and added, "One of Ramiro's crew used to come by to visit Kayla. He's the one who told us the sector was clear. When he saw our bikes that day, he stopped by to see her."

Kayla shot Veridian a warning glance. There were some things she wasn't willing to discuss. "It was piss-poor timing. He saw my bag and called it in to Ramiro. A few minutes later, there was a freaking party in our tent. Ramiro demanded the cube, and I refused. It got ugly. Vex broke Veridian's arm, and Ramiro took the cube from me."

She paused for a moment before continuing the story. "After we got Veridian back to camp, I worked on a program to send false data readings to the UV guard at Ramiro's camp. I drove out the next day by myself and told Ramiro I had reconsidered his offer. He took me into his office, and I activated the program. When the alarm went off, he left me to go check the equipment. I broke into his safe, took my data cube back, and ran."

"Holy shit," Cruncher muttered.

Kayla took another sip. "I knew Ramiro would be hunting me down, so I drove straight to Warig's camp. I told him I'd found it in a cleared sector, and he bought it on the spot for forty thousand credits."

Xantham let out a low whistle. "Damn, girl, that's a lot of credits."

Kayla shrugged. It was strange how some things seemed so important at the time. "It was fine until Ramiro found out I'd sold it to Warig. He flipped out and told Warig I had stolen it from him. Both traders blacklisted Leo's camp on the spot. Leo was pretty pissed about it, but the forty thousand credits helped smooth things over. He decided it would be a good idea to get out of the area, so we picked up and moved closer to Henkel and Carl."

"So that's why you came this direction," Carl mused. "You first popped up on our radar about a year ago, right after that incident."

"Yeah, well, it's not like we had a lot of choice." Kayla finished her drink and pushed away from the table. "So, thanks for the drink and the entertainment, but I think it's time for us to head out. Come on, V."

Kayla dropped the cold pack on the table and avoided looking at the surrounding faces. She knew she'd see a mix of emotions on them, some with awe and others with pity. She'd seen it before and wasn't any more prepared to deal with it now. None of it changed anything. The past couldn't be rewritten. There was no use dwelling on it.

Veridian moved to stand beside her, offering her the opportunity to retreat. With a smile, he took control of the conversation at the table and gave her a gentle nudge toward the door. She tossed him a grateful look.

Barely registering Veridian's voice saying his goodbyes, Kayla headed toward the exit and nearly ran into Carl leaning against the wall by the door. When she met his eyes, he gave her a small smile and a brief nod. Her face flushed at the approval in his expression. Turning away, she hurried out the door, wanting to leave and rebuild her emotional shields before they collapsed.

CHAPTER FOUR

A FEW DAYS LATER, Kayla was underground. Against Veridian's advice, she snuck out of camp and headed back to the ruins. Veridian grudgingly followed her, unwilling to let her scavenge alone. She knew he was apprehensive about making Leo angry.

In Kayla's opinion, she'd stayed above ground long enough. Sitting in camp made her stir-crazy, and she found herself snapping at people left and right. She figured Leo wouldn't be all that upset at her leaving. In fact, she reasoned he would probably end up welcoming a more relaxing day without having her yell back and forth with him.

"Dropping down to level four," Kayla announced over her headset. The cable lowered her into the ruins in Sector Twelve. Once her feet touched the floor, she pressed the button to signal she'd stopped her descent. Kayla unhooked the harness and looked around the room again.

This is where I belong.

Most other ruin rats might look at scavenging as a way to survive, but there was something eerily calming about being in the ruins. Walking through rooms forever frozen in time allowed her a glimpse of another world. She could almost get lost in other people's memories.

Kayla smiled to herself as she moved through the old bedroom and spotted the empty jewelry box she'd thrown in the corner. She picked it up and stuffed it into her bag. It probably wasn't worth much, but it might get them a few credits.

Making her way across the room, she climbed over a partially collapsed wall separating the bedroom from the hallway. Working her way through the hall, she was careful to check the stability of the ground before each step to avoid another collapse.

She came to a large hole in another wall, which appeared to lead to another bedroom. This room was remarkably well preserved and appeared to have belonged to a child. Kayla began sorting through debris for any salvageable items.

She moved to the other side of the room and discovered what looked like an old toy chest in the corner. Grinning, she knelt on the ground. It might not look like much from the outside, but sometimes the contents were in decent shape.

Kayla pried open the rusted lid and discovered a few old-fashioned toys inside. One looked like some sort of worn, plastic music player. She put it in her pack and picked up a ceramic doll wearing a long, faded red dress. It was in better condition than she expected. She added the doll to her pack as well.

The rest of the items looked like trash. She doubted they would bring in many credits but made a mental note in case she ever wanted to come back. There wasn't much else in the room she could carry, so she headed back to the hallway.

"Kayla," Veridian's voice called over her headset, "we've got a problem. I've got three riders on approach. It looks like Carl again."

"Shit. That guy is seriously becoming a pain in my ass. It

can't be a coincidence he knew we'd be here today. How long do I have?"

"Less than five minutes. If you get up here now, we might be okay."

Kayla dashed to the harness, strapped herself in, and hit the button for the cable to lift her to the surface. The time would be close, but it was possible. "Disengage the UV guard and get the hell out of here, V. I'll take care of the cabling device and meet you where we discussed."

"On it," he replied.

By the time she climbed out of the hole, Veridian was already driving away. She grabbed the cabling device and attached it to her bike. Glancing up, she saw three bikes rapidly approaching. She leaped on to her speeder and fired up the engine.

With a grin, she pulled back on the throttle and took off speeding over the landscape with the three bikes following her.

Leaning forward, she pulled back on the thrust lever. The bike engine roared and shot forward at near breakneck speed. *Let's see how well you can ride, Carl.*

Kayla crouched low, the wind rushing around her as she pushed the bike to its limits. Angling into a turn, she shifted herself slightly toward the edge of the seat and brought the bike nearly to the ground before pulling out of the turn. She glanced into her mirror and saw she'd left the other bikes far behind.

Kayla continued driving for another ten minutes until she was sure she'd lost them. She and Veridian had designated meeting locations for those times they needed to outrun traders and their crew. She turned her bike around and went the long way back toward Sector Three, one of the few cleared sectors, making sure not to cross Carl's path.

When she arrived, Veridian was already waiting for her

under the UV guard. He was clearly agitated, pacing under the artificial shade. "You lost them?"

Kayla pulled off her helmet. "Of course. I drove around making sure before heading here."

She removed the cabling device from her bike and handed it to Veridian to reattach to his bike. "I didn't think they'd be onto us so quickly. Carl must have known you'd try to go back into the ruins before the week was up."

Kayla shrugged and opened her backpack to make sure the artifacts hadn't been damaged. A beep from Veridian's bike radar made her look up.

"What is it?"

He stared at the radar. "Shit, we've got three bikes headed this way. They must have followed you."

She shook her head in denial. "No freaking way. I lost them."

"Could they have gotten back into our comms?"

Kayla considered the possibility for a moment. "I don't see how. Why the hell are they chasing us down for a couple of stupid artifacts? He's worse than a rash that won't go away."

"Do you want to take off?"

"Nah." Kayla stretched her arms over her head and leaned against the bike. "Not much point if the bastard is tracking us. Let's find out what he wants."

Veridian frowned but didn't object. They waited while the three bikes pulled up and Carl dismounted, along with Xantham and Cruncher.

Xantham pulled off his helmet and stared at Kayla. "Fuck me sideways. Where the hell did you learn to ride, girl? I've never seen anyone with moves like that."

She grinned and winked at him. "You pick it up quick when you have to outrun traders and their crew."

Carl tucked his helmet under his arm. "Kayla, we need to talk."

She yawned. "Nice to see you, too, Carl. But I'm a little busy right now getting my much-needed rest. You see, I'm still technically grounded, but I thought the fresh air might do me some good."

"You sure looked pretty damn healthy for someone flying out of Sector Twelve earlier."

Kayla blinked at him. "Business for you traders must be really slow if you're willing to chase me across half the district. If you need the credits so bad, go ahead and search us, but keep Leo out of this. He didn't know I was coming here. I waited two days, which was more than fair."

Carl shook his head. "No, it's not that. I need to talk to you about Ramiro."

Kayla's shoulders tensed. She wasn't about to discuss Ramiro beyond what she'd revealed the other day. "There's nothing to talk about. The guy's an asshole, and I plan on staying as far away from him as I can get. I'm more interested in knowing how you knew I'd be here. I know for a fact my comms and Leo's system are squeaky clean. I spent the last two days—" Kayla's eyes widened as a thought struck her and she jerked upright. "You sneaky bastard. You put a tracker on my bike when I came to your camp the other day, didn't you?"

"Kayla, that's not important right now," Carl began.

She ignored him and crouched next to her bike, pulling a flashlight out of her pocket. If there was a tracking device somewhere, she'd find it.

"Ramiro's gone off the deep end. He's looking for you."

Kayla ran her fingers along the underside of the engine, wondering what it would take to get him to drop the subject. "Yeah, yeah, what else is new?"

"Dammit, Kayla." Carl sighed, then walked over and pulled the miniature tracking device off her bike. He handed it to her, taking away her distraction. "Will you please talk to me now?"

She looked at the device and pouted. "I would have found it."

He nodded. "I know. I'm trying to save some time. We have a problem with Ramiro. He's been trying to access my comm system."

"That sounds like your problem, not mine." She stood up and brushed the dirt off her pants.

"I'm afraid it's not. Xantham went ahead and let him into our system enough to find out what he was looking for. He's looking for *you*. Cruncher did some checking and found Ramiro's put a price on you."

Kayla paused while she tried to wrap her mind around what he was saying. Her brow furrowed, and she gave a slight shake of her head. "That doesn't make any sense. He might have gotten a little worked up the other day, but the Aurelia Data Cube incident happened a year ago. Why would he bother doing something now? Besides, he already knows he hurt—" She pushed away those thoughts and straightened her shoulders. "Never mind. It doesn't matter. It's done. It's in the past. I stay out of Ramiro's way, and he leaves me alone."

A look of guilt flashed across Carl's face but disappeared so fast Kayla wondered if she'd imagined it. "I'm afraid it's not that simple anymore. Ramiro broke the rules. You may think that as a trader we can do whatever the hell we want, but that's not the case. Based on his own admission, I petitioned OmniLab to have his trader status revoked."

Kayla's eyes widened. "Why the hell would you do a thing like that? Shit, Carl, he's going to blame me. If he didn't already want to permanently dump my databanks, he will now. If you wanted me out of your district so badly, you could have at least given me a head's up to get the hell out of OmniLab territory."

Veridian ran a jerky hand through his hair, looking worried. "Can you call OmniLab and tell them you made a mistake?"

"I can't," Carl said simply. "The other two traders have signed off on the petition, and OmniLab is investigating. But even if I could call it off, I wouldn't. As it is, you don't trust us. The only way we're ever going to be able to repair the relationship between traders and ruin rats is if we're held accountable for our actions."

"At the risk of getting Kayla *killed*?" Veridian demanded.

"Not if I can help it." Carl turned to Kayla, holding out his hands in apology. "I wasn't expecting Ramiro to respond this way. For that, I take full responsibility. I know what you think of traders, but I can protect you. Ramiro's going to be throwing all his resources into hunting you down. He seems to think if he gets rid of you, he'll eliminate the threat of being removed as a trader. If you accept the offer I made, I can help you. I can keep you safe."

Kayla's eyes narrowed. "How?"

"If you join my crew, you'll be in a secure base. You'll have my resources backing you. Otherwise, you won't last more than a couple of days on your own. Look how easy it was for me to track you down. It'll be just as easy for Ramiro."

She gaped at him. Were they really back to that again? She didn't bother to hide the sarcasm in her voice. "Oh, isn't that convenient? Forget it. I'll take my chances with Ramiro. At least if he kills me, there'll be some poetic justice in that."

"Kayla." Veridian's voice was soft but insistent, his eyes full of concern.

She shook her head. "Oh no, V, don't you look at me like that. You know I can't. I won't do it."

Veridian walked up to her and took her hands in his. "Carl's right. You need to do this. I've been trying to help you pick up the pieces for the past year, but I can't help you with this. You owe it to Pretz to accept this offer. Don't let Ramiro hurt you."

Kayla tried to pull away. "Don't you dare bring him up."

Veridian gripped her tighter, not letting go. "I can't lose you, Kayla. You're the only family I have left."

His pained words tore through her, and she bowed her head, closing her eyes tight. She wanted to scream in frustration. The thought of hurting Veridian was like a knife in her gut, but she didn't know how she could reconcile her emotions enough to work for OmniLab.

As though sensing her need for movement, Veridian released her. She stepped away, feeling conflicted. Pacing around the small area under the portable UV guard, Kayla kicked at her bike. Running her hands through her hair in agitation, she contemplated her options. Sadly, there weren't many. She turned to Carl, who seemed to be waiting for her to come to the conclusion he'd already reached. She swallowed and hung her head. "How long?"

"The contract would be for a year," Carl replied and exhaled as though he'd been holding his breath. "It's an OmniLab contract and their requirement, not mine. You can leave after that if that's what you still want."

She turned away and stared off into the horizon. The sun was beginning to set. *Fitting.*

"Kayla, I'm not trying to force you into this. I honestly had no idea Ramiro would target you. If anything, I figured he would have gone after me. It was never my intention to put you in danger. If I could protect you at Leo's camp, I would. I wanted you to join my crew willingly, not like this."

"I know," she said in annoyance and turned around to look at him. "Dammit, I know. For what it's worth, I appreciate it. You're not a bad guy, Carl. You're a pain in the ass, but you're not a bad guy."

Veridian looked hopeful. "So you'll agree to join him?"

"Yeah," she said in dejection, shoving her hands in her back pockets. "Doesn't seem like I have much of a choice if I want to keep breathing."

Carl nodded, and Cruncher handed him a small computer tablet. He pulled up the contract and offered it to her.

"It's the same contract you reviewed the other day," he explained. "Just press your thumb on the bottom panel. It'll scan your thumbprint and take a small blood sample to record your DNA."

Kayla took the tablet from him. "And Veridian?"

Carl nodded. "His contract is already prepared. It would be in his best interest to join us too. I'm sure Ramiro knows the easiest way to get to you is through Veridian."

Kayla looked down at the tablet. The moment she pressed her finger against the panel, her fate would be sealed. Even Leo wouldn't risk taking her back if she broke an OmniLab contract. She hesitated, lifting her head to meet Veridian's gaze, silently asking if he was sure. He gave her an encouraging nod. Dammit. It was going to be a long year.

She pressed her thumb against the bottom panel until she felt a slight pinch. The tablet beeped its acceptance of her sample. It was such a small thing, but she felt like she'd just signed part of herself away. Struggling to keep her hand from shaking, she handed it back to Carl. If he noticed, he didn't say anything. He pressed a few buttons before passing it to Veridian.

Veridian scanned the document and pressed his thumb against it. When it beeped, Carl took the tablet. "Well, it didn't happen quite the way I hoped, but I'm glad you're part of the team. I've sent your contracts directly to OmniLab to be recorded. You're now authorized to act on my behalf throughout this district."

Cruncher grinned and shook Veridian's hand, then gave

Kayla a big bear hug. "Welcome to the dark side, kiddo. I'm glad you came around."

She couldn't help but smile at his enthusiasm. "Yeah, well, let's see if you're still saying that after a year."

Xantham grabbed her, picked her up, and swung her around. A laugh bubbled out of her before she could help it. He kissed her cheek. "Shit, girl, this is going to be great!"

Carl smiled at them. "If you don't mind, I think it might be safest if you came directly to our camp, Kayla. Veridian, Cruncher can go with you to pick up your things and escort you back."

Kayla and Veridian exchanged a look, and Veridian shook his head. They both knew Leo was going to lose his shit when he found out. Bringing Cruncher to the camp would put him directly in the line of fire. "That's okay. Take Kayla with you, but I think I should go alone. I need to talk to Leo and explain it to him. It'll go better without someone from a trader camp there. I'll stay there tonight and come over tomorrow with our things."

Carl nodded in agreement.

Veridian hugged Kayla. "Thanks. You're doing the right thing."

"Yeah, yeah," she muttered but squeezed him tightly as she returned his hug. After she pulled away, she picked up her helmet and glanced back at her bike where the purloined items were hidden.

"So, now that I'm part of your crew, do I have to turn over the loot I scavenged earlier?"

Cruncher and Xantham chuckled while Carl closed his eyes and shook his head in exasperation. Kayla gave them a small shrug. Did they really think she'd been taking in the view?

"We'll figure it out," Carl said with a sigh. "It's getting late, and I want to get back to camp and find out what's going on with Ramiro. They've been monitoring his chatter back at camp. I had to bring Xantham with me to help track you."

"All right," Kayla agreed and mounted her bike with the others. Veridian disengaged the UV guard and gave her a wave before taking off toward Leo's camp. She hesitated a moment, wanting to follow him but dutifully turned her bike to follow Carl and the others back toward their camp.

———

WHEN THEY ARRIVED, Kayla dismounted and followed Carl inside. Even though she'd been to his camp a few days ago, things were entirely different now. It was strange to think she'd return here each day after scavenging in the ruins. She'd spent so long avoiding traders and now she was living with one. Steeling her resolve, she followed the example of the men and hung her helmet and jacket at the entrance.

"Let me show you where you'll be staying," Carl offered. She bit her lip but nodded in agreement. Her feet felt heavy as she trudged behind him into the crew's quarters.

Someone had already set up two additional sleeping areas, complete with privacy dividers. Enclosed within each area was a bed, storage locker, and desk. The personal areas were about three times the size of what she had at Leo's camp. She couldn't help but feel annoyed at the sight though. These areas hadn't been there a few days ago.

Cocky bastard knew we'd accept before he even came out to find me.

Her first instinct was to snap at him for his assumption. But when she looked up at him, his brows were furrowed as though he was unsure about her reaction. She faltered, wondering if she could be reading him wrong. Most traders wouldn't have cared about what happened to someone like her, much less sought her out and offered to protect her. Biting back her retort, she said, "Pretty nice."

Carl gave her a warm smile, looking relieved and somewhat pleased by her comment. "If there's anything else you need, let me know. I want you to be happy here, Kayla."

She looked up in surprise, the intensity of his gaze making her stomach do a neat little somersault. *Oh, crap, he's got the most incredible eyes.*

"Thanks, Carl," she managed with a weak smile. "I can't imagine needing anything else."

"She needs some spare clothes," Jinx called out from her private area, making it obvious she'd been listening to their conversation. She popped her head out with a grin, her eyes twinkling. "I'm glad you decided to join us. I know you probably weren't ready to make the leap, but we're happy to have you on the team. You can borrow some of my clothes until you get your things. I'll leave them in your locker."

Surprised, and a little touched by the offer, Kayla nodded her thanks.

Carl cleared his throat, drawing her attention back to him. "Kayla, if you want, I'd like to take you over to the tech room. You should become familiar with our system, and we need to configure your commlink for our frequencies. We can check with Xantham, too, and find out what's going on with Ramiro."

"Sure." With a wave at Jinx, she followed Carl out of the crew's quarters and into the tech room. Cruncher and Zane were in the room working on one of the systems.

When she walked in, Zane stood up and greeted her. "Welcome to the crew."

Xantham came skidding into the room. His face lit up at the sight of her and he flashed a huge grin. "This is going to be great! Kayla, wait until you see some of the toys we're getting in the next few weeks."

Kayla laughed at their enthusiasm. Although she still felt a little uncomfortable, they seemed to be going out of their way to make her feel welcome. "Thanks, guys. I appreciate it."

———

CARL AND XANTHAM had disappeared and left her with Cruncher, explaining they needed to configure their communication settings to allow her access to their frequencies. Cruncher was in the process of giving her an overview of their system map, and she leaned over to get a closer look. It looked like a security grid around the camp.

Kayla had to remind herself she was playing for the other team now as Cruncher pointed to the screen and launched into an explanation. "These systems track any movement within range. Any guests, invited or uninvited, are picked up. Our bikes have monitors that let us know when it's one of us approaching or someone else. We'll install one on your bike tomorrow morning."

She nodded. The system appeared much more sophisticated than what they had at Leo's camp, but there were some similarities. She made a mental note to investigate it more fully later on. For research purposes, of course. After all, her contract was only for a year.

Cruncher moved over to another computer that monitored the camp's UV guard, air flow, temperature, light, and energy. Kayla looked at it and frowned, pointing to some numbers. "You guys are using way too much energy on your cooling unit."

He looked at her in surprise. "Oh? You think you can do better?"

"Pfft," she said with a grin, unable to resist a challenge. "Watch and learn."

He turned over the controls to her and watched as she rerouted the energy fields throughout the camp. After about thirty minutes, she turned the controls back over to him.

"Damn, girl," he muttered as he reviewed her work. "Where did you learn to do this?"

She gave a small shrug. "Our cooling system is always crapping out on us. I had to get creative. You know, when I was rerouting the power, I noticed some potential conflicts with the new gizmos you're testing. I think they might be causing a few hiccups in your system. A few months ago, I wrote a program that can help smooth some of these out. Mind if I upload it and run a scan to fix the problems?"

"Not at all." He pointed to another monitor. "You can set it up over on that screen."

Kayla scooted over to the far side of the desk and pulled up an additional monitor. Scrolling through the data on her commlink, she found the program and uploaded the file. As she went to put down her commlink, an old video file caught her attention. She'd never been able to bring herself to delete it.

Glancing up, she saw Cruncher was still engrossed with whatever was on his screen. She slipped on her earpiece and watched the video in silence. A soft smile crept on her face, and she blinked back the tears that threatened when the video ended.

With a sigh, she unplugged her earpiece and put her commlink on the desk. If this was going to be her new life, she needed to fully embrace it. The best way to start was with a project. Kayla rolled her shoulders, determined to focus on her task and find trouble spots in Carl's system.

———

AN HOUR LATER, Carl walked back into the tech room. He

was anxious to find out how his newest recruit was getting along. Cruncher was hunched over a monitor reviewing the security system data.

"Where's Kayla?"

Cruncher turned to look at Carl and put a finger to his lips, motioning to him to keep his voice down. He nodded over to the corner of the room where Kayla was sitting with her head in her arms on the desk. She'd fallen asleep at the computer.

Carl's mouth twitched in a smile. She was always so fiery and passionate. It was strange seeing her like this, and he felt as though he were witnessing some forbidden rite. Some of her dark hair had fallen over her face, accentuating the paleness of her skin. She appeared almost angelic in her repose. He knew once she was awake, though, that devilish glint would reappear in her eyes and make the current sight a dim memory.

Cruncher's whisper cut through his musing. "That girl is freaking unbelievable. I showed her the systems, and she jumped right in. She's got some serious tech skills. Within minutes, she ended up recalibrating the cooling system here in camp. It's some damn nice work too. She's got it running about thirty percent more efficiently. When she finished that, she reconfigured a bunch of our new equipment that was causing glitches."

Carl rubbed his chin in thought. He'd known she was talented, but Cruncher didn't hand out praise lightly. She must have really impressed him. "She's definitely a find. Thanks for your help today, Cruncher."

"Did you hear anything more about Ramiro?"

Carl bit back a curse, thinking about the unscrupulous trader. "Yeah, he got the notification from OmniLab about Kayla joining us. Xantham tapped into his comms and heard him yelling about it. He's going to start targeting us, so we're going to have to focus on security here and out in the field. I want groups of at least four people at every scavenge site until this is done. He's getting desperate."

Cruncher nodded and turned back to his monitor. "I'll get started on it."

Carl glanced at Kayla again, debating whether to disturb her. She'd been through a lot over the past few days. All things considered, she'd handled it well. He tucked her hair behind her ear, letting his fingers trail along her cheek. She didn't stir.

Making the decision to let her sleep in her own bed, he picked up her commlink off the desk and tucked it in his pocket.

"It's bedtime," he whispered before scooping her out of the chair.

At the sound of his voice, she snuggled into his chest. He felt a moment of surprise at the feeling of possessiveness that coursed through him. Something about her got under his skin. Her intriguing mix of contradictions fascinated him. She seemed to have no problem going toe-to-toe with him and anyone else, but he also sensed her vulnerability below the surface.

He carried her to the crew's quarters and gently laid her on the bed. She curled up in a ball as he pulled the blanket up over her, tucking her in. Unable to resist, he brushed a small kiss along her temple before activating the privacy setting for her personal area and leaving.

Carl headed toward his office and sat down at the desk, the movement making him realize he still had Kayla's commlink in his pocket. Determined to give it back to her in the morning, he dropped it on the desk and pulled out his own to scroll through his messages.

In addition to his daily trader responsibilities, he still tried to maintain an active presence within the towers. It was difficult, but he was determined to eventually move up into a director position at OmniLab where he could try to make some real changes. He was the youngest trader to have ever been recruited, a fact which had earned him some notoriety.

Carl sighed and rubbed his forehead, feeling the beginning of a headache as he read through his messages. The corruption and animosity on the surface between the ruin rats and OmniLab seemed to be reaching a crescendo. The latest situation with Ramiro and Kayla seemed to reinforce his concerns. Something needed to be done before the situation deteriorated even more.

It took him almost an hour to finish corresponding with his contacts and set up necessary appointments. When he finished, he pushed away from the desk and stretched his tired muscles.

His gaze fell on Kayla's commlink and he picked it up, considering the worn device. It was an older model, and he wondered if she'd enjoy receiving an upgrade. He still chuckled at the wonder on her face when she'd seen their newly acquired prototypes. So much for her being a hard-hearted thief.

He flipped open her commlink to get a better idea of which model style she preferred and noticed she'd been watching a video file. There was a moment of hesitation before his curiosity got the better of him and he hit the replay button.

The video had been recorded down in the ruins some time ago. It was obvious Kayla had been the one filming since she was laughing while a young man with shoulder-length brown hair tried to explain how to pick a complicated lock. Carl smiled at the sound and wondered about the identity of the young man whose eyes twinkled as he tried to keep from laughing.

"Kayla, knock it off and pay attention. We don't have a lot

of time down here. Ramiro's going to be pissed if he catches us."

Her teasing voice came over the audio. "I can't help it, Pretz. You sound so serious."

Pretz cleared his throat and tried to maintain his composure. "This is the 8600, and it's tough as hell. When you can crack this baby in under a minute and a half, this will be worth it. Now here we— Damn you, Kayla! You look ridiculous."

His face broke into a grin and he laughed, tossing his lockpick aside. "You're impossible."

With a mischievous glint in his eyes, he made a grab for the camera. There was a squeal from Kayla and more laughter as the video ended.

Carl flipped the commlink closed, a wave of mixed feelings coming over him. He'd seen a hint of Kayla's playful side when they battled wits against each other, but there was an edge to it that wasn't present in the video. He wasn't sure if it was because he was a trader or if there was something else.

Veridian had mentioned the name Pretz when he was trying to talk Kayla into joining earlier. Carl rubbed his chin, recalling her agitation, but he'd assumed they were talking about another ruin rat from Leo's camp. There were too many of them, and they were much too secretive for him to know all their names. Some memory tickled in the back of his mind, but he couldn't put his finger on it. He frowned and headed out of his office toward the tech room.

Cruncher looked up when he entered. "You're still up, Boss?"

Carl handed Kayla's commlink to Cruncher. "There's a video on her commlink she was watching right before she fell asleep. Do you know a ruin rat named Pretz? I keep thinking his name is familiar, but I can't remember where I've heard it before. He mentioned Ramiro on the video."

"Just a second. I've heard that name before." Cruncher turned to his computer and entered in a few commands. Almost immediately, an image appeared on the screen.

Carl leaned over to get a better look at the screen and saw the young man in the video. His name appeared, along with an OmniLab contract and identification number. "He's not a ruin rat. He's part of Ramiro's crew."

Cruncher shook his head and pointed toward the bottom of the screen. "Not anymore, Boss. According to this, he was killed in a scavenging accident about a year ago. His body was discovered by Ramiro."

"That's around the same time the Aurelia Data Cube incident happened," Carl mused, considering the potential implications. "I wonder if they're connected."

Cruncher leaned back in his chair and tapped his fingers on the desk. "I still have a contact in Ramiro's crew who might talk to me. We go way back. I could ask him about this guy and find out what he knows. Something about this doesn't feel right."

Carl nodded. "Yeah, if you can trust him, go ahead. Let me know what he says. My gut says there's more to this story."

CHAPTER FIVE

"WE FINISHED RUNNING the additional security scans last night. The problem is going to be traveling outside our monitoring areas."

Carl nodded at Cruncher's assessment and took another bite of food. He glanced around the table at his crew and considered his options. They couldn't close up shop while they waited for a resolution of the issue with Ramiro. No matter what he decided, their productivity would take a hit.

Xantham leaned over, swiping a fruit stick off Jinx's plate. She glowered at him and snatched it back, bopping him on the head in the process. Ignoring their antics, Carl turned back to Cruncher with the intention of continuing their conversation. He fell silent at the older man's expression.

"Hot damn." Cruncher's jaw dropped.

Carl looked up to see Kayla striding into the room. With a cheerful "Good morning," she flashed a smile to the group and headed toward the cabinet that stored their prepared meals.

Carl swallowed and couldn't help but gape as she bent over the cabinet. Her shorts hung low on her waist and hugged her curves seductively. The small top was low cut and accentuated her breasts while leaving her midsection bare. Oblivious to the reaction she'd caused, she pulled out one of the breakfast meals and programmed the computer to heat it.

"You're going to have to beat off the potential recruits if they get a look at her."

Carl eyed her appreciatively, silently agreeing with Cruncher's comment. It was more than her appearance though. There was such an effortless sensuality to her movements. Something about her captivated him, and judging from the reactions of the other men in the room, he wasn't alone.

Elyot was close to drooling, and Xantham nearly fell out of his chair trying to get a better look.

Jinx looked at the men in mock disgust. "You know, I don't remember getting that kind of reaction when I wore the same outfit."

Xantham's eyes didn't leave Kayla. "Much love to you, Jinx, but you don't have a body like that."

Jinx rolled her eyes, taking a large bite of her fruit stick. Carl cleared his throat, and Xantham had the grace to look abashed. Kayla brought her food tray to the table and sat down.

"Sleep well?" Carl leaned forward, watching while she uncovered her plate.

Kayla nodded. "Yeah. Those privacy dividers are nice. I didn't mean to sleep so late."

He gave her a reassuring smile. "Don't worry. You haven't missed anything."

"Oh, thanks again for the clothes, Jinx. I'm hoping Veridian will be here this morning with my things."

"Yeah, thanks for the clothes, Jinx," Xantham echoed, putting his head in his hands to gaze at Kayla.

Jinx kicked him under the table. He jerked upright and

grimaced at her. Jinx turned back to Kayla and smiled. "Anytime, Kayla. Ignore Xantham. He was dropped on his head when he was a kid."

Kayla arched a brow, then looked at the faces seated around the table. "So where are Lisia and Zane? Did they head to the ruins?"

Jinx looked slightly uncomfortable and so did the men. "Uh, Lisia wanted to get out of camp for a bit. They're running the perimeter to check for security flaws."

Kayla cocked her head. "Oh?"

Before Jinx could reply, Carl pushed away his plate and changed the subject. "Kayla, I have some commlink appointments this afternoon, but before that we're going to run some preliminary tests on the new equipment. If everything is quiet with Ramiro, we're planning on going underground tomorrow to see how some of these new toys handle. You interested?"

"Are you fucking kidding me?" she exclaimed, acting shocked he would even consider the alternative. "I'm in."

Xantham gave a dreamy sigh. "The face of an angel, the body of a goddess, and the mouth of a ruin rat. I think I'm in love, Boss."

Jinx smacked him in the back of the head, causing him to yelp. "Excuse us." Jinx stood and grabbed the back of Xantham's shirt to pull him away from the table. With an apologetic smile, she said, "I think Xantham needs to go take a cold shower."

Carl shook his head at Kayla's look of confusion, while Cruncher and Elyot both laughed.

Elyot stood and dumped out the empty plates before turning to Kayla. "I'm going to be working on the system maintenance while you guys are testing. If you get some time later, Kayla, I'd love to see what you can do with some of the locks. Zane wouldn't shut up about it the other day."

"Sure."

"Sounds good. I'll see you a bit later." He waved and headed out of the room.

Cruncher finished eating, stood up, and dumped his plate before looking at Carl. "I'll start prepping in the tech room while you two finish your meals."

Carl nodded and turned back to Kayla. She glanced around at the empty room and observed, "It sure cleared out fast around here."

He watched her pick at her food for a moment. A strand of hair fell across her cheek, and he resisted the urge to tuck it behind her ear, not knowing if he'd be able to stop touching her once he started. "Sorry for not waking you. I thought you'd enjoy sleeping in today since we didn't have anything on the schedule."

In an effort to keep his hands busy, he reached into his pocket, withdrew her commlink, and slid it over to her. "You left your commlink in the tech room. I would have returned it to you last night but didn't want to wake you."

"Thanks." She flipped it open and read through her messages. A small frown marred her features. "Well, it looks like you were right."

"About what?"

"V says someone from Ramiro's crew contacted Leo last night asking about us. Leo told him we were both gone and staying at your camp now." She took another bite of her breakfast, chewing while she finished reading the message.

Carl's jaw tightened at the news. It wasn't any more than what he had expected, but it still pissed him off. "Veridian is okay?"

She flipped her commlink shut and pushed away her plate. "Yeah, he should be here in an hour or two."

Carl stood up. He'd feel better once Veridian had arrived.

Both Kayla and Veridian fell under his protection the moment they agreed to work for him, and it was a job he didn't take lightly. "If you're finished eating, let's go check out the new equipment. I know you've been dying to get your hands on it."

Kayla nodded eagerly and dumped her plate. He led her into the tech room where Cruncher had pulled out some of the new sensors.

"Great," Cruncher said when he saw her. "Kayla, grab that one there and see if you can configure the uplink to our system. Then you can start calibrating it."

Kayla knelt to pick up the unit he pointed out. There was no hesitation in her movements as her nimble fingers ran across the monitor to locate the specific uplink frequency. She scrolled through the data until she detected the frequency and then initiated the connection.

Cruncher motioned to Carl, letting him know he wanted a private word. "I'll be right back."

She gave an absent nod, completely engrossed in her project. Anxious to learn what Cruncher had found, Carl followed him into the next room.

When Cruncher was sure Kayla was out of earshot, he said, "I managed to touch base with my contact in Ramiro's camp. Minko has been working with Ramiro for several years. He was more forthcoming than I expected. I don't think he likes Ramiro much."

"What did he say?"

"He said Pretz was a good guy. Solid. Brought in a steady stream of profit and could work locks like no one he's ever seen. They were trying to recruit his brother, too, but didn't have much luck."

Carl rubbed his chin, glancing toward the tech room. "Did he say anything about Kayla?"

"Not by name," Cruncher admitted. "He said Pretz was

head over heels for some ruin rat. I got the impression it caused some problems with Ramiro."

"Did he know anything about how he died?"

Cruncher shook his head. "Not much. Ramiro discovered Pretz had fallen through two levels in one of the cleared sectors. It surprised everyone since Pretz wasn't careless and those sectors had already been cleared. Minko said he never found out why Pretz was in a cleared sector on his scheduled day off. But Minko saw the body, and it was mangled pretty badly."

Carl frowned. It was unfortunate, but accidents sometimes happened in the ruins. The fact he was in a cleared sector was suspicious though. "Thanks, Cruncher."

"No problem, Boss." Cruncher leaned forward, lowering his voice even more. "There was one more thing though. The day after Pretz died, Minko said Pretz's girl showed up and demanded to see Ramiro. He said she was a hot little number with dark hair and a lot of attitude, which sounds a lot like our Kayla. Ramiro took her into his office, and the next thing everyone knew, the Aurelia Data Cube had been stolen."

"So the timing fits," Carl mused, glancing at the door where Kayla was working. "It sounds like I need to have a talk with Kayla. I think we're missing a pretty big part of the story."

Cruncher nodded, folding his arms across his chest. "Sounds that way. I'm not sure how well it'll go over, talking to her about it though. Ruin rats don't like discussing their private lives, especially with traders. It doesn't matter that she's part of the crew now."

"I'll figure something out," Carl promised. The alternative wasn't acceptable.

———

Kayla looked up as he entered and flashed him a huge smile. He nearly stumbled, entranced by the way she lit up the room. She was sitting on the floor, surrounded by equipment, and her eyes sparkled in excitement. Her earlier reservation was gone in the face of new technology.

"You guys have got some amazing toys here. Carl, I want to show you something."

She jumped up and crossed over to him, handing him one of the sensors. He took it and flipped it over the way she instructed. Leaning over him, she rested her hand on his arm to point out some of the displayed readings. He took a deep breath, capturing her alluring scent. Having her this close was distracting, but her enthusiasm was infectious. He found himself smiling while she explained the settings she had configured.

"That's great work, Kayla." He handed back the sensor. She reached up to put it back on one of the higher shelves, and Carl noticed her shirt creeping up, barely stopping at her breasts. He inhaled sharply but couldn't bring himself to look away.

Cruncher sat down and said under his breath, "Hot little number is right."

Carl forced himself to breathe normally. "Kayla, if you've got a few minutes, I wanted to talk to you."

"Sure. Let me just clean up this mess."

She bent down to grab another piece of equipment, awarding them with another spectacular view of her curves. Carl cleared his throat and wondered if he should stop to take a cold shower himself.

"Uh, just leave it. Cruncher can take care of it."

Cruncher gave him a pained look. "I can?"

Carl smirked at Cruncher. The older man was enjoying the show a little too much.

Kayla hesitated, looking between them. "I don't mind."

"That's nice of you, but let Cruncher do it. I'm not sure his heart can take it otherwise." Carl took her hand to lead her out of the room. "Let's go to my office."

"I'll remember this, Boss. You owe me!" Cruncher called out.

Carl snorted and continued walking.

"What was that about?"

Carl looked down at Kayla's confused expression. "You have no idea the effect you have on people, do you?"

She threw up her hands in exasperation. "Well, shit. I pissed him off already?"

Carl chuckled. She really was adorable. Unable to resist, he tucked her hair behind her ear. "Not even close. It's just distracting having such a beautiful woman around."

Kayla raised an eyebrow, but before he could say anything further, Xantham walked around the corner and called out to them.

"Hey, you two! There's a solo rider on the radar. Looks like your boy, Veridian, will be here any second. At least I hope it's him and not one of Ramiro's punks."

Looking pleased by the news, Kayla turned to Carl. "It probably is. He sent me a message saying he'd be here around this time. Mind if we talk a bit later?"

"Sure. It'll wait. I'd like to say hello to Veridian too."

Taking a detour, they reached the entrance just as Veridian stepped inside and dropped a bag on the ground. He pulled off his helmet and ran his fingers through his disheveled, light-brown hair, his eyes lighting up when he saw Kayla. She let out a squeal and flung herself into his arms. He dropped his helmet in surprise to catch her and hugged her tightly before setting her down. Kissing the top of her head, he teased, "So how much trouble did you manage to get into so far?"

Kayla laughed. "Not enough. But the day is young."

He looked skeptical. "I'm not surprised. But I'm glad you're safe."

Carl waited until they were finished before stepping forward. He found their dynamic interesting. Kayla wasn't as reserved around Veridian, and he obviously doted on her. Carl extended his hand in greeting. "Glad you made it, Veridian. Do you need help bringing anything in?"

"Yeah, if you don't mind. I've got a few boxes with me. They're on my bike." Veridian gestured to the bag on the floor. "Kayla, that's some of your stuff. Where do you want me to put it?"

She picked up the bag and slung it over her shoulder. "I'll take care of it while you grab the rest of the stuff."

Xantham stepped forward to help, and each of the men grabbed their jackets and helmets to bring in the rest of the supplies. Once they came back inside, Carl directed Veridian down the hall. "We set up your private area in the crew's quarters."

Carl looked down at his box as they entered the crew's quarters. "Is this box yours or Kayla's?"

Veridian glanced at it. "That one belongs to Kayla."

Hefting the box, he carried it over to Kayla's private area where she was unpacking her bag. She looked up as he walked in and put the box on her desk.

"Thanks, Carl."

"No problem. Let me know if you need any help."

She opened up the box he had brought into the room. A picture of the young man from Kayla's commlink rested near the top.

Deciding it was a good opportunity to bring him up, he gestured to the image. "Is that Pretz?"

Kayla froze. "How do you know him?"

"I've heard about him," he replied neutrally, watching her expression. "Wasn't he part of Ramiro's crew?"

"Yeah, he was." Kayla squeezed her eyes shut and turned away from Carl, shoving the picture in the back of her locker.

Her visceral reaction surprised him. He hesitated, debating how far to push her. Unfortunately, if Pretz was tied to the situation with Ramiro, he needed to know. The more information he could provide to OmniLab, the more likely Ramiro would be punished.

"I heard he was great with locks," he prompted, hoping she would open up a bit more.

Kayla whirled on him. "You seem to know an awful lot for someone who didn't know a damn thing about the Aurelia Data Cube the other day."

Taken aback at her sudden anger, he held up his hands. "I'm sorry. I didn't realize he was a sensitive subject."

Kayla slammed the locker shut and stared at the closed door for a minute. She took a deep breath before turning around and resting the back of her head against the door. "Forget it. It's in the past."

Carl frowned. The look in her eyes was haunted, and he felt the sudden urge to comfort her. Before he could move toward her, Xantham poked his head in. She immediately straightened and forced a smile.

"Hey, girl. You need some help?"

Kayla shook her head, glancing at Carl. "Nah, think I've got it covered."

"Okay, cool. Hey, Boss, I'm going to get Veridian set up on our frequencies, unless you needed me for anything else?"

"That sounds good. Thanks, Xantham."

Xantham winked at Kayla before heading to the communications room. Carl studied Kayla thoughtfully. As Cruncher predicted, she wasn't going to be forthcoming with information, and he didn't want to push her away. Deciding it was better to retreat while they were still on a positive note, he said, "I'll let you finish unpacking then."

He turned and paused when he saw Lisia in the doorway watching them. He opened his mouth to call out to her, but she turned on her heels and stormed off. His lips pressed together in a slight grimace.

Kayla touched Carl's arm to get his attention. "What's the deal with Lisia? Every time I see her, she looks like she wants to throw a screwdriver at my face."

He sighed, rubbing the back of his neck. Lisia's childish behavior needed to stop. He'd been hoping her attitude would have improved by now, but it seemed to have gotten worse over the past few days.

"It's not you. It's me. I, ah, got involved with her a few months back. It was a mistake, and I ended it almost immediately after it began. She didn't take it well."

Kayla's eyes widened as she looked down the hallway where the girl disappeared. "She still has a thing for you?"

"It looks that way. I'm hoping she'll get over it soon."

"Hmm..." Kayla crossed her arms and studied him. "I guess I can't blame her. You're kinda nice to look at."

Carl chuckled, returning her assessment with a long look of his own. He leaned forward and lowered his voice. "I could definitely say the same."

He brushed her hair behind her ear and trailed his fingers down her cheek. When he rubbed his thumb over her lower lip, her cheeks flushed, and her mouth parted slightly. Although he wanted nothing more than to pursue her, he recognized the need to give her some time to adapt to her new surroundings. Summoning his willpower, he took a step back, giving Kayla a long perusal.

"I need to take care of a few things. If you need anything, let me know. Otherwise, I'll see you a bit later."

————

KAYLA WATCHED HIM WALK AWAY, trying to ignore the familiar flutter in her stomach she seemed to get every time he was around. Leaning against the wall for support, she mentally kicked herself.

Damn, damn, damn. Get it together, Kayla. He's a trader.

Forcing herself to turn away from his retreating figure, she looked at the box with disinterest. The thought of unpacking wasn't appealing. Instead, she headed over to Veridian's private area.

Shoving a box aside, she sprawled out on his bed.

Veridian cocked his head at her and then gave it a slow shake. "I haven't been here for an hour and you're already taking over my area."

"Oh, shush. If you really minded, you'd kick me out."

He chuckled but didn't argue with her. Taking that as a victory, she fluffed up his pillow behind her. "What did Leo say? Was he pissed?"

He shrugged, but Kayla noticed his shoulders tense. "It's probably for the best you didn't come back last night. I got stuck listening to a Leo rant that should have been directed at you. He's worried about Ramiro though. To be honest, I think he's going to miss you."

Kayla frowned. She'd known Leo was going to be upset, and she felt guilty for letting Veridian take the brunt of it. More than anything, though, she was worried about how the camp would fare without her. She guessed that was Leo's main concern too. She hoped Carl would keep his word and allow her to transfer some credits back to them. Until they found a replacement scavenger, it would be difficult on them. "I doubt that. He'll just miss having someone to argue with."

"That's probably partly true. You know, he wants us to come back when we're done after the year. He wanted me to tell you that."

Kayla propped herself up on her elbows to see him better.

She was normally pretty good at reading Veridian, but she couldn't tell how he felt about the turn of events. When they were younger, he had joked about joining a trader camp, but he hadn't said anything about it in recent years. In fact, he'd always supported her anti-OmniLab campaign, especially after the situation with Ramiro.

"We'll see. You know, we could always take off and start our own camp or something. We could even leave OmniLab territory. There are other places where we could start over."

Veridian gave her a sharp look, and she barely managed not to flinch. "You'd better be considering options for a year from now and not thinking what I think you're thinking. We're not breaking the contract. We'd be blacklisted by every single OmniLab trader. There's no going back from that, Kayla."

Kayla groaned and fell back on the bed in frustration. So much for her fantasy. Staring up at the ceiling, she declared, "Fine. Have it your way. I won't do anything crazy."

Veridian turned back to the box. "Carl and his crew seem like decent people. You said yourself he wasn't a bad guy."

Kayla couldn't stop the silly grin from spreading across her face. "He's too damn pretty to be a trader."

"Kayla!" Veridian stared at her in shock.

"What?" she asked, feigning ignorance. "He's got these amazing eyes. And his body... Oh man, I want to bite his ass." She let out a dreamy sigh.

Veridian threw a shirt at her in disgust, and she laughed. Unable to resist teasing him, she added, "Don't get me started about the way he kisses."

"I left you for one night!"

"Yeah, but nothing happened last night. I fell asleep." *Unfortunately.*

"Then when did you... Oh." Veridian frowned. "That's

why you didn't kick his ass when he paid Leo to keep you above ground."

"Yeah, he distracted me." Kayla bit her lip, thinking of that day. The man wreaked havoc on her senses. "I really like him, V. There's something about him. It feels like he actually sees me. I haven't felt that way in a long time."

Veridian's brow furrowed, and he sat down next to her. His voice turned serious. "Kayla, tread carefully. There's no future with him. At some point, he's going to go back and live in those towers. This is temporary for him. Not only that, but he's technically our boss now. If things go bad with him or you piss him off, we're stuck."

Kayla looked away, knowing he was right. Yet, she wasn't willing to dismiss her feelings based on some future possibility. It might not be the practical thing to do, but she knew better than anyone how short life could be. She might as well live her life to the fullest. There might not be a tomorrow.

Kayla offered a weak smile. "When have you ever known me to do anything sensible?"

He shook his head and sighed. They both knew there was no good answer to that question.

CHAPTER SIX

KAYLA STARED at the monitor in amazement. The security system in Carl's base was more sophisticated than she'd first guessed. Numerous, seemingly independent layers actually overlapped each other to create a complex web.

Her fingers flew across the screen. Fascinated by the intricacies of the design, she shifted through yet another layer and admired the way it aligned with its predecessor. She pulled up another monitor to line up the two layers side by side. There were definitely some security holes, but she could fix them.

Marking off the vulnerable areas, she shifted the screen to pull up the next layer. She would work on reinforcing those areas once she had them mapped out, but she wanted to see what she was up against first.

Cruncher leaned over her shoulder. "What was wrong with that last one?"

She pulled the previous layer back up and pointed to the areas she had isolated. "You've got some holes in your system, pal. It's leaking like a sieve."

"Shit, you're right."

"It's not that bad. This is actually a sweet system. Who designed it?"

"OmniLab, but I made a few tweaks. Unfortunately, Ramiro's security is similar. He'll be familiar with the ins and outs."

Kayla's eyes glinted mischievously. "Oh, really?"

Cruncher nodded. "Yeah. The system was designed to protect against ruin rats and other troublemakers. Traders don't usually go up against traders."

Kayla pulled out her commlink and scrolled through her files. "I had to analyze Ramiro's system when I scouted his base a year ago. I didn't bother with his security system because it would have taken way too long, but I did play around with the maintenance and monitoring systems. They weren't well protected."

"What are you saying?"

"You can circumvent the security by going through the maintenance and monitoring systems. Your security system isn't linked to everything. We need to fix that."

Kayla located the file she was looking for and uploaded it. She displayed the code on the screen. "I can make a few changes to this and link them together. I'll essentially add another layer, rather than modifying the existing ones. I still need to plug those other holes, but this is a pretty big threat."

Shock and disbelief came over Cruncher's face as he looked through the complex code. "You wrote this?"

She looked at the screen, trying to see it from his point of view. It was decent, but nothing spectacular. "Yeah. It's a little sloppy. I didn't think I'd have much reason to use it again, but I didn't want to get rid of it."

Cruncher let out a low, appreciative whistle. "Why do you even bother going into the pits, girl? You're a natural tech."

She wrinkled her nose. It might be okay for some people, but she prided herself on her ability to recover artifacts and wouldn't change that for anything. The tech stuff was more of a hobby. "No way. I belong in the ruins."

Cruncher shook his head. "Most techs I've seen can't work this level of technology."

She shrugged and finished modifying the code. Linking it to the security system, she fashioned another layer of security over the existing ones.

"I'll need to polish this up a bit later, but it'll provide some basic coverage for the time being. I need to go stretch my legs or something though. I've been sitting here too long."

"Yeah, go ahead." He waved her off with a nod. "Do you mind if I check out your code some more?"

"Not at all." Kayla rubbed the back of her neck, trying to stretch out the kinks, and headed toward the practice room. She was hoping Elyot was around so she could work on some locks with him. Engrossed with the idea she might be able to talk him into making a small wager, she nearly bumped into Lisia and Jinx just inside the room.

Lisia glared at her. Jinx glanced at her friend before giving Kayla a hesitant smile. "Hey, Kayla. What's up?"

"Sorry if I interrupted something. I was actually looking for Elyot. He wanted to work on some locks with me."

"Carl wasn't enough for you?" Lisia asked coldly. "Now you're planning on moving in on Elyot too?"

"Whoa there, kitten," Kayla said in surprise. "You might want to sheathe those claws before you get hurt."

Lisia turned to Jinx. "I'll talk to you later. I have things to do." Without another glance at Kayla, she walked out of the room.

"Sorry about that," Jinx apologized, shifting her weight uncomfortably. "I hope you don't judge Lisia too harshly over it. She's a good person, she's... well, she's got it pretty bad for Carl."

Kayla tried to keep her expression neutral. She wouldn't

normally be interested in camp gossip, but given her own interest in Carl, she couldn't help herself. "Carl mentioned they had been involved."

Jinx nodded. "Yeah, it was pretty stupid of Carl. He started trying to recruit Elyot about a year ago. Elyot was interested in joining up but didn't want to leave his sister behind. They went back and forth about it for a while. Lisia isn't a scavenger, and we weren't looking for more techs. They eventually came to some sort of agreement and Elyot signed up."

Kayla's eyes widened, surprised at the news. "Lisia is Elyot's sister?"

"Yeah, I thought you knew."

When Kayla shook her head, Jinx shrugged. "Well, when Elyot brought her here, Lisia sort of developed this hero-worship mentality about Carl. You know how some ruin rats are around traders. I think he was flattered at first and thought it was cute when Lisia would trail him. But it got a little intense. He screwed up and ended up fooling around with her. Carl immediately regretted it and tried to call things off with her."

Kayla knew exactly what she was talking about. She'd seen quite a few ruin rats fall all over themselves in an effort to get into a trader's good graces. She couldn't help but feel a little disappointed in Carl that he'd gone along with it. At least he realized his mistake and tried to put a stop to it though. "Did that cause problems with Elyot?"

"Yeah, some. After Carl told her he wasn't interested, she freaked out and was pretty miserable around here for awhile. But after a few weeks, it started getting a bit better. Then, when Carl started telling Xantham and Cruncher to track your movements, she lost it again."

Kayla frowned. "How long was he tracking me?"

Jinx grinned. "The past few months. We'd all heard about

you. Carl was wondering if you'd be a good fit for the team. He had Xantham hack into your comms a few times, but you kept finding out. That impressed the hell outta both Carl and Xantham. Most scavengers don't have a lot of tech skills. But then he had Cruncher manually install a sniffer directly into Leo's system a few weeks back, figuring you didn't handle the system comms. It was pretty risky, but he didn't think you'd find that one."

Kayla swallowed, not sure how she felt about the news. She knew Carl had been watching Leo's camp, but she didn't realize she was the reason. It seemed Leo was right; she wasn't good at staying under the radar. "We found it. But not until a few days ago."

"Yeah, I heard about that. Pretty awesome work routing it to that awful sound clip."

Kayla shrugged and managed a small smile. "Not really. It looked like it had been on there for weeks. Our techs didn't catch it."

Jinx nodded, looking proud. "Xantham designed it. He's good at what he does. Carl had him capture your transmissions. He started tracking your movements and Leo's financials. When he realized how much you were scavenging right under his nose, he decided to be more aggressive in recruiting you."

"But why is Lisia upset if I was just a potential recruit? She's had a problem with me since I met her."

Jinx was thoughtful for a moment. "At first, I think it was because Carl was focused on something other than her. But then she overheard Cruncher and Carl talking about the run-in they had with you over at Sector Twelve. Cruncher made some comment about how you were the most skilled ruin rat he had ever seen, and Carl told him you were also the best-looking one. It pissed Lisia off."

"Look," Jinx continued. "We're a small crew. You can't

sneeze in here without someone knowing the color of your snot. It sounds like the boss is probably into you. You seem like you can handle yourself, so play him or not, it's up to you. You know the risks. I hope you don't judge Lisia too harshly. She's normally a sweet girl, just a little confused."

Kayla nodded. "I get it. Thanks."

Jinx gave her a dismissive wave and turned back to her equipment. "No problem. If you're looking for Elyot, I think he's either in the comm room or the crew's quarters."

Still mulling over her conversation with Jinx, Kayla headed back toward the communications room. Carl and Xantham were leaning over the desk studying some readouts on a monitor. Xantham had an earpiece on but lowered it when she entered the room.

"Damn, girl, you're a sight for sore eyes."

"That she is," Carl agreed, his eyes warming. He stepped away from Xantham and motioned for Kayla to come closer. "We're still monitoring Ramiro's chatter."

"Oh?" She moved to peek over Xantham's shoulder.

Xantham tapped on the screen. "Yeah. He's been trying to get into our system for the past two days. He hasn't been able to do it yet, but he's persistent. I imagine he's pretty pissed off about it."

Carl nodded. "Xantham's been doing an excellent job at keeping him out."

"Shit, Boss," he said, grinning at Carl's compliment. "I could do this with my eyes closed."

Although Kayla was appreciative of their efforts, she felt a pang of guilt at being the one responsible for the heightened security. Although, she reasoned, it was Carl's fault for contacting OmniLab. If he'd left things alone, they wouldn't be in this situation. Xantham didn't have anything to do with it, though, and she didn't like having anyone else take care of her problems. "Anything I can do to help?"

Carl shook his head. "Xantham has this under control. But I still need to speak with you in my office if you have a few minutes."

Kayla gave a half-hearted shrug. There were worse things than being alone with a gorgeous specimen of a man.

———

CARL SLIPPED his hand around her waist to lead her toward his office. He seemed to take every opportunity to touch her. She normally didn't enjoy unsolicited touches, but Kayla found herself craving his. For someone who had prided herself on not needing anyone, this growing addiction made her feel unsettled.

Once they were inside his office, Carl enabled the privacy divider and pulled out the bottle of scotch and two glasses. She raised her eyebrows as he poured her a glass and handed it to her.

"What's this for? I managed to get through the day injury free so far."

He smiled. "I just thought you'd enjoy it."

Far be it for her to refuse his generosity. She picked up the glass and took a sip. Deciding to take the opportunity to explore, she wandered around his office. It was surprisingly neat and organized with a few old-world artifacts on display. She recognized some items from previous scavenges but others were unfamiliar.

A strange vase on one shelf caught her attention. She studied the lines of it, admiring the way it had been painted. It was simple but extraordinarily beautiful.

Carl approached her and gestured to the item. "Do you like it?"

"Yeah. I've never seen anything like it before. It almost seems to change colors when you move past it."

"That's one of my favorites. I purchased it from Warig. One of his scavengers found it. I had to have it."

"It's beautiful." Kayla took another sip, moving away to continue her exploration. She paused at a small, red button on the wall. Curious, she pressed it and a panel slid open. "You have another entrance to your private quarters through your office?" She looked inside. It would have been handy if she'd known about it the other day. All the stupid shit with Ramiro could have been avoided.

"Yes. It's convenient, and I enjoy my privacy."

Kayla remained at the doorway and glanced around the room. It was almost as neat as his office. There were a few personal touches, but not many. Based on his office and bedroom area, she figured he was a man who enjoyed simplicity and beauty. There was more extravagance in these two rooms than she'd seen in her life. It was just another reminder they were from two very different worlds.

Finished with her brief tour, Kayla turned around to face him. "So what did you want to talk to me about?"

"A few things." He took the empty glass from her and refilled her drink before handing it back to her. "Mainly, I wanted to see how you were doing."

Kayla sat down on the edge of his desk and twirled the scotch around, trying to figure him out. Perhaps it was paranoia, but she wasn't used to such scrutiny. "What do you mean?"

"I know it was a difficult decision for you to join. I hope you're not regretting it."

"Nope, I don't believe in regrets."

"No?"

She took another sip. "It's our mistakes that make us who we are."

He regarded her for a long moment. "You continue to surprise me, Kayla."

She shrugged. "I get that a lot. It's not usually meant in a good way either."

He laughed and refilled her glass again. Kayla eyed it skeptically. "I thought you warned me against drinking too much of this."

"I did," he admitted. "It definitely sneaks up on you. But I didn't think you backed away from a challenge either."

There was a mischievous glint in his eye, and she couldn't help but smile in response. This playful side of him was appealing. "What are you up to, Carl?" He didn't reply. Instead, he took a long drink and put his empty glass on the desk. Kayla laughed in delight. "All right then."

She drank the scotch and put her empty glass on the desk next to his. He refilled the glasses and moved hers toward her.

Kayla watched him toss back his drink before she grinned and did the same, wincing slightly as the liquid burned her throat. She tapped her finger on the desk, indicating she wanted another one. She was beginning to understand what he meant about it sneaking up on you. A pleasant warmth filled her belly, and her limbs were feeling much more fluid.

"You're right, you know," she admitted after he poured another round.

"Oh?"

Feeling bolder than usual, she sauntered over to him. She ran her fingers up his chest and wound her arms around his neck. "I've never been known to back away from a challenge."

Carl slipped his hands around her waist and raised an eyebrow at her. "I've noticed."

"So is this why you lured me into your office?"

"In part." He reached up to caress her face, his touch sending little shockwaves through her. "But I also wanted to talk to you."

Talking seemed highly overrated. She was enjoying the

euphoric sensation brought on by his touch. Letting her body mold to his, Kayla gave him a teasing smile. "I'm not in the mood to talk right now."

Desire flashed in his eyes, but he shook his head as though trying to clear it. "I'm not, either, but I think it's important."

She trailed small kisses up his chest and smiled inwardly when she felt his grip tighten on her hips. The problem with this trader was he liked to talk too much. It seemed like every time she turned around, he tried to have another discussion. She could tell by his body's response that he wanted her as much as she wanted him. Carl needed to learn how to live in the moment.

"You know, OmniLab is investigating the issue with Ramiro. It's likely they'll remove him as a trader."

"Mmhmm." She ran her fingers along his arms, feeling him tremble when she lightly scratched him with her nails.

He took a ragged breath. "They need to know everything that happened."

"That's nice." Kayla reached up and tugged out his ponytail. She'd wanted to see it loose for months. Running her fingers through his hair, she demanded, "I want you to kiss me."

"Kayla, I don't think you realize how irresistible you are."

"Then show me."

His mouth crushed hers as his tongue thrust forcefully into her mouth, sweeping against her own. When his hands slid upward from her hips to work their way under her shirt, she moaned in approval. He cupped her breast and rubbed his thumb against her nipple. It hardened in response, and she whimpered, wanting more.

With a curse, he broke their kiss. Resting his forehead against hers, Carl took a deep breath and groaned. "Kayla, I want you so badly right now. But not like this."

She blinked up at him in confusion. Of all the things she expected, that wasn't one of them. "Why not?"

"Because you've had too much to drink. I can't take advantage of you like that. I think we should just talk."

"Then let me take advantage of you," she insisted and kissed his neck. "I want you, Carl."

With a pained expression, he unwound her hands. "I know you think you do, but that's the alcohol talking. Wait until you're sober."

A small giggle bubbled out of her. Go figure. A trader being noble. She touched the ends of his dark hair and decided she liked it much better down. In fact, she was hard-pressed to find something about him she didn't like. Except for him wanting to talk. She could definitely do without the conversation. "I feel pretty good right now though."

"I'm sure you do."

Kayla frowned when he eased her into a chair, taking the seat beside her. He took her hand in his and began drawing small circles across her palm. "I'm worried about Ramiro, sweetheart. I don't want him to hurt you. I need you to be honest with me and tell me what happened."

She stared down at their entwined hands, remembering another time when someone else used to do the same thing. Her chest tightened, and she tried to push away the memories. "I told you already. That son of a bitch stole my damn data cube, and I got it back."

He gave her an encouraging nod. "But you didn't tell me how Pretz was involved."

The sound of his name sliced through her heart. Guilt and loss rushed over her, and she took a ragged breath. Her emotions were too close to the surface, and she was having trouble keeping them in check. Kayla looked away, unable to meet his gaze. "I don't talk about Pretz."

"Why not?"

Because it was my fault! she wanted to scream. She blinked back tears, knowing she was responsible for what happened to him. Carl lifted her chin, forcing her to look at him.

"What happened, Kayla?"

She felt her emotional walls crumble at the compassion in his eyes. With that one look, he was offering her a chance at redemption. She choked on a sob, unable to hold in the words. "It was my fault. He died because of me."

There was a long pause. When he finally spoke, there was no judgment in his tone. Instead, his voice was gentle. "What do you mean?"

Kayla squeezed her eyes shut, remembering the weeks before he died. "Pretz wanted me to try to join Ramiro's crew, but I didn't want to. I didn't like Ramiro. He and Vex were... cruel. Pretz said he treated all ruin rats like that, but he would treat me differently if I were part of the crew."

They had argued about it. Pretz had the same hero-worship mentality as Lisia when it came to traders. He'd been blind to Ramiro's faults and only saw the possibilities afforded by working for OmniLab. Even Pretz's brother had warned him about Ramiro, but Pretz wouldn't listen.

"Pretz was waiting for me above ground when I found the cube. He was thrilled when he saw it. He was sure Ramiro would make me an offer to join in exchange for the cube. I didn't think it was a good idea, but Pretz called him anyway. Ramiro and Vex showed up and demanded the data cube."

She hiccupped and rubbed her arms, wishing she could erase the painful memory. "Ramiro told Pretz women like me were only good for one thing and not worth joining a trader's crew. He said if I played nice with him, though, he'd give me a finder's fee and other special perks. When I told him no, he said since we were in his sector, he could take anything he wanted, including me. He grabbed me and pushed me to the ground and ripped my clothes. I fought him, but he's a big bastard. Veridian tried to stop him, but Vex broke his arm and dislocated his shoulder."

"Jesus, Kayla. How did you get away?"

"Pretz," she said softly. "Ramiro was on top of me, and Pretz grabbed him and fought him off. He told us to run, so we did. Later that day, we heard that Pretz had an accident in the ruins."

Kayla couldn't stop the tears from spilling down her cheeks. "We knew it was a lie, but no one would believe us over an OmniLab trader. That bastard killed Pretz. He told us to run, and we did. I didn't know they would kill him."

Lowering her voice to a whisper, she spoke the words that had been haunting her for over a year. "I loved him, and Ramiro killed him because of me."

"Shh," Carl hushed her and pulled her onto his lap. Burying her face against his chest, she let go of the emotions she had suppressed for so long. His hands stroked her hair, and she was dimly aware of his voice murmuring soothing words.

Lost in her grief, Carl's comforting presence wrapped around her until her sobs subsided and she fell into a troubled sleep.

CHAPTER SEVEN

KAYLA WOKE up disoriented and confused. Rubbing her eyes, she wondered if the scotch had something to do with it. She was still dressed in Jinx's clothes, and she recognized Carl's private quarters. With horror, she recalled what she'd told Carl. Shame and embarrassment flooded through her as she dropped her head in her hands.

Not only did she practically throw herself at him, she'd turned into a blubbering idiot and poured her heart out. Feeling raw and wanting to escape, she stood up and crossed the darkened room toward Carl's office. His light was on, and she could hear two low voices talking. She paused outside the door, not willing to face anyone until she got her emotions under control.

"That's some nasty business if Ramiro tried to force himself on Kayla and killed that poor kid."

Kayla started, recognizing Cruncher's voice. Shame quickly turned to anger at the realization they were discussing her. This was exactly why she didn't talk about her personal life. She should have known better than to trust a trader with her secrets.

"It fits," Carl was saying. "It explains why Pretz was in a cleared sector that day. It also explains why Ramiro's determined to get rid of Kayla and Veridian. When OmniLab finds out what he did and how he killed one of his employees, they'll strip his status and freeze his assets."

Kayla didn't want to hear anymore. Backing away, she stumbled to the other door leading out to the hallway. She grabbed her UV gear out of the sanitation machine and pulled it on.

Veridian was just coming out of the crew's quarters when he spotted her.

"Kayla? You okay?"

She put one hand against the wall to steady herself and managed to nod. "Yeah. I... I can't talk about it right now, V."

Concern etched on his face, he bent down to look at her closely. "You're acting strange. What's wrong?"

Kayla shook her head, trying to blink back the tears that threatened. Even though she knew Veridian would understand, she couldn't revisit her emotional torment twice in once night. She never should have told Carl what happened with Pretz.

"I talked when I shouldn't have," she said angrily as a tear rolled down her cheek. "I hate crying. I need to go clear my head." Pushing away from the wall, she took off down the hallway, intent on escaping.

———

"WHAT DID YOU DO TO HER?" Veridian stormed into Carl's office, looking furious. "I just saw Kayla, and she was crying. Kayla doesn't cry! She gets pissed off, yells, hits, and throws things. But she doesn't cry."

Carl stared at him for a moment in confusion. As his words registered, Carl darted to his private quarters and swore at the sight of the empty bed. "Damn, she woke up. I thought she would have slept longer."

Cruncher frowned, eyeing the bottle and empty glasses on the desk. "How much did you give her to drink?"

Carl rubbed his forehead. "More than I should have. She's such a little thing. She seemed pretty smashed and probably still is. I should go talk to her."

Veridian looked back and forth between them. "What are you talking about?"

"She was drinking scotch," Cruncher explained. "That stuff has a pretty high alcohol content, lowers your inhibitions, and gives you a hell of a buzz."

Veridian's expression let Carl know exactly how stupid he thought that idea was. "Why would you give that to her, of all people? Why not just let Ramiro have his way with her? Lowering Kayla's inhibitions is like throwing her off a cliff. She's reckless enough as it is."

Carl raised an eyebrow, unaccustomed to being reprimanded by a ruin rat. Apparently, Kayla and Veridian had more in common than he thought. Nevertheless, he couldn't exactly dispute Veridian's assessment. He'd been hoping she would have slept it off.

Before Carl could formulate a reply, Veridian's gaze landed on his desk. His eyes widened when he recognized the image on the tablet. "Oh shit. She told you about Pretz?"

"You knew him well?"

Veridian nodded, still looking at the picture. "Ramiro sent him to our camp one day to drop off some equipment, and he met Kayla. He fell for her pretty hard. He used to go with her into the ruins whenever he had a day off. He told her if she didn't join Ramiro's crew, he was leaving after his contract was up to be with her. He was crazy about her."

Veridian sighed. "She was really messed up after Pretz died. She lost it. That's why she went to Ramiro's camp the next day. I think part of her wanted to get caught. She blames herself for what happened."

"That's ridiculous. It wasn't her fault."

"Yeah, you try explaining that to her and let me know how it goes," Veridian retorted, crossing his arms over his chest. "I can't even bring up his name without her jumping down my throat."

He had a point. Kayla hid her emotions pretty well, but it was obvious she was still grieving. Feeling responsible for her current emotional state, Carl said, "I'll go talk to her."

He took a step toward the door and nearly ran into Xantham.

"Uh, Boss?" A look of confusion came over Xantham's face as his gaze darted between the three men.

Carl tried to brush past him. "Not now, Xantham. I need to find Kayla."

"Yeah. That's why I'm here. She took off on her speeder a few minutes ago."

He shut his eyes, hoping he'd misheard. "What?"

"Yeah, I can't get over how fast that girl drives. If the size of her bike's dust cloud was any indication, she's pretty pissed."

"Shit."

"It gets worse," Xantham told him hurriedly, shifting his weight from foot to foot. "I don't know how it happened, but Ramiro got into our system through a backdoor. I also picked up another bike on the radar that's not one of ours. It's trailing her."

Carl felt the blood rush from his face. He turned to Veridian. "Do you know where she would have gone?"

"To the ruins. That's where she always goes."

"But it's in the middle of the night and she's alone," Carl protested in disbelief.

Veridian gave out an impatient snort. "You don't have a

clue about her, do you? Day, night, alone, whatever. None of it matters to her. She says the only time she feels alive is when she's in the ruins."

"We need to find her before Ramiro does or she hurts herself. Do you have any idea which sector she would have gone to?"

Veridian shook his head. "There's no way to know. She could be anywhere. She could have even gone back to another district if she was upset enough."

"She headed east," Xantham volunteered.

"Then we'll head in that direction," Carl replied and headed toward the camp entrance. "Xantham, track her bike and send me the coordinates the minute she stops. Cruncher, come with me."

"I'm going with you too," Veridian insisted.

Carl spared him a nod and continued issuing orders. "Xantham, do whatever you need to do. I don't care what rules you break, but get into Ramiro's channels. Find out what's going on and if he's the one trailing her."

"On it, Boss."

———

THE THREE MEN headed east for what seemed an eternity. Exasperated, Carl barked into his headset, "Dammit, Xantham, give me something."

"I'm working on it, Boss. But someone's scrambling the system so I can't lock on a trace. Give me a second. I'm trying to shut down the backdoor and flush our system."

"Just do it."

A few minutes later, Xantham's voice came back over the headset. "I've got her. I'm sending the coordinates to you now. It looks like she stopped, but I don't know how long she's been there."

Carl glanced at the coordinates that flashed on his onboard screen. "Is that Sector Twelve?"

"Affirmative."

Carl swore angrily and turned his bike north toward Sector Twelve. They were at least twenty minutes away, which was twenty more than they could afford. He pushed the speeder into a higher gear, determined to cut down the time as much as possible. When they arrived, two bikes were parked above the entrance to the ruins. He recognized Kayla's bike as one of them.

"Shit," Carl muttered and yanked off his helmet. "They're both down in the ruins. Let's get the cables set up. Cruncher, I'm going to need you to go down with me. Veridian, can you handle monitoring from here?"

Both men agreed immediately. Cruncher began setting up the equipment with Carl while Veridian crouched down near Kayla's equipment.

"Something isn't right," Veridian announced. "Kayla doesn't set up her equipment like this."

Carl looked up to see Veridian raise the cable. Almost immediately, the cable came to the surface. "The end of the cable's been cut. He either dropped her or didn't want her to be able to get out."

Carl pushed aside his growing concern. He needed to focus on facts. Crouching down, he examined the frayed end. Whoever had cut the cable wanted it to appear an accident.

"Xantham, connect me to Kayla," Carl instructed over his headset.

"You're patched through. Go ahead, Boss."

"Kayla? You there?"

There was only silence on the other end. Ignoring the dread in the pit of his stomach, Carl grabbed the harness from Cruncher and strapped himself in. Cruncher did the same, and they began the long descent.

As they moved slowly downward through the levels, Carl peered around with his flashlight looking for any sign of Kayla. He finally saw her when he reached the fourth level. She was lying on the ground, not moving. The rest of the cable had fallen around her. From the amount, he estimated she'd fallen at least two or three levels.

Fear gripped him as he said over his headset, "I found her."

He stopped the cable's descent and climbed out of the harness. Another figure was facedown a few feet from her.

"Cruncher, check him out," he instructed and went directly to Kayla. He dropped to his knees next to her, calling out her name. She didn't respond.

Her helmet had been tossed aside, and her dark hair covered her face. He moved to unzip her jacket and realized her harness was missing. She couldn't have fallen. Ramiro must have been trying to recreate Pretz's accident.

Hoping they weren't too late, he felt for a pulse. It was weak, but she was alive. He brushed her hair back from her face and his hand came away wet. It was covered in blood. Her lip was cut, and there was a deep gash near her temple. Dark bruises were forming around her throat where it appeared someone had choked her.

"Shit," he said into his headset. "She's alive but unconscious. She didn't fall. She was practically beaten to death. Call Zane and Elyot. Tell them to get out here now. We're going to need a lift to bring her up. I don't want to move her more than necessary. Drop a med kit down to me, and tell Jinx to get the med room ready."

Cruncher moved over to the large man lying near Kayla and rolled him over. Vex's fixed gaze stared back at them. A deep cut was across his neck, and he was covered in blood. Cruncher shook his head at the brutality. "He's dead, Boss. It looks like she hit an artery. What the hell happened down here?"

Carl didn't bother to respond. He pulled off his jacket and shirt to rip them into makeshift bandages. Pressing firmly against Kayla's head, he tried to slow the bleeding. Her skin felt cool and clammy, and her pulse seemed to be weakening. He cursed himself for letting this happen to her.

Cruncher grabbed the med kit the moment it was lowered. He pulled out two monitors and handed one of them to Carl. "These are the new vital sign monitors. Attach one of the monitors to the inside of her wrist and one near her heart. It'll give us a more accurate reading."

Following Cruncher's instructions, Carl pressed one of the monitors on the inside of her wrist. He lifted her shirt to place the other monitor and faltered at the sight of the dark bruises around her rib area.

Cruncher shook his head, shaken by the sight. "Oh shit. What the hell did he do to her?"

Carl's jaw clenched, but he kept his hands gentle as he pressed the other monitor to her chest just below her breast. If Vex wasn't already dead, he'd be tempted to kill him again. When he was confident the device was in place, he nodded to Cruncher to activate the monitor inside the med kit.

"We're picking up her vitals now, Boss, but they're faint."

Carl leaned over her. "Kayla, can you hear me? We're going to bring you up soon. You've got a nasty bump on your head and some bruises, but you're going to be okay."

Saying a silent prayer, he hoped his words weren't superfluous. The alternative was unthinkable.

He glanced up as Cruncher moved away and picked up a knife off the ground. Examining the blade, Cruncher spoke into the headset. "Veridian, does Kayla usually carry a knife?"

Veridian hesitated before answering. "Yeah. Ever since the incident with Ramiro and Pretz, she's kept one on her. It's embedded into her belt and isn't noticeable unless you know it's there."

Carl exchanged a look with Cruncher and observed, "There's no doubt how this would have turned out if she didn't have that with her."

Cruncher made a small noise of agreement and packed the knife away in the medical kit. Carl turned back to Kayla, knowing Cruncher would probably return it to her at some point. The two of them had developed a relationship of mutual respect and even affection.

Although Cruncher had been working in the trader camp for years, even before Carl had taken over the camp, the older man had grown up as a ruin rat. He didn't speak much about his origins, but Carl had learned to value his opinions when dealing with the surface-dwellers. Cruncher had proven to be an excellent judge of character, and Carl was thankful for his guidance.

It was Cruncher who had first brought Kayla to his attention. He'd initially been skeptical when he heard about her abrasive nature, but he'd been fascinated from the moment they met. Carl was inexplicably drawn to her. His attraction went far beyond her skill as a scavenger.

She constantly challenged him, forcing him to stay one step ahead of her. Her brilliance and passion inspired him to look deeper within himself. It was so easy to get caught up in the politics of the tower and planning his future, but she reminded him of the importance of focusing on the present.

Kayla was wild and impulsive, but in the rare moments he'd been able to lower her defenses, he'd glimpsed a fragile softness within her. He wanted to draw it out and see it blossom.

His throat tightened at the thought of losing her now.

Xantham's voice came over the headset, interrupting his thoughts. "Zane and Elyot are a few minutes out. They've got

114 · JAMIE A. WATERS

the lift and the extended bike to bring her back. Jinx is setting up the med room now. She wants to know if you want her to contact OmniLab to get any additional equipment."

"Not yet. It looks like she may have some bruised or cracked ribs, but I can't tell beyond that. The head injury worries me. She's lost a lot of blood."

"She's tough. She'll make it," Cruncher said in a low voice.

Carl continued pressing the makeshift compress against her head, hoping Cruncher was right. Time seemed to move in slow motion while they waited. When Zane and Elyot finally dropped down, Carl breathed a sigh of relief. Kayla's pulse had grown even weaker.

Both men were equally shocked when they witnessed the violent scene, but they quickly worked together to transfer Kayla to the lift. The mood was subdued as they lifted her out of the ruins. Veridian nearly lost it when he saw Kayla's still figure covered with blood. Cruncher put his hand on Veridian's shoulder. "Keep it together. You won't do her any good if you fall apart right now. We've got to get her back to camp."

Veridian squared his shoulders and bent down to help reattach the lifting board to the extended bike. His hands trembled, and Carl stepped forward to take over. He motioned for Veridian to climb up next to Kayla. "She needs you."

Veridian's head jerked up, his expression one of surprise but quickly changing to one of gratitude. Carl offered him a reassuring nod before directing the rest of his men back to camp.

———

JINX WAS ALREADY in the medical room when Carl entered with Kayla in his arms. The moment he laid her on the examination table, activity erupted around him. Jinx bent down and cut off her jacket while Zane grabbed the I.V. and inserted the needle into Kayla's arm. Jinx glanced at the monitor readings with a frown. "Her blood pressure is dropping."

Carl grabbed a pouch of synthetic blood and handed it to Zane, who immediately hooked it up to the I.V. along with the saline solution. Jinx jerked open one of the drawers and pulled out a needle. She slid the needle into the I.V. and pushed a clear liquid through the line.

"What are you giving her?" Veridian leaned forward, peering over Jinx's shoulder.

"Just something to help boost her blood pressure," Jinx explained without looking away from the monitor. As soon as Kayla's blood pressure stabilized and her vital signs moved into a more acceptable range, Jinx gave her another injection. "This is a metabolic booster. It'll speed up her healing rate."

Carl adjusted the scanner hanging on the wall. "Everyone step back for a minute."

Zane and Jinx moved away from Kayla while Carl activated the scanner. A thin beam of light moved over her form and then beeped loudly. Carl studied the images that flashed on the screen.

"She's got a concussion. Her left wrist is fractured, and it looks like she has two cracked ribs. With the head wound too... This was way too close."

Carl gripped the edge of the counter and took a deep breath. It was his fault this happened. He'd known Ramiro was unbalanced since he witnessed his reaction to her in his office. He could have pushed OmniLab harder to step in immediately. Instead, he wasted time playing games trying to get her to open up to him.

Jinx put her hand on Carl's arm. "It could have been

worse. We can fix those. She'll be okay, Carl. You got to her in time."

A chair squeaked across the floor. Carl turned to see Veridian sit beside the medical bed. The younger man stroked Kayla's hair and kissed her forehead, whispering reassuring words in her ear.

Carl felt a pang of jealousy at the display of tenderness. He longed to be the one next to her, but he hadn't earned that right. He might not be able to erase what happened, but he could make sure Ramiro never hurt anyone again.

Determination in his gaze, he declared, "It shouldn't have happened in the first place." He pressed the button on his commlink. "Xantham, what have you learned?"

"Just a second, Boss. I'll be right there."

A minute later, Xantham appeared. When he saw Kayla, his eyes widened in shock. "Holy shit. What the hell did he do to her?"

"From the looks of it, he smacked her around and tried to strangle her," Zane said in a dry voice and crossed his arms over his chest. "But it looked like Kayla was able to drop the bastard before he could finish the job."

"Oh man."

Carl turned to him. "What did you find out?"

Xantham tore his eyes away from Kayla. "Ramiro didn't want to get his hands dirty, so he sent Vex. Vex had been camping right outside the range of our perimeter. They locked onto her bike signal as soon as she left. Ramiro told him to make it look like an accident."

Carl's eyes hardened. "Did he say anything else?"

Xantham looked uncomfortable. "Vex... uh, laughed and said the little whore was going to meet the same end as her boyfriend. Ramiro's been freaking out for the past hour since Vex stopped transmitting."

"Tell me you have it recorded."

"Yeah, but Boss, I don't think OmniLab will be real happy if they find out I hacked into Ramiro's comms."

"I don't care," Carl dismissed his concerns. Playing by the straight and narrow hadn't prevented two people from dying and another from being seriously injured. "You acted on my orders. I'm sending the recording to OmniLab. He's not getting away with this."

Xantham nodded. Jinx waved her hands, motioning everyone toward the door. "Everyone out except Veridian. I need to put on the bone molds and get her cleaned up."

"I'm staying," Carl said firmly.

Jinx frowned. As the crew trickled out, Jinx said, "Fine. But you don't need to watch. She deserves some privacy after what she's been through."

Carl obediently averted his eyes while Veridian and Jinx undressed Kayla and cleaned her wounds. After Jinx wrapped her ribs with the bone molds, Veridian pulled a blanket over Kayla. "Okay, Carl. We're done."

Carl turned back around. Kayla's dark hair fell around her face and was still damp from where Jinx had washed the blood out of it. Her eyes were closed, and she looked extraordinarily pale. The bruises around her neck were darkening. Carl could see the outline of where Vex's fingers had gripped her.

Jinx pointed to the bone mold on the counter. "Carl, would you mind putting that on her wrist?"

He nodded and gently lifted Kayla's hand to wrap her wrist in the mold. Jinx adjusted the I.V. "It'll take a few hours for the bone molds to finish regenerating her bones. She'll need at least one more bag of synthetic blood, but at least her vitals are stable now. With that concussion, she'll probably be confused when she wakes up. I don't want to give her a painkiller until then. Right now, being unconscious is the best thing for her."

"I'll take care of it," Carl offered.

"In that case, I'm going to go get rid of these clothes. We're going to need to get her some more UV gear. These are trashed."

"That's fine. I'll arrange it." It was the least he could do. Hell, he'd buy her a new speeder if he thought it would make it up to her.

Jinx stepped out of the room, carrying the ruined clothes. Veridian held Kayla's uninjured hand and watched her silently. Carl pulled up another chair and sat on the other side of Kayla. He put his head in his hands and sighed.

"So what happens now?"

He glanced up to see Veridian's worried expression. "I'll send the recording to OmniLab. They need to know what happened. They have an obligation to protect her as part of the contract." He wished he felt as confident as he sounded. OmniLab should never have put Ramiro into a position of authority.

"She won't get into any trouble over killing Vex, will she?"

Carl shook his head. He'd make sure of it. "No. There's no doubt she was simply defending herself."

"I'd love to be alone with Ramiro for five minutes right now."

Carl nodded in agreement. "You're not the only one."

They both fell silent for several minutes. "She's going to be pissed when she wakes up and sees this. She hates being sick or injured."

Carl's mouth twisted into a smile, remembering how she'd objected to using the medicinal cream. "I believe it."

"Thanks for going down to get her. Most traders wouldn't have done that."

"I don't think she would have been down there if it weren't for me," Carl admitted in frustration. "I gave her the scotch hoping to get her to open up and talk to me about

Pretz. I knew there was more to the story than she originally told me. I should have waited for her to come around in her own time."

Veridian shook his head. "I'm not sure about that. Don't get me wrong, I'm angry this happened, but I don't know about the rest. It's been a year, and she hasn't opened up about Pretz. Tonight was the first time I actually saw her cry. She's kept all those feelings bottled up for a long time. She needed to let them out."

"She told me she loved him."

Veridian looked at him in surprise and then considered Kayla thoughtfully. "She never told me that. I knew she cared about him, but I didn't realize..." His voice trailed off, indecision playing across his face. After a long moment, he said, "She can sometimes come across as being a sarcastic hard-ass, but that's not who she is. Kayla's got one of the biggest hearts I've ever seen. She's either been hurt or has lost everyone she's ever cared about. She doesn't like to let people get too close."

Carl raised an eyebrow, surprised at the volunteered information. From everything he'd seen, Veridian was a staunch defender of Kayla's privacy. Wondering where this sudden loquaciousness was coming from, he observed, "She seems to be close to you."

"I guess, but I've hurt her too. After my mother died, Kayla needed me and I wasn't there for her. She turned to Pretz instead."

"Kayla was close to her?"

Veridian rubbed Kayla's hand and didn't answer right away. When he did, his voice was quiet. "Yeah. Kayla grew up in our camp. There was some sort of collapse in the ruins when she was a kid. Leo and my mother heard screams and went to investigate. Several people were down there when the beams fell. One of the women in the group was badly hurt but conscious. When she saw Leo and my mother, she pushed Kayla through a small opening and begged my mother to take her. My mother pulled Kayla out right before another beam fell. Leo and my mother were lucky to make it out of there alive."

"What the hell were they doing taking a kid into the ruins?" Carl had difficulty imagining taking a child down into the ruins. There were far too many dangers.

Veridian shrugged. "She was a little young, but it's not that unusual. We have to learn sometime. Leo tried to find out what camp she was from. He asked some other scavengers, but no one seemed to know anything about them. He gave up and figured they were new to the area, maybe starting a new camp."

"I wasn't much older than Kayla when she came to live with us." Veridian smiled at the memory. "She was headstrong, even then. She had to know how everything worked. I think she drove people crazy with her nonstop questions, but she was absolutely brilliant. If you showed her something once, she immediately caught on. She was easily out-scavenging seasoned ruin rats by the time she was twelve."

"How long ago did she come to live with you?"

Veridian thought carefully. "I don't know. I'm guessing it was about sixteen years ago. That would make her around twenty or twenty-one now."

Carl sat back, somewhat surprised. He'd known she was young, but it was strange to have it confirmed. Most people with her level of skill and experience were several years older. It seemed they both had one more thing in common: responsibility had been put on both of them at a young age.

Glancing down at her, his heart thrummed in his chest. She looked so vulnerable surrounded by the medical equipment. He ached to pull her into his arms and hold her. He swallowed and looked up to see Veridian studying him with an uncanny awareness. Carl cleared his throat. "I'm surprised you're being this open with me."

Veridian rubbed his thumb across the top of Kayla's hand. "Kayla's been living in a fog since Pretz died. She's gone through the motions but there's been something missing. She might kick my ass for telling you everything, but I doubt it. Scotch or not, she wouldn't have opened up to you about Pretz if she didn't want you to know. It's more than that though." He looked up to meet Carl's eyes. "She lights up when she's around you. I've missed seeing that spark in her. I know it won't last, but I'm thankful you brought it back."

Carl opened his mouth to object, but words failed him. Veridian was right. Anything between him and Kayla could only be temporary. He had less than three years left on his contract. After that, he had to return to the towers. No matter what was growing between them, it wasn't fair to her to begin something he couldn't finish.

A monitor beeped, and Carl stood to replace the pouch of synthetic blood with a new one. He adjusted her I.V. line, and she moved slightly.

"I think she's waking up. Kayla? Can you hear me?"

Her green eyes slowly opened, and Carl sighed in relief. She squinted at the bright light and tried to look around the room. Crying out in pain from the effort, she fell back again.

Veridian stood, putting his hands on her shoulders to prevent her from trying to sit up. "You need to stay still, Kayla. You were hurt. You've lost a lot of blood and broken a few bones. It'll take a few more hours for them to be repaired."

Kayla lifted her broken wrist and stared at the bone mold.

"Shit." Dropping her wrist back down, she winced in pain. "My head is freaking killing me. What happened?"

"What do you remember?" Veridian sat back down beside her.

She frowned. "Uh, crap. I think... I was in the ruins?"

Carl picked up the painkiller and brought it toward her I.V. line. "That's right. You should feel better pretty soon though. You need to rest right now."

She held up her hand when she saw the needle. "Wait. Stop. Don't give me that yet. It makes me stupid. I need to remember. Oh shit. It even hurts to breathe."

Carl paused, the needle hovering by the I.V. line. "Kayla, it'll stop the pain."

"No, dammit. Hang on. Let me think a minute," she insisted stubbornly. She closed her eyes and concentrated. Her eyes flew open. "Where's Vex?"

"He's dead." Veridian's voice was matter-of-fact.

"He is?" She reached up with her uninjured hand to touch her throat, wincing in pain at the movement. "He was choking me. I grabbed my knife and tried to stop him. He... Did he throw me into the wall?"

Carl nodded. "Kayla, it's going to be all right. I'm going to give you the painkiller now."

When she didn't offer any further objections, he pushed the medicine into the line and watched as she began to relax. "Oh, crap... that's... that works. I guess I needed that."

"You're actually admitting I was right?"

"Maybe," she murmured and looked up at him. With her uninjured hand, she reached out to grasp his hand. He pressed a kiss on the inside of her palm, careful not to hurt her further. She gave a long, drawn-out sigh. "Too damn pretty. Why did you have to be a trader?"

Carl chuckled. "So I could get stubborn ruin rats out of trouble. Now you need to close your eyes and get some rest."

Once he'd made sure she was sleeping comfortably, Carl headed toward the common room. His crew was standing around talking but fell silent the moment he entered.

Jinx took a step toward him. "Is she awake?"

"She's sleeping again, but she regained consciousness for a few minutes. I gave her the painkiller, and it knocked her out." Carl turned to the rest of the crew. "I know you're concerned, but she's going to be fine. We're going to need to take shifts around the clock for a while until this issue with Ramiro is settled. I'll push on OmniLab to try to get them moving."

Xantham scratched his head. "I'm going to need to take the first shift then. Zane, you mind joining me? I need to make sure our comms are locked up tight after they infiltrated them earlier."

After Zane agreed, Cruncher spoke up. "Elyot and I will take the second shift."

"Carl, I think I should stay with Kayla tonight," Jinx suggested. "She seems to be out of danger, but I don't want to take any chances."

Carl threw her a grateful look. "Thanks, I was going to ask you to check in on her throughout the night. Veridian is going to stay with her, but I would feel more comfortable if you watched her too."

She turned to Lisia. "Would you mind checking in on her tomorrow during the second shift? Or would you rather help out with the security systems?"

Lisia looked up from the ground when everyone's gaze fell on her. "I-I'll work security tomorrow," she stammered before turning away and striding out of the room.

Elyot frowned at his sister's behavior. "Jinx, I can check on her tomorrow instead."

Carl held up his hand, waving off Elyot's excuses. "That's all right. Why don't you guys get some rest? I need to go give Ramiro a call and tell him to get Vex's body out of my district."

CHAPTER EIGHT

ELYOT STARED at the code on the screen. "No way! She wrote that? I thought she was a scavenger."

Cruncher chuckled at Elyot's reaction. "Yeah. That's what I thought too. This is the same code she wrote to distract Ramiro so she could steal the Aurelia Data Cube."

Elyot let out a low whistle and gestured to his sister. "Lisia, you're a tech. You should see this."

"I'll pass." She waved him off, not bothering to turn away from her screen. Elyot started to make a comment but fell silent when he noticed Carl standing in the doorway.

"Hey, Boss. Didn't know if we would see you today."

"Yeah, I've been on my commlink all morning." Carl leaned over the desk to see what they were working on. "What's this?"

Cruncher sat back in his chair and gestured to the monitor in front of him. "I was showing Elyot the code Kayla wrote when she stole the data cube. She modified it so it'll protect our system from the same type of attack. Apparently, some of our critical base systems were vulnerable."

At Carl's obvious interest, Cruncher entered a few

commands. The new code appeared on the screen, along with the overlay system Kayla modified.

Carl looked at the code in surprise. "When did she do this?"

"She started working on it yesterday. Then, this morning when she woke up, she insisted I hook her into the system so she could work on it from the med room. For the past several hours that girl has been tearing apart our security and rebuilding it."

Carl chuckled, imagining the scene. "She's been doing all this from the med room?"

"Yeah, she was pretty pissed with Veridian for not letting her get up. Veridian compromised by letting her work from the med room. That girl is something else. I've never seen anyone with her skills either above or below ground. I don't know how the hell she does it."

Lisia turned away from her screen and stared at the three men, not bothering to hide her disgust. "How much longer are you going to keep going on about this? I'm sick and tired of listening to you guys fawn over her."

Cruncher raised an eyebrow. "When you start bringing in a fraction of the credits that girl does in a week, let me know. Then I'll start singing your praises too."

Elyot moved between them and held up his hands. "Come on, Cruncher. Leave her alone."

Lisia shook her head and pushed away from her desk. "No, Elyot, I'm sick of this. Every single one of you has been going on about her since she came up on your radar. But how much of it is her so-called talent you're admiring? From the looks of things, she's been nothing but trouble since you first saw her. She's got us on lockdown over here, and we're working around the clock because of *her*. Personally, I think it's her assets that have you drooling."

Carl had just about reached his limit with her attitude.

Cruncher wasn't helping matters either; he'd never been fond of Lisia. "That's enough. All of you. Lisia, you're a good tech and we appreciate everything you do. You and Kayla are both valuable members of this team. We need to work together and try to get along."

Lisia let out a forced laugh. "So maybe I should mimic your behavior and try sleeping with her? Because from where I'm standing, that's what it looks like you want."

Elyot's eyes widened. "Lisia... don't," he said in a low whisper.

Anger floored Carl, but he managed to rein it in. "This conversation is over."

"Fine." Lisia slammed her monitoring station shut. Without another word, she stormed out of the room.

Elyot looked sheepish and ran his hand through his hair. "I'm sorry about that, Boss. I'll talk to her."

Carl shook his head. He'd put off dealing with Lisia long enough. "No. I appreciate the offer, but I'll speak with her. I've given her more leeway than I should have because of what happened. That was my fault. I need to be the one to work this out with her."

Elyot hesitated. "I suppose you're right. I'll stay out of it as much as I can, but she's still my sister, Carl."

"I know. That's why I haven't pushed until now."

Elyot nodded and sat back down. With a deep breath, Carl headed down the hallway after Lisia. When he reached the crew's quarters, he found her talking to Zane. Judging by Zane's discomfort and relief at seeing Carl, it was clear she was complaining again. Carl clenched his jaw and tried to maintain his composure. "Lisia, I need to speak with you in my office."

Her shoulders stiffened, but she gave him a curt nod before turning to Zane. "Sorry, I'll catch you later."

Carl ignored the questioning look on Zane's face and

followed Lisia. She flounced into his office and turned to him when she reached the desk.

Even in her anger, Carl couldn't deny she was extraordinarily pretty. Her long, blond hair was piled on top of her head with a few curls falling around her face. She was tall and slender with delicate features. Her blue eyes were full of a mixture of hostility and apprehensiveness. Unfortunately, her once sweet nature had been replaced by an angry bitterness.

"You need something, Carl?"

He didn't answer immediately. Instead, he engaged the privacy controls. There would be enough rumors circulating over their previous argument in the tech room. He didn't need to add more fuel to the fire. "We need to talk about your attitude, Lisia."

She leaned against his desk and crossed her arms over her chest. "What's to discuss? You've made it clear you're no longer interested in me."

Carl sighed and tried to remain diplomatic. "Lisia, you're a good person and a good tech. What happened between us shouldn't have happened. I crossed a line when I kissed you. I gave you the wrong impression and I apologize."

Lisia's expression clouded as her shoulders slumped. "I thought there was something between us. I don't understand what changed. I care about you."

Carl could see the pain in her eyes. He wanted to be gentle with her, but she'd gone too far. "I don't want to hurt you. I've never wanted to hurt you. But this has got to stop."

She frowned. "This is because of Kayla, isn't it? Until she came into the picture, everything was fine. What's so special about her?"

"You're wrong. This has nothing to do with her," Carl insisted, although part of him wondered if she might have a point. The more he was around Kayla, the more he wanted her, even to the point of being distracted from his responsibilities. On some level, he recognized he was approaching dangerous territory. A relationship between a ruin rat and a trader could be disastrous.

"I don't believe that. I've seen the way you look at her. She has every single man in this camp practically falling over himself trying to get her attention. It's too bad Vex wasn't able to finish what he started." Her hand flew to her mouth. She shook her head and whispered, "I didn't mean that."

Her words were the last straw. Carl gave her a hard look. "Are you sure about that?"

She didn't answer. Carl leaned across his desk. "You signed a one-year contract with me. That contract is up in two months. Unless I see a dramatic shift in your attitude and you begin treating everyone on this team with respect, your contract will *not* be renewed."

Her blue eyes widened in shock at his declaration. "Elyot won't stay without me."

"If that's what happens, so be it. I'm prepared to lose both of you, if that's what you decide. You need to figure out if that's what you want, and if you're willing to go back to your old life."

Lisia swallowed and straightened her shoulders. She placed her hands on her hips and gave him a cold stare. "I understand. Is there anything else you wanted to discuss with me?"

"No, that's all."

She started to turn away, but Carl held up his hand to stop her. "Lisia, I hope you consider this carefully. Your decision will also affect your brother."

"You've made yourself clear, Carl." Lisia turned on her heels and left his office.

Carl slumped down in his chair and ran his hands over his face in frustration. He supposed his confrontation with her could have gone worse. At least she hadn't tried to take a swing at him.

A beep from his commlink interrupted his musing. Flipping it open, he stared at the message from OmniLab. A representative from the towers was coming to the camp to discuss the situation with Ramiro. He sighed and tossed it on his desk. If it wasn't one thing, it was something else.

He pushed away from his desk. If OmniLab was coming, he needed to let Kayla know and prepare her. There was no doubt they were going to want to speak with her about the Aurelia Data Cube incident. The representatives from OmniLab would probably be in for a shock when they realized how large of a rift there was between themselves and the so-called ruin rats.

———

THE MOMENT CARL left his office, he heard shouting. Alarmed, he ran down the hall where the yelling seemed to be originating from.

Jinx, Veridian, and Xantham were standing in the hallway outside the medical room. Veridian was leaning against the wall and seemed undisturbed by the noise. Jinx was chewing on her lip anxiously and looked as though she wanted to intervene while Xantham tried to stifle his laughter.

"What the hell is going on?" Carl demanded.

Veridian shrugged. "Leo stopped by to see Kayla. He wanted to see for himself what Ramiro did to her."

Jinx shook her head in exasperation. "They've been yelling at each other for about twenty minutes now."

"At least they aren't breaking anything." Veridian grinned.

"Is this normal?" Carl glanced at the closed door, incredulous at their behavior.

"This is relatively tame. Usually it's much worse, but I

guess it's to be expected since Kayla isn't running at full capacity yet."

"You should hear some of the insults, Boss." Xantham chuckled. "Kayla's got some especially creative ones."

"This is absurd. I'm putting a stop to this." Carl reached for the door, narrowly avoiding being hit when it swung open. Leo stormed out, his face red and furious. When he saw Carl, he squared his shoulders and puffed out his chest.

"Good. It's you. Maybe you'll have better luck getting that screeching harpy in there to listen to reason."

"I heard that, you snot-nosed, scrawny-assed half-wit!" Kayla shouted. "How the hell did you learn to walk on your hands and teach your asshole how to talk?"

"Shut up, you pit-diving, self-absorbed shrew. Your betters are talking!" Leo shouted over his shoulder and winked at Carl.

"What betters? You can't count your balls and get the same answer twice!" Kayla yelled from inside the room.

Xantham burst out laughing. Veridian grinned, and Jinx tried unsuccessfully to hide her smile. Carl stared at Leo. The man had to be insane.

"What the hell do you think you're doing, Leo?" Carl demanded in a low whisper.

"I should ask you the same question. You take my best scavenger for the sake of protecting her and let *this* happen?"

Veridian interrupted. "Leo, Carl was the one who saved her. She wouldn't be here if it weren't for him."

"Don't think I don't know that, boy," Leo reproved and turned back to Carl. "I'm grateful for what you did for her. When Veridian called me and told me what happened, I needed to come out here and see how bad off she was. Now that I've seen for myself, I know she'll be okay. She's still got her fight left in her."

"You were intentionally trying to provoke her?"

Leo grinned, rocking back on his heels. "Of course. How else do you get through to her? She's got more spit and vinegar in her than anyone. If she wasn't bitching and yelling, I'd know it was serious."

Carl rubbed his forehead, trying to stave off the headache that threatened. "Xantham, can you show Leo out? Kayla needs rest, not... whatever this is."

Xantham grinned and led Leo toward the exit. One hurdle overcome, Carl took a deep breath and stepped into the medical room prepared to face a bigger challenge. How such a willful personality could fit inside a petite, curvy body was a mystery.

Kayla was sitting up looking down at her legs as they dangled off the side of the bed. Her head shot up when he entered.

Her eyes were bright, and her skin was slightly flushed from yelling back and forth with Leo. Her dark hair was loose around her face, and Carl noticed the bone molds had been removed. Someone had brought her some clean clothes, and the bruises were barely noticeable.

"Are you all right?"

"Oh. Hey, Carl. I thought you were Leo coming back to go another round."

"You seem to be feeling better," he observed.

"Yeah. I'm tired of sitting here though," she complained. "Veridian wouldn't let me get up. Then he stuck Leo on me."

"Oh?"

Veridian stepped into the room. "Only because you were bound and determined to try to get up and go running around. Kayla, you nearly died! You need to rest. Let your body heal."

She waved her hand, dismissing his objections. "So you've been telling me all day. I get it."

Carl sighed in exasperation. "Kayla, you're a piece of work. Veridian, give me a few minutes with her."

Veridian raised an eyebrow but didn't object. He left the room, closing the door firmly behind him.

Carl crossed the room to stand in front of Kayla. He gently tilted her head back and studied her. The cut on her head appeared to be rapidly healing, thanks to the OmniLab medicine.

"How do you feel?"

"Other than wanting to drag Ramiro through the district tied to the back of my speeder? Much better, thanks."

"Don't worry. He'll get what's coming to him," Carl promised. "You had us worried, Kayla. We thought we were going to lose you."

"Yeah, I heard." She glanced away and bit her lower lip. When she turned back to look at him, her face was filled with uncertainty.

"I'm not very good at this, but I... um... wanted to thank you. Veridian told me you were the one who stayed with me and brought me up from the ruins. He said you sat in here with me afterwards for a long time too."

A small smile touched his face. "Yes, I did, and you're welcome. I'm glad you're all right."

Clearly uncomfortable with the direction of the conversation, she tugged at a loose thread on the blanket. "So did you find out anything more about Ramiro?"

He shook his head. "Not much. I called him last night and told him where to retrieve Vex's body. I'm sure he's done it by now. He was pretty pissed about it. But you don't have anything to worry about. I contacted OmniLab to escalate the petition and they're reviewing it now."

"I didn't know I'd killed him until Veridian told me."

Carl sat down on the edge of the bed next to her. "What do you remember?"

Kayla frowned. "I had just gotten down to the fourth level and I was sitting there, thinking. I remember hearing the motor of a cable and I thought it was either you or Veridian. I figured you guys had come looking for me. When my cable fell down, I realized it was probably one of Ramiro's goons.

"Next thing I knew, Vex knocked me to the ground. He kicked me, but I managed to get back up. He lifted me up and started choking me. I couldn't breathe," she recalled, rubbing her throat absently. "I didn't even think about it. I grabbed my knife and lashed out. I must have cut him. I didn't even realize I'd hurt him. I think he threw me into the wall. I don't remember anything after that."

Carl reached out, putting his hand over hers. "You did what you had to do, Kayla."

"I know," she said in a soft voice. "I don't feel any guilt for killing that bastard. I just wish it had been a year ago."

Carl squeezed her hand, wanting to reassure her. "You did the right thing."

"Yeah," she murmured and let her gaze drop to the floor. She bit her lip and looked up at him hopefully. "Think this mess with Ramiro will be cleared up and I can go back to scavenging in a couple days?"

Carl shook his head, unsurprised by her eagerness to get back to work. He'd known she was going to be a terrible patient. "No way. You need to stay above ground a bit longer than a couple days. The petition against Ramiro should be resolved soon, but you still need to heal."

Her lips turned down into a pout. "What kind of time frame are you thinking? Two days? Three?"

"Why don't we take it a day at a time and see how you're progressing. You're healing rapidly, thanks to the booster we gave you, but you still need to give yourself some time."

Kayla blew out a breath, and he could tell she was frustrated. "Well, can I at least get out of this stupid room? It's making me crazy. I'm not an invalid."

"That's fine."

"Good. I want to see what Cruncher's been doing with my security modifications. I also want to get Xantham to show me the comm system so I can figure out how they managed to get through to your system."

Carl chuckled at her enthusiasm. "I'm sure Cruncher would be happy to show you. He was admiring your work earlier. You're very talented, Kayla. Where did you learn your tech skills?"

She bumped her shoulder against his playfully. "You should know better than to ask. Ruin rats don't tell traders their secrets."

Carl raised an eyebrow, pretending to scrutinize her. "Hmm. Now that I think about it, you're not looking as well as I first thought. You may need to stay in bed for at least a week. I'm not sure you should overly excite yourself by looking at security or communication systems either."

Kayla's face fell at his words and she scowled. "Why, you lousy, sneaky—"

"Careful, Kayla," he warned teasingly. "You might even need two weeks to recover if you get yourself worked up again."

Her eyes narrowed, and she glared at him, clamping her mouth shut.

"So you were about to tell me where you learned your tech skills," he hinted.

"You're almost as bad as Veridian," she accused and then shrugged. "Well, there's no big mystery. I've always had a knack for it. It sounds kinda silly, but I've always thought computers were a lot easier to understand than people."

"What do you mean?"

"They do what you tell them to do, and if it doesn't

work, it's not because they're mad at you, or feel threatened by you, or think you're a smartass. It's because you didn't do it right. They're infinitely patient too. You can keep trying until it's finally right. They don't ever give up on you."

Carl watched her quietly for a moment. Her head was slightly lowered, and she was intently studying the blanket on the bed. The tough exterior she portrayed to the world had slipped away. She looked so uncharacteristically vulnerable that he wanted to take her in his arms and reassure her everything would be all right.

"That makes sense."

Kayla looked up at him and blushed when she realized she'd said too much. Carl smiled at her. The light flush on her cheeks was endearing and so unlike the normal façade she presented to the world.

He took her hand in his again. "Well, since you were forthcoming with me, I think we should see about getting you into the tech room. Are you still interested?"

"Hell yeah!"

"And she's back," he said, chuckling at her exuberance. He helped her up and put his arm around her waist to steady her. "Go ahead and lean on me. Take it slow."

She took a few tentative steps and muttered, "Okay, maybe you were right about keeping me above ground for a few days. This sucks."

He chuckled and slid the door open to find Veridian and Jinx waiting outside. Veridian gaped at Kayla. "She shouldn't be out of bed yet."

"It's okay, Veridian. I'm taking her into the tech room for a few minutes, and then she promises to go to bed."

"What? No, I didn't," Kayla protested.

"Yes, you did. If you've forgotten already, maybe you should lie down now."

"You're too damn sneaky." She sighed in resignation. "I guess I did then."

"Good girl," he whispered in her ear, giving her a slight squeeze. She laughed at his teasing.

Veridian started to object again and then shrugged. "I guess you know what you're doing."

Carl walked her into the tech room, impressed with her determination. Cruncher jumped out of his chair and gave her a gentle hug, careful to avoid her injuries. The two men helped ease her into a chair in front of the monitors.

"Glad you're okay, kiddo. You had us worried."

Kayla offered him a smile and gestured to the monitors. "I'm just glad to be out of the med room. Bring on the goodies, Cruncher. Let me see what you managed to do while they had me locked up all day."

"You're gonna love this," Cruncher predicted and pulled up the security overlay. Kayla's eyes immediately fixed on the screen.

"I'll be back in a few minutes," Carl promised. "And then you're going to bed."

"Yeah, sure, whatever." She waved dismissively, not bothering to look away from the screen.

Carl chuckled. "Mind keeping an eye on her, Cruncher?"

"No problem, Boss." Cruncher sat next to her and rested his arm on the back of her chair. He leaned over her to point out some areas of the screen.

Pleased she was recovering well, Carl was still smiling when he left the room and headed to his office.

————

KAYLA STUDIED the security images Cruncher pulled up on the screen. She was impressed with how far he'd gotten on her designs since this morning. He'd incorporated a few new ideas into them, and she wondered how she could apply it to other programs she'd worked on.

"How does it look?"

Kayla turned at the sound of Carl's voice. "Fantastic. I think we've got everything locked down tight. I want to make a few more tweaks, but even I would have a hard time getting through this system now." She beamed with pride. It was some of her best work. "I haven't looked at the communication system yet though."

"Soon. But you need to get some rest now."

She started to object but fell silent at the look on his face. With a sigh, she stood up. Carl took a step toward her. "Do you need help?"

"No, I can do this." She shook her head, squaring her shoulders in determination. "I need to do this."

Carl kept pace with her as she made her way toward the crew's quarters. Even though he didn't insist on helping her, she enjoyed his reassuring presence. He was quieter than usual, though, and Kayla wondered about it.

"Is everything okay? You seem distracted."

"I'm fine." He darted a quick glance at her. "There is something I need to tell you though. I got a message from OmniLab earlier. They're going to send someone out to talk about the petition against Ramiro. They'll probably want to speak with you. I'm hoping you'll be nice."

Kayla rolled her eyes. Be nice? To a bunch of Omnis? "Are you asking me to be nice or kiss their ass? Because it'll be a cold day in hell before the latter happens."

He chuckled in spite of himself. "I suppose I'll be thankful for nice."

She winked at him and offered, "In that case, I'll see what I can do."

When they arrived at her private area within the crew's quarters, he followed her inside and activated the privacy settings. Kayla raised her eyebrows. "Don't tell me you're going to get frisky with me while I'm recuperating," she teased.

His mouth twisted into a grin. "As tempting as that would be, I'll try to restrain myself. I wanted to let you know there's a good chance they're going to ask you about Pretz. I understand it's painful for you, but you'll need to tell them what happened."

She sat on the edge of her bed. "Screw that. You want me to tell a couple of pompous Omnis about my personal life? Keep dreaming, pal."

Carl opened her locker and took out the picture of Pretz. Her heart pounded. Why was he bringing this up again? He tried to hand it to her, but she pushed it away.

"Put it back."

He put the picture on her lap. "Kayla, I want you to look at him. He meant a great deal to you. I'd like you to tell me about him."

She stiffened. It was bad enough she'd poured her heart out to him before. She didn't need to do it again. "I'm not interested in your games. Take it, Carl. Put it away. Leave the past in the past."

He shook his head and said stubbornly, "He was important to you. That memory deserves to be honored."

Kayla looked down at the picture. Pretz's smiling face stared up at her, and she studied it for a long time. She traced her fingers over his image. She felt a pang of sadness, remembering his laughter. "Why are you pushing this, Carl?"

"It's important for you to talk about it. The more you talk about it, the easier it'll get. You've kept this bottled inside for almost a year. Don't you think it's time you let some of your pain out?"

He didn't understand. It wasn't just about losing Pretz. She'd lost part of herself when he died. "What do you know about it? You know absolutely nothing about losing someone you care about! He was one of the only people who ever gave me a second thought. Because of me, he's gone. If I had only..." Her eyes welled with tears as she looked away.

"Kayla, it's not your fault. It's Ramiro's and Vex's fault. If it weren't for them, he'd still be alive. You need to stop blaming yourself."

Carl's voice was full of compassion, and it made the heaviness in her chest even worse. Kayla put the picture aside, not wanting to look at it anymore. "Go away, Carl. I don't want to talk about this."

He ignored her request. Instead, he sat next to her and put his arm around her. She stiffened but didn't pull away.

"What was he like?" he asked and put the picture back on her lap again.

He was torturing her. She wanted to lash out and push him away, but she doubted it would do any good. That tactic had proven ineffective with him. She hung her head in resignation. "He... he was the only person in Ramiro's crew with an ounce of talent and charm."

"You met him when he came to your camp?"

Kayla nodded, smiling at the memory and brushing tears out of her eyes. "Yeah, he was an impossible flirt. He used to wait for me outside Leo's camp and follow me to our scavenge sites. He was incredibly annoying and sweet at the same time."

"Was he the one who taught you how to work locks?"

"Mmhmm," she murmured and traced his outline on the photograph. "I was already pretty good at locks, but he was amazing. He knew how competitive I was and turned it into a game. There was this stupid song he used to hum while he was working the locks. It drove me crazy because it was so distracting, but I'd love to hear it one more time."

"What was it that you liked about him?"

Kayla sighed and leaned into Carl, letting his warmth surround her. "He loved being in the ruins. Although I think part of him said that because he knew how I felt about them. He used to sneak off from Ramiro's camp to go scavenging with me. We would end up sitting there and talking for hours. He was such a dreamer."

"What do you mean?"

"He always had these big plans for the future," she explained with a laugh. "He wanted to one day run his own camp or make some kind of outrageous discovery and try to buy his way into the towers."

"What about you? Did you want that too?"

She shook her head. "No. Until Pretz, I'd never thought about the future. If I spent all my time fantasizing about the future, I'd forget to live in the present. But he seemed to enjoy it, and I liked listening to him." Kayla put the picture on the small table next to her bed. "I never told him I loved him. I didn't even realize I did until after he was gone."

Carl looked at her in surprise. "I'm sure he knew how much you cared for him."

"Maybe," she said in a quiet voice. She hoped he did. "If there's one thing I've learned, it's that life is far too unpredictable."

"I agree, but that's part of what makes it precious." Carl reached up to tuck her hair behind her ear. His hand caressed the side of her face, sending chills through her. "I should probably let you get some rest."

"Carl, wait." She put her hand on his arm to stop him. "Don't go yet."

He raised an eyebrow. "You're still recovering, Kayla. You should try to get as much rest as you can. We can talk more tomorrow. The sooner you heal, the sooner you can go back into the ruins."

"I know," she said impatiently, but her thoughts weren't

on scavenging. In forcing her to confront her demons, he'd loosened something inside her.

What she felt for Carl wasn't the same as what she'd felt for Pretz. There was no substitution. Her relationship with Pretz had been consummated in innocence. They'd both been blind to the realities of their harsh world. With Carl, there was no future, and he'd never make empty promises. In some ways, it made it easier. She could live fully in the moment with him and not worry about tomorrow.

Kayla leaned toward him and pressed her lips against his. When he didn't immediately push her away, she wrapped her arms around him. There was only a moment of hesitation before Carl deepened the kiss and pulled her closer to him. She shifted herself so she was straddling his lap and could more easily tease his mouth with her lips.

He broke the kiss. "Kayla, you're still injured."

"Shut up, Carl." She pushed him back on her bed. She didn't want words right now. She needed to just... *feel*. Kayla kissed his neck and nipped at his earlobe while his hands roamed up her thighs toward her waist. She sat up and ran her fingers lightly over his chest before reaching down and pulling her shirt over her head. Tossing it across the room, she looked down at him intently, waiting to see if he would accept what she offered.

———

CARL TOOK a deep breath as he looked up at her partially nude body. She was breathtakingly beautiful. Her dark hair fell around her face, and her green eyes were full of desire. His hands wandered from her slim waist up toward her breasts. Her skin was incredibly soft, and the scent of her was intoxicating.

"Kayla," he murmured, not wanting to break the moment

but needing to say the words. "I'm a trader. Are you sure about this?"

She paused for a moment, and Carl started to wonder if she'd changed her mind. He was about to reach for her shirt when she said, "Just tell me you can't get me pregnant."

His eyes widened, and he shook his head. *Of course she'd worry about such a thing.* A pregnancy for a ruin rat could be disastrous. "OmniLab carefully controls procreation so we can maintain our resource levels. We're all required to—"

"I don't need a birth control lesson, Carl," she interrupted. As she tugged on his shirt, he sat up to help her remove it. Kayla threw it on the floor and turned to him with a look of fierce determination. "And yes, I'm sure. I'll face whatever comes. I don't want to wait. I don't know what's going to happen tomorrow or the next day, but right now, this is what I need. I need to feel alive."

Carl stared at her, powerless to refuse her. She was offering a large part of herself to him, and selfishly, he wanted to take it. He couldn't remember ever wanting someone the way he wanted her.

She ran her fingers across his chest, and he pulled her close to him. When his mouth found hers again, he flipped her over, pinning her to the bed. As she wrapped her legs around him, he was struck by the intense need to be inside her.

This woman drove him to the edge of sanity. Her smell surrounded him, intoxicating him, and driving him to possess her. He forced himself to slow down and bent down to take one of her nipples into his mouth. Kayla gasped as he flicked his tongue against her nipple and suckled gently.

"Carl. I want... I need..."

"Shh. I know."

He pulled off her shorts with nimble fingers while his mouth teased her navel. When he reached the soft mound of dark curls, he gently spread her open and tasted her sweetness. Kayla gasped, her hands fisted in the blankets.

Finding the sensitive nodule above her opening, Carl gently worked it with his tongue. When she cried out, shuddering in release, he moved back up to cover her body with his. Unhooking his pants and slipping them off, he positioned himself against her and paused.

"Kayla, look at me."

Her eyes fluttered open, still dazed from her orgasm. He held her gaze as he began to push inside her, not stopping until he was fully seated within her. Kayla gasped, her fingers digging into his shoulders, pulling him toward her.

She was so tight and hot, it took all of his control not to lose himself completely. He forced himself to move slowly inside her, trying to give her time to get used to him.

Carl shifted her slightly and found the sensitive nub again with his fingers. He rubbed against it while she clung to him. His rhythm increased as her body responded to his. Feeling her writhing beneath him with her soft cries in his ears was a heady combination.

When she wrapped her legs around him again and whimpered in his ear, Carl felt as though he was already lost. He plunged into her depths without abandon as she met him stroke for stroke. When Kayla trembled with her release a second time, he couldn't hold back anymore. He pushed into her once more and exploded inside her.

Collapsing on top of her, Carl buried his face in her hair. After a moment, he became dimly aware he was probably crushing her. He rolled over to give her a chance to breathe and looked down at her.

Her skin was flushed from their lovemaking, and she had a small smile on her face. Her eyes were closed, and he was struck once again by how stunning she was. Bending down to kiss her softly, she wrapped her arms around him in response.

He felt a faint stirring inside him already and was mildly surprised at the reaction she evoked from him. "Kayla?"

"Hmm?" she replied, lazily opening her eyes.

Carl propped himself up on his elbow, worried he'd been too rough. In the heat of the moment, he'd forgotten about her injuries. "Are you all right?"

She lifted her hand to touch his face and murmured, "Mmhmm. I'm better than all right. I feel wonderful."

Carl lightly brushed her hair out of her face and kissed her forehead. "Get some rest, sweetheart."

Kayla closed her eyes and snuggled against him. He wrapped his arm around her and held her while she slept.

CHAPTER NINE

SEVERAL HOURS LATER, Kayla woke up with Carl's arm draped over her. Warm and content, she cuddled up next to him and watched him sleep. He normally kept his dark hair pulled back in a ponytail, but it fell loose around his face while he slept. She definitely preferred it down. Part of her was surprised he'd stayed, but she was secretly pleased. *He looks so relaxed and peaceful.* She lightly traced her fingers along the contours of his face.

His brown eyes opened, and she offered him a smile. He pulled her closer, and she kissed his neck, teasing the sensitive areas with her tongue. She felt him shiver, and she hid a smile against his skin, loving the effect she had on him.

Continuing to kiss his neck, she moved down toward his chest, taking her time to tease him along the way with small flicks of her tongue. Seeming impatient, his hands found her waist, and he pulled her on top of him. His voice was husky in her ear. "Your kisses are driving me crazy."

Resisting the urge to smirk, Kayla continued her tactile exploration with her hands and lips. He'd been driving her crazy since the moment she'd met him. If she could return the favor through sensual torture, she'd somehow manage to suffer through it. Especially if the benefits were as delicious as the previous night.

Shifting so she was straddling him, Kayla ran her fingers down the course of his firm chest, delighting in his reaction. As though unable to help himself, Carl reached up to cup her breasts, rubbing his thumbs against the hardened buds. When he sat up to take one of her nipples into his mouth, the pull went straight to her core. All reasoned thought deserted her, and she ran her fingers through his hair, pulling him close to her. *To hell with sensual torture.* She wanted this man, now as much as ever.

Carl's commlink flashed and beeped, interrupting them. Kayla felt a moment of annoyance but ignored the call, going back to kissing his shoulder. She ran her hands down his muscular arms, and he cursed when the commlink beeped again. Reaching over and glancing at the communication device, he hit the button to enable audio. "What is it?"

Cruncher's voice came over the com. "Sorry to bother you this early, Boss, but we've got two riders approaching."

"Thanks." He cut off the call with a sigh.

Kayla sat back. "You have to go?"

He cupped her face and kissed her deeply. She melted into his embrace, disappointed when he pulled away.

"I can't tell you how much I wish I didn't, but Cruncher wouldn't have called me if it wasn't important."

She slid off his lap. He stood and grabbed his clothes off the floor.

"Do you know who it is?"

Pulling on his clothes, Carl tied his hair back from his face. "I'm not sure, but I suspect it's the representatives from OmniLab."

Kayla groaned. "So the impressive Omnis actually decided

to come down from their lofty towers and slum it with the rest of us."

He held out his hand for her and helped her up. Pulling her close once more, he lowered his mouth to hers. "I'd rather be here right now than anywhere near those lofty towers."

Her stomach fluttered at his words, and she smiled at him. Grabbing her shirt off the floor, she pulled it over her head. "I'm going to go take a nice long shower and think about all the things I want to do to you when I get you alone again."

Carl stared at her with a mournful expression. "You're an evil and cruel woman, Kayla."

Kayla laughed and pulled on her shorts. "Go take care of your guests. I'll see you a bit later."

———

ONCE HE WAS GONE, Kayla poked her head out of her private quarters. Most of the other privacy dividers were still enabled, indicating people were still sleeping. She pulled out some clean clothes and headed to the lavatory.

She was feeling much better. The soreness from her injuries was barely noticeable. After checking in the mirror, she decided the bruises had pretty much completely disappeared. She went through her morning ritual unhurried before wandering out to the common room. Xantham and Lisia sat at the table eating breakfast and chatting.

"Good morning," Kayla called out as she walked over to the food preparation area.

Xantham grinned at her. "It's always a good morning when you're around. Want to join us?"

She returned his smile. "Yeah, one sec." She programmed the computer to heat her food before bringing it over to the table.

Xantham patted the chair next to him and she slid into it. Lisia gave her an annoyed look before going back to her meal. Kayla was determined to not let Lisia's attitude get to her. "How are you, Lisia?"

The blonde stiffened slightly but replied, "I'm fine."

"Glad to hear it." Kayla took a bite of the rehydrated prepared food and considered Lisia. The girl stared down at her plate with a dour expression and picked at her food. Her curls were pulled back in a high ponytail away from her heart-shaped face. Her skin was fair, and her eyes were a pale-blue Kayla thought was rather nice.

Aware Kayla was watching her, Lisia looked up and snapped, "Don't you have anything better to do than to stare at me?"

Kayla raised her eyebrows in surprise. "No harm meant. I was just thinking that you have pretty eyes."

Lisia's eyes narrowed as she glared at Kayla.

So much for playing nice. Kayla leaned back, considering her options. If she were back in Leo's camp, she'd have already smacked Lisia down. Since she suspected that wouldn't go over well, she'd have to call her on her bullshit instead. "You know, I think this is the first time I've sat in the same room with you for more than five minutes. I'm just wondering how long it'll take before you stop looking at me like you wish I'd go ruin diving without a cable."

Lisia pursed her lips. "We should both be so lucky. Obviously, Carl's personal ministrations last night have you feeling much better."

Xantham's eyes widened. "Oh man, if you two are going to start a catfight, let me know. I've gotta get a video of this."

Kayla took another bite of her breakfast and shrugged. Inwardly, she agreed. It was hard not to feel much better, thanks to Carl's "personal ministrations," but she wasn't inclined to discuss that with Lisia, although the look on her face might be worth it.

"If Lisia needs a catfight to get this out of her system, I'm down. But she doesn't strike me as the type."

Lisia gave her a look of disgust and stood, dumping her plate into the recycler. "I don't know what Carl sees in you. You walk in here and act like you own the place and everyone starts swooning over you. You're unreservedly pathetic, crude, and even Carl thinks you're reckless and irresponsible."

Kayla stood up and leaned over the table. "Watch it, Lisia. Right now, I can empathize with what you're going through, but if you keep walking down this line, you'll find out how much of a bitch I can be."

"I think I've already figured that out," Lisia replied and strode out of the room.

"Damn," Kayla muttered and sat back down, poking at her breakfast.

Xantham gave her a sympathetic look. "It's okay. She'll eventually get over it."

Kayla shook her head. "No, not that. That was a damn classy exit. I hate not getting the last word."

Xantham roared with laughter. Kayla grinned at him and took another bite.

"Did I miss something?" Kayla turned to see Cruncher standing in the doorway watching them.

"Nah," Kayla said dismissively.

Cruncher shrugged. "Kayla, if you've got a minute, Carl's meeting with two representatives from OmniLab. Couple of strange characters, if you ask me. They want to meet you though. Carl thought you might be interested in joining him now since they're going to start negotiating on the items you scavenged."

"Fun stuff. I'll be there in a minute."

"Thanks. Come on into Carl's office when you're done."

Xantham let out a low whistle. "Omnis are here? This is turning out to be one strange week. I've gotta go outside and check out their bikes."

He jumped up and practically ran toward the entrance. Kayla couldn't blame him. If she thought she could get away with blowing off the Omnis, she'd do it. With a sigh, she dumped her plate and headed to Carl's office. The door slid open when she pressed the button on the wall.

Carl looked up and smiled at her in greeting as she entered. "Thanks for coming. I'd like you to meet Director Borshin and Master Tal'Vayr from the OmniLab Towers. Gentlemen, this is our newest recruit."

Director Borshin was an older man, shaped a little like a barrel. He was completely bald with a smooth, polished dome and gray eyes that regarded her with polite interest. He was dressed in UV-protective gear that looked similar to the equipment Carl had acquired from OmniLab. The Director could possibly pass as a trader or as someone on a trader's crew, but the other man was a different story.

Master Tal'Vayr appeared to be a few years older than Kayla, but he had a commanding presence. He was tall, with fair skin and blue eyes. His golden hair fell neatly to his shoulders. He wore a long, white tunic over a pair of white pants and several pieces of gold jewelry. Kayla thought he was a little too polished for her tastes, but she couldn't deny he was an extremely attractive man.

He sat in a chair next to the Director, and two of his fingers tapped against the Director's wrist. He watched Kayla with mild curiosity as she stepped into the room.

For some reason she couldn't name, Kayla felt uncomfortable. Few things bothered her, but her senses went on alert the minute she stepped through the doorway and Master Tal'-Vayr's eyes met hers.

"A pleasure to meet you," the Director offered. He turned to Carl and joked, "I wasn't aware scavengers were so lovely. Perhaps I should consider replacing Ramiro personally."

"Nice to meet you both," Kayla said, and the Director smiled at her. Master Tal'Vayr gave her a polite nod but kept silent and continued to study her.

Carl cleared his throat and pulled out the lockbox from under his desk. "We've already negotiated on some other pieces we've obtained," he explained to Kayla. Turning to the other men, he added, "These other items were found by Kayla in the past few days."

He pulled out the jewelry and carving she'd collected and spread them on the desk. He then reached into a bag and brought out the two toys and jewelry box. Kayla leaned against the wall to watch. Carl had promised her a percentage of whatever she scavenged, and she was curious to find out what kind of money they were talking about.

Director Borshin leaned forward and began to sort through the items. "These pieces are very well preserved."

"Open at ten thousand. No more than twenty thousand credits total for the jewelry and the box."

Kayla started at the sound of the voice in her head. She was sure she'd heard someone, but it didn't appear as though anyone had spoken. Her eyes were drawn to Master Tal'Vayr's fingers still resting on the Director's wrist. Something about it set off her internal creep-factor alarm.

The Director cleared his throat. "I'm prepared to offer ten thousand credits for the jewelry and the box."

Carl frowned. "These pieces are in excellent condition. I'd say they are definitely closer to being worth fifteen thousand."

"Very well. We have an agreement at fifteen thousand."

Kayla's jaw dropped at the Director's formal announcement. She had no idea the profit that traders made from their excavations was so high. She wondered how much Warig had gotten from the Aurelia Data Cube.

"Open at eight thousand. The limit is fifteen thousand for the toys. The doll is unusual."

Goose bumps broke out on her arms at the sound of the mental voice. Kayla struggled to maintain her composure, but she was freaking out inside. Her eyes were drawn to Master Tal'Vayr's fingers again as they rested on the Director's arm. Was there some strange Omni ability that allowed them to communicate through thought? If so, why was she able to hear it and Carl couldn't?

"I'm prepared to offer eight thousand credits for the doll and the music machine."

Kayla's gaze darted to Carl as he considered the offer on the table. It might be foolish, but she couldn't let him agree. Not when she was due a percentage of the take. "I don't mean to interrupt, but I've been scavenging for a while now. I've never seen a doll like that before. I think, oh, say, fifteen thousand credits would be far more reasonable."

Carl gave her a sharp look but didn't contradict her. Instead, he turned to the Director. "Your thoughts?"

The Director nodded. "We have an agreement at fifteen thousand credits."

Woohoo! Kayla did a mental victory dance.

"Interesting," the voice mused.

Kayla's exhilaration faded, and she swallowed hard. Master Tal'Vayr was staring directly at her. Carl and Cruncher seemed oblivious to the exchange and instead waited patiently for the Director to offer on the next item.

"Open bidding at five thousand credits for the dragon carving. But accept up to twenty thousand credits."

What the hell is a dragon?

Master Tal'Vayr gave her a startled look. The Director

cleared his throat and bid on the final item. "I'm prepared to offer five thousand credits for the carving."

Carl rubbed his chin. "I'm surprised. The material seems rare. It seems to be worth closer to ten thousand credits."

Kayla bit the inside of her cheek to keep from saying anything. Master Tal'Vayr leaned forward in his chair, not taking his eyes off her. He almost seemed to be daring her to speak up. She shifted her weight from foot to foot. "Would you mind waiting a minute before you come to an agreement?" Carl looked as though he was about to object, but she held up a finger and gave him a pleading look. "Don't agree to anything yet. I'll be right back."

Once Kayla was out of their sight, she ran toward the crew quarters. She ignored Veridian's privacy divider and barged into his personal quarters.

"V, get up." She climbed on the bed and shoved him awake. "I need your help."

Veridian sat up, rubbing his eyes. "What's wrong? Are you okay? Did Ramiro come after you again?"

She grabbed his pants off the floor and threw them at him. "No, I'm fine. Get dressed. I need your help. Hurry up."

Confused, he pulled on his pants. She gestured for him to move faster. "I need you to tell these guys the carving we found is a dragon, and it's extremely rare. Tell them you believe it's worth twenty thousand credits. I don't care what else you say, but insist on that number."

Veridian pulled a shirt over his head. "Kayla, what are you talking about? What the hell is going on?"

"Just do it." She grabbed his hand and dragged him out of the crew's quarters. "I'll explain later."

Veridian tumbled after her. When they entered the office, she pushed him forward unceremoniously. "This is Veridian. My previous camp considered him to be an expert at appraising artifacts. He told me some interesting things about that particular piece. I thought you should hear them before deciding on a final number."

She stepped back, leaving everyone staring at Veridian. He scratched his head, looking bewildered, and turned to give her an annoyed look before smiling apologetically at the newcomers. It was obvious he'd just stumbled out of bed by the state of his disheveled hair and wrinkled clothing.

He cleared his throat. "Uh, right. The piece she's talking about is a dragon carving, and it's extremely rare. Based on my extensive experience appraising artifacts," he glared at Kayla, "I'd have to say it's worth at least twenty thousand credits."

"Interesting," Master Tal'Vayr commented and stood from his seat. Kayla blinked at him. It was the first time he'd spoken, and his voice flowed over her like a caress. He crossed the room toward them. "I'm curious though. You seem well versed in the appraisal amount. But do you know the lore behind the dragons?" He directed his question at Veridian without taking his eyes off Kayla.

Veridian hesitated, glancing nervously at Kayla. She ignored his "What the hell have you gotten me into?" look.

"Uh, sadly, my experience is limited to only how much it's worth."

"How unfortunate." Master Tal'Vayr turned to Kayla. "It was quite industrious of you to bring your friend here to appraise the piece."

She shrugged. Sticking her hands in her back pockets, she rocked back on her heels. "I'm just trying to be helpful. I figured V's experience would help you agree on a reasonable amount."

"And how much do you think the dragon carving is worth?"

She looked into his cool blue eyes, feeling disconcerted.

"I'm just a scavenger. But Veridian seems to think it's worth twenty thousand credits."

He gave her a curt nod and picked up the small dragon carving from the desk. He studied it carefully before walking back toward Kayla.

"Trader Carl, we have an agreement at twenty thousand credits," Master Tal'Vayr announced. Then he turned to her and held out the small dragon carving. "I want you to keep this artifact as a gift. I suspect it's more suitable than you realize."

At her confused look, Master Tal'Vayr explained, "A dragon is what some people believe to be a mythological beast. Some others believe they have withdrawn to other worlds. Either way, the sculpture is a reminder of the reverence and belief in something greater."

Master Tal'Vayr reached for her hand, and she gasped at his touch. Electricity seemed to flow through her as she tried to pull her hand away, but he gripped her hand tightly. He placed the carving into her palm and covered it with his other hand.

Images and thoughts seemed to flow through Kayla at a rapid pace, making her dizzy. Master Tal'Vayr stared at her in shock and demanded, "How... Who are you?"

Kayla snatched her hand away, nearly dropping the artifact, and exhaled deeply. She took an uneasy step back trying to distance herself from him.

Master Tal'Vayr turned to Carl, who had watched the exchange. "This is the young woman who discovered the Aurelia Data Cube?"

"Yes," Carl said, glancing at Kayla in confusion.

Master Tal'Vayr's eyes narrowed as he studied her. "How old are you?"

"None of your business." She'd be damned if she was going to answer his questions. She didn't understand everything that was going on, but this whole situation was getting out of hand. "I'll either answer questions about Ramiro or not, but my personal business is my own. It doesn't concern you."

Master Tal'Vayr stared at her in shock, clearly not used to having his orders questioned. He turned to Carl. "You obtained her DNA when she signed the contract?"

"Of course," Carl replied with a frown.

"Put her information on the display."

Carl entered the command to pull up her information on the monitor in his office. Master Tal'Vayr barely glanced at it, completely fixated on Kayla. "Run a cross-check through OmniLab records for the past twenty years. Use Clearance Code X59BN23."

Carl entered in the information. The computer began scanning through its databanks.

Kayla had a sudden sinking feeling in the pit of her stomach. She didn't like the way this was going or the way this Master Tal'Vayr guy kept staring at her.

A minute later, the computer beeped, and a warning displayed on the screen. Carl looked up in confusion. "It's blocked. Restricted Access."

Master Tal'Vayr turned to the computer. He pressed his palm against it and announced, "Override System Access. Master Alec Tal'Vayr. L561N836."

The computer beeped in acknowledgment and an image appeared on the screen. Kayla stared at the eerily familiar child with dark hair and large, green eyes. She looked at the name next to the image and shook her head in disbelief. She stepped back, whispering, "No. It's not true."

Master Tal'Vayr looked at her sharply. "You've been missing a long time, Kayla Rath'Varein."

Carl looked shocked at the mention of the name. "Rath'-Varein? That's impossible."

"Apparently not."

Carl stared at the picture of the young girl and scrolled through the text. He looked up to meet Kayla's panicked expression. "Veridian told me Leo found you after a ruin collapse. OmniLab thought everyone had been killed, including you."

Veridian scratched his head. "Uh, Kayla? What's going on?"

"Oh, *hell* no." She shook her head, denying the implications of what they were trying to tell her. "You guys have been sucking on vent exhaust for too long if you think I'm an Omni. No freaking way. Forget it."

Master Tal'Vayr took a step toward her. "DNA doesn't lie, Kayla Rath'Varein."

"I'll tell you exactly where you can shove your DNA crap. And quit calling me that. My name is Kayla. Period. That's it."

"This woman belongs in the tower," Master Tal'Vayr announced. "Her contract is null and void. She'll be returning with me."

His words were like cold water pouring over her, and anger flooded through her at the idea that this stranger—this Omni—was trying to control her. "The only thing you're going to be getting from me is my boot up your ass if you think I'm going to take one step inside those freakish towers of yours. If you want to cancel my contract, great. Fantastic. Wipe your ass with it for all I care. But I don't belong to OmniLab, and I damn well will *not* be going to that tower with you."

"You are a member of the Inner Circle by right of birth. You have no business being outside the towers. It was a mistake to allow you to set foot here sixteen years ago."

"To hell with this. I'm out of here."

Finished with the conversation, Kayla turned to head toward the door, but Master Tal'Vayr made a grab for her. A rush of energy flowed through her the moment he touched her. Sights, smells, and sounds flooded her mind. She felt as though she were drowning in a river of someone else's memories.

You belong with us, Kayla Rath'Varein. I can guide you through this, if you'll let me. Open yourself and let me show you how to navigate.

Dizziness threatened to overwhelm her, and she started to falter. Suddenly, without knowing how, she found a calm oasis within the storm of senses raging around her. Kayla managed to get control of herself enough to realize Master Tal'Vayr was toying with her. It pissed her off.

Something inside her snapped. She pushed the foreign images out of her mind and back toward Master Tal'Vayr. He stumbled backward and broke contact with her.

"Unbelievable," he murmured in shock, gaping at her. "You're untrained. How did you do that?"

"You revolting, puerile, slack-jawed, drooling piece of garbage," Kayla snarled. "If there's such a thing as a higher being and he decides to give the planet an enema, you'd better run like hell because anywhere you're standing is a suitable place for the insertion."

He blinked, as though her words confused him, and shook his head in disbelief. "You didn't just resist me. You completely deflected my influence."

Kayla's eyes narrowed. "I don't know what kind of world you live in up in those towers, but you're in *my* playground now. You guys may go around zapping each other with electricity left and right, but I'm not into that freaky shit. Don't fuck with me."

She spun on her heels and stormed out of the room.

Too bad Lisia didn't see that exit.

CHAPTER TEN

KAYLA STARED at the mapping images on the screen and impatiently tapped the keys in front of her. She cycled through the diagrams so she could start rendering them in three dimensions.

Carl walked into the tech room and sat down next to her. "Kayla, we need to talk."

"If it's about that OmniLab crap, I'm not interested."

"Master Tal'Vayr didn't handle the situation well. I tried to explain it to him, but things are different in the towers. He's not used to being questioned."

Kayla entered some additional commands into the computer. She felt him watching her and tried to ignore him. "I know what happened just now came as a shock. It shocked me too. But there's no denying you're the child in that picture."

She glanced at him briefly. "It doesn't matter. This is who I am now."

"It *does* matter. Yes, you're still Kayla, but you're more than that. You're a Rath'Varein."

She made a face. They could give her any name they

wanted. It wouldn't change anything. "That name means absolutely nothing to me."

"Dammit, Kayla. This is so difficult because you didn't grow up in the towers." Carl took a deep breath, exhaling slowly. "You should know this. Dmitri Rath'Varein was one of the founders of OmniLab. He enlisted the help of Marsin Tal'Vayr and some others to build the towers."

Kayla turned her chair to look at him. "Are you trying to tell me you think I'm related to the guy who built those ugly-ass towers?"

"Yes, but it's more than that. OmniLab didn't just build the towers. They built a lot of other things too. They knew our world was headed for trouble, and they wanted to save certain parts of it. Dmitri Rath'Varein was trying to save something he considered more precious than humanity."

Kayla tapped her fingers on the desk in annoyance. "What the hell are you talking about, Carl?"

Master Tal'Vayr stepped into the room. "I think I should explain."

Kayla scowled at him. He was the last person she wanted to see right now.

Master Tal'Vayr walked over to her, and she scrambled to her feet, preparing for a quick exit. He paused and clasped his hands in front of him, looking harmless, but she knew the effects of his zappy fingers now. "I want to apologize to you, Kayla. Trader Carl has tried to explain the way things work here on the surface. It's much different than what I expected. I would imagine you're as unfamiliar with our ways as I am about your life here. Do you have any memory of living with us?"

"Look, Master Tal'Vayr, or whatever the hell your name is," Kayla began, eyeing the distance to the door. When he didn't make any sudden movements, she relaxed. "I don't know anything about you, and I don't *want* to know anything about you. As far as I'm concerned, you can go back to your big towers and leave me the hell alone. The only reason I'm even in this trader camp right now is because I didn't have a choice. Ramiro, another one of you Omnis, decided the planet would be a little more pleasant if I didn't exist."

Master Tal'Vayr frowned. "Please, call me Alec. You are a member of the Inner Circle and it's not fitting for you to call me by my title."

Kayla snorted and sat back down in the chair. What kind of guy insisted on people calling him Master anyway? She dismissed him with a wave of her hand. "Fine, Alec. Go away. I'm busy. I don't want to listen to you anymore."

Alec looked at Carl questioningly, and he motioned for him to keep talking to her. Kayla narrowed her eyes at Carl. *Traitor.*

"Ah, I suppose you don't remember, but I knew you when you were young. I was several years older than you. You were extremely talented, even then. You had the ability to locate items people had lost or hidden. That's why the High Council agreed to let you travel to the ruins. A lot of our people objected, though, because of your age."

Kayla pretended to ignore him and continued studying the images. Out of the corner of her eye, she saw Carl nod at Alec again, encouraging him to continue. She was tempted to kick him in the shins.

"I used to have a small, glass globe you were obsessed with. You would sneak it out of my quarters whenever you got a chance. You always found it, it didn't matter where I hid it. It had little flecks of green and..."

"Gold," Kayla whispered in surprise and looked up from the monitor. He now had her full attention. "I used to have dreams about a glass ball that flashed green and gold when it moved."

Alec nodded. "That would be it. I still have it. I would

have given it to you when we were children, but you seemed to enjoy finding it almost as much as you enjoyed playing with it."

Kayla shook her head. The whole thing was too far-fetched to believe. "This doesn't mean anything."

"No? When I first entered, Trader Carl was trying to explain to you a bit of our history. A bit of *your* history. It was our ancestors who built the towers to protect those of us with certain distinctive traits. Specifically, those of us with unique bloodlines."

She'd never heard that before. "Huh? I thought everyone paid their way in."

Alec hesitated and glanced at Carl before explaining. "Some did, yes. We needed the funding, of course. But before entrance to the towers was opened to the highest bidders, certain people were targeted. OmniLab was originally a company that operated as a medical research facility, dedicated to compiling information on the millions of people populating the planet. Based on the information OmniLab obtained, we were able to determine some people carried certain markers in their DNA which set them apart from others."

"What sort of markers?"

"Your senses are different from other people. You have a unique ancestry. I'm sure you've noticed you're able to hear and see things other people are unable to sense. I would imagine with your unique skill set, you've been quite successful in discovering artifacts."

"I've had some luck," she admitted grudgingly.

"I'm sure that's an understatement." He gave her a knowing smile. "But regardless, there are several of us who share these same DNA markers. You would have trained to use your innate talents and develop others if you had grown up in the towers. As it is, there's a great deal of raw potential within you that's waiting to be unlocked."

Okay, this was too bizarre, and she needed to shut him down. "Are you always this creepy?"

Carl smothered a grin and pretended to be fascinated by the wall. Alec returned her look. "Are you always this difficult?"

She shrugged, turned back to the computer, and entered in a few keystrokes to download the data to her commlink. "So I've been told." Standing up, she offered them both a smile. "Well, it was interesting meeting you, but it's time for me to head out. Carl, thanks for everything, and I'm sure I'll see you around."

Surprised, Carl stood. "Where are you going?"

She winked at him. "My contract is null and void. I'm a free agent again."

"Dammit, Kayla, don't do this. What about Veridian?"

Understanding hit her like a punch in the stomach. "Damn you and your stupid contracts. He's not released, is he?"

"No, Master Tal'Vayr only released your contract, not his."

Master Tal'Vayr listened to their exchange and offered, "If that's an issue, I have a proposition."

Kayla's lips formed a thin line. A proposition was how she got into this mess to begin with. "Fine, I'll bite. What is it?"

"I want you to come back with me to the towers. In exchange, I'll release Veridian from his contract, if that's what he wishes."

"Like hell. I'm not going anywhere with you."

Alec held up his hand. "I'm not asking you to come permanently, unless you decide otherwise. Instead, I would like to invite you to visit the towers. It's my hope that some of your childhood memories may return."

"Forget it." Kayla shoved her commlink in her pocket and

headed toward the door. She'd figure out some other way to get Veridian out of the contract. Her idea about leaving the district was beginning to look more appealing.

Alec took a step toward her and said quickly, "Wouldn't you like to see your mother again?"

Kayla froze. Of all the things she'd expected him to say, that wasn't one of them. She turned around slowly and narrowed her eyes at him. "My mother died in the ruins helping me escape."

Alec shook his head. "Whoever it was, she wasn't your mother. A team of people from OmniLab, scientists and several Inner Circle members, took you into the ruins. Your mother has never left the towers."

"I don't believe you," Kayla argued, but he'd placed a niggle of doubt in her mind.

"She's very much alive," Alec informed her. "She's spent the last sixteen years believing her only child was killed. It would mean a great deal to her to see you again."

Kayla shook her head, feeling overwhelmed. The possibility she could have family had never dawned on her. It was too much for her to wrap her head around. "I... I have to go. I need some air." Not caring what they thought, she ran out of the room toward her private area in the crew's quarters.

She enabled the privacy setting and sat on the edge of the bed, putting her head in her hands. Realizing she was shaking, she took a deep breath and tried to calm down. Things were moving way too fast, and she felt powerless to stop them.

Screw that. I'm only powerless if I let them control me.

Kayla stood and looked around the small room, wanting to escape. She opened the locker and pulled out the empty bag Veridian had brought with him. Running away could be an option. If she scavenged enough, maybe she could pay for Veridian's contract or pay Leo off to hide Veridian. There were other facilities out there. She didn't know where, but they existed. Somewhere.

Possibilities ran through her mind, each more absurd than the last. She tossed the bag on the bed, ready to have a panic attack, when the door slid open. Kayla looked up to see Veridian standing in the doorway.

His gaze fell on the open bag. "Kayla, what's going on?"

She sat on the bed, pushing the bag aside. "I don't know anymore, V. It's all getting away from me. That Master What-shisface seems to think I'm an Omni and wants me to go visit the towers. He says my mother is still alive, and that she believes I've been dead for the past sixteen years."

Veridian's eyes widened, and he sat next to her. "Wow. Do you believe him?"

She shrugged. "You saw the picture. I don't know what to believe."

"What are you going to do?"

"I was thinking about going back to Leo's camp," she admitted, nudging the bag with her foot. "My contract's been thrown out, but I didn't realize it didn't apply to yours too."

Veridian put his arm around her and gave her a reassuring squeeze. "If going back to Leo's camp is what you want to do, then go. Don't worry about me. Staying here is temporary. Quite honestly, living in a trader camp isn't half bad."

Kayla gave him a weak smile. Even though it had only been a few days, she liked being here too. She wasn't ready to admit it out loud though. But no matter how much she liked or disliked it, Kayla couldn't imagine being somewhere without Veridian. "That Master guy said if you wanted to be released from your contract, he would do it. But I have to visit the towers with him."

"Kayla, seeing the inside of the towers is something most ruin rats dream about. Aren't you curious?"

"No. I've always hated those stupid towers. They freak me out for some reason."

Veridian fell silent for several long moments. "I shouldn't be the reason you go. Don't worry about my contract. But if what he said is true, I think you should consider meeting your mother."

Kayla felt a sudden uncontrollable fear at the thought. "Why? She's just some woman I don't remember. It was your mother who raised me."

The words sounded crass even to her, and she flinched at Veridian's disapproving look.

"Family is important, Kayla. She's your mother and deserves to see the woman her daughter has become. It would have broken my mother's heart if she thought she lost me."

Kayla frowned and picked at a piece of lint on her blanket. He was right. If what Alec said were true, she could be getting a second chance. The door beeped, and Kayla glared at it in annoyance. She wasn't ready to agree to anything yet. "If it's that Omni guy again, tell him I'm washing my hair or something."

Veridian chuckled and opened the door to find Carl standing in the doorway. "Sorry to interrupt, but I was hoping to speak with you, Kayla."

Kayla looked up at him and gave a nod. He stepped inside. "Would you mind giving us a minute, Veridian?"

Veridian hesitated before nodding in agreement. "Think about what I said," he reminded her before leaving the room.

She grumbled under her breath and stood. Needing to keep her hands busy, she picked up the bag and tossed it on the desk. No matter what she decided, she needed to pack. Carl walked up behind her and slipped his hands around her waist. She stiffened slightly, but then relaxed against him as he brushed his lips against her hair. "It's a lot take in, I know. I don't blame you for wanting to leave."

She turned around to look up at him in surprise. "You don't?"

He shook his head. "No, I don't. I know you don't want to be controlled or manipulated. That's exactly what's happening. I don't want you to leave, but I understand if you do."

His easy acceptance was surprising, but Carl never did anything expected. Overwhelmed with gratitude, Kayla rested her head against his chest. He seemed to understand what she needed, even when she didn't. She inhaled his masculine scent, wanting to memorize it. "Well, it's not like you won't ever see me if I go back to Leo's camp. I'm sure I'll piss you off again before you know it."

Carl paused for a minute and then tilted her head up to look at him. "I don't think you understand the enormity of what's happened, Kayla. I'm just a trader working on behalf of Omnilab. OmniLab controls the district. You're part of that, whether or not you want to admit it. You can scavenge whatever the hell you want in whatever district you want and no one can say a damn thing to you now."

Confused, she pulled back. "What are you talking about?"

"Tower politics. There's a hierarchy, and the Inner Circle is at the top, right below the High Council. Many members of the Inner Circle are also part of the High Council, the governing body of the towers. I guess you could say the Inner Circle acts more as advisers to the High Council.

"Before your father died, he ran the High Council. The High Council appoints traders to act on behalf of OmniLab. In exchange, they provide generous compensation for securing artifacts and resources. All traders answer to the High Council and the Inner Circle. You're part of the Inner Circle by right of birth."

Kayla laughed. "Are you trying to tell me I'm your boss now?"

Carl smiled wryly. "In a strange twist of fate, yes."

Hmm. This has possibilities. Kayla gave him a wicked smile. "So you have to do whatever I want?"

"Technically, yes," he admitted and tucked her hair behind her ear. "But to be honest, I shouldn't even have my hands on you. You're... ah... quite a bit out of my league now. Members of the Inner Circle keep to themselves. They don't usually pay much attention to us lowly traders."

Kayla raised an eyebrow as she ran her hands across his chest. "What if I want your hands on me?"

His eyes darkened with desire. "Kayla, I don't think there's a man alive who could resist you, Inner Circle or not." He bent down, his lips ravishing hers. She put her arms around him and returned his kiss with equal fervor.

They were both breathing heavily when the kiss ended. She rested her head against his chest while he threaded his fingers through her hair. His voice was low and husky as he said, "Part of me wants to say to hell with everything and run off to Leo's camp with you."

"Let's go right now. We can even go start our own camp."

He chuckled, then his smile faded as he searched her expression. "You're serious, aren't you?"

"I don't like people telling me what to do or how to live my life. It seems like that's all I've been getting lately."

He considered her for a long moment. "I think you have a lot of your father in you."

Kayla blinked, momentarily taken aback by his words. She'd occasionally wondered about her mother, but she'd never given much thought to a father. Leo was probably the closest thing she had to one, and she wasn't convinced he'd bother with her if she weren't consistently turning in a profit. He'd taken her in as a kid, and she'd been paying him back ever since. "What do you know about him?"

"From everything I've heard, he was a great man. He never backed away from a challenge and had an incredibly strong will. Everyone admired him. It was a huge blow to the High Council when he died, and things were in an uproar for a while. Master Tal'Vayr stepped in and took control of the Council. It was the first time in history the towers weren't run by a Rath'Varein. A lot of people were upset."

She glanced toward the closed door, thinking of the pompous Omni running around Carl's camp. "Wait, *Alec* runs the High Council now?"

"No, his father does," Carl said with a chuckle. "Alec is part of the Inner Circle though. It's just a matter of time before he's on the High Council. Your existence is going to upset the balance, but in a good way, I think. If you decide to visit the towers, you would definitely cause a stir."

Kayla pulled away from him, still feeling defensive. She wasn't ready to agree to anything. "You're assuming I want to go there."

"No, I'm not. I'm just speculating." He took another step toward her and brushed his lips against her forehead. "Kayla, your life is your own. You just have more options now than you did yesterday."

She considered his words and what Veridian had said. "Do you know my mother?"

Carl shook his head. "Not really. I've seen images of her, but I've only met her once. I didn't realize it, but you look a bit like her. She has dark hair like yours, and she's petite. I don't remember much else, except that she's quite beautiful."

When Kayla didn't respond, Carl continued, "She stays out of politics for the most part. I've heard she was much more involved with the towers before the ruin collapse. Since losing you and your father, she's kept to herself."

Kayla bit her lip, indecision weighing heavily upon her.

"Are you thinking about meeting her?"

She lifted a shoulder in a half-hearted shrug. "I don't know. Maybe. V seems to think I should. I don't have any memories of her though. I always thought my mother had been killed. Now I find out that wasn't true, and there's this woman who exists that I know nothing about."

"You could always try visiting the towers for a few days," he encouraged. "You could meet her and see if anything there resonates with you. If not, you can always leave and come back here or go to Leo's camp."

Kayla looked away, her gaze landing on the small table next to the bed where she'd placed the image viewer the night before. Just like Veridian, family had been important to Pretz too. Maybe they were right. If she didn't take this opportunity, she'd always wonder. "You think they'd let me bring V? He's always been curious about the towers."

A thoughtful look crossed Carl's face, and he shrugged. "I've never heard of a ruin rat being allowed entry into the towers, but he's part of a trader's crew now. I've taken Cruncher with me to the towers to collect supplies. Not only that, but Master Tal'Vayr seems eager for you to visit. I'm sure he'd be willing to make some rather large concessions for you."

"What about you? You're from the towers. Would you go too?"

"That's a little different," he said with a frown. "I've been assigned to stay here until I'm recalled or my contract expires. I'll need to head to the towers in a few days when the High Council replaces Ramiro. As part of my trading agreement with OmniLab, I'm supposed to meet with the other traders to establish guidelines for working with the new one. If you want to go on ahead with Master Tal'Vayr, I could bring you and Veridian back in a few days."

It was a reasonable suggestion, and she was hard-pressed to find a flaw in it, but she couldn't shake the sense of foreboding at the idea of going to the towers. "Something about

Alec bothers me," Kayla admitted. "I don't like the way he looks at me."

Carl chuckled. "He looks at you the same way most men do. You're the most beautiful, talented, and passionate woman I've ever met, Kayla."

She looked up at him, her stomach fluttering as he gazed down at her. The man was dangerous. She couldn't seem to keep her hands off him and, in return, his touch made all her concerns seem insignificant. Kayla reached up to kiss him again.

"He's kinda pretty, in a strange sort of way," she told him with a teasing smile. "But he doesn't make me feel the same way you do."

"I'm glad to hear it." Carl laughed, then whispered huskily in her ear, "I hope you'll keep giving me the opportunity to make you feel that way."

Kayla shivered. Both the promise in his words and his warm breath against her skin created delicious tingles through her body. Oh, she could definitely keep giving him opportunities.

He pulled back a fraction, his expression becoming thoughtful. "So do you think you'll go? This would give you something to do while you're healing and not able to go into the ruins. Ramiro can't touch you in the towers. Besides, think of all the technology you could get your hands on."

Her eyes widened as she considered his words. Holy smokes! She'd never even considered the possibilities. "You're right. I wonder if they'd let me see some of their prototypes?"

"I imagine they would," he admitted with a trace of a smile. "Your name holds far more weight than you realize."

Kayla cocked her head. "When do you think you'll be coming to the towers?"

"I suspect things will happen fairly quickly with Ramiro

now. My best guess would be two or three days at the most. They can't leave Ramiro's camp without a trader for long."

She could handle that. "All right. I'll take Veridian and go check out these towers." She paused for a moment, glanced at the door, and frowned. "I guess I should go tell Alec he can dislodge the stick from him ass and that I'll go."

Carl laughed. "Having you in the towers is definitely going to liven things up. I wish I could be there to see it."

CHAPTER ELEVEN

KAYLA DISMOUNTED from her bike and stared up at the huge towers. The buildings were larger than she'd thought. Curious, she touched the wall with a gloved hand. It was somewhat reassuring to know it was just a regular building.

Veridian put his hand on her arm to get her attention. "You okay?"

Feeling sheepish, she pulled her hand away from the wall and nodded. Veridian gave her a reassuring smile. Taking a deep breath, she put aside her reservations and followed Master Tal'Vayr and Director Borshin into the entrance area. When the door sealed behind Veridian, she pulled off her protective gear and helmet.

A young man tentatively approached her. He bowed and reached out to take her belongings. At Kayla's hesitation, Alec motioned for her to hand them to the man. Puzzled, she watched as the man hung them on a nearby rack.

"I could have done that."

"M-my apologies if I have offended, M-mistress Rath'-Varein," the young man stammered. He seemed troubled at the possibility he had displeased her.

"What the hell?" Kayla jerked back, alarmed by both his actions and the use of the unfamiliar title. She looked at Alec, determined to put a stop to it. "Oh no, you tell him to cut that out. I'm Kayla. *Just* Kayla. You start calling me something else and I'm out of here." She crossed her arms and muttered under her breath, "And I can hang up my own shit."

Alec's lips twitched as though he were suppressing a smile, and he handed over his equipment. "It's fine, Melvin. You may call her Kayla, if that's her preference."

Melvin looked puzzled but nodded in agreement. He reached out to take Director Borshin's and Veridian's belongings.

Kayla looked around the large, open room. The floor tiles sparkled and shone, and the walls were a brilliant white. A desk sat in the center of the room with flowering, green plants on both sides of it providing a splash of color in an otherwise sterile environment. A woman stood behind the desk, gaping at Kayla. When Kayla returned her look, the girl immediately looked away and pretended to be engrossed with the screen on her desk.

Kayla leaned toward Alec and whispered, "Is everyone going to stare at me?"

He smiled at her. "Probably at first. You've been dead for sixteen years."

"Great," she muttered, following him into the next room.

Sunlight filtered through the main common area of the towers. An enormous waterfall cascaded down into a pool at the ground level surrounded by lush plants and greenery. Kayla's eyes widened in disbelief; she'd stepped through to another world.

She reached out to touch one of the plants, entranced by the smooth texture of the leaf. Alec's observation of her tactile exploration made her flush in embarrassment and she dropped her hand. He seemed pleased by her reaction, though, and held out his hand to her. "This is the main entrance area. We'll be traveling up the elevators toward the quarters of the Inner Circle. You'll probably want to spend most of your time there."

Kayla hesitated before taking his hand. "Are you going to zap me again?"

Alec shook his head. "I will not attempt to influence you in any way, Kayla. You have my word."

"All right." She tentatively slipped her hand into his. His skin was warm, and there was a slight tingle, but it was an eerily familiar feeling. A flash of a memory floated at the edge of her mind, but it was gone before she could fully recall it. She felt a distinct pull toward Alec, and she looked up at him in surprise. His blue eyes were watching her intently.

"Are you sure you're not doing something?"

"No. Whatever you're feeling is of your own design, not mine. You may not believe you remember your past, but I suspect part of you does."

Kayla frowned but let him lead her toward the elevator. He pressed the button and the door immediately slid open. Alec turned to Director Borshin. "Thank you for your help, Director. I'll meet with you later."

Director Borshin bowed to Alec and walked away. Once he was gone, Alec turned to Kayla and Veridian. "The priority elevator is typically closed to the general public. It will take us directly to the Inner Sanctum."

They stepped inside the elevator, and Alec pressed his hand against the panel on the wall. "Welcome, Master Alec Tal'Vayr," a computerized voice greeted them. A moment later, the elevator shot upward.

Veridian let out a low whistle and looked out the glass window. Kayla looked down, her eyes widening as the levels flew past. They were traveling at a fast rate toward the top of the tower. Kayla pressed her hand to her stomach, the sudden rush of speed similar to the feeling of riding on her speeder. It was exhilarating, but nothing was familiar.

When the elevator stopped, Kayla couldn't help but stare. A miniature river flowed through the corridor surrounded by trees and foliage. The soft sounds of burbling water echoed throughout the passageway. Soft, ambient lighting cast a warm glow over a cobblestone path that twisted through the landscape. She bent down beside the water, unable to resist dipping her fingers into the cool stream.

"It's beautiful," she said in wonder, amazed such a place existed.

"This is where you were born." Alec pointed to the path in front of them. "You used to run down that path when you were a child. Your family's quarters are down this way."

She bit her lip and looked in the direction Alec had gestured. An older man was walking down the path toward them. Kayla stood, rubbing her wet fingers against her pants. Alec straightened, his entire demeanor changing as the man approached. Kayla had thought him uptight before, but his body language was now almost rigid. She glanced over at Veridian. He shook his head, letting her know he'd caught it too. Wary now, she turned back to the newcomer.

The man inclined his head. "Mistress Kayla Rath'Varein, I presume?"

Alec gave a shallow bow to the man. "Yes, however, she prefers to be called Kayla. Kayla, please allow me to introduce you to my father, Master Edwin Tal'Vayr, leader of our High Council and a member of the Inner Circle. I've also brought a close friend of hers to visit. This is Veridian Levanthe."

Kayla studied the tall man in front of her, trying to see a resemblance between him and Alec. They both had the same golden hair, but his was graying slightly. He kept it pulled away from his face and tied neatly at the base of his neck, the same way Carl wore his hair.

Must be an Omni thing.

Unlike Alec, he carried a bit of extra girth around his midsection. She couldn't call him soft though. This was a man confident in his own authority and who commanded power. If her time around the ruin rats had taught her anything, it was that showing weakness around someone like him would be a mistake.

There was a weight to his gaze, as though he were assessing her. She lifted her chin, returning his gaze evenly. After a long moment, he gave a curt nod. "Welcome back to the towers, Miss Rath'Varein. It's been far too long since you wandered these halls. We were quite surprised to discover you were alive and living on the surface."

"Apparently, I don't die so easily."

"Ah, yes," Edwin replied with a smile that didn't meet his eyes. "I heard about your unfortunate incident with Trader Ramiro. His title has been stripped, and we will appoint a replacement within the next few days. Unfortunately, Ramiro's disappeared from his camp. We're monitoring the surrounding areas and will detain him once he reappears."

Great. She resisted the urge to wrinkle her nose. It didn't say much for these Omnis that someone like Ramiro had given them the slip. "Good to know."

Edwin turned to his son. "I presume you're taking her to receive a security access bracelet?"

"No," Alec replied with a determined look. "It was a long trip, and she wants to meet her mother. I'll make sure she has access to whatever she wishes. A bracelet can be given to her later, if necessary."

The leader of the High Council paused, and his eyes narrowed. Alec's mouth formed a thin line, but he remained silent.

Edwin turned back to Kayla. "It's against policy, but I'll permit it for now."

She glanced back and forth between father and son. "What's a security access bracelet?"

"The bracelet identifies you and will allow you access to most areas of the tower. It's only fitting someone of your stature and lineage should wear one."

Kayla examined the man's wrists and noticed he wasn't wearing any jewelry. A quick glance at Alec also confirmed that even though he also wore several pieces of jewelry, his wrists were bare. She turned back to Edwin and cocked her head. "Where's yours?"

Edwin studied her for a moment. "I'm the leader of the High Council, dear. I'm known on-site."

"Right." The man's creep factor was off the charts. She hadn't survived this long by buying this guy's version of bullshit. She gestured to Alec. "What about your son?"

Edwin gave Alec a sharp look. Alec shook his head, holding out his hands. "I haven't needed one, Kayla. You don't strike me as the type of woman to need embellishments either. Your beauty speaks for itself. A bracelet would only detract from your presence."

Kayla gaped at him. *Holy shit! Is the freaking Omni hitting on me?*

Alec coughed and looked away. Kayla's eyes narrowed suspiciously, but before she could question him, Alec composed himself and turned back to his father. "If you'll excuse us, I'm going to escort Kayla to her family's rooms. I'll bring her to dinner this evening."

"Very well, Alec. I'll see you later this evening. Make sure you take special care of our guest."

Alec bowed again to his father. Turning to Kayla, he gave her a charming smile. "Are you ready to meet your mother?"

The ground fell out from under her, and reality crashed in.

She'd known it was coming. It was the whole reason she was here. She swallowed, shoving her hands in her pockets, and resisted the urge to run. Veridian gave her a nod of reassurance as though saying she could do this.

"Yeah, I guess," she managed. "That's why I came, right?"

Taking a deep breath, Kayla squared her shoulders and followed Alec down the path until it stopped at an ornate door. It was an old-fashioned wooden door carved with several old-world images. A large tree encompassed most of the design, with strange flying creatures perched in the branches.

She turned to Alec. "What's this?"

"These are your family's quarters. Your mother has been informed of your arrival. Go ahead and press your palm against the panel by the door."

Kayla stared at the door, gathering her courage. It was now or never. She pressed her hand against the small, white panel, and the door slid open to reveal a large circular-shaped living area. The room was airy and bright, decorated in soft creams. Several flowering plants were positioned throughout the room. Curved sofas provided seating and were centered around a small, gurgling fountain in the living area. The room was decorated simply, but it was warm and elegant.

A petite, dark-haired woman rose from one of the sofas when they entered. Her hand flew to her mouth as she stared at Kayla.

Alec stepped forward. "Mistress Seara Rath'Varein, allow me to introduce Mistress Kayla Rath'Varein and her friend, Veridian Levanthe."

Kayla stared at the beautiful, middle-aged woman in front of her. This was her mother? She was slender and dressed in a long, white dress with a light, almost translucent robe thrown over her shoulders. Her dark hair was pulled back from her face and pinned up in an elaborate style. Her face was kind and younger than Kayla had expected. The only signs of age were the small lines etched around the corners of her lips and green eyes. It was her eyes, though, that were the most startling. Kayla had spent her life looking at those same eyes every time she'd seen her reflection. They were the same as hers.

Seara took a tentative step forward, her eyes filling with moisture. "It's true. I never wanted to believe you had been killed, but..." Her voice trailed off.

Kayla bit her lip and turned to Veridian in a panic. He stepped forward to intervene. "It's nice to meet you, Mistress Seara Rath'Varein."

Kayla peered around him and watched the woman wipe her eyes, giving a nervous laugh. "I'm sorry. I kept telling myself not to make a spectacle, but you know what they say about good intentions. Please, call me Seara. There's no need to be formal."

"Thank you, Seara," Veridian said politely. "I imagine this must be shocking to you."

She gave him an appreciative smile. "Please, all of you, have a seat. I'm sorry if I made you uncomfortable, Kayla."

Following Veridian's lead, Kayla took a seat next to him and rubbed her hands together, feeling like she was about to come out of her skin. She'd never thought of herself as self-conscious before, but then again, she never thought she'd be in this sort of situation. "That's all right. This whole thing is sort of awkward."

Alec walked over to Seara and leaned against the column next to her. Seara sat across from them, still staring at Kayla as though trying to memorize her. "You're even more beautiful than I imagined. I wish your father could be here to see you. You were so little when I last saw you. I'll never forget the way you looked when your father agreed to take you down to the surface. Your eyes lit up with excitement.

You were adamant you were going to find something special."

Kayla shook her head. "I'm sorry, but I don't remember."

Seara nodded sadly, clasping her hands together on her lap. "You were very young. If you want, I have some videos of the three of us together. Maybe you'd like to see them at some point?"

"Sure, I guess."

Alec gestured to Veridian. "Seara, Veridian's mother was the one who saved Kayla from the ruin collapse. They grew up together."

Seara's gaze turned to Veridian again, her face filling with gratitude. "Your mother sounds like a truly great woman. I'd be honored to meet her one day and offer my thanks."

"I believe she would have enjoyed meeting you too. Unfortunately, she passed away almost two years ago."

"I'm sorry to hear that." Seara's expression darkened. The depth of the emotion on her face made Kayla's heart go out to the older woman. "It's incredibly painful to lose someone you love. I owe you and your family a great debt for the life of my daughter."

In an attempt to lighten the mood, Veridian bumped shoulders with Kayla and teased, "I could have gotten worse in a little sister, but not much."

Kayla laughed, relaxing a fraction, and gave him an affectionate shove. "You jerk. Your life would be impossibly dull without me. Admit it."

Veridian chuckled. "You're definitely right about that. I wouldn't have gotten into nearly as much trouble."

Seara smiled at them. "It sounds like you two have quite a few stories to tell."

" They're mostly Kayla's stories. I was usually just along for the ride to try to keep her out of as much trouble as possible."

"Oh, please." Kayla crossed her arms in a playful pout. She knew he was trying to make the situation easier for everyone, and she loved him all the more for it.

Veridian leaned forward, resting his elbows on his knees. "There was this one time when she was about thirteen, and she was really getting into scavenging. She heard one of the other scavengers in our camp talking about how there wasn't anything of value in a particular sector. So she snuck out of camp the next morning and dropped down into the ruins. She ended up coming back to the surface a couple hours later with almost five thousand credits worth of loot."

"You know, the way I remember it, you were just as anxious to go down there as I was."

Veridian winked at Kayla and continued his story. "Mack, the scavenger who had been complaining, was furious. He was convinced she was trying to make him look bad. He went to Leo, our camp master, and demanded she be grounded on the surface until she learned her place."

Seara leaned forward, her hands resting on the edge of her seat. "What happened?"

Kayla grinned. "I clocked him."

Seara's eyes flew open. "You hit him?"

Veridian nodded and laughed. "This little, dark-haired, skinny girl went right up to Mack, who's actually a pretty big guy, and... Wham! She punched him right in the face and told him to suck it up. She told him if he couldn't handle a little competition, he should go play in the tech room."

"Oh my," Seara gasped. "What did he do?"

"He was pretty pissed, but it got him to wake up. When he realized Kayla wasn't a pushover, he actually started to respect her. Most of the other scavengers did too. Mack ended up teaching her quite a few of his tricks in the pits."

Kayla smiled. "He's a good guy. He'd freak out if he saw me here in the middle of OmniLab."

Seara sat back, pride shining in her eyes as she beamed at Kayla. "It sounds like you have a lot of your father in you. There was a fire in him, and he never let anyone or anything hold him back. It was one of the things I admired most about him. I believe you have that same fire, Kayla."

Veridian snorted. "She's a freaking inferno."

Kayla stuck her tongue out at him.

Alec, who had been quiet up until then, cleared his throat. "It's getting late. I'm sure there's much more you'd like to discuss, but if you don't mind, my father is expecting us for dinner tonight."

Seara stood and smoothed the wrinkles from her dress. "Oh, of course. If you'll find something suitable for Veridian to wear, I'll take Kayla to my room. I believe I have something appropriate for her."

Kayla followed her down the long hallway, stopping when Seara paused outside a door. She turned around to face Kayla, her expression hopeful. "Would you like to see your old room? The furnishings are the same, but most of your things were put in storage years ago for safekeeping. I'll have them brought back up for you. They might jog some of your memories."

"My room?"

Seara nodded and pressed the button outside of the room to open the door. Kayla stepped inside and looked around, not sure what she'd been expecting. A large canopy bed stood in the center of the room. The walls were a pale-blue while thick, cream-colored carpeting covered the floor. An expansive mural of the sky was painted on the ceiling. As Kayla stared at it, the mural seemed to change, and she realized it represented the time of day. The sun was beginning to set, and the room was filled with soft pinks and gold. A large desk stood on one side of the room, and there were two other doors on the opposite wall.

"Wow, it's big," Kayla said in surprise. "Where do those doors go?"

Seara smiled. "I've always loved this room. That door leads to your private bath area, and the other is your closet."

"All this space for one person?"

"Yes. This room is actually smaller than some of our others. We selected it when you were a child because we wanted to keep you close to us. Our room is down the hall. We would have given you larger and more private quarters as you grew up."

"Will I be staying here tonight?"

Seara nodded. "It's yours for as long as you want. If you'd rather have a different room, you can take your pick. Veridian can stay in the room next door, if you'd like."

"No, this is fine. Thanks." Kayla trailed her fingers along the edge of the desk, not quite believing this was real. The varnished wood was smooth to the touch and had been well tended over the years. This one piece of furniture was more beautiful and elaborate than anything she'd ever seen.

She caught her reflection in the mirror and paused. With her faded clothes and tousled hair, she was a stark contrast to the richness of her surroundings. Kayla bit her lip, feeling out of place. She was better suited to wielding a wrench than living amongst this luxury.

"You don't need to thank me, Kayla. All of this belongs to you. It's as much yours as it is mine."

Kayla jerked her hand back and frowned. "Uh, let's just say it's yours for now. This is a little overwhelming."

"I understand," Seara said quickly. "I don't want to pressure you."

Kayla slipped her hands back into her pockets to resist touching anything else. "So what's this thing about dinner? Why do we have to change?"

"Right. Let's go to my room." Seara led the way back

down the hall. "We occasionally have formal dinners. This one is political and social. The High Council will be there, along with many from the Inner Circle. They're entertaining some prospective traders and will decide on one of them in the next few days. I imagine there will be more people than usual since you'll be there. They're going to be curious."

"Great, more people staring at me," Kayla muttered.

Seara smiled at her daughter. "Well, we'll make sure we give them something to really stare at then."

She led Kayla a few doors down the hall and stepped into a large room that was almost the size of Leo's entire camp.

"This is *your* room?" Kayla asked in amazement, trying to take in everything at once. There was a large, intricately carved canopy bed against the far wall. One wall had a mirror with lights and a counter filled with strange bottles. Ornate pieces of furniture, including a seating area, were placed throughout the room. This ceiling also had a similarly strange mural that seemed to reflect the outside sky.

"Yes. The closet is through here." Seara pressed a button on the wall, and a door slid open. Racks of clothing lined the inside with floor-length mirrors on the back wall. Seara stepped inside and began browsing through her clothing. Kayla walked over to the closet and stared in shock.

"These all belong to you? You have a whole room for clothing? I think you have more clothes than Leo and Carl's camps combined."

Seara paused, turning back to Kayla with an apology in her eyes. "I'm sorry. I know this is new to you. I've heard some stories about what life is like outside of the tower, but most people only hear things second-hand. Is it bad?"

Kayla shook her head. "Not at all. It's not anything like this though. I suppose it's what you're used to. Your entire bedroom is larger than the camp where I grew up."

"Were you... happy growing up?"

Seara's worried expression tugged at Kayla's sympathy. It was as though one more emotional blow would topple her. Something about her provoked Kayla's protective instincts. "I suppose," she said with a shrug. "Happiness isn't really something you think about. I mean, I love scavenging and being in the ruins. There's nothing like the freedom and feeling you get when you race your speeder across the district. So yeah, I guess so."

Seara smiled, looking relieved at her response. "You seem like you really enjoy it. Veridian appears to care about you a great deal too. I'm glad you had someone like him growing up. I used to wonder what you would look like or what you would be like as you got older. I'm so glad to have this chance. I..." Her voice broke as tears filled her eyes.

She stepped toward Kayla and hugged her tightly. Kayla floundered, startled at the unsolicited display of affection. Not sure what else to do, she tentatively returned the embrace.

Seara stepped back, wiping away her tears. "I'm sorry. I shouldn't have done that. I've wanted to hug you since I first saw you."

"Uh, that's okay," Kayla said, not wanting Seara to feel uncomfortable. Despite the awkwardness, the hug was sort of nice. "I'm just not sure how to handle this yet."

"I understand." Seara took a deep breath and turned back to the clothes in the closet. She selected a dress and held it out to Kayla. "I think you would look fabulous in this one."

Kayla cocked her head and stared at the long skein of white fabric, trying to figure out how she was supposed to put the thing on. She reached out to touch it, the fabric impossibly soft as it glided across her palm. "You expect *me* to wear *this*? It's beautiful, but how the hell do you guys get anything done dressed like this?"

Seara laughed. "I would imagine it's not suitable to ride on a speeder or go scavenging in the ruins, but it works nicely for dinner. I'll show you how to put it on and help you with your hair."

Kayla pulled back and touched her hair self-consciously.

Seara frowned at the gesture. "Oh dear. I hope I didn't offend you. You have beautiful hair, but these dinners tend to be formal affairs."

Kayla stared at the dress with skepticism. No matter how much you polished a waste-recycling canister, it wouldn't change its function. She looked up, prepared to voice her doubts, but words failed her at the eager look on Seara's face. Kayla swallowed and managed a weak shrug. "All right. I'll give it a shot."

Seara's eyes lit up in excitement as she clasped her hands together. "Wonderful! Let's get started."

CHAPTER TWELVE

KAYLA LOOKED down at the dress. "I feel ridiculous."

The gown was pure white and made from some sort of impossibly soft material. It had a revealing neckline and spaghetti straps that crossed her back. Except for the two small straps, the back was open and accentuated her curves before cascading nearly to the floor. A high slit in the side reached almost to her hip. Kayla wondered why these Omnis even bothered wearing anything at all.

Her mother had twisted Kayla's hair into a complicated up-do, leaving a few wisps to fall around her face. She'd allowed Seara to paint her face using the strange bottles on the counter. Kayla stared at herself in the mirror and had a hard time believing it was her reflection staring back at her.

Seara practically beamed. "You look exquisite. That dress looks far better on you than it ever did on me. It looks like it was made for you."

"You guys seriously wear this stuff to *eat*? I'm going to end up spilling something on it or worse," she complained, looking down at her cleavage on display. "I think my boobs are going to pop out."

Seara laughed in delight, waving off her concerns. "You'll be fine. If it gets ruined, I have plenty more. I can't remember when I've ever had this much fun dressing for dinner."

Kayla laughed in spite of herself at Seara's giddiness. Her mother was wearing a long, cream-colored dress with intricate, golden threading, and her hair was pinned up in some sort of bun fastened with sparkling clips. She was absolutely breathtaking.

Seara reached up to adjust Kayla's hair, and she noticed the strange bracelet around her mother's wrist. Kayla frowned, remembering the earlier conversation with Alec and his father. "Hey, is that one of those security bracelets?"

Seara's eyes widened, and she pulled back, self-consciously twisting the bracelet around her wrist. "Who told you about them? Did Alec say something?"

"No," Kayla replied, puzzled by Seara's reaction. "We ran into his father outside, and he mentioned I should get one. He said it gives you access to secure areas?"

"Something like that. What did Alec say about it?"

"He said I didn't need one. He wanted me to meet you first. I'm guessing he wanted to show me around himself. Maybe I should get one though."

A security access bracelet might come in handy. She'd like to investigate some of OmniLab's new prototypes. An all-access pass could get her into the restricted areas without too much trouble. Although, even without one, it wouldn't stop her planned exploration.

Seara touched Kayla's arm and vehemently shook her head. She held her finger to her lips to indicate silence, then pointed to her ear and gestured to the entire room. "That's an option. You may not need one though. Wait and see."

Kayla's brow furrowed. They were being monitored? She looked around the room trying to figure out a likely place for listening devices. In a room this size, it would be easy to plant something. Deciding it would probably be best to play along until she could learn more, she said, "Uh, okay. I don't want to wear something around my wrist anyway."

Seara nodded emphatically and kept her finger pressed against her lips. "We can talk more about it later. Let's go show Veridian and Alec your dress. I can't wait to see their faces."

Kayla let Seara lead her back down the hall to where Veridian and Alec were waiting. Both men stood as they entered, looking polished in formal suits.

Veridian's eyes widened as he tugged at his collar, looking as freaked out as she felt. "Kayla? Wow, um... wow."

She flushed. Veridian looked uncomfortable in his suit, but Alec seemed to be perfectly at ease in his. He was exotic, elegant, and incredibly sexy all at once. He studied her intently, and Kayla noticed the heat in his eyes. "You're absolutely stunning, Kayla."

Oh man, an Omni shouldn't look that good.

The corners of his mouth tilted upward into a smirk. Kayla's eyes narrowed in suspicion, wondering if he was reading her thoughts again. Before she could ask him, Seara clapped her hands together to get everyone's attention. "We should probably head to the meeting room. Your attendance is going to cause something of a stir."

Kayla grimaced at the thought of parading around a bunch of Omnis. These were the same people who controlled the lives of her friends on the surface, and she was about to go socialize with them wearing a borrowed dress worth more than her camp's annual income. She squared her shoulders and nodded. She could do this. If not, she'd see just how well this dress would hold up on a speeder.

"Time to show everyone what a reanimated corpse looks like," Kayla muttered under her breath.

Veridian heard her comment and smothered a laugh.

"Veridian, would you escort me?" Seara linked her arm with his. "I'd love to hear more of the stories from when you two were growing up."

Veridian flashed her a huge smile. As they headed out the door, he launched into a story about Kayla sneaking off into the ruins when she was ten years old.

Alec approached Kayla. "May I have the honor of escorting you?"

She looked at him in alarm. "I knew it. I told Seara these shoes were death traps. Is that why someone has to escort us? So we don't fall on our face?"

Alec chuckled. "No, although I'm quite sure if you wanted to take them off at some point, no one would mind. They definitely won't be looking at your feet."

Okay, now he's definitely flirting with me.

Alec's eyes warmed, and he leaned close to her. "And for the record, you're the most beautiful reanimated corpse I've ever seen."

"You weren't supposed to hear that."

Alec's mouth twitched into a smile, and he held out his arm for Kayla. She linked her arm in his and warned, "You better catch me if I fall on my ass. Preferably before. With my luck, I'll end up ripping this dress and giving the entire room a show."

Alec laughed. "You're one of the most unusual and outspoken women I've ever met. It's rather refreshing. Is it just you or because you grew up on the surface, I wonder? I never know what you're going to say next."

Kayla shrugged. "It's probably me. Judging by the number of people I've managed to piss off over the years, yeah, it's me."

He smiled at her, and they headed out of the Rath'Varein private quarters. They followed Seara and Veridian down the pathway toward a central meeting room area. Dozens of people milled around, sipping on drinks and chatting with one another.

Seara turned to Kayla and whispered, "They usually mingle for about twenty or thirty minutes before anyone is even seated. It's all about politics here."

At the sight of their group, the majority of the people fell silent and openly stared at Kayla and her companions. Kayla ignored the stares and strode into the room on Alec's arm.

Edwin spotted them from across the room and approached. "Seara, you look wonderful as usual, my dear. Your daughter definitely takes after you."

Without waiting for a response, Edwin snapped his fingers at someone. They immediately came over carrying a tray of tall, slender glasses. Edwin lifted two glasses and handed one to Seara and the other to Kayla.

Alec accepted a glass from the server and motioned for Veridian to take one too. Kayla studied the bubbling golden liquid. "What is this?"

"It's called champagne. It's a little sweet. You might enjoy it."

Kayla sniffed the glass, decided it wasn't too offensive, and took a cautious sip. The bubbles tickled her tongue and mouth, but it was a pleasant enough taste.

Alec's mouth twitched in a hint of a smile. "Do you like it?"

She nodded and took another sip. "Yeah, I've never had anything like this. I like the bubbles."

Seara turned to Edwin. "I need to speak with you privately."

"I'm sure you do. In the meantime, Alec, why don't you take Kayla and Veridian around and introduce them to a few people? There are two potential traders here. I'm sure Kayla and Veridian can give them some unique insight as to what to expect on the surface if they're selected."

Alec inclined his head and led Kayla and Veridian away, while Seara and Edwin disappeared into another room. Kayla turned to watch them go, wondering about the tension between them.

"The potential traders are Milo and Rand," Alec explained, interrupting her thoughts. "They've both studied the pre-war history extensively, are technical experts, and the High Council believes either one would make a suitable trader. They've never been to the surface, though, so they'll probably be interested in speaking with you both."

"How do you decide who you're going to send?"

"Becoming a trader is actually quite difficult. Usually, it requires extensive study, and we test them thoroughly on their knowledge. They also have to share similar ideologies to OmniLab's High Council and Inner Circle."

Kayla frowned. "Then how the hell did Ramiro get in? That guy was a couple sandwiches short of a picnic."

Alec lowered his voice. "Occasionally, such as the case with Ramiro, bribes are accepted. Becoming a trader and fulfilling the terms of the contract boosts a family's status considerably."

Kayla's eyes narrowed. "Did either of these two buy their way in?"

Alec shook his head. "No, they were selected on merit and achievements alone. An inquiry into selection status is occurring as a result of the petition against Ramiro. The High Council is being cautious with this next selection."

Well, maybe they don't have their heads completely up their asses. "I see. What about Carl? Why was he selected?"

Alec hesitated. "He was actually recruited, not selected. The removal of the previous trader was rather sudden. Carl's been on the fast track for an assistant director position, and a few of our directors thought the experience would benefit him. He's young for it, but based on his merits and achievements, we decided he would be a good fit. So far, he's exceeded all expectations."

Kayla nodded in agreement. "For a trader, he's a pretty good guy."

Alec brought them over to a tall man in his thirties. He had short, dark hair and wore slightly less ostentatious formal wear. He was considerably shorter than Alec and appeared to be far more of a tech room junkie than someone who could navigate the pits. His brown eyes were intelligent, and they widened considerably as he recognized them.

"Oh goodness! Mistress Kayla Rath'Varein, Master Alec Tal'Vayr, it's truly an honor to meet you. My name is Milo Orwin."

"Hi, Milo. Nice to meet you. But call me Kayla. I don't get into the fancy names and crap."

At Milo's shocked expression, Alec added, "Kayla prefers to avoid formalities. It appears to be a trademark on the surface. And this is Veridian Levanthe."

"This is so exciting," Milo said with a bow, twisting his hands nervously. His words flew together in rapid succession. "I can't express how honored I am. To meet both of you is truly a wondrous thing. Thank you for taking the time to speak with me."

Holy shit. If this guy gets flustered this easily, the ruin rats are going to chew him up and spit him out.

Alec smiled at Milo and said with a trace of laughter in his voice, "Please be at ease, Milo. As you know, Kayla and Veridian recently arrived from the surface. The culture there is quite different than what you're accustomed to here in the towers."

"Yeah," Kayla muttered. "We don't dress up for dinner."

Alec barely managed to keep a straight face. Milo looked

at Kayla and Veridian eagerly. "Would it be okay if I asked you a few questions? I'd like to have some additional background. I've studied quite a bit about what life is like on the surface, but there's so much more to learn."

Veridian smiled at him. "Sure, I'd be happy to answer your questions."

Kayla finished her glass of champagne. "Uh huh. V's better with questions than I am."

"In that case, why don't we let Veridian and Milo talk?" Alec suggested, sweeping her empty glass from her hand. "I'll get you another drink and introduce you to Rand."

"All right." Once they were out of earshot, she blew out a breath and shook her head. "You're not really going to send that guy to the surface, are you? He won't last a week."

Alec chuckled and waved over a server. Taking another drink off the tray, he offered it to her and leaned close, his breath warm against her ear. "You are truly a gem, Kayla."

"Hmm," she murmured, ignoring the goose bumps his nearness caused, and took a large sip. Too much was happening that was outside her realm of experience. She was attracted to Alec, but he was like one of the relics she discovered when scavenging. He was nice to look at, but he belonged in the towers and not in her hands. She looked around the room for a distraction. "So where's this other trader?"

"I'll introduce you to him now," Alec offered and pressed his hand against the small of her back. A shiver went through her at the contact, but she didn't pull away.

He led her across the room and stopped in front of a tall man who didn't look like he spent all his time in the tech room. His blond hair was pulled back in a ponytail, and he had an air of confidence about him.

"Master Tal'Vayr and Mistress Rath'Varein," he acknowledged with a polite smile.

"Kayla," she said firmly. "Just Kayla. You must be Rand?"

He bowed briefly. "Yes. I've been looking forward to meeting you. I understand you're familiar with the district I'm hoping to oversee?"

Okay, this one has potential. A little formal, but he'll get over that. Not bad to look at either.

"You could say that."

Rand studied her for a moment, his curiosity evident. "Are there many surface camps in that area? Our data is sketchy since they seem to move around frequently."

"Surface camps? I think you mean ruin rats." She laughed at the polite description. "There are some. Ramiro wasn't good at what he did so it was easy to scavenge under his nose. His prices sucked though. A lot of the camps scavenged in his district and then sold to Warig or Carl."

If Rand was surprised at her candor, he hid it well. She got the impression he was filing away her observations for later. He gave a thoughtful nod and mused, "I'm surprised they wouldn't feel some loyalty toward the trader in the district they scavenged from."

Kayla smirked at him. "If you become a trader, you're going to learn one thing real quick. Ruin rats don't like traders or Omnis. You're a necessary evil, and the less contact with you, the better."

Alec looked at her in surprise. "*All* ruin rats feel this way?"

Kayla sipped her drink. "Pretty much. Sure, there are a few exceptions. But generally speaking? Oh yeah. Most traders tend to screw over ruin rats every chance they get. There's no loyalty on either side. Don't expect to be welcomed with open arms."

"I see. It sounds like this will be more challenging than I anticipated." Rand turned to Alec. "I look forward to meeting with the High Council and Inner Circle representatives when I present my final bid for the trader position."

Alec inclined his head. Rand turned to Kayla and bowed low to her. "It was truly a pleasure to meet you. I hope I'll be given the opportunity to try to repair the rift between the surface camps and the traders."

Kayla looked at him in surprise. "You sound like Carl."

He raised an eyebrow. "Trader Carl Grayson?"

When she nodded, he chuckled and admitted, "We know each other well. We studied together before he was recruited for his current position."

She smiled, beginning to like the trader recruit even more. "It figures. He's one of the only decent traders I've ever known. Sneaky bastard, but fair. Most ruin rats don't like him simply because he's a trader, but he's respected."

Rand nodded thoughtfully. "I'll be interested in speaking with him when he comes to the meeting."

A soft chime echoed throughout the room. Alec put his arm around her waist. "That's our cue, dear." He offered a polite nod to Rand and led her away.

"I take it you approve of him?" Alec asked her quietly as they stepped into the large banquet hall area.

"Yeah, he's better than the other idiot." Kayla looked around at all the tables decorated with white tablecloths covered with strange dishes and flowers. "What the hell is this? It's supposed to be dinner. You sit, you eat, and you're done."

He gave her an encouraging smile. "It's not too bad. You might even enjoy yourself. I'll show you to your seat and then go check on Veridian."

Alec led her to a large table at the far end of the room. The table was situated near a strange glass wall that had water droplets falling in artistic patterns. Once she was seated in the chair he held out for her, he briefly rested his hands on her bare shoulders. His touch sent warm tingles over her skin. Leaning close to her ear, he whispered, "I'll be right back."

Kayla studied the table in front of her. There were several silver eating utensils and crystal glasses at every place setting. She picked up a fork, wondering how many credits it was worth. With a sigh, she replaced it and shook her head at the opulence.

Wow, I can't believe people actually live like this.

She finished her champagne while watching people stroll into the room and find their seats. The moment she put the empty glass in front of her, a woman approached her. "Would you care for another glass of champagne, Mistress Rath'-Varein? Or could I interest you in a glass of wine?"

Before Kayla could reply, Alec reappeared with Veridian. "Another glass of champagne for now. The wine tends to be more suitable with dinner." The server nodded and quickly walked away.

Veridian leaned down to Kayla. "Hey, do you mind if I sit with Milo? He's studied ancient pre-war societies, and he's been telling me about them. We've been comparing them to the culture of ruin rats and traders."

Kayla stared at him for a moment and then burst out laughing. She shooed him away and teased, "Go play with your new friend. It figures that a freaking Omni shares your obsession."

He grinned at her and headed over to another table. Alec sat down next to her and casually rested his arm across the back of her chair. "Veridian enjoys studying history?"

Kayla nodded. "Yeah, he loves that kind of stuff. It isn't very helpful in the ruins, but he's into it."

The server reappeared and placed another glass of champagne in front of her.

"Thanks."

The woman looked startled at her appreciation. Her eyes darted between Kayla and Alec. She swallowed nervously and stammered, "You're welcome, Mistress Rath'Varein."

"I need a damn sign with my name on it," Kayla muttered, annoyed with the whole title nonsense. Alec smiled in amusement. He leaned close to her, lifting one of the loose tendrils of hair around her face and rubbing it between his fingers. "You make the servers nervous. They aren't used to us acknowledging them."

"That's weird," she returned and sipped her drink. She leaned back in her chair, enjoying his attention. "Why wouldn't you acknowledge them?"

Alec shrugged and continued to play with her hair. "In part, we're different. We usually keep to ourselves, and they seem to prefer it that way."

Kayla's mother and Alec's father appeared at the table. Edwin held out Seara's chair for her while she took a seat. "Would you care for another glass of champagne, Seara?"

"No, thank you," she said softly and turned to her daughter. "Did you have a chance to meet the potential traders, Kayla?"

"Yeah, Veridian's talking shop with one of them right now."

Seara smiled and placed her napkin in her lap. Kayla looked at the napkin and followed suit, earning a look of approval from Seara. "I'm glad he's enjoying himself."

Edwin took his seat, his gaze falling on Alec's arm still resting on her chair. He nodded, looking pleased, and then said, "Ah, there's Keith and Marcus. They decided to join us after all."

Kayla sat up, pulling away from Alec. Even though she'd been comfortable, she wasn't inclined to do anything to make Edwin happy. Something about him rubbed her the wrong way.

Two older men approached, and Edwin stood and shook hands with them. After making their introductions, they sat at the table.

"Kayla, you're as lovely as your mother," Keith said. "It's our great fortune you survived all these years."

Marcus nodded and added, "It's nice to know the Rath'-Varein line continues. We still mourn the loss of your father."

Before she could think of an appropriate response, the servers appeared and began placing plates in front of them. Kayla stared at the food. It was unlike anything she'd seen before. The colors were vibrant, and the smells were incredible.

"What is this?" she whispered to Alec.

He smiled at her. "Grilled vegetables and pasta with a basil sauce."

She watched him lift his fork and place it in his mouth. Curious, she picked up her fork and took a bite. Her eyes widened as she chewed her food.

"Holy shit! This is freaking unbelievable."

Alec burst into laughter, and Seara's hand flew to her mouth to suppress a laugh. Marcus and Keith exchanged amused glances, but Edwin frowned at her outburst.

"This is what you guys normally eat?"

Alec nodded. "I'm glad you like it. Our chefs are always coming up with new dishes."

She took another bite and then a sip of the wine. Her senses were in overload.

"The flavors are amazing. I never thought food could taste like this. What did you do to it?"

"We grow our own vegetables here," Seara explained. "We have extensive laboratories and greenhouses to grow our own food."

"I'd love to see that."

"I'd be happy to take you on a tour tomorrow," Alec offered.

She nodded eagerly. Edwin leaned forward. "So, Kayla, what do you think of our potential traders?"

Kayla shrugged, still enraptured by the meal. "They both seem nice enough, but Rand is probably better suited for the job."

"You were able to make a judgment like that without seeing their qualifications?"

Kayla looked up from her plate to find Edwin looking down his nose at her. He was the quintessential Omni—pompous and condescending.

"I don't need to see their qualifications. It comes down to a matter of will, drive, and confidence. There won't be a ruin rat in your entire territory that won't take advantage of someone who has their head up their ass or jumps when you say boo."

"You don't think having knowledge or expertise is important when it comes to collecting artifacts?"

"Some, sure," she agreed, "but do you think ruin rats have had any sort of formal training? From what I've seen, most traders don't crawl through the ruins anyway. They run their camps and negotiate with the rest of us who do the actual work. That's why Ramiro sucked. He didn't give a shit about his crew, and he took advantage of the ruin rats whenever he could. He wasn't exactly bright, though, so that didn't happen often."

"I see. You seem to have strong opinions on the matter," Edwin observed.

Keith leaned forward, looking interested in the discussion. "She may have a point, Edwin. Ramiro's profit margins were low, and he had trouble keeping people under contract. Tell me, Kayla, what are your thoughts of our current traders?"

"Warig is okay," she admitted, taking a liking to the other council member. "He's not as easy to take advantage of as Ramiro was. His prices are average, but he's a little too cautious. His crew seems to respect him though. Most ruin rats prefer dealing with him rather than Ramiro simply because Ramiro was a jerk."

"Warig's profits have been stable but nothing spectacular," Keith mused. "What about Henkel and Carl?"

Kayla took a sip of her wine and considered the question. She didn't think he'd be interested in hearing Carl was as delicious as the pasta thing.

"Henkel's an idiot. His crew thinks he's an idiot too. Negotiating with him is a pain in the ass. He takes forever to figure out his numbers and what he wants to spend. His district is crowded with ruin rats since it's so easy to scavenge under his nose. Carl's about the only trader you've got that's worth a damn. He runs a tight crew, and they respect him. He's sneaky, devious, and it's hard as hell to scavenge in his district without getting caught. He takes it in stride when you get away with it, though, and he's fair. His prices are better, too, so more people come to him to trade."

"Interesting. Carl's profits have been substantially higher than the other traders," Keith observed. He turned to Edwin. "Perhaps we've been approaching this the wrong way. It seems we may need to look at different qualifications in our traders."

"Perhaps," Edwin conceded.

The servers reappeared and removed their empty plates, replacing them with small bowls of colorful fruit.

Kayla looked at it in surprise. "What's this?"

"It's a fruit medley," Alec informed her. "But just a moment. There's something else I think you should try."

He waved over one of the servers and whispered in her ear. She nodded and disappeared.

Kayla looked at him curiously, and he said, "Go ahead and try the fruit. It's a light and refreshing dessert. But I suspect you may enjoy this other one a bit more."

She took an experimental bite. "Wow, this is amazing. I've had fruit substitutes before, but this is completely different."

A moment later, the server reappeared holding a small plate with a slice of a dark cake drizzled with some sort of red liquid. At Kayla's questioning look, Alec took a small forkful and leaned over toward her.

She hesitated for a moment and then opened her mouth to taste it. "This is chocolate cake with a raspberry sauce," he explained as her lips closed around the fork.

Her eyes widened, and she looked down at the dessert in amazement. She swallowed and murmured under her breath, "I think my mouth just had an orgasm."

Alec dropped the fork on the table and turned away laughing. Kayla grinned and pulled the plate closer to take another bite.

"Kayla, your reactions are priceless."

She closed her eyes and waved Alec away. "Shh. I'm savoring this moment."

He chuckled. "When you're finished, I have something I'd like to show you."

She opened her eyes and put her hand on her stomach. "I hope it's not more food. I've eaten way too much tonight."

Alec turned to Seara. "Do you mind if I borrow your daughter for a few minutes? I have a small gift I'd like to give her."

At Seara's hesitation, Kayla looked up. Tension radiated from Seara, and she darted a quick glance at Edwin. Alec shook his head and placed his hand over Kayla's. Even though he'd been somewhat flirtatious toward her all evening, the gesture seemed almost protective.

"It's something from her childhood, Seara. It may bring back some of her memories."

The older woman looked relieved. "Of course, Alec. I trust you'll act in Kayla's best interest."

Edwin cleared his throat. "While our children are off dallying, I'll escort you back to your quarters, Seara."

Seara turned to Kayla. "Don't worry about your charming friend. I'll bring Veridian back to our family's quarters when he's finished. Go ahead and enjoy yourself."

Kayla agreed, thankful to get away from the table. There were things going on and politics at play she didn't understand. Alec said goodnight to everyone and held out his arm for Kayla. She put her arm through his and let him lead her out of the room. She was acutely aware of the looks and comments the two of them were generating.

Although she wasn't sure about Alec's motives, Kayla was confident in her ability to handle him. She had doubts about the zapping thing he'd done to her, but he seemed genuinely remorseful about upsetting her. Seara also seemed to trust him, and Kayla liked—even admired—the older woman.

When they left the dining area, Kayla stopped. "Okay, these shoes are coming off. I feel like I'm about to fall over."

She sat on a nearby bench, and he knelt in front of her. His eyes held hers as he lifted the hem of her dress above her ankles. His hands were gentle, brushing against her skin as he removed her shoes. His touch sent those strange little tingles through her, and she couldn't decide if she wanted him to keep touching her or ask him to stop.

Once he had removed her shoes, Alec stood up. With one hand holding her shoes, he offered his other hand and helped her to her feet. She swallowed, feeling strangely off-balance. Trying to lighten the mood, she teased, "So is shoe removal part of a Master's job?"

Alec put his hand around her waist and looked down into her eyes. "If I remember correctly, you instructed me not to let you fall earlier. I'm merely honoring your request."

"Thanks," Kayla whispered, caught by his gaze. His eyes

were an almost impossible shade of blue with shimmering gold flecks.

"My pleasure," he replied, taking her hand. He led her down the path and brought her to another ornate door. It was similar to the design outside of her family's quarters. He pressed his palm against the panel, and the door slid open.

The colors inside the Tal'Vayr family quarters were much bolder than Seara's living area. Instead of the flowering arrangements Seara preferred, there were several abstract and geometrical pieces of art hanging on the walls. Kayla was surprised at the style. It didn't seem to represent Alec well.

"The decor is my father's personal taste. My private quarters are through here." He pressed a button, and another door opened.

This area appeared to suit Alec better. The colors were softer and more muted. There was a large seating area in the front room and a small food preparation area off to the side. There were several other doors down another hallway.

"Wow, this place is huge."

Alec looked around, and Kayla got the impression he was trying to see the room through her eyes. "It gives me a bit of privacy since families tend to share living quarters."

"So what did you want to show me?"

Alec dropped her shoes on the floor and took both of her hands in his. "Think of this as a memory exercise. I want you to close your eyes and imagine the glass globe from your dreams."

It was a strange request, but she was intrigued enough to play along. She closed her eyes and imagined the sparkling gold and green globe.

"Do you see it?"

She nodded. "Yes, I can see it."

"Now, hold it in your mind and think beyond the globe.

Imagine its location. Is it on top of something? Is it inside something?"

She frowned in concentration as he released her hands. "It's in a box of some sort."

"Can you tell where the box is located?"

She reached out with her hand as though trying to touch it, feeling a slight tingle ripple through her.

Kayla's eyes flew open. She pointed across the room. "It's there!"

She headed toward a desk in the corner and opened up a small chest. There, on a velvet cushion, sat the strange glass globe from her dreams.

Kayla stared at her hands in disbelief, wondering about the tingle she'd felt. She'd have thought it was some sort of elaborate trick if she hadn't experienced it. "How is this possible?"

"This is only one of your abilities, Kayla. You're extraordinarily talented."

She carefully lifted the glass globe. It was identical to the one from memory. Green and gold flecks swirled inside it. "It's beautiful."

"I want you to have it. I should have given it to you years ago."

Kayla jerked her head up, shocked he was trying to give her such an expensive gift. She put it back in the chest, feeling a twinge of regret, but she couldn't take it. "I can't accept this. You've kept it all these years. It must mean a lot to you."

Alec put his hand on hers. "Kayla, it would mean a lot more to me if you accepted it."

She hesitated but looked at the globe with longing. "Are you sure?"

"Yes," he insisted and stepped closer to her. "I'd like you to have it. It belongs with you."

She pulled the box toward her and trailed her fingers over the globe once more. She'd never owned anything so beautiful. "Thank you."

"Kayla," he murmured. She looked up at him, and he lifted his hand to stroke her cheek. "You're exquisite."

He tilted her head back and pressed his lips against hers. She closed her eyes and leaned into the kiss. Her senses went into overload. Everything felt sharper and clearer. His touch sent energy flowing through her.

But he's not Carl.

She pulled away. "I'm sorry, Alec. I can't do this."

He looked at her in surprise. "Because of Carl? Kayla, he's just a trader."

"How did you..." her voice trailed off and her eyes narrowed. She'd had her suspicions, but she hadn't been sure until now. She took a step back. "Are you listening to my thoughts?"

He hesitated for a moment before admitting, "Yes. Not all of them, but I can hear some. You haven't learned to think quietly yet."

"All this time?" she accused angrily, mentally kicking herself for letting down her guard. She'd been so focused on all these strange new experiences that she hadn't been paying enough attention to what was right in front of her. How much had he been manipulating her by listening to her thoughts? For all she knew, he had been directing her like some mindless puppet.

"Kayla, I was waiting for the right time to teach you. Most people can't communicate with thought. I usually have to be touching someone for them to hear me. You're one of the rare exceptions."

Well, didn't she feel lucky.

"You sick and twisted bastard." Her hand clenched into a fist and she swung.

He caught her hand easily. "You don't want to do that."

She snatched her hand away from him and hissed, "Everyone deserves the right to be a jackass, but you abuse the privilege."

Alec followed her as she stormed out of the room. "Wait a minute, Kayla."

She ignored him and headed straight for the door, walking right into Master Edwin Tal'Vayr.

The older man glanced back at Alec. "Is there a problem, Kayla?"

She scowled at him. "Yeah, your son. Now, if you'll excuse me, I'm done with this. I'm beginning to see why my subconscious wanted to avoid the towers all these years. At least things make sense on the surface and there isn't any of this woo-woo crap."

"You're planning on leaving the towers?" Edwin's eyes narrowed.

"I'm definitely thinking about it."

"Kayla, wait a minute," Alec protested. "This was just a misunderstanding."

Edwin gave Alec a hard look and grabbed Kayla's wrist. "You had your chance, Alec."

"What are you doing? Get your hands off me!"

She tried to pull away from him, but his grip was ironclad. Suddenly, Kayla felt a sharp, piercing energy flow through her. She gasped and struggled against him.

More energy poured through her, and Kayla started feeling dizzy. She desperately searched for the calm oasis she'd found before. Relief flooded through her when she found it. Gathering as much of the energy as she could, she flung it back toward Edwin.

He relaxed his grip slightly, and his eyes widened in surprise. There was admiration in his voice as he said, "You said she was strong, but I had no idea."

"Let her go," Alec demanded angrily. "She was upset because of a misunderstanding. This isn't necessary."

"Forget it," Edwin snarled. "She's an untapped resource. I'm not risking her leaving the tower. I had no idea she was this powerful."

His words didn't make complete sense to Kayla, but she was having trouble focusing on both the energy and their argument. If she could clear her head of the energy rush, she could think and get out of this mess. She pushed more energy back toward Edwin. He tightened his grip on her wrist, and she cried out as her senses were once again flooded.

The assault continued to increase in intensity until Kayla finally closed herself off in the dark abyss of her mind.

CHAPTER THIRTEEN

EDWIN LOWERED Kayla's unconscious form to the floor. Alec knelt beside her and looked up at his father in anger.

"She was upset because she found out I was reading her thoughts. If you'd given her a few minutes to calm down or let me talk to her, this wouldn't have been necessary."

Edwin gave his son a hard look. "This was inevitable. She's her father's daughter in every sense. I haven't seen anyone with this much raw talent since he died."

Alec returned his father's look. He should have known his father wouldn't be reasonable where Kayla was concerned. She was too headstrong and too much like her father for him to view her as anything other than a threat. He'd hoped his obvious interest in Kayla would be enough of a deterrent. "And what do you plan to tell Seara? Or her friend Veridian?"

Edwin walked over to the communications device on the wall and pressed a button on the control panel. "Seara will be told the truth. She has no choice but to accept it. I made that clear to her tonight. Kayla's little outsider friend is of no interest to me. Send him away."

"Send him away?" Alec asked dryly, trying to keep his

temper in check. If he lost it now, he wouldn't be in a position to help anyone. "You think he's just going to accept the fact Kayla's disappeared and doesn't want to even say goodbye?"

"Then you'll have to *make* him accept it," Edwin ordered as the door opened. Director Borshin and another man entered the Tal'Vayr family quarters.

"Borshin, Cessel." Edwin nodded at the two men he summoned. He gestured to Kayla. "Take her to Observation Room A. Cessel, I want her outfitted with a bracelet immediately."

Director Borshin scampered out of the room to retrieve a transport while Cessel looked down at Kayla as though examining a specimen on a microscope. "Forgive me, but we received reports of some disturbing fluctuations in the energy field. Was this woman the cause?"

Annoyed with the callousness of Edwin's head scientist, Alec corrected the man. "This *woman* is Mistress Kayla Rath'Varein."

Cessel's eyes widened, and he backpedaled quickly. "My apologies, Master Tal'Vayr. I didn't intend any disrespect."

"Enough," Edwin ordered. "What do you mean by 'disturbing fluctuations'?"

Cessel cleared his throat and looked at Kayla's unconscious form on the floor in front of him. "There was a significant energy drain on our pooled resources. Five of your sources have been temporarily depleted."

Alec's head jerked up. "It took five people to subdue her?"

Edwin regarded Kayla with new interest. "Cessel, I want you to attune her bracelet directly to me. I want to test the limits of her strength."

Alec stared at his father and clenched his fists, furious at the covetous look on his face. It took everything he had not to give in to his impulses. Forcing his body to relax, he shook his head. "Absolutely not. She's untrained. If you try using her that way, it could kill her."

Edwin regarded his son coolly. "Then feel free to train her. But my order stands."

Director Borshin returned with Seara following on his heels. He pushed the medical transport cart into the room. "My apologies, Master Tal'Vayr, but Mistress Rath'Varein saw me in the hallway."

"Edwin, what have you done? We all felt the drain on the energy pool."

When she saw Kayla, she gasped in horror, ran over to her daughter, and knelt beside her. She looked up at Alec pleadingly. "Why now? You said you wouldn't do this now."

Her look of betrayal pained him. He shook his head, holding out his hands in regret. "I'm sorry, Seara. I didn't want this either. It wasn't my decision."

Seara stood and turned to look at Edwin, hate filling her eyes. "You bastard! She's of no use to you right now. She doesn't remember anything of her past with us, and she hasn't been trained yet."

Alec stood and approached Seara. He rested his hand on her arm, allowing his thoughts to flow through to hers. Her eyes filled with tears as he shared what had transpired and she learned what Edwin had ordered.

"Please don't do this, Edwin. Putting a bracelet on her now without the support of all of us to tamper the flow will destroy her. She couldn't possibly know how to properly channel that sort of energy."

When Edwin didn't reply, she reached for his arm. "She's my daughter, Edwin. I'll do whatever you want, but please don't do this to her."

Edwin gave her a bored look. "Seara, once upon a time that offer may have intrigued me, but I already control you.

You have nothing left to propose. Your daughter, on the other hand, has potential."

Director Borshin pushed the medical transport into the center of the room. Tears ran down Seara's face as they moved Kayla into the transport and activated the privacy setting to hide her from view.

"At least tell me where you're taking her," Seara begged.

"Oh, don't be dramatic," Edwin said in annoyance. "She's going to Observation Room A. They'll put on the bracelet, and she'll be returned to you tomorrow."

Alec gave his father a dark look before turning back to Seara. He put his arm around her, trying to offer some reassurance. Where his father was concerned, he couldn't make any promises. "Seara, I need to speak with Veridian and explain things to him. When I'm finished, I'll check on Kayla for you. In the meantime, let me take you back to your quarters."

Seara nodded and wiped away her tears. Borshin and Cessel pushed the medical transport out of the room. Alec led the older woman out of his family's quarters and toward her rooms. When they were outside, she turned to him. "I don't understand, Alec. What happened?"

"Kayla was angry when she realized I could hear her thoughts. My father overreacted and thought she intended to leave the towers."

Seara stopped and looked at Alec harshly. "You haven't listened in on private thoughts since you were a child. Why would you do such a thing?"

Because he was a cad? Because he enjoyed experiencing Kayla's refreshing way of looking at the world? Alec resisted the urge to flinch under Seara's accusatory stare. "It wasn't intentional in the beginning. I suspect we have similar talents. I was able to hear her without touching her. She hasn't learned how to guard her thoughts, and I wanted to give her some time before explaining this to her. She seemed apprehensive about our abilities."

Seara's eyes widened as she absorbed the news. "She can read thoughts too? That's not something that usually runs in our family."

"I don't believe she can read everyone. Perhaps because I'm already sensitive to it, she's able to tap into it somehow. I'm not sure. But that's what originally caught my attention. She appeared to be able to hear me influencing Director Borshin while standing on the opposite side of the room."

They approached the door to Seara's quarters, and she clutched his arm to stop him. "I have a request, Alec."

He looked at her expectantly as she explained, "When you speak with Veridian, be kind. I owe him and his family a debt which can never be repaid. Kayla seems to care about him a great deal."

"Of course, Seara. I'll try not to upset him, but this is necessary." He didn't need to remind her of what his father would do to Veridian if he didn't leave the towers of his own volition.

She nodded and opened the door to find Veridian sitting inside the common area. When he didn't see Kayla, a look of confusion came over his face.

"Where's Kayla?"

Alec walked over to him and held out his hand to shake it. "It's been a great pleasure meeting you, Veridian."

Veridian accepted the man's handshake. "You too. What's going on?"

The moment Veridian touched his hand, Alec wove a subtle thread of influence around his next words. "I gave Kayla a toy from her childhood. It triggered a number of memories. She asked to be alone for a while so she could sort through her thoughts. She wants you to return to Trader Carl's camp."

Veridian shook his head and tried to pull away. "That doesn't make sense. She wants me to leave without her?"

Alec was surprised at Veridian's resistance. The bond between Veridian and Kayla must have been extremely strong for him to believe his convictions so vehemently. Alec increased his influence. "Yes. She wants some time to sort through her memories. She'll contact you when she's ready."

Veridian's shoulders slumped. "I guess... I guess I should go back now?"

Alec released Veridian's hand. "Yes. We can have someone escort you back."

Veridian scratched his head and turned to Seara. "It was nice meeting you, Seara. I'm glad Kayla found you."

"Goodbye, Veridian. Thank you," Seara said softly.

"I'll walk you out," Alec offered, sensing the man was still having difficulties making sense of the story he'd been given. He led Veridian out of the Rath'Varein quarters and back toward the main elevator. They rode the elevator down in silence. When it arrived on the ground floor, Alec took him to the main entrance area where they'd first arrived. Melvin looked up in surprise and bowed low when he recognized Alec.

"Melvin, contact Director Borshin and tell him to come down. I want you both to escort Veridian back to Trader Carl Grayson's camp."

If Melvin was surprised, he didn't show it. He merely nodded. "Right away, Master Tal'Vayr."

Alec turned once more to Kayla's close friend. "Veridian, I wish you the best of luck."

Veridian nodded. "Thanks."

Without another word, Alec turned and left the room, knowing his request would be fulfilled. He headed straight for the observation room where Cessel was holding Kayla. Dealing with Veridian had taken more time than he'd expected, and he didn't want to leave Kayla alone longer than necessary. Upon entering the large laboratory, he found Cessel arguing with his assistant.

"Cessel? What's going on?"

Cessel frowned and shifted his weight from foot to foot. "We have a small problem. I contacted Master Edwin Tal'-Vayr and asked him to come down."

"What sort of problem?"

"We ran a blood test on Kayla to properly configure the bracelet. Unfortunately, she must have some sort of metabolic booster in her system because we're unable to get a stable reading. Was she given something within the past few days?"

Alec nodded, keeping his face impassive. "I believe so. She was injured the other day. They probably gave it to her then. Why is that a problem?"

Cessel gave a long, drawn-out sigh. "The bracelets are sensitive devices. If I can't get a stable reading, I can't properly attune it. It'll be worthless. It could take several more days for the booster to get out of her system."

Alec's initial relief quickly dissipated. This news wouldn't deter his father from pressing forward. He'd insist on keeping Kayla here until the drug was out of her system.

"Is she awake yet?"

Cessel shook his head. "Not yet, but soon. She's in restraints at the moment. We weren't sure how she'd react."

"You put her in restraints?"

"Well, of course. The energy reserves are low. Five people are drained, and we won't be able to subdue her again easily without more drastic measures being taken."

"Release her," Alec ordered, resisting the urge to pummel the man. "*Now*. She's untrained. She won't hurt you."

"Of course." Cessel hastened to the door where Kayla was being held. Alec followed him into the smaller observation room.

Kayla was lying on a table with her eyes closed. Her arms and feet were bound with electronic restraints. Cessel walked around the table and deactivated the restraints. Once she had been released, Alec crossed the room to stand over her.

Alec looked down at Kayla and frowned. He hadn't been feigning his attraction to her. If things had been different, he would have enjoyed taking his time getting to know her. After what happened tonight, though, he doubted she'd ever trust him again.

Pushing aside his regret, he brushed his hand against her cheek. He caressed her tenderly for a moment before opening his senses toward her. Closing his eyes, he found himself surrounded by darkness.

"Kayla?"

She remained silent, but he could sense her. He tried to navigate toward her but found it difficult without being able to see the familiar threads of thoughts and memories. He sifted through the darkness and hit a strange sort of wall. Confused, he tried to feel his way around it, but it resisted all of his advances.

Understanding finally hit him and shocked him to his core. She hadn't been subdued; she'd crafted some sort of mental wall to keep the assault at bay. Her lack of consciousness was of her own design. It was an instinctual method of self-preservation.

"Kayla? You can lower the wall. I'm not going to hurt you."

"Alec?" she asked, sounding hesitant and unsure.

"Yes, it's me. I won't hurt you."

The wall dropped suddenly. A rush of anger and fury hit him. The sudden assault left him reeling. Her thoughts and emotions swirled around him, and he struggled against her assault.

"Kayla, stop," he thought in her direction.

"You want me to stop? Get the hell out of my mind, you decomposing, maggotous bungweed!"

"It's a little difficult to withdraw when you're attacking me," he gasped.

The assault stopped abruptly, and he caught his breath. The darkness had been stripped away and he could see the vibrant lines of thought and energy linking them. Kayla's thoughts were clear and well-defined. For a moment, he was captivated by the brilliant rainbow of color.

"Kayla, I had no idea you could do this. It's beautiful. How did you learn to do that?"

"Do what?" Her mental voice was cautious.

"The intricate weaving and the colors. I've never known anyone who could craft something like this without years of training."

He could sense her anxiety, confusion, and fear. She was probably weaving these complex energy fields intuitively.

"I'm not trying to frighten you."

"Get out of my mind!" With a great force of energy, she pushed him out of her thoughts.

———

THE CONNECTION TO ALEC VANISHED, and Kayla's eyes flew open. She scrambled off the table and backed away from him. Her eyes darted around the unfamiliar room. "Where did you take me?"

"Kayla, it's going to be all right. I didn't bring you here. My father did."

"Why?" Alec didn't reply immediately, and her eyes narrowed at his hesitation. "Don't you dare lie to me, Alec."

———

HE SIGHED and clasped his hands behind his back. "My father

and some of his scientists developed these bracelets several months ago. He wants you to wear one."

"What are these things? Seara was upset when I asked her about it."

"They call them security access bracelets, but that's not exactly an accurate representation. Kayla, those of us in the Inner Circle have special talents. The bracelets harmonize with your DNA and actually connect to the energy you're able to channel. It siphons off your energy into a pool that can be tapped into when someone needs it to do things that wouldn't normally be possible."

She blinked. What the hell kind of freak show had she fallen into?

"What are you saying, Alec?"

"My father has created an energy pool he can use to enhance his own abilities or divert it to other areas. The goal was to discover untapped natural resources throughout the planet. Our towers are no longer fully self-sustaining. We were only supposed to live here until the world was viable again. We need to supplement our resources with whatever we can find."

Well, that's interesting. Looks like the Omnis aren't much better off than the ruin rats. "Why was my mother upset about the bracelet then? And why don't you have one?"

Alec frowned. "My talent is unique, and it's more beneficial for me not to wear one. The bracelets siphon off your energy. You don't have any control over how much is taken or how it's used. Seara and many others originally agreed to wear the bracelet to help OmniLab. They felt it was their duty, but they didn't realize what that meant. None of us did."

"Your father isn't trying to help the towers, is he?" she guessed.

"Yes, he's trying to find resources to help the towers." Silently, he added, *"He's also using the bracelets to control the*

Inner Circle and High Council into doing his bidding. He's become power hungry. Be careful what you say, Kayla. He's probably watching right now."

"I see." She still didn't like that he could pick thoughts out of her head, but it might come in handy. She just wished she could read him as easily and figure out his angle. *"Why not take them off then?"*

Alec sighed and thought back, *"It's not that simple. It's linked to your DNA. If you forcibly remove them, it destroys your ability to properly channel your energy. It's essentially a death sentence."*

Kayla shook her head and declared aloud, "I won't be a puppet."

"As long as you're here, you don't have a choice in wearing the bracelet. But I need to train you properly. If too much power is channeled through you and you're not prepared, it could hurt or even kill you."

She laughed. "You think I'm going to let you near me? Go ahead and try it. I can't remember the last time I wanted to break somebody's fingers so badly."

Alec looked at her for a long time and then shook his head. "I'm not your enemy, Kayla."

The door slid open, and Kayla's eyes narrowed as she studied the newcomer. He was a short and thin older man. His dark hair was cropped close to his head, and he seemed overly nervous.

"Who are you?" she demanded.

He bowed to her. "I am Cessel Witlanger, Mistress Rath'-Varein. I'm a scientist here."

Alec turned to him. "What is it, Cessel?"

"Master Tal'Vayr has been advised of the situation. He has insisted Mistress Rath'Varein remain here until she's stable."

"What the hell are you talking about?" Kayla demanded.

"You were given a metabolic booster when you were injured the other day. Cessel won't be able to fit you for a bracelet until your system stabilizes. My father intends to keep you here until then," Alec explained.

"Right." Kayla snorted. She had no intention of sticking around long enough to receive a new piece of jewelry.

Alec looked regretful as he said, "I'll let you get some rest. There's a private bath through that door. If you get bored, there's a computer on the wall for you to view. Access is restricted though. If you need anything else, ask Cessel to call me. I'll check back with you tomorrow."

"Gee, I can't wait."

"Goodnight, Kayla," he said quietly and left the room with Cessel trailing behind him.

As soon as they left, Kayla studied her surroundings. Her eyes were drawn to an air vent high on one of the walls. The bed, a small counter, and the computer were the only furnishings in the sparse room. There were two cameras installed in the ceiling that provided complete surveillance coverage of the entire room.

Kayla crouched down to examine the bed. As she suspected, it was affixed to the floor and couldn't be moved.

She headed for the private bathroom, where she quickly determined surveillance didn't extend to this room. There was a sink, a shower station, and a toilet, along with some basic toiletry items. Another vent was situated high on the wall. She picked up the comb and wondered if she could use the edge to pry off the vent cover.

Kayla held the comb between her teeth and hiked up her dress. She'd known this formal gown wouldn't be conducive to life as a ruin rat. Next time she was invited to an Omni party, she'd wear her own clothes.

She carefully climbed on top of the toilet and stepped over to stand on the sink. Stretching as far as possible, she reached up toward the vent. Dammit. She was too short.

Blowing out a frustrated breath, she climbed back down

and headed out to the main room. She tapped the comb thoughtfully on her hand, surveying the room again. Out of curiosity, she pressed the small panel next to the exterior door. Nothing happened.

Of course they wouldn't make it that easy. She studied the cover plate carefully. If she had some tools, she could probably override it. But then what? She didn't know the layout of the towers or their security system. It didn't matter either way. The panel cover was securely affixed to the wall.

Annoyed, Kayla walked over to the computer and turned on the screen. She entered a few keystrokes and realized Alec wasn't exaggerating when he mentioned the limited access. She scrolled through the menus on the terminal, considering her options. The biggest problem was the surveillance in the room. A plan formed in her mind, and she dimmed the monitor before shutting it off.

Kayla made an elaborate show of yawning and stretching before grabbing some additional blankets off the counter. She spread them out on the bed as though getting ready to sleep and then turned off the overhead lights. Once the room was flooded in darkness, she yanked the blanket off the bed and threw it over the top of the monitor, making sure it reached the floor. She crawled under the blanket and turned the monitor back on.

Satisfied the thick blanket was keeping the light from showing, she used the edge of the comb to pry off the bottom front panel of the screen. As she suspected, they had simply disconnected the communications line. Using her nails and the edge of the comb to pull apart the wiring, she twisted the wires together and connected them to the computer.

Kayla bit back a grin when the computer linked to the communications system. She typed in a few commands and was able to pull up the entire database of residents within OmniLab. She located the name Carl Grayson and pulled up his information. This next part was a bit tricky. She worked her way through the system until she was able to access his communications account.

Kayla tapped her finger quietly against the screen and typed in a quick message, marking it as urgent and saving it as a draft. An outgoing message might raise a flag in the system, and she wasn't willing to risk it. She just hoped Carl would notice the message.

Now to figure out how these bracelets work.

She cleared the screen and pulled up a new command prompt, determined to learn as much as she could about what Edwin Tal'Vayr was planning.

CHAPTER FOURTEEN

CARL LOOKED through the report Jinx had given to him. Her numbers were usually right on target, and this report didn't appear any different.

"Yeah, it looks sound. I'll request this inventory from OmniLab in the morning. Is there anything else you needed?"

Jinx leaned across the desk. "Actually, yeah. You look like crap, Carl. What's going on?"

He chuckled at her frankness and leaned back in his chair. "It's nothing. I've just got quite a bit on my mind."

"Would that something have dark hair and green eyes?"

When he didn't reply, she said, "I'm not trying to pry. Well, maybe a little. But ever since she left, you've been pretty cranky. I was wondering if you wanted to talk about it."

He sighed and pushed the tablet away. "Not particularly. She's gone, and that's all there is to it."

"Aha, I was right." Jinx grinned, waving her finger at him. "But I think you're wrong about that. I saw the way you two looked at each other. Hell, everyone in this camp did. Why do you think Lisia got pissed off? Sparks were flying every time you two set foot in the same room. She'll come back."

He hoped so, but he wouldn't count on it. Even though he'd made some headway with her, he hadn't been able to alleviate all her reservations about working in a trader camp. In fact, with the latest OmniLab development, it had just complicated issues. "We'll see."

Jinx rolled her eyes. "Can you honestly picture her living up in those towers permanently? I mean, hell, she wasn't here for long, but she didn't strike me as the type to enjoy complacency."

Carl smiled at her words. "I suppose you're right. I'll see her in a few days when I head to the towers. She seemed convinced she would want to come back by then."

Jinx nodded encouragingly. "I wouldn't doubt it."

The door to Carl's office beeped. He pressed a button on his desk to admit Xantham. The dark-skinned man entered the room. "Boss, we're picking up Veridian's bike on the radar. He's got two other OmniLab vehicles with him too."

Carl frowned, uneasy at the news. "That soon? Something must be wrong. Was Kayla with him?"

Xantham shook his head. "Not unless she's on an OmniLab speeder."

"All right, thanks." Carl left his office and headed toward the entrance to meet Veridian. The ruin rat barely glanced at Carl when he entered and hung up his gear. He shoved his hands in his pockets, visibly upset.

"Veridian? Is everything okay? I wasn't expecting you back so soon. Where's Kayla?"

"Yeah, it's fine. At least, I think it's fine. I don't know." He ran a shaky hand over the top of his head, frowning as though something confused him.

"Come on in and have a seat," Carl suggested, motioning

for Veridian to follow him to the common room. He slumped down in a chair looking more than a little lost. Jinx handed him a hydrating pack, and he drank it automatically. Carl frowned. He didn't know Veridian well, but this wasn't like him. "Why don't you tell us what happened, Veridian. Where's Kayla?"

"I don't know. We got there, and she met her mother. That seemed to go well, although Kayla was a little freaked out. Then we went to dinner. I don't know what the hell happened after that." Veridian crushed the hydrating pack in frustration and tossed it on the table.

Jinx sat beside him. "Did something happen at dinner?"

Veridian shrugged. "I don't know. I got caught up talking to one of the potential traders. I shouldn't have left her. Kayla and Alec disappeared at some point. Seara, that's Kayla's mother, came over to me after dinner and asked me to accompany her back to her family's quarters. We sat around for a while talking and waiting for Kayla to come back. Suddenly, Seara got this strange look on her face, jumped up in a panic, and ran out of the room."

Veridian scratched his head and continued, "Seara came back a little later with Alec. She was quiet, and it looked like she'd been crying. Alec said Kayla started remembering things. He told me Kayla wanted to be alone for a while and asked me to come back here."

Carl frowned, his unease growing. "You didn't talk to Kayla?"

Veridian threw up his hands in frustration. "No. Alec said she didn't want to talk to anyone. Next thing I knew, I was on my speeder heading back here."

Carl shook his head. "This doesn't make sense. There's no way Kayla would have told you to leave. She's always been adamant about not being separated from you."

"I thought so too. But maybe remembering her past

changed things? I don't know. It seemed to make sense at the time."

Carl drummed his fingers on the table. Jinx rested her hand on Veridian's arm. "Veridian, why don't you call her and find out if she's okay?"

Veridian pulled out his commlink, but Kayla didn't answer. He sent a message asking her to contact him and closed his commlink. His shoulders slumped. "I shouldn't have pushed her. She told me she didn't want to go to the towers. I should have listened."

Jinx shook her head. "I'm sure everything's fine. She's probably just sleeping. You can try her again in the morning."

Hope filled Veridian's eyes as he raised his head. "You think so?"

Jinx offered him a reassuring smile and nodded. "Yes. You should get some rest too. You look exhausted. We'll find out what's going on. Don't worry."

"Yeah. I guess." Veridian stood and muttered a goodnight before heading out of the room.

"Anyone else think this reeks?" Xantham said when he was gone.

Carl nodded. If there was one thing beyond reproach, it was Kayla's loyalty to Veridian. "Kayla wouldn't have sent him away. I don't care what she remembered."

"Maybe you should go to the towers a day early," Jinx suggested. "Go check on her and find out what's going on."

"That's not a bad idea. We're low on inventory anyway. I could use that as an excuse," Carl mused. "In the meantime, we should get some rest. Maybe Kayla will call Veridian in the morning and straighten this out."

They murmured their agreement. Carl said goodnight to the group and headed back to his office. Pushing aside the inventory list Jinx had given him earlier, he pulled up a copy of Kayla's OmniLab contract. He stared at her picture for a long moment and then shut it off in annoyance. He was acting like a lovesick teenager.

You were the one who encouraged her to go.

Mentally kicking himself, he headed to his bedroom. He pulled off his shirt and threw it on the floor in frustration. Resting his head in his hands, he sighed. Sleep would be a long time coming.

———

SEVERAL HOURS LATER, Carl woke to the sound of his comm-link. He grabbed it and flipped it open. Sitting up, he rubbed his eyes and read the message from OmniLab.

So they narrowed down the selection of potential traders.

The message requested his presence at the towers in two days for the final decision. He studied the qualifications of the proposed trader candidates and chuckled when he saw Rand's name on the list.

Carl scrolled through the rest of his messages and was about to close his commlink when he noticed a draft message marked urgent. He couldn't remember creating an urgent draft. Curious, he opened it up and stared in shock at the short message.

Carl,

Hope you're doing well. If you happen to stop by OmniLab, I'd love it if you could break me out of here. Seems like these zap-happy circle freaks are into some weird shit and have decided they want me to join their little club. Apparently, they don't like to take "no" for an answer either.

Oh, you might not want to tell Veridian about this little mix-up. I don't want him to worry—not to mention I'll never be able to live this down once he finds out.

K.

His fingers tightened reflexively on the commlink.

Jumping to his feet, Carl headed out into the common room. Cruncher and Zane were sitting at the table having breakfast and talking.

"Morning, Boss," Cruncher said. "I heard Veridian came back last night."

Carl tossed Cruncher his commlink. "Read the draft message."

Cruncher opened the commlink and read through it quickly. When he finished, he looked up at Carl, his eyes filled with worry. "Shit, Boss, is this for real?"

Carl nodded grimly. Given Kayla's penchant for getting into trouble, he shouldn't be surprised. "Get Xantham and Veridian. We're going to the towers early. I want to find out what the hell is going on."

Zane looked confused. "What happened?"

"I don't know. Kayla hacked into my commlink somehow and sent me a message. She indicated she's being held against her will."

"But I thought her family was one of the higher-ups in those towers."

"They are," Carl informed him. "That's why this doesn't make any sense."

Jinx walked into the room and saw the tense faces. She frowned. "Did something happen?"

"We got a message from Kayla. I think she's in trouble," Carl explained. "Cruncher, I want Xantham and Veridian ready to leave in thirty minutes. It'll take us a couple of hours to get to the towers."

Cruncher nodded and headed out of the room. Jinx walked over to Carl and put her hand on him reassuringly. "Don't worry. Kayla's proven to be pretty resourceful. I'm sure she'll be fine."

Carl hoped she was right, but the incident with Ramiro was too fresh in his mind. If he managed to get her out of this mess, he was going to have to find a way to keep her permanently out of trouble.

––––––––

LESS THAN THIRTY MINUTES LATER, Carl, Cruncher, Xantham, and Veridian were on their speeders heading toward the OmniLab towers.

As they approached the towers, Carl frowned. It had been almost a year since he'd last visited the towers. Surprisingly enough, he realized he didn't miss it. He understood why many traders ended up extending their contracts and staying in the field longer. There was something about being on the surface and working daily with your crew that made it feel more like home than anywhere else.

Carl pressed a button on his speeder, triggering the large overhead doors. As they opened, Xantham whistled and said into the headset, "Damn. I never thought I'd see these towers this close."

Carl chuckled and replied, "Wait until you see the inside."

They climbed off their speeders and entered the lower level entrance area. Three armed men wearing the distinctive Omni security uniforms stood near the door, eyeing them with suspicion. An elderly blond woman with a stern expression pointed to a panel on the wall. "Identify yourselves."

Carl pulled off his helmet and hung it up on the rack. Pressing his hand against the panel, he spoke his name in a clear voice.

The woman glanced at the tablet she was carrying. "You're early, Trader Carl Grayson. We weren't expecting you for another day. Welcome back to OmniLab Towers."

Carl motioned for everyone else to do the same. They each checked in one by one. Once they identified themselves, the woman said, "Traders don't usually bring so many of their crew members to the towers. Is there a problem?"

Carl gave her his most disarming smile. If they were turned away now, there was little he could do about it. "We need to pick up some supplies. I'll need their help to bring the items back. Veridian Levanthe is a close friend of Mistress Kayla Rath'Varein. He intends to visit her while he's here."

The woman eyed Veridian speculatively and didn't appear impressed. "We haven't received a notification from the Inner Circle about any guests. I'm sorry, but without authorization, access to their tower is denied."

He'd expected as much. "That's fine. We'll contact her directly after our other business is concluded."

The woman hesitated and then nodded. She motioned for the guards to step aside and let them pass.

Carl headed out of the entrance area and into the main tower. Xantham and Cruncher looked around in amazement as Carl led them to an elevator.

Veridian frowned when they stepped inside. "Where are we going? This isn't the same elevator Kayla and I took yesterday."

"We're going to my family's quarters. Notification of our arrival has already reached the Inner Circle and High Council. I'm guessing someone will contact us fairly soon to find out why we're here."

The elevator stopped, and they stepped out. Carl led them down a long hallway and stopped at a door. He pressed his palm against the panel, and it slid open.

The living area was decorated in a waterfall of color, somehow complimenting the otherwise minimalist design. He couldn't help but smile at the contrast. It represented his parents' relationship completely. They were vastly different, but it worked. Not for the first time, he believed their differences made them stronger.

He waved his crew inside and called out, "Hello? Is anyone here?"

"Oh my word! Is that you, Carl?" a woman's voice answered. A huge smile spread over his face when his mother emerged from another room. She was tall and slender, with light streaks of gray in her dark hair. It was grayer than the last time he'd seen her, but it was hard to tell. She had it pulled back in a bun, as it often was when she worked on her art. Her brown eyes twinkled, lighting up at the sight of him.

"Carl!" she exclaimed, rushing over to give him a hug.

Hugging her tightly, Carl pressed a kiss against her cheek. He caught a whiff of nuts and varnish, confirming that she'd been painting. "Hi, Mom. I'm here for the traders meeting. I've brought some of my crew with me."

She stepped back, ran her hand over her hair, and chided, "Shame on you, Carl. You didn't tell me you were coming today, and you brought all these handsome men with you. What are you thinking?"

Carl laughed. "You're beautiful, Mother. I can tell you've been painting though. I'd like you to meet Xantham, our communications expert, Veridian, our newest recruit, and Cruncher, our amazing tech and former scavenger."

"I'm so glad to meet all of you. Please, call me Rina. If there's anything I can get for you while you're here, let me know."

"It's nice to meet you, Rina," Cruncher said and kissed her hand.

She beamed at him. "Oh, I like your friends, Carl."

Veridian gave her a polite smile. Xantham piped up, "Thanks, Rina. Maybe while we're here, you can tell us all the embarrassing stories about your son?"

Carl gave Xantham a dark look. "Don't count on it."

Rina laughed in delight. "Well, come on in. Carl, you can stay in your room. We'll get your friends set up in some of the other guest rooms."

Carl followed his mother down the hall. "Where's Dad?"

"Oh, he's over at the school. He can't seem to stay away. Seems like he's constantly taking on new students."

Carl nodded. His father was a scientist and professor at the school. Learning was his passion, and even when home, he was usually engrossed in some sort of project. His office was frequently scattered with a wide assortment of projects in various stages of completion.

"Here we go." Rina opened one of the doors. "Maybe two of you can share a room, if you don't mind. We're a little low on space right now. Your father's taken over one of the other rooms with more of his projects."

"That's fine," Carl replied. "Xantham and Veridian, do you mind staying together?"

Xantham chuckled. "Works for me. Cruncher snores."

Cruncher scowled and made a move to swat him, but Xantham quickly ducked away.

Rina smiled at them. A strange chime sounded at the door and she faltered. Her smile fell and her eyes grew large. She turned to Carl, not bothering to hide her shock.

"Someone from the Inner Circle is here? What's going on?"

"I'll handle this, Mom," Carl replied, returning to the entrance. He opened the door to see Alec and Director Borshin.

"Master Tal'Vayr, Director Borshin," Carl greeted them and invited them inside. "I was wondering if a representative from the Inner Circle would be showing up. I wasn't expecting anyone quite so quickly or so notable though."

Alec entered and looked around the room at Carl's crew. When he spotted Veridian, his eyes narrowed. "I received a report you had arrived early and brought unexpected guests, Trader Carl. Your attendance was not required until tomorrow. Is there a problem?"

Carl kept his tone casual, not wanting to confirm his real reasons for arriving early. "Not at all. I have some inventory to pick up, and Veridian was having second thoughts about leaving Kayla. I thought it might be a good idea to come a little early to check in on her and see how she's doing."

"Mistress Kayla Rath'Varein is no longer your concern," Alec replied coldly. "I'll let her know you asked after her. She may contact you if she wishes."

Carl frowned. "That doesn't sound like Kayla. She wouldn't have cut Veridian off like that. What's going on?"

"You overstep yourself, *Trader* Carl Grayson. As a courtesy, I have tolerated your questions, but that ends now. You are free to remain here and conduct your trader business. But after the appointment of the new trader within the next two days, you are to leave and return to the surface to fulfill the terms of your contract. I suggest you focus only on your trader business while you're in the towers, or we may find ourselves looking for someone to replace you too."

"I see."

Alec nodded, seeming to be satisfied he'd made his point. He turned and left with Director Borshin following him.

When the door closed, Rina stepped forward. "Carl? What's going on? That wasn't just anyone from the Inner Circle. That was *Alec Tal'Vayr.* He's to be appointed to the High Council any day now."

"Politics," Carl muttered in disgust. He was beginning to think Kayla had a point in not trusting OmniLab. He'd originally hoped to join the political arena to make some changes, but if the corruption went as high as he feared, he wasn't sure that was possible. At the very least, Alec Tal'Vayr's presence confirmed the High Council's knowledge of Kayla being held against her will. He turned to his mother. "Everything's fine, but I think it would be best if you knew as little as possible."

She frowned. "All right. But you're going to have to explain how you know Mistress Kayla Rath'Varein. The entire tower has been talking about her return and how she was living on the surface all these years."

"Up until yesterday, she was living in your son's camp and working as a scavenger for him," Cruncher volunteered with a chuckle.

Rina gasped, her eyes lighting up at the gossip. "She worked for you? What's she like?"

Carl ran his hands over his face. "Yeah. She was only a member of my crew for a few days, but she's been a pain in the ass since I first met her."

Rina's eyes widened in shock. "Carl!"

Xantham laughed. "It's true. If you meet her, you'll understand. But she's wicked-good at what she does. She's got some crazy skills."

Veridian nodded. "Yeah. Kayla tends to get into more trouble than anyone else I've ever known."

Rina looked at her son with a knowing expression. "Trouble, huh? Is she pretty too?"

Xantham grinned. "She's got to be the finest-looking ruin rat I've ever seen."

Carl gave Xantham a warning look. "She's not a ruin rat anymore. Be careful what you say about her. If anyone in the Inner Circle or High Council hears you, it won't end well."

Xantham made a face but didn't make any more comments.

Veridian rubbed the back of his neck. "What happens now? How can we find her?"

Carl turned to his mother. "Mom, do you mind giving us a bit of privacy? I don't want you involved in this."

She hesitated but agreed. "I hope you know what you're doing, Carl. Be careful."

After his mother left the room, Carl turned back to Veridian. "Do you know how to get to Kayla's family quarters?"

"Yeah, but we have to take that big elevator up."

Carl looked at Xantham. "Run through our system comms and files over the past few days. When Alec Tal'Vayr was in our camp, he used a palm print and override code to get into Kayla's file. I'm hoping he hasn't changed his code yet."

Xantham pulled out his commlink and started working on Carl's request. Carl turned to Cruncher. "Do you think there's a way you can get into the OmniLab system and find out if they're holding Kayla somewhere?"

"I can try to have a look. I'm sure they have all sorts of safeguards in place though. I'm good, but I'm not an expert. Kayla would be better at this."

"Do what you can but don't get caught. Kayla's got to have access to a computer if she sent me that message. Maybe she'll reach out to us again."

Xantham looked up from his screen. "I've got it, Boss. I have the voice recording."

"Okay," Carl said and took a deep breath. Once they did this, there was no going back. It could end very badly for all of them. "Cruncher, stay here and work on locating Kayla. Xantham and Veridian, let's go pretend to be a member of the Inner Circle."

———

CARL GLANCED DOWN THE CORRIDOR. "Luckily, this is a quiet time of day. We're not as likely to be noticed. They have surveillance, but as long as we get in to see Kayla's mother before they notice us, we should be fine."

They stepped into the priority elevator, and Carl

motioned for Xantham to use the override code. Xantham connected his tablet to the elevator panel, scanned in the palm print, and played back the code. They all breathed a collective sigh of relief when a computerized voice said, "Welcome, Master Alec Tal'Vayr."

The elevator shot upward and Xantham said, "Wow, it actually worked. Go figure. Their security kinda sucks."

"Most people wouldn't dream of impersonating an Inner Circle member," Carl said dryly. "The consequences aren't pretty."

When the door opened, Carl let Veridian take the lead toward the Rath'Varein quarters.

"No offense, Boss, but this is a hell of a lot fancier than your digs," Xantham observed.

Carl looked around at the expansive hall lined with a cobblestone walkway, lush greenery, and gurgling stream. "No kidding."

Veridian pressed the button outside the ornately carved door and waited. A few moments later, the door slid open. Although Carl had met Seara before, he hadn't paid much attention. He was taken aback at the similarity between the petite woman and Kayla. If he'd had any question in his mind about Kayla's heritage, it was now gone.

Seara gasped at the sight of Veridian, her green eyes widening in surprise. "Veridian, you're back. I thought you'd left."

"I did, but I came back. Seara, this is Carl and Xantham. We'd like to see Kayla."

Seara lowered her gaze and shook her head. "Kayla's not here. She's in seclusion. I'm sorry you came back all this way, Veridian. I'll let her know you stopped by when she returns."

Veridian's face fell. "Please, Seara, I know something's happened to her. I know she's your daughter, but she's my family too."

Seara looked torn for a moment. Seemingly coming to a decision, she pressed her finger to her lips indicating for them to keep quiet. She furtively glanced out into the corridor before motioning for them to follow her into the common living room area. Walking over to a painting on the wall, she pressed a button hidden underneath. An unobtrusive door slid open, and she walked inside.

Curious, they followed. When the door slid shut behind them, Seara said, "This is a safe room my husband built. We can talk freely in here, but only for a short time. I'm sure they know you're here. You shouldn't have come back."

"We don't mean to intrude, Mistress Rath'Varein, but Kayla sent me a message. She said she's being held against her will and asked for my help." Carl pulled out his commlink and showed her the message.

Seara read over the message and sighed. "I'm sorry, but all I know is she's in Observation Room A. They're keeping her locked up until the metabolic booster is out of her system and they can put a security bracelet on her."

At the sight of Carl's confusion, she held up her wrist to show them her bracelet. "The Inner Circle has essentially been imprisoned for the last nine months. These bracelets around our wrists are just another way for the High Council to control us."

"How is that possible?" Carl shook his head in disbelief. "With the combined abilities of the Inner Circle, the High Council should be no match for you."

"The bracelets damper our abilities," she said angrily, showing a trace of the fire he was used to seeing in Kayla. "We originally offered to wear them, hoping to use the combined energy of the Inner Circle to locate new resources. But now, Edwin Tal'Vayr and the High Council use them to siphon our power for their own purposes. We don't have the strength to fight them. They were supposed to help our people, not imprison us."

Xantham looked back and forth between them. "Um, I think I'm missing something. What power? What abilities?"

Carl frowned. He wasn't part of the Inner Circle and knew very little of their ways. He knew more than most others because of his association with them, but they were secretive. Most of what he knew was in the form of rumors and speculation.

Seara lowered her gaze and sighed. "We don't discuss this with outsiders, but Kayla trusts you. I would ask you to not repeat this to anyone else."

When they all nodded their consent, she continued, "Some of us in the towers have certain extraordinary talents. Our abilities vary from person to person. Although many of us don't share the full scope of our talents with each other, Kayla was a bit different. At a very young age, she displayed a talent for locating missing objects. We thought she might be able to help find resources. After we lost her, though, we began searching for other ways to find resources. The bracelets were one of our best hopes."

Cruncher shook his head. "That explains why Kayla's the best scavenger we've ever seen."

Veridian looked down at Seara's wrist. "Maybe it's a stupid question, but why don't you remove the bracelet?"

"It's a complicated design. It's impossible for us to remove it on our own. The material embedded within the bracelets actually encodes itself somehow with our DNA. If I were to forcibly remove my bracelet, it would strip me of my abilities. Losing my senses like that would be..." Seara shuddered. "Those who have removed their bracelets have either gone mad or died within hours. We haven't found a way to escape from it successfully. The technology was too new when we originally agreed. We had no way of knowing these bracelets would end up being permanent."

The news shocked Carl to his core. This was more than corruption. The entire foundation and social structure of the towers was built around the Inner Circle and the High Council. If they were being imprisoned, there had been a major shift in the tower's power structure. "Who's responsible for this?"

"Edwin Tal'Vayr is the one who implemented the design. A few other council members are also strong supporters. Essentially, anyone not wearing a bracelet is in control."

"Alec doesn't wear a bracelet," Veridian observed.

Seara bristled in defense. "No, but he's a special case because of the unique nature of his talents. He doesn't like the bracelets and was trying to keep Kayla safe. Edwin wanted to put it on her immediately, but Alec convinced him to wait. I think Edwin was actually pleased Alec seemed interested in Kayla. A union between our families is something he's always wanted."

Carl's eyes narrowed, but he put his personal feelings aside for the moment. "So what happened? Did Kayla reject him?"

Seara shook her head. "Alec can influence people and read the thoughts of other sensitives. He has to be touching them for it to work, but apparently Kayla was an exception. He can read her thoughts, and she can hear his even if they're across the room. When Kayla realized he was reading her thoughts, she got angry and threatened to leave the towers. Edwin overheard and had her taken to an isolation room to be fitted for the bracelet."

Xantham cringed. "Reading Kayla's thoughts? That's kinda scary. I can only imagine how pissed she was when she found out."

Carl frowned. "Do you know where the observation rooms are?"

"No, but I can point you in the right direction. They won't allow me to see her in person, but Alec arranged for me to have a video feed."

Seara turned on the computer in the safe room and entered in a code. A small observation room appeared on the screen. Kayla was inside and appeared to be yelling at someone.

Seara pressed a button to enable audio, and they could hear Kayla shouting. "Go ahead and try it! I dare you. Next time I won't be gentle."

"Please, Mistress Rath'Varein," a voice in the background pleaded. "I just need a small blood sample to check your progress."

"Are you always this stupid, or are you making a special effort today?" She waved what looked like a food tray in a threatening manner. "Let me make this clear since you obviously have some sort of brain damage. If you try coming near me again, I'll kick your ass."

"I've had enough of this," a new voice announced. Edwin Tal'Vayr appeared on the screen and walked purposefully over to Kayla. She managed to swipe him once with the tray before he grabbed her. He was considerably larger and easily deflected her blows before finally subduing her. She struggled against him as he lifted a small metal device. Pressing it against her, she cried out and crumpled to the floor.

"Take your sample and put her back in restraints. If my son has a problem with that, direct him to me. You have about five minutes until she regains consciousness. I'm not dealing with this nonsense again."

CHAPTER FIFTEEN

CARL LOOKED up and saw tears in Seara's eyes. He turned to Xantham. "Can you get a lock on this signal and try to figure out where it's coming from? Once you get it, send the information to Cruncher and tell him to run a search for Observation Room A."

"I'll see what I can do," Xantham replied and bent over the computer. He worked diligently for several minutes. "Boss, I think we've got a problem."

"What is it?"

"They know we're in this part of the tower."

Seara straightened, her gaze darting around the room. "You have to leave immediately. I can't let them know about this room. Follow me and remain quiet. I'll take you to the staff elevator. That will buy you a little bit of time. I'll help you any way I can, but my usefulness is limited as long as I wear the bracelet."

Seara led them out of the small room and back toward the front door. She cautiously looked outside before motioning for them to follow her down the cobblestone path. They raced down the hall and around the corner to an obscure door that led to the service elevator.

"We'll find her, Mistress Rath'Varein," Carl promised.

Seara blinked the gathering moisture from her eyes. "Thank you, Trader Carl Grayson. Kayla spoke highly of you, and now I see why. I'm sorry I can't do more. If you're able to get my daughter out of there, please take her as far away from these towers as you can."

Carl nodded and stepped inside. When the elevator door closed, Carl opened his commlink and called Cruncher. "Have you learned anything?"

Cruncher replied, "Yeah, actually. It was hit or miss until Xantham sent over that link, but I've been able to track the signal and compare it with some floor plans. It looks like the signal is originating from the ninety-second level of your tower. I can give you better directions once you're there."

Xantham reached over to program the elevator to take them to Kayla's floor. "So what's the plan?"

"We don't have much time to work out an extensive plan. In many of the common areas, the towers use biometric identification. They've probably already flagged Alec's identity and changed his code. We need to try to stay one step ahead as much as possible. You and Cruncher will need to create a distraction. Veridian and I will go in and grab Kayla. We need to get in and out as quickly as possible."

"I can create a temporary system shutdown in that area. That will distract them for a few minutes and set the biometrics offline," Cruncher offered.

"Let's do it. When we get her out of there, I know a safe place to take her until we can get her out of the towers." After that, they'd have to play it by ear. It was likely that neither the trader camp nor the towers were going to be safe for any of them.

The elevator door opened, and they stepped outside. Carl plugged in his earpiece. "Which way, Cruncher?"

"Follow the hall down. It looks like it's the third door on the left."

There were a few people moving throughout the hallway, but they seemed to be focused on their tasks and paid little attention to the group. This level appeared to be a scientific research area from the number of people wearing lab coats. When they reached the door, Xantham looked at the metal plate on the wall. "I can get us through here, but I'll need a minute."

Carl and Veridian pretended to be discussing something on Carl's commlink while they hid Xantham from view. Xantham crouched down and removed the cover plate. He pulled out the wires and grabbed a tool from his belt. Splicing the wires together, he connected them to his commlink. "Go ahead, Cruncher," he said when he was ready. "Throw the switch."

"You'll have three minutes, starting... now."

Carl and Veridian slipped inside the door while Xantham leaned casually against the wall to wait.

The room was dark except for the emergency lighting. Carl could see the one-way glass mirror they had observed in the video. Two people were at the far side of the darkened room shouting about the system shutdown and trying to reactivate it. Carl quickly headed toward the room where they were holding Kayla. He whispered to Veridian to keep a lookout and opened the door.

Kayla's eyes widened when she recognized him. He deactivated her restraints, and she threw her arms around him gratefully. He lifted her off the table and set her down on the floor. "We have to get out of here." She nodded. He took her hand in his, and they ran out of the room. "We've only got another minute. Let's go."

The three of them exited the laboratory and met Xantham in the hallway. They fled back toward the service elevator, and Kayla breathed a sigh of relief as the door closed behind them.

"Thanks," she said breathlessly.

Xantham scanned her up and down with his eyes. "Damn! If that's how they dress the prisoners in these towers, maybe I should become a guard."

She rolled her eyes at him while he grinned. Veridian gave her a hug. "I'm sorry I left you, Kayla. I don't know what got into me."

"I don't think you had a choice, V. It was probably Alec. I think he must have influenced you and sent you away."

Veridian frowned, looking affronted. "That bastard."

"I'm not sure about that," she admitted. "There's something about him. I get the feeling he has his own agenda in this."

She turned to Carl, her green eyes softening with emotion. "I know what you risked by doing this. You didn't have to do it. Thank you."

He smiled at her. "I'm starting to get used to bailing you out of trouble."

Kayla laughed and threw her arms around him. Relieved she was all right, Carl slipped his arms around her and buried his face in her hair. He held her close and inhaled deeply, her alluring scent surrounding him and dissipating his fear.

She pulled back slightly to look up at him. "Then I'll just have to keep thanking you." Standing on her toes, she pulled him down toward her and kissed him.

"Now why don't I get that kind of thank you?" Xantham complained.

Kayla broke the kiss and turned to Xantham. Her eyes twinkled as she leaned over and kissed him lightly on the lips.

"Now *that's* what I'm talking about. I could definitely get into this whole damsel rescuing thing."

She laughed, and Carl shook his head in amusement. He pulled off his jacket and slipped it over Kayla's shoulders. "Keep this on," he instructed. "It's not much better, but walking around in an evening dress is going to draw quite a bit of attention."

She slipped her arms through the jacket. "Where are we going?"

"We're stopping at the level where my family's quarters are located. Xantham and Veridian are going to wait there. I'm taking you to a friend. You'll be safe there until we can figure out how to get you out of here."

The elevator stopped, and Carl turned to Xantham and Veridian. "Go back to my quarters and wipe your system files on your commlinks and terminals. They're going to launch an investigation and that's the first place they'll look."

Xantham nodded. "We're on it."

Veridian gave Kayla another hug. "I'm glad you're okay."

She kissed his cheek. "Take care of yourself, V."

The door closed, and Carl programmed several floors into the controls. At Kayla's questioning look, he said, "I don't want them tracing us. When we get out, try to keep your head down as much as possible."

She nodded, and when the door opened for a third time, they stepped out. He took her hand and led her down a crowded hallway. They walked for nearly ten minutes before they came to a less congested area. Carl turned a corner and walked a few doors down before pressing a button. The door slid open, and Kayla recognized one of the trader recruits from last night.

"Carl? It's good to see you, my friend!" Rand shook Carl's hand and clapped him on the back. "I didn't think you'd be here for another day or two."

Carl glanced around to make sure the corridor was still empty. "May we come in?"

"Of course," Rand replied, and then noticed Kayla. His expression changed to one of surprised confusion when he recognized her. He stepped back and said more formally, "My apologies, Mistress Rath'Varein. It's a pleasure to see you again."

"Thanks, but you should probably call me Kayla, especially since I'm appearing on your doorstep like this."

Carl led her inside. "We have a little problem and need your help."

Rand closed the door behind them. "What's wrong, Carl?"

"I'm sorry to put you in this position, but I needed someone I could trust." He explained the situation, and Rand's eyes widened as he listened. He turned to Kayla with a combination of shock and horror on his face.

"They've been doing this for that long?"

Carl nodded grimly. "I need to get Kayla out of the towers, but I need time to figure out how to do that. They're going to suspect me, so I can't take her back to my family's quarters."

"She can stay here," Rand offered.

Kayla shook her head. "Carl, I'm not leaving the towers. Not yet anyway."

He turned to look at her in exasperation. "Kayla, you can't stay here. They're going to keep looking for you until they find you."

Stubbornly, she insisted, "No. I'm going to put a stop to this. Running away won't fix anything. It's my fault this happened in the first place."

"What are you talking about? You didn't step foot into the towers until yesterday."

"I hacked into OmniLab's files and read about the security bracelets. They learned how to make them from the Aurelia

Data Cube—the same data cube I stole. Cessel, one of the scientists here, discovered a layer of encrypted data that described a way to combine energy resources. The High Council modified the design on the data cube to develop the bracelets. If I can study it a bit more, I think I can figure out how to deactivate them."

Carl swore. Of course it would all come back to that damn data cube and she'd feel responsible. Kayla had one of the most ass-backward moral compasses of anyone he'd ever met. He shook his head to refuse. His first priority was making sure she was safe. He just needed her to see reason.

"When we get you out of here, you can take your time and study the information. We'll come back, and you can try deactivating them."

"No." Kayla crossed her arms over her chest, and he grimaced at the stubborn set of her jaw. "I'm not leaving. I'm responsible for this, and I'll be damned if I'm going to leave these people under the thumb of that asshole."

Rand had been silently watching the exchange but decided to interrupt. "Carl, she's right. If she can do this, she can shift the balance of power back the way it's supposed to be. You haven't lived here for several years. Life under Edwin Tal'Vayr hasn't been pleasant. He's got a chokehold on everyone."

Carl sighed and ran his hands over his face in resignation. The last thing Kayla needed was another ally supporting her insane plan. Rand had no idea what he was encouraging. "Kayla, you make it incredibly difficult to keep you alive."

She laughed and kissed his cheek before turning back to Rand. "Thank you for allowing me to stay here. I have a small favor to ask though."

"What do you need?"

She gestured to her rumpled evening gown and grinned. "Can I use your shower and borrow some clothes?"

He chuckled. "Of course. My bedroom is right through that door. Grab whatever you need. The bathroom is next door to my room."

She thanked him again and headed toward the door he indicated.

Rand shook his head as she disappeared through the door. "If anyone had told me Andrei Rath'Varein's daughter would be borrowing my clothes and taking a shower in my bathroom, I never would have believed them."

"No kidding," Carl muttered, still debating on whether it might be safer for everyone to simply knock Kayla unconscious and drag her out of the towers. "I need a drink."

"I imagine so," Rand said with a chuckle. He walked into the living area and stepped up to a small bar built into the wall. He poured two glasses and handed one to Carl.

Carl took a sip. "Of course it would be scotch. You might not want to let Kayla know you have this."

Rand raised an eyebrow. "She doesn't like it?"

"She likes it a little too much." He chuckled and took another drink. "You met her yesterday?"

Rand nodded. "Alec Tal'Vayr brought her to the introductory dinner last night. The two of them together caused quite a stir."

"What do you mean?"

"Alec's in line to take one of the empty positions on the High Council in the next few weeks, maybe even sooner. If so, he'll be the youngest High Council member in history. Having Kayla Rath'Varein on his arm last night was a pretty significant boost to that claim. It weakened the arguments of the holdouts. A lot of people are interested in seeing those two families merge. He didn't leave her side all night."

"So I heard," Carl replied in a dry voice, his fingers tightening around the glass in his hand. The thought of Alec's hands on Kayla made him see red.

Rand studied his friend. "I know that look. You're into her, aren't you?"

Carl put his glass down to keep from breaking it and scowled.

Rand laughed at his reaction. "Carl, as your friend, I agree she's absolutely gorgeous. I mean, hell, she's a knockout. But I'd stay away if I were you. Not only is she a Rath'Varein, but it's pretty obvious Alec Tal'Vayr's got his eye on her."

"Don't bother. I've already given myself the lecture."

"Have another drink, my friend. You need it," Rand said with a grin and leaned forward. "So tell me how you met her. I've heard the rumors, but I'm curious about the truth."

Carl poured himself another drink and launched into the story about Ramiro. By the time he finished, Kayla reappeared wearing a long T-shirt. Her hair was slightly damp and fell loose around her face. Her legs and feet were bare. She walked over to them and looked at Carl's glass with interest.

"Is that what I think it is?"

Carl stared at her for a long moment before he realized she'd asked him a question. He blinked, trying to clear his head from the lust-induced haze. "I think I need to pick you up some clothes."

Rand coughed. "Please don't on my account."

Carl shot him a dark look, and he glanced away, pretending to be interested in a spot on the ceiling. Kayla looked down and shrugged. "I'm wearing more now than I was last night in that dress."

Carl admired her legs. Modesty had never been a virtue shared by the ruin rats. "I'm not so sure about that."

She tapped on his glass. "Are you going to share?"

"Only if you promise you'll stay in this room."

"Fine," she agreed, and he poured her a glass. She took a sip, leaning against him while he slipped his arm around her waist. Rand raised his eyebrows at Carl but didn't comment.

"For what's it worth, you've got my support on the whole trader thing," Kayla told Rand.

"For what it's worth, I appreciate it," he returned with a chuckle and lifted his glass in salute.

She grinned at him. "If you've got access to a computer, I can get started working on the Aurelia Data Cube."

"Sure. I'll be right back. I can set up a terminal for you out here."

After he left, Kayla put her glass down and turned to look up at Carl. "Thanks for helping me with this. I owe you."

When she looked at him like that, he wondered what he wouldn't do for her. "You don't need to thank me for anything, Kayla."

"You sure about that? You might like what I had in mind." She smiled and wrapped her arms around his neck.

Her suggestive teasing made the blood rush to other parts of his anatomy. "Damn, woman, you're going to be the death of me." He pulled her close and kissed her deeply. His hands wandered down her slim figure, and he wrapped his arms around her possessively. He wanted to press her up against the wall and devour her right there.

Rand cleared his throat loudly as he stepped back into the room with the computer terminal. Kayla spun around to face Rand. "Oops."

"Don't mind me," Rand said and began setting up the terminal.

Carl sighed and released Kayla. "We need to talk about your timing, Rand."

Rand smirked. "Yeah, considering you're in enough trouble as it is, my timing is the least of your worries."

Carl's commlink beeped, and he flipped it open. Xantham's voice came over the device. "Boss, Alec just showed up. They're searching your family's quarters right now. You might want to get over here."

"I'll be there in a few minutes." He disconnected the call and turned to Kayla. He hated to leave her, but he had little choice. At least Rand would look out for her. "Don't worry. We knew this was going to happen. Just stay here and you'll be fine."

She nodded, and he kissed her again. He turned to Rand. "Thanks again for this. I'll be back in a few hours. I just need to make sure they don't follow me here."

"No problem," Rand replied. "Kayla, you can get started using the system. I'll walk Carl out."

She agreed and sat in front of the computer terminal.

Rand led Carl to the front door and said quietly, "You didn't mention she was into you too. Alec Tal'Vayr isn't going to like that."

With more cockiness than he felt, Carl replied, "He'll have to get over it." He had no intention of letting her go, Inner Circle or not. Someone like Alec Tal'Vayr couldn't even begin to understand Kayla or make her happy. "Thanks again for this. I'll see you a bit later."

Carl left Rand and went to the supply station to drop off his inventory list and make arrangements to pick up the new shipment. He made it a point to chat with the woman behind the counter to make sure she'd remember him. Once he'd established an alibi, he headed back to his family's quarters.

OmniLab Security was still searching his family's quarters when he arrived. Rina rushed up to him, wringing her hands worriedly. "Carl, what's going on? They're searching your father's office and going through his files."

"I'm sorry, Mom. I'm sure they'll be finished soon."

Cruncher approached him. "They have techs working on our computers right now."

Carl nodded, confident they wouldn't find anything, and walked into the common room. Alec was standing over a technician while they searched Xantham's computer.

Alec gave Carl a sharp look and demanded, "Where is she?"

Carl made a show of looking around the room. "Who?"

Alec's eyes narrowed, and he said in a low voice, "Don't play games with me. Where is Kayla?"

Carl shook his head. "Don't ask me. I was on Level Eighteen dropping off my inventory request. You're welcome to verify that. As far as Kayla is concerned, I can assure you she's not here. But I can empathize with your frustration. It's difficult trying to keep track of her. Trust me, after having her hound my district for about a year, I've learned just how difficult."

"You're making a huge mistake," Alec warned. "Are you prepared to take on the entire High Council?"

"I have no interest in taking on the High Council. I'm sure wherever Kayla may be, she's there of her own free will. Unless you know something I don't."

"Then you've made your decision. So be it."

Alec turned to Director Borshin. "Arrest him. Bring Xantham and Veridian too. I want them taken to a holding cell for interrogation."

"On what grounds?" Carl demanded.

Alec's expression was cold as he said, "Our surveillance cameras observed you in a restricted area."

Carl remained silent while electronic holding bracelets were attached to each of them. Director Borshin motioned for the security officers to escort the men from the room.

Cruncher stepped close to Rina and whispered, "Don't worry about Carl. He'll be out of there before you know it."

She nodded, but from the expression on her face, it was clear she didn't believe it.

CHAPTER SIXTEEN

CARL DRUMMED his fingers impatiently on the table in the interrogation room while he waited. It was nearly an hour before Director Borshin and Alec entered. Director Borshin sat at the table across from Carl while Alec casually leaned against the wall and observed.

Director Borshin cleared his throat and said formally, "You're being charged with accessing a Priority One restricted area. As you know, conviction of this crime will automatically bring your trader status into question, and a review will determine your continued eligibility."

Carl was quiet for a moment before he spoke, "What area am I being accused of accessing?"

Director Borshin glanced down at his tablet before answering. "You were recorded accessing the Inner Sanctum earlier today without authorization. More charges may be pending upon further review."

Carl looked at Alec. "You must be desperate to find her if you're going to these extremes."

Alec didn't reply, and Director Borshin continued, "We're

prepared to dismiss all charges related to this crime for information on the whereabouts of Mistress Kayla Rath'Varein."

"I'm sure you are, but I can't help you."

The alarm on the door beeped, and it slid open. Seara stepped into the room and glanced at Carl before turning to Alec.

"I believe there's been a misunderstanding. I received the notification of their arrest, and I'm here to dispute the charges. They were in the Inner Sanctum at my request. I heard Veridian had returned to the towers and wanted to speak with him."

Alec studied the woman for a long moment. "Are you prepared to make that an official statement, Seara?"

She inclined her head. "Yes, I am."

"Very well," Alec replied. "I hope you know what you're doing." He gave Seara a long look and then turned to Director Borshin. "Release them and take her statement."

She gave him a curt nod, and Alec walked out of the room. Seara turned to Director Borshin. "Director Borshin, I'd like a minute alone with Trader Carl."

Director Borshin acquiesced, leaving them alone in the room. Seara held up her hand before he could speak. "I apologize for any confusion. I must have forgotten to submit the notification of your visit."

Realizing they were still being monitored, Carl forced a smile and stood. "No problem. It happens to all of us."

Seara led him out of the interrogation room. "Director Borshin, I'm ready to give my statement. I trust you've released Trader Carl's crew members?"

Director Borshin looked up. "Yes, Mistress Rath'Varein. They're in the hallway waiting. If you'd care to have a seat, I can take your statement."

Seara sat in the chair and darted a quick look at Carl, nodding toward the door. The meaning in her eyes was clear:

she wanted him out of there. He had no idea what this was going to cost her, but she appeared to have control of the situation for the moment. Heeding her unspoken request, he headed outside to where Xantham and Veridian were waiting for him.

"Damn, Boss, that was a little too close."

"Let's go," Carl replied, not comfortable with the listening ears around them. "I don't want to talk here."

―――――――

RINA GASPED at the sight of them and hugged Carl tightly. "I was so worried. You need to tell me what's going on right now. Don't you dare even think about giving me any of that nonsense about trying to protect me. OmniLab Security just arrested my son and searched my home."

He hadn't wanted to get her involved, but it was a little late for that. "You're right. I owe you an explanation."

She was quiet as he told her the entire story. When he finished, he said, "I'm sorry I brought you into this, Mom, but I'm trying to protect someone I care about."

Rina sat down in shock. "This is unbelievable."

Carl crouched down beside her. "I need to go check on Kayla and find out if she's learned anything about removing the bracelets. We're running out of time. They're determined to find her."

Cruncher paced the room. "I'm sure they've got surveillance all over the place, Boss. They're going to be waiting for you to make a move."

"Can you see if there's a way to access the security system? I want to find out if there's any way I can get out of here without them detecting me."

"Yeah, I think we can figure something out."

While Cruncher, Xantham, and Veridian began working

on the problem, Rina pulled on Carl's arm to get his attention. "I don't think you should go, Carl. Let me go check on her. They won't be expecting me."

Carl looked at his mother in surprise. Although he was touched by the courageousness of her offer, he wouldn't risk it. He already had to deal with one woman he cared about who was intent on putting herself in danger; he wasn't sure his heart could handle another. "Absolutely not. I'm not going to drag you into this any more than I already have. If this goes badly, I won't risk anything happening to you or Dad."

She frowned. "I had a feeling you were going to say that."

What he didn't say was that if things went badly and he was exiled, he had more options than she did. But judging by the worried expression on his mother's face, he didn't have to say it. The threat was very real.

Carl offered her a reassuring smile before turning away to join the rest of his men in trying to access the security system.

———

SEVERAL HOURS LATER, Cruncher announced, "Boss, I think I've got it!"

Carl's head jerked up. "What? How?"

"I'm not sure, but I used one of the tricks Kayla showed me with the security layers. There were some holes, and I managed to slip inside."

Carl moved over to look at Cruncher's screen. "You sure about this?"

"I can't say for certain," Cruncher admitted. "Kayla told me the security systems were similar in design."

Xantham leaned over to view the screen. He ran his fingers over the tablet and entered some commands. He shook his head and clucked his tongue. "I'm not sure, Boss. It looks like he's in clean, but I don't have a good feeling about it. It's a risk."

Carl swore. "The longer we wait, the riskier this becomes. We have to be out of the towers in two days, but I need to get Kayla out sooner. She might have figured out how to remove the bracelets, but I won't know until I speak with her. It's too risky trying to contact her through comms."

"Why not use me as a decoy?" Veridian suggested.

"What do you mean?"

"If it's a setup and they're monitoring, I can be the one who will go and lead them around for a while. You can sneak out and go check on Kayla."

It had a high potential for failure, but it was their best option. Veridian's ties to Kayla were well known. "Let's do it," Carl agreed. "How long do you need until you can deactivate the cameras in this area?"

"Five minutes," Cruncher replied.

"Okay," Carl said. "Veridian will head out one minute before you deactivate them. I need about thirty seconds to make it to a service elevator."

"That shouldn't be a problem."

When Cruncher gave the signal, Veridian headed outside. Carl waited until Xantham gave him the next signal before slipping out of the room and walking in the opposite direction. The hallway was empty at this time of night, and he moved quickly around the corner toward a service elevator.

Carl punched in a code and the elevator shot downward toward a busy shopping and entertainment level. He moved through the crowds and slipped down a hallway toward another service elevator. Taking this elevator to another level, he continued to work his way through the towers.

When he was confident he wasn't being followed, Carl took another service elevator to Rand's floor. He walked quickly to Rand's door and pressed the button. The door slid open, and Rand waved him inside.

"Sorry it took so long," Carl greeted his friend. "I got tied up."

"I heard. Kayla said you'd been arrested."

He shouldn't have been surprised she knew about the arrest. Leaving her alone with access to a computer in Rand's suite probably meant she had her fingers in all sorts of OmniLab pies.

Rand chuckled. "You didn't tell me she was a first-class tech. She's the one who sent the notification to her mother telling her you'd been arrested."

"Where is she?"

Rand pointed to his office. "She fell asleep a couple of hours ago. Poor thing was exhausted. I don't think she slept all night. But even so, she made me promise to tell you to wake her when you got here."

Carl walked into the darkened office where Kayla was curled up on a couch with a blanket thrown over her. He sat on the edge of the couch next to her and smiled as he studied her sleeping form. It was a mystery how such a troublesome creature could appear so innocent. He brushed her hair back from her face and kissed her temple.

"Kayla?"

Opening her eyes, she smiled as she recognized him. "Hey." She yawned sleepily and wrapped her arms around him. "You made it."

He kissed her lightly and pulled her into his lap, where she cuddled up against him. "I heard I have you to thank for that."

"Mmm," she murmured, nuzzling his chest. "You wouldn't have even been there if it weren't for me. I'm glad you're okay."

"Rand says you've been asleep for a couple of hours. I

would have let you sleep longer, but I'm not sure how long I can stay."

"Crap, I didn't mean to sleep so long." She sighed and pushed the blanket aside.

Carl's eyes lingered over her figure, and he lightly ran his fingers up her bare leg. "I can't tell you how much I want to take you back to bed."

She laughed as he tickled her. "And you call *me* distracting?"

"You're very distracting. Especially when you're wearing nothing but a T-shirt."

She gave him a seductive smile. "I could always take it off."

Carl raised an eyebrow. She shifted so she was straddling his lap. Carl ran his hands up her thighs until they found their way under her shirt and rested on the gentle curve of her waist. "Yeah, you could do that, but I'm not sure we'll have time for what'll happen if you do."

A loud chime echoed throughout the entire quarters, and Kayla looked around in confusion.

"What's that?"

"Shit!" Carl moved her back onto the couch. "Kayla, stay here. Whatever you do, don't come out."

She frowned as he left the room and closed the office door behind him. Rand met him at the door. "This isn't good."

"I'll take responsibility for this, Rand," Carl promised.

A moment later, the front door opened. Alec stepped inside, along with Director Borshin and half a dozen security officers.

"Master Tal'Vayr," Rand greeted him. "It's an honor to see you again."

Alec looked amused. "Is it?"

Carl held out his hands. "I'm not sure what this is about,

Master Tal'Vayr. Rand and I go way back. When I heard he was a trader applicant, I stopped by to catch up with him."

"I see. Then I'm sure you won't have a problem with us conducting a search of the premises. Director, go ahead. She's here."

Director Borshin directed the security officers to begin searching the quarters. Alec turned toward Rand. "I'm surprised you agreed to this. You realize your decision has jeopardized any chance you had of becoming a trader. As for you, Carl, I'll see your title stripped by morning. I warned you not to play games with me."

"Alec, stop it," Kayla's voice interrupted him.

Carl turned and nearly groaned when she stepped through the doorway. Her hair was slightly disheveled, and it was obvious she had just stumbled out of bed. Rand's shirt had slipped off her shoulder, its length barely falling mid-thigh. Oblivious to the stares, her eyes glittered with angry determination.

"Kayla," Alec greeted her in a low voice.

She looked around the room at the security officers and then turned to Alec. "I want to speak with you privately. Get them out of here."

Carl expected Alec to object, but he simply motioned for the Director and security personnel to wait outside.

———

Kayla waited until they were gone before approaching Alec. She'd spent hours scouring through emails and correspondence, trying to get a better understanding of the political structure in the towers. Although her knowledge was still somewhat rudimentary, she had more than enough experience with the dark side of human nature to give her additional insight.

She also trusted her gut. Even though she still had reservations about Alec, she suspected he was her best chance to redeem herself and fix the situation. The fact Alec had asked everyone to leave gave her hope she was right in her estimation of him.

"You know damn well Carl and Rand haven't done anything wrong. As an Inner Circle member, I asked them both for help. They honored that request."

Alec's mouth twitched into a smile. "Is that so? You're claiming your title now?"

Kayla knew what he was asking. By acknowledging her title, she was agreeing to be subject to the laws and guidelines of the towers. Her independent nature made her want to kick him in the shins and run for the door, but she couldn't allow Carl or Rand to be punished because of her decisions. Her eyes narrowed, and she hissed, "Yes, damn you. Now back off and leave them alone."

"Of course, Mistress Kayla Rath'Varein," he replied with a small bow. She grimaced at the title but didn't object. "If you're willing to take your place as an Inner Circle member and vouch for them, my business with them is settled. Are you prepared to return with me to the Inner Sanctum now?"

Before she could reply, Carl stepped forward with his fists clenched. The anger roiling off him was nearly tangible. "So you can keep her imprisoned with the rest of the Inner Circle?"

Alec raised his eyebrows. "Interesting. It sounds like someone has been telling you some rather fanciful stories."

Kayla considered reminding Alec about the cute little holding room but held her tongue. The tension in the room was nearly suffocating. Carl had gone into protective mode and seemed to be looking for an excuse to go after Alec. She sighed, dropping her shoulders, and looked up at Alec. The time for games was over. What happened in the next few minutes would affect all of them.

Abandoning all pretenses, she lifted her hands in a pleading gesture. "Alec, please, I need your help. I know how to remove the bracelets, but I can't do it without you."

Alec paused at her announcement. He glanced at Carl and Rand before returning his gaze to Kayla. She didn't blame him for looking skeptical.

"How?"

It was time to lay her cards on the table. She stepped forward and grabbed Alec's hand. "I'll show you."

Surprised, he followed her into Rand's office.

"Sit," she ordered. Alec raised an eyebrow, but he took a seat while Carl and Rand remained standing.

"If this day wasn't weird enough with Andrei Rath'Varein's daughter wearing my clothes and sleeping on my couch, it just got even more bizarre. I've got the next member of the High Council sitting on my couch too," Rand muttered in a low voice.

Carl nodded in agreement as Kayla turned the computer terminal back on. She ignored them and climbed on the couch next to Alec. He glanced down at her bare legs.

"Do you usually make it a habit of running around only half dressed?"

She rolled her eyes. "Don't abduct me when I'm wearing an evening dress and I'll see what I can do. Now shut up and look."

Alec chuckled and looked at the screen. Pulling up Cessel's research, she pointed to an image of the bracelets and zoomed in on the diagram.

"The way these are designed is tricky," she explained and pointed to two areas. "If you were able to direct two powerful energy bursts simultaneously here and here, it should flood the bracelet and deactivate them."

Alec leaned forward and shook his head. He didn't look surprised at her revelation. He'd obviously already considered and discarded the notion. "It's not possible, Kayla. You're talking about more energy than I can generate. Even if you were able to generate that much energy, you don't have the precision yet to hit one of those targets, much less both."

Kayla nodded. "Right. But what if you were to use my energy along with yours to send the pulses into the bracelet?"

Alec gave her a sharp look. "What are you saying?"

"I read through Cessel's notes. He said there's a way you can link with individual people without the use of a bracelet. Can't you tap into my energy and use it to give yourself enough power to deactivate the bracelets?"

Alec's voice came into her head. *"This is not something to be discussed in front of outsiders."*

Alec stood and flipped open his commlink. "Director, you can dismiss all but the required security personnel. Remain outside, though, and arrange to have someone go to the Rath'Varein quarters to pick up Kayla some suitable attire. I'm going to be a bit longer."

He snapped his commlink shut before turning to look at Carl and Rand. "Would you mind giving us a moment? There are some things I need to discuss with Kayla in private."

Carl looked at Kayla questioningly. She nodded at him to let him know it was okay. Carl didn't look happy about it, but he and Rand left the room and slid the door shut behind them.

Kayla watched as Alec let out a long exhale. "You knew about the weakness in the bracelets, didn't you?"

Alec met her gaze and nodded. "I've been looking for a way to deactivate the bracelets for months. I came to your same conclusion, but too many of us are wearing the bracelets. I don't think anyone here has the potential to generate enough energy to short-circuit the bracelets."

Kayla cocked her head. "If you show me how, I can help."

He rubbed the back of his neck, looking weary. "Kayla, I don't think you understand what you're asking. Don't get me wrong, your solution is a very attractive offer, and in another time and place, I would be extremely open to it. But not until you fully comprehend exactly what you're asking."

Kayla looked at him in confusion. "I don't understand. It's pretty straightforward. You take my energy, zap those bracelets, and the Inner Circle is freed and can take back their power from the High Council."

Alec chuckled at her description. "Yes, that sounds pretty straightforward. But what you're talking about doing is not something that's done casually. Sharing energy creates an extremely close bond between the two individuals."

"But the bracelets do it."

"Yes, but it's not the same."

"Alec, please," Kayla said softly. "This is our best shot. It's my fault these people are wearing those stupid things. I found the data cube that started all of this. Let me help fix it."

He studied her for a long time. "I think you need to see what you're asking."

She looked at him in surprise. "You'll do it?"

"I didn't say that," he corrected her. "I want to show you what you're asking. If you still want to go through with this afterward, I'll agree."

Kayla pulled back, her misgivings growing. She wanted to help but there were limits. "Why? Is it going to hurt?" She considered herself tough, but she wasn't into pain.

He shook his head. "Sharing energy doesn't hurt. I'll walk you through every step. If you want to stop at any time, just say the word."

She stood, determined to do this. "Okay. What do I do?"

He stood in front of her and looked down into her eyes.

"Relax. I have to touch you to do this. It won't hurt. You'll feel a slight warmth."

"All right."

He lifted both of his hands, gently laying them on her face. She felt his fingers warm, but it wasn't an unpleasant sensation. It was actually rather soothing, and the strange sense of intimacy was nice. There was a slight vibration coming from him, similar to what she felt when she had imagined the sparkling globe.

"You're right." His voice was in her head again. *"Think about the vibration. That's the energy flowing through you. Just listen to it and follow it."*

Kayla's immediate reaction was to shut him out of her mind, but she forced herself to relax. She focused on the link between them and saw it strengthen and shift. Hundreds of colors appeared, and she followed the threads in her mind. They formed a beautiful web, and she admired it for a few moments. *"Am I doing it right?"*

"Yes. I want you to see how the energy works and how it flows. I've never met anyone able to weave such pure and brilliant colors without any form of training."

"I'm doing this?" she asked in alarm.

"It's okay, Kayla," he reassured her in a soothing mental voice. *"You're not even aware of it. I'm not directing this flow at all. This is all you. You can push me out of your mind at any time. The only time I direct the flow is when I'm trying to influence someone. One day, if you want, I'll show you the way that pattern looks."*

"Maybe." She wasn't willing to commit to continuing these lessons beyond her current goal. She was already outside her comfort zone.

Alec didn't push and instead directed her attention to the threads of energy. *"Right now, some of your energy threads are woven together but others are loose and floating. You need to rein them in. If you're not using them, it's usually a good idea to keep them woven together. If you need them quickly, it's easier to gather them if they're already together."*

"How do I do that?"

"Pick a thread that's floating unbound and weave it together with another thread. Keep it loose though. You want to keep control of them, not build an impenetrable wall."

Intrigued by the wall idea, she asked, *"Why not?"*

"Because you need to be able to see and feel what's going on around you. If you close yourself off to the world, you'll end up back in that dark area you were in yesterday when you were unconscious."

"Oh." Kayla did as he instructed and focused on one of the free-flowing, loose threads. She pulled it toward her and was surprised when it seemed to understand what she wanted. With little effort, she held onto it. She reached for another thread and wove them together. The colors seemed to mesh together and collide. Fascinated, she studied them for a long moment.

She felt Alec's approval and began pulling the other loose threads together. When she finished, she took hold of the thread between the two of them.

"If you weave that thread into the mix, our connection will be severed. If I touch you again, I won't be able to connect with you unless you're willing. You'll need to remove a thread of energy from your web and reach for me."

"Wait, that's how I can block you from reading my thoughts?"

"Yes."

She released it. *"How do I hold this together? Won't it become unraveled if I'm not thinking about it?"*

"It may take some concentration initially, but not much. You seem to be picking up on this quickly. You're already subconsciously weaving some threads. Once you get used to doing it, it will become second-nature to you."

Practice. She could do that. This process was much less complicated than Kayla had expected. *"Okay, now what?"*

"This is where it gets a little tricky. You need to take all of your threads and give them to me. Connect them to mine."

Kayla stared at the large number of threads. *"All of them?"*

"Yes," he replied dryly. *"You'll be opening yourself up to me completely by doing this. You won't be able to push me out. The same goes for me. The connection can only be severed by mutual agreement. It also cannot be formed without this step. This is why it's uncommon. It's an act of complete trust. The only way to possibly generate the amount of power necessary is through this step."*

Kayla hesitated, uncertainty filling her. It had seemed like a good idea at first, but she wasn't sure she could willingly give up control to another person. It went against everything she'd ever learned.

"You don't have to do this, Kayla. I can train you how to use your energy and become precise in targeting. It'll take some time, but you can eventually learn how to form a smaller bond so we can target them together."

"No." It could take months or years to gain the level of expertise she needed and even then, there was no guarantee. Veridian had once told her everything happened for a reason. She'd never given much thought to the concept of fate, but maybe he was right. Maybe everything was inter-connected, and perhaps this was a lesson she needed to learn. She needed to take that leap of faith.

She took all of her threads and sent them toward Alec. She gasped when she felt herself connect with him. Kayla realized he was taking as much of a risk as she was. She opened her eyes and looked up into his clear-blue ones.

Kayla could feel everything he was experiencing and understood he was able to do the same. Curious, she reached up to touch his face and marveled how she was able to experience the duality of the sensation of touch. She could sense his thoughts and emotions and knew her touch affected him deeply. She felt his desire and realized he knew exactly how she felt in return.

"*Shit,*" she thought in alarm. "*Okay, fine, I think you're incredibly sexy and the thought of jumping you is pretty damn attractive. Okay, it's a lot more than just attractive. But I have a thing for Carl. I'm not going to act on it.*"

She sensed a combination of amusement and irritation emanating from him. He cleared his throat. "*Do you want to continue?*"

Kayla hesitated briefly. "*There's more to this?*"

"*Quite a bit. If you're ready, I'm going to send you some energy. When you receive it, I want you to try to send it back.*"

"*I'm ready.*"

He sent a small pulse of energy toward her, and Kayla laughed in delight as the energy tickled her senses. Alec smiled at her, and she carefully returned the pulse.

"*Good,*" he said in approval. "*In order to accomplish what you're talking about doing with the bracelets, we have to establish a steady flow of energy. I'm going to send you a larger stream of energy so you can see what I'm talking about.*"

More prepared now, she said, "*Okay, go ahead.*"

He sent a steady stream of energy toward her, and she marveled at the feeling as it washed over her. She felt as though she was showering in the clearest of thoughts and colors. She had never felt so safe or as alive as she did at that moment.

Kayla explored the way his energy poured through to her and noticed she felt a slight pull toward him. She wondered if she was depleting his energy and supposed she should probably return some to him.

"*Kayla, wait,*" he urged. "*Don't close the circuit.*"

His thought came too late. Following his example, she sent her own stream of energy toward him. She gasped when their energy linked together and rushed through both of them. Kayla couldn't help but close her eyes and simply feel the exquisite sensations rushing through her. She'd never felt so connected to anyone before and wanted nothing more than to have him touch her and claim her.

The foreign thought surprised her, but it felt so natural and right that she was confused for a moment.

"Break the circuit if you can," Alec instructed.

Bewildered by his request, she wondered why he would ever want this feeling to end. She wanted his hands on her more than anything else. She reached up and pressed her lips against his and felt his desire match her own. It only made her want him more. She wanted more energy from him and increased her flow of energy in an effort to entice him into responding.

"Stop the flow of energy, Kayla. I don't think I can resist much longer."

She hesitated a moment before pulling her energy back from him. She felt him shudder at the sudden withdrawal. He looked at her with such an aching need that she wanted to return the connection.

"No, don't. Just give me a minute."

Alec closed his eyes and took a few deep breaths. She felt him carefully withdraw his energy from her. She winced at the sudden intimate and painful loss. He wrapped his arms around her and held her close to him.

"Take your time," he suggested. *"You can still feel the connection, just not the energy."*

Whimpering slightly, she leaned into him and rested her head against his chest. She heard and felt the beating of his heart in sync with her own.

"When you're ready, go ahead and take your energy threads away."

Kayla shook her head, unwilling to break the connection.

He said gently, *"You need to do it, Kayla. I know it's hard, but I won't go away. I promise. You can always reach for me, I'll be here for you."*

She felt the truth in his thoughts. He felt the same way she did. She also knew he was worried about her. He was concerned he had taken her too far too quickly. Reluctantly, she pulled the energy threads away.

Alec released her, and she stepped back, trembling slightly.

"Are you all right?"

She looked up at him and blushed at the intimacy they'd shared. "Yeah. I, um, see what you mean now."

He gave her an understanding smile. "I wasn't expecting to show you quite that much."

Kayla bit her lip, unsure about this whole energy thing. "Is it going to be like that when we fry the bracelets?"

He shook his head. "No. You'll be the one sending your energy toward me. As long as the energy flows in one direction, it's fine."

"What happened just now?"

"Ahh, well…" He cleared his throat, looking uncomfortable. "Mutually sharing energy is usually only done between two people who are seeking a stronger bond than a physical one."

Kayla stared at him. "Are you trying to tell me in your polite Omni way that we just mind-fucked each other?"

Alec's mouth curved into a grin. "I think that qualified more as mind-foreplay. That's why you didn't want to stop."

"Holy shit." She dropped down on the couch, completely stunned.

He nodded. "It's a powerful thing. That's one of the reasons we tend to keep to our own kind. It's not only our regular abilities. You could easily have a physical relationship with someone else, but you won't find that complete connection outside of the Circle."

"You mentioned bloodlines and our unique heritage before," Kayla recalled. "Why are we different?"

Alec smiled and sat next to her, taking her hand in his. "Do you remember the dragon statue you discovered in the ruins?"

"Of course. What about it?"

"The dragons have had countless names over the centuries. But here, in the towers, we usually refer to them as the *Drac'kin*. Thousands of years ago, when our world was still linked to other worlds, the *Drac'kin* were a dominant force. They waged a war in the Otherworld which nearly destroyed this world and several others in the process."

Kayla looked at him skeptically. "This sounds like a fairy tale."

"I suppose it does," he agreed. "But regardless, during this battle, one of the *Drac'kin* betrayed her kind. She gave others the knowledge to close the rifts between the worlds. They followed her instructions and some of the *Drac'kin* became trapped here on this world. Their descendants lived on. Some intermingled with the humans while others tried to keep their bloodlines pure."

"You're saying we're related to these *Drac'kin*?"

He nodded. "The most powerful talents usually have the purest bloodlines. OmniLab was created to try to preserve as many of our kind as possible."

CHAPTER SEVENTEEN

"Our kind?" Kayla repeated, pulling her hand free and standing. "Do you know how crazy this sounds?"

He sighed and leaned back, waving a hand casually in the air. "How would you explain what just happened between us, Kayla? How would you explain your talents and everything else you've seen here in the towers?"

She looked away. Drugs? Illness? Mental breakdown? She wasn't sure which of those was more attractive. "I don't know."

"I know this is probably difficult to accept," he admitted. "It would have been easier if you had grown up here with other people like you."

"Look," Kayla began pacing back and forth within the small room, "I admit what happened between us was bizarre, but I don't believe the rest of it. Dragons? Other worlds? It sounds crazy." *Hmm. It looks like I'm leaning toward a mental breakdown.* "And for the record, I can have a relationship with anyone I want. If I want to be with Carl, that's my choice. I don't care about this pure bloodline crap. I'll be damned if someone's going to tell me who I should or shouldn't be involved with."

The thought made her blood boil. She spun around to glare at Alec, who was calmly watching her rant. His serene composure just pissed her off more. She was having a break-down over here, and he was completely unruffled.

"You can do what you'd like, Kayla, but it doesn't change who or what we are."

"Damn you!" she shouted. "How can you sit there and say this to me? You don't know anything about me."

"Are you sure about that, Kayla? After what just happened between us?" Alec took a step toward her, his knowing look reminding her of their shared intimacy.

She blanched, recalling the way she'd shamefully begged him not to sever their connection. Up until then, she'd never realized how alone she was and how different. It was just one more thing she could blame him for. Sometimes ignorance *was* better.

Alec's eyes glinted meaningfully. "I'd say I know you far better than anyone else ever has and far better than anyone else ever could. I can give you what you want, Kayla."

How dare he dangle such a promise in front of her? She was a woman on the edge of going ballistic. He'd felt her emotions and the depth of her pain, even if she were reluc-tant to admit it out loud. Now he was exploiting those emotions, using them against her to get her to agree to his way of thinking.

Kayla glared at him for a moment before launching herself at him. Alec grabbed her easily and tossed her on the couch. Holding her down, he said quietly, "I see we're going to have to work on your temper."

"You bastard," she hissed. He was doing this on purpose, trying to rile her up. She pushed a wave of energy toward him, and he pulled back, eyeing her appreciatively. "You learn quickly. Good. When the High Council finds out you're trying to deactivate those bracelets, they're going to come after you to stop you. How well do you think you can you defend yourself or your friends?"

Better than he thought. She climbed off the couch and scowled at him. He might excel at mind manipulation, but she wasn't afraid to get physical. Grabbing a glass off the table, she threw it at him. He dodged, and it shattered when it hit the floor.

At the noise, Carl and Rand came rushing back into the office, stopping when they saw the mess. "What's going on? We heard a crash."

"Kayla's a little distressed," Alec explained.

Alec's lackadaisical description infuriated her. In the span of a few minutes, he'd turned her entire world inside out. She'd laid her soul bare to a complete stranger, learned she was some sort of alien freak, and that OmniLab wanted to oversee the distribution of visitor passes to her ovaries.

"A little distressed? You drop these huge bombshells on me and say I'm a little distressed? You vomitus, slack-jawed, freakish cretin! You're about as subtle as a well-thrown brick."

Carl walked around the broken glass toward her. "Kayla?"

"Stay out of this, Carl." She couldn't explain. Not now. She was having trouble getting her head around it herself. Not only that, but the thought of Carl's reaction scared her. How do you tell the man you're sleeping with that your ancestors had wings?

Alec chuckled. "Good advice. It would be a shame for Carl to get involved with something he doesn't understand."

Carl looked back and forth between Alec and Kayla. She scowled at Alec, wanting him to shut up. Snatching a computer tablet off the table, she threw it at him. He caught it easily and circled Kayla.

Furious, she glared at Alec. "You leave Carl out of this!"

"I intend to. I'm much more interested in finding out if that's your intention as well." His voice seemed casual, but she caught the edge of challenge in it. The bond between them flared and understanding hit her. He was asking if she was willing to let Carl go now that she knew the truth.

She wasn't. Kayla understood the reason Alec had been hunting her down in the towers wasn't because he was trying to turn her in to Edwin. He'd been trying to keep her away from Carl and corral her back to her own kind.

Sick and tired of people trying to control her, she said angrily, "I'd call you a parasite but that would be injurious and defamatory to the thousands of existing parasitic species."

"You are truly a fascinating creature, Kayla Rath'Varein. I've never met anyone so completely ruled by their passions."

Kayla lunged for him again. Alec grabbed her this time and pinned her against the wall. She threw more energy in his direction, but he was expecting it and somehow wrapped it around her. Her anger evaporated, replaced with surprise and fear. Her voice came out barely more than a whisper. "How did you do that?"

Alec's eyes widened. He immediately released her and stepped back a split second before Carl rushed forward to insert himself between them. Glaring at Alec, he said, "I don't care if you're an Inner Circle member or not. Keep your hands off her."

Alec glanced at Carl in annoyance. "This doesn't concern you."

He turned back to her and his expression softened. *"I would never hurt you,"* Alec promised. *"But you need to learn to protect yourself."*

Kayla felt the sincerity of his thought and nodded at Alec. She put her hand on Carl's arm. "It's okay. He just surprised me."

Carl looked at her curiously but made no move to step out of the line of fire. She crossed her arms and asked Alec, "So what happens now?"

"You can either wear the bracelet or we can try to upset the balance of power. It's up to you. You know the risks and consequences of both."

She blinked, surprised he would even bother to ask. "Gee, let me think. I'm going to go with kicking some High Council ass."

———

WHILE KAYLA CHANGED into the clothing Director Borshin had retrieved, Carl waited in the living area with the other men. Alec was on his commlink, looking out of place in the trader applicant's surroundings.

Rand poured everyone a drink while Alec spoke with Seara and asked her to meet him at his office. When he disconnected from the call, he accepted the drink Rand offered.

Carl looked at Alec. "I don't get it. Why the change of heart? You were ready to put a bracelet on Kayla and now you're going to take on the entire High Council?"

Alec took a drink and regarded him. Carl had the feeling Alec was weighing the merit in answering his questions. "My motivations are my business. However, I never intended to allow Kayla to wear a bracelet."

"Then why did you hunt her down? Why didn't you let her escape?"

Alec raised an eyebrow. "She belongs here. You may believe you understand her, Trader Carl Grayson, but you would be sorely mistaken."

Carl's expression darkened. "I understand her far better than you think."

Alec chuckled. "Go ahead and enjoy her while you can, but she belongs to me. That's something you won't ever be able to change." He put his glass down. "I'll be waiting outside. I need to make a few more calls."

Carl's jaw tightened. He made a move to go after him, but Rand's hand on his shoulder stopped him. Rand shook his head, letting him know it was a bad idea. "You know, I've been called cocky and arrogant in my life, but I don't come anywhere close to that."

Carl's voice came out as a low growl. "I don't trust him."

"You don't have to trust him. It's whether or not Kayla does that matters. From all appearances, there's something going on between them."

"Going on between who?" Kayla stepped into the room. She wore a simple, white dress that stopped just above her knee. The light fabric moved with her as she walked and enhanced her femininity. The sight of her completely distracted Carl from his thoughts.

"It's nothing," Carl replied, not wanting to discuss Alec. "You look beautiful, Kayla."

She looked down at the dress. "Why the hell don't Omni women wear any practical clothing?"

Carl admired her figure. "From my point of view, I'm glad they don't."

Rand held up his drink in salute and added, "You won't hear me complaining either."

Kayla sighed. "Where's Alec?"

"He's waiting outside to take you to his office to meet with Seara. We should get going. Thanks for your help, Rand."

Kayla kissed Rand lightly on the cheek. "Yeah, thanks for letting me crash here. You've been great."

Rand's eyes lit up, and he smiled at her. Carl chuckled, realizing she'd just charmed another soon-to-be trader.

"You're definitely the most memorable Inner Circle member I've ever met, Kayla. If you two don't mind, I think it would be best if I stayed here. Getting involved in Inner Circle business tends to have long-lasting repercussions."

She grinned at him and headed toward the door. Carl stopped her. "Are you sure you want to do this? I don't trust Alec."

Kayla looked up at him, determination in her gaze. "I need to do this. Alec is the only one who can help me get those bracelets off."

Carl frowned, wishing he had a better feeling about this. "I'm going with you then. I don't want anything to happen to you."

"I was hoping you'd say that." She smiled, slipped her hand in his, and they headed outside.

———

ALEC LOOKED up when they emerged. "Seara will be meeting us in my office in about an hour. That gives us a little time to discuss our options."

Kayla and Carl followed Alec toward one of the priority elevators. They filed inside, and Alec pressed the button.

"Maybe it's just me, but isn't Edwin going to be pissed off when he finds out you're not sending me back to that little room?"

"I'm sure he will," Alec replied, clasping his hands behind his back and watching the numbers increase on the screen above them. "However, he considered you a flight risk at the time. You're accompanying me willingly, and he gave me permission to train you. That's what I intend to do."

She had to give him credit. "Sneaky. I like the way you think."

The elevator doors opened, and they stepped out into a

large lobby area. Tables and seating were scattered around a cascading waterfall in the center of the room. A small restaurant area was off to the side. Several people were milling around the area.

"This is the entrance to the administrative offices," Alec explained, leading them through a pair of double doors.

As they walked down the hall, a woman called out, "Alec! There you are."

The woman appeared to be a few years older than Kayla. She was tall with long, straight blond hair falling nearly to her waist and bright-blue eyes. Her features were delicate and well-defined. She wore an elaborate and sophisticated pantsuit with several pieces of strange jewelry. Sauntering over to Alec, she kissed his cheek affectionately.

"I've missed you," she cooed, fluttering her eyelashes at him.

Kayla raised her brows. She'd never seen anyone flutter their eyelashes before. She blinked rapidly to see if she could pull it off. A quick glance at Carl smothering a laugh let her know she wasn't successful.

Alec paused and greeted the woman politely. "Celeste, I don't believe you had the opportunity to meet Kayla Rath'-Varein last night. The gentleman with her is Trader Carl Grayson." He turned to Kayla. "I'd like to introduce you to Mistress Celeste Staghorn. Celeste's father is Master Marcus Staghorn, one of our High Council members."

Celeste ignored Carl and focused her attention on Kayla instead. "So this is the woman who has the entire circle gossiping. It's a pleasure to meet you." Celeste gave Alec a teasing look and added, "Maybe next time Alec takes you to dinner, he won't keep you all to himself. Speaking of which, Alec, you still owe me dinner since you canceled on me last week."

Alec inclined his head. "Of course, Celeste. I'd be happy

to escort you to dinner later this week. Just let me know which day is best for you. I'll make the arrangements."

Celeste put her hand on his arm and said suggestively, "I'll check my schedule. But I'm thinking I'd like to have dinner at my place instead. There's so much we should catch up on."

Kayla frowned at the woman's blatant invitation. Alec stepped away from Celeste. "If you insist. However, you'll need to excuse us. We have some pressing matters which need to be handled."

"I wouldn't dream of keeping you." Celeste smiled at him. She gave a brief nod to Carl before turning to Kayla and holding out her hand. "It's been wonderful meeting you."

Kayla hesitated before accepting her offered hand. The moment her fingers touched Celeste, she felt the familiar energy tingle. Celeste's blue eyes widened, and she pulled her hand away quickly. The blond woman stared at Kayla for a moment before turning to Alec in alarm. "So this is why you're so drawn to her. Does the High Council know how much energy she can channel?"

"Yes." He stepped in front of Kayla protectively and reached out to touch Celeste's arm. Kayla felt a shift in the energy current around Celeste as Alec spoke his next words. "I trust you'll keep your observations to yourself."

Celeste nodded, looking slightly dazed. Alec removed his hand and the energy web dissipated. "It was a pleasure seeing you again, Celeste."

Kayla gave Alec a questioning look when the young woman walked away. He shook his head, indicating he would explain later, and motioned for them to continue following him.

Alec led them down the hall to a large office. The room was spacious with a wide desk in the corner of the room. Video screens were mounted on two adjacent walls. Another wall had an enormous fish tank while the last had a built-in cabinet with numerous artifacts and other decorations.

"Wow," Kayla murmured and walked around the office.

"Nice setup," Carl said appreciatively.

Alec leaned against his desk, watching Kayla. When she stopped at the fish tank, they darted away from her. She tapped on the edge of the glass. "They're real?"

"Yes," he replied, looking pleased at her interest. "We have large tanks on some of the lower levels. I'll take you to see them at some point, if you'd like."

"I think I could spend years here and not see everything."

"That's entirely possible," he admitted. "Before Seara gets here, we need to discuss the best way to proceed with removing the bracelets."

Kayla walked over to the desk and sat on the edge of it. Her dress hiked up slightly, and she dangled her legs off the side. Leaning back, she said, "Okay, go for it."

Alec glanced down at her legs and offered, "I have chairs, if you prefer."

"I get a better view of the room this way," she said with a laugh. Besides, she enjoyed the advantage it gave her. It threw people off balance and served as a great distraction. The dress she wore seemed to enhance the effects. Maybe the Omnis did know what they were doing with their strange clothing. "So what's the best way to handle the bracelet thing?"

"As you know, the bracelets act as an artificial bond and combine energy," Alec explained, tearing his gaze away from her legs. "They can be used at will by some High Council members. Our scientists continuously monitor the energy pool. If there's a sudden depletion in resources, such as by having the bracelets removed, they'll know immediately."

"So we have to try to remove them all at once?"

"That's one option," he admitted. "But I'm not sure it's the best solution. I don't know how removing a bracelet will affect either of us. It's possible we'll experience a significant drain on our energy that could leave both of us vulnerable. Even if we take away the pooled energy, the councilors are still powerful in their own right."

"And they'll come after us," she guessed.

Alec nodded. "Yes, there's no doubt. There may be a way to give false data readings to the monitoring system to cover our activities, but we'll have to plan a time when the High Council will be distracted and not using the pooled resources. Otherwise, they'll notice the depletion for themselves."

"What are you thinking?" Carl rubbed the back of his neck.

"The final bid for the trader position is happening tomorrow," Alec explained. "I think we should try to do this before then. That doesn't give us much time, but they'll all be focused on the trader meeting. Otherwise, if we wait, my father will put a bracelet on Kayla and we'll lose our chance."

It sounded good to Kayla, but her scope of experience was limited to taking advantage of traders. She looked at Carl, hoping to get his opinion. He paced the room, rubbing his chin in thought. "Xantham and Cruncher can work on developing a program that can send these false readings, but they'll need your access codes to get into the system."

Alec nodded. "That's fine."

Carl flipped open his commlink and called Cruncher. He explained what they were looking for, and Alec supplied them with his codes.

When they finished with their call, Alec turned to Kayla. "I'll need to teach you some basics in how to defend yourself against a mental attack. There's a good chance that once they realize what's going on, they'll try to stop us. I can shield you in part, but I'm sure some of them are already aware of your potential. If they focus on you, you'll need to learn how to circumvent their attack."

She sat up straight. "Is that what you did to me earlier?"

"Yes. I turned your energy back toward you with a shield. That's one technique. There are several others you can learn. You're able to channel a great deal of energy, but it's chaotic and not well-developed because you haven't been trained."

"The woman in the hall mentioned that," Kayla recalled. "How did she know?"

"Celeste has a talent for detecting energy potential. She can sense if someone is channeling or directing energy too. When she touched you, she picked up on that. I helped her 'forget' so she won't think to tell anyone else before we're ready."

"So *that's* what you did," Kayla mused. "I felt a shift in the energy, but I wasn't sure if that's what it was."

"You felt me influencing her?" Alec frowned.

She nodded. "Yeah. You touched her and there was this weird shift around her when you spoke."

Alec shook his head, looking troubled. "You shouldn't have been able to detect that."

Kayla shrugged. It was an advantage as far as she was concerned. If she could detect when someone was using energy around her, she could avoid it. "Well, at least this way I'll know when you're up to no good."

The door beeped. Alec pressed a button and Seara entered the room. When she saw Kayla, she rushed over and hugged her.

"I'm so sorry," Seara gushed. "I didn't know how to warn you about Edwin and the bracelets. I'm glad you're safe."

Kayla hugged her awkwardly. She was growing more accustomed to Seara's frequent displays of affection, but she wasn't sure she'd ever feel completely comfortable with it. "Uh, don't worry about it. Thanks for bailing my friends out."

"Yes, thank you again, Seara," Carl added.

Seara turned to look at Carl and offered him a warm smile. "I'm glad it worked out."

"Thanks for coming," Alec greeted her. "We wanted to take a closer look at your bracelet. Kayla discovered some information in Cessel's notes indicating there's a way to safely remove the bracelets."

Seara's eyes widened in shock and she whispered, "Truly?"

Kayla nodded at her hopeful expression. "Yeah. I can show you, but it involves directing a great amount of energy in two specific locations. It'll fry the bracelet and render it useless. It won't affect you at all."

"How much energy is required to deactivate it?" Seara asked Alec.

"More than most of us are able to channel alone," he admitted. "But I suspect Kayla can channel that kind of energy easily. The difficulty is that it requires pinpoint accuracy."

Seara's shoulders slumped at the news. "At least we know there's a way this can eventually be accomplished."

Kayla shook her head. "Alec is going to do that funky-connection-energy-transfer thing with me. He'll use my energy to zap those suckers. We don't have to wait."

Seara gaped at her and whirled around to glare at Alec. "Absolutely not! You are *not* going to link with my daughter when she hasn't learned anything about our ways. I can't believe you're entertaining the idea."

Alec cleared his throat and tugged at his collar. "We've already attempted some preliminary trials, Seara. I explained to Kayla what was involved and showed her how the connection would work."

"Yeah, it was fine," Kayla agreed and gave Alec a sheepish look. "It was a little intense when our energy mixed together, but Alec said we don't have to do that again to break the bracelets."

Seara's eyes widened in horror at Kayla's words. She turned to Alec and slapped him across the face. His eyes narrowed slightly, but he didn't move. "How could you? It's one thing to be forced to wear the bracelet, but it doesn't require us to share that level of connection with anyone. You've created a permanent link with her!"

Carl's head jerked up to focus on Alec. "Is that what you meant earlier?"

Kayla's jaw dropped. "Whoa, did I miss something? What's this about a permanent link?"

Seara looked shocked and asked in a whisper, "Alec, you didn't tell her?"

"Carl, none of this is your concern. You're here as a courtesy, nothing more," Alec replied icily. He turned back to Seara. "It didn't get that far, Seara. The connection was shared, but it was not completed."

"You stopped it? How?"

"With great difficulty," Alec admitted and darted a glance at Kayla.

Kayla slid off the desk. If there was one thing worse than people trying to control her, it was when they were talking about her like she wasn't in the room. She put her hands on her hips, determined to get some answers. "Uh, excuse me, but I'd like to know what the hell you two are talking about."

Seara took a deep, steadying breath and turned to Kayla. "We may, in the heat of the moment, toss energy back and forth with someone. But sharing energy at the same time can create a permanent link with the other person. This is usually only done by two committed mates and both parties fully understand what's involved."

Kayla shook her head. This sounded like one of those birds-and-the-bees talks. "Um, still not understanding this permanent link stuff."

Seara looked weary and took a nearby seat. "We essentially claim one another. It's a way of committing to that one other person. No matter where you are or what you're doing, you'll always feel a permanent connection with the other person."

"Wait, you *claim* one another?" Kayla asked in alarm. She felt the blood drain from her face. "But that's what I wanted when... Oh shit."

Her gaze flew to Alec, and he nodded. "I know. That's why it was difficult to stop it."

"I'm surprised you had that sort of willpower," Seara said thoughtfully. "It's an almost overwhelming force to complete the claim."

"No kidding," Kayla muttered and rubbed her arms. The idea of irrevocably bonding to another person gave her chills. She'd enjoyed the moment they shared. Okay, that was a lie. It was one of the most intense and profound experiences of her life. But she was much safer flying solo. She took a quick peek at Carl and wondered what it would have been like to share the moment with him instead.

"Your father and I shared that bond," Seara recalled sadly. "When I lost him, I knew it immediately. I felt the connection disappear. I didn't think I'd survive it."

Alec was quiet for a moment and then said, "Seara, I told you before that I would do everything possible to protect Kayla. I admit, not forging that connection was incredibly difficult, but I assure you I will not intentionally put her in that position again unless she is fully cognizant of what it means."

Carl glared at Alec. "From where I'm standing, it would be better for you to keep your distance from her."

Alec looked amused. "I'm sure you'd like that. But that won't ever happen."

Kayla looked back and forth between the two men. This

wasn't good. If they were going to succeed, they all needed to work together.

She glanced at Seara and saw the older woman had come to the same conclusion. Before Kayla could say anything, Seara neatly changed the subject, preventing a more heated argument. "You wanted to examine my bracelet?"

"Yes, if you don't mind." Alec motioned toward the seating area. "With Kayla's help I can take a closer look at it. I don't want to deactivate it, though, until we know we can mask it properly."

"Of course."

Kayla and Seara sat on the couch. Alec pulled up a chair to sit across from them and held out his hand for Kayla. Carl frowned when she slipped her hand into his.

"Kayla, you'll need to connect to me the same way you did earlier," Alec instructed.

She nodded. Closing her eyes, Kayla gathered her threads of energy and sent them toward Alec. The moment she did, the same familiar intimacy from before returned. This time she was more prepared for it. She couldn't help but take a moment to revel in the sensation. The pull toward him was becoming stronger, and she felt the urge to share energy with him again.

"I feel it too," he told her. "It's possible that even though we didn't complete the connection earlier, it created a small bond between us. People don't normally initiate a bond without completing it, so I can't be sure."

Kayla opened her eyes and bit her lip. It seemed like they were both in new territory. Seara looked between them. "What's wrong, Kayla?"

"Nothing," Kayla replied. "It's fine. Let's do this."

Alec reached for Seara's wrist to examine her bracelet, and Kayla leaned forward to get a better look. It was a small, braided-gold band interlaid with strange stones. The colors in the stones appeared to shift and change when it moved. It reminded Kayla of the colors she saw when the energy threads blended together.

"Go ahead and send a large, steady stream toward me, Kayla," Alec instructed.

She did as he asked, and she could feel his urge to match her energy flow with his. He closed his eyes for a moment, and Kayla could sense his struggle to control his desire before turning back to the bracelet. Once he'd gotten it under control, Alec began gently probing the bracelet with her energy in the areas she had identified. She could see the small fluctuations of the energy surrounding the bracelet as he studied it.

After a long time, he lowered Seara's hand. Kayla stopped the flow of energy and felt Alec's longing from the withdrawal. He closed his eyes, and she felt him trying to steady himself.

He took a deep breath and said, *"Go ahead and break the connection."*

She pulled back and broke the connection. He squeezed her hand before releasing it.

Seara watched them for a minute. "Will it work?"

Alec nodded. "Yes, but it'll take a great deal of energy to deactivate them. We'll have to wait for the masking program before we try anything though. I don't want to risk alerting the High Council too soon."

When Seara nodded in agreement, Kayla offered, "I can help Cruncher and Xantham write the masking program. It shouldn't be too difficult if they already have your access codes."

Carl pulled Kayla up and wrapped his arm around her waist. "I'll take Kayla back to my family's quarters. She can work with them there. That is, unless you're planning on raiding us again."

Alec stood, not bothering to hide his irritation at the question. "It would be better if she stayed here in the Inner Sanctum. As long as she's here and the High Council believes she's willing to wear the bracelet, they won't pursue her."

Kayla scowled. Alec had a lot to learn if he thought she was going to roll over for the OmniLab bigwigs. "The High Council can kiss my ass. Seara's quarters are under surveillance. At least if I'm with Carl, you don't have bugs there. Besides, I need to be able to work with Xantham, Cruncher, and V to get this program going."

"I'm afraid that won't work, Kayla. The High Council will insist you remain in the Inner Sanctum until the bracelet is equipped. As long as you're here, I can claim you're cooperating fully and we're waiting for the metabolic booster to leave your system. If you leave, they may employ more drastic measures."

Seara had been quiet up until now. "Everyone could stay in our family's quarters. We may have surveillance, but you could use the safe room while you're working on the program."

Alec's eyes narrowed. "You have a safe room?"

Seara smiled. "Yes. My husband had a great many secrets, Alec. It was originally designed to be a hidden storage room, but Andrei had some concerns and turned it into a safe room."

Carl's arms tightened around her waist. "What sort of concerns?"

Seara hesitated. "There were some political power pulls going on for a few years before he died. He suspected there was a plot to have him removed from the High Council."

Carl frowned. "From everything I've seen, Andrei Rath'-Varein was a great leader. Why did they want to remove him?"

The memory was obviously painful for Seara. She twisted

her hands in her lap, her voice quiet. "Some people weren't happy with the pace we were obtaining new resources. There were arguments that we should be more aggressive and even target other communities. My husband believed we could locate new resources using our talents cooperatively rather than coercing other communities into submission."

Kayla bit her lip, not wanting to upset Seara, but she was curious about getting more insight into her background. "Is that why he took me into the ruins?"

Seara nodded and offered a sad smile. "When we realized you had the talent for locating objects, the High Council urged your father to take you into the ruins. He had some reservations because of your age, but the council put a lot of pressure on him. He finally decided he would take you himself with several handpicked people he trusted."

Seara stood and took Kayla's hand in hers. "I don't know what happened or what went wrong. Everyone who went on the expedition was killed. We were monitoring it from here, and everything appeared stable. We sent out an additional team immediately, but it was too late. I'm just thankful you survived."

She turned to Alec. "Is there any objection to Kayla returning with me and having her friends join us? It would give me a chance to spend more time with her."

"I suppose there wouldn't be any objections," Alec said in resignation.

Seara inclined her head. "Carl, why don't you get your friends and have them join us? I'll let an attendant know they have access to the priority elevators. We should head back now so they can continue working on this project."

CHAPTER EIGHTEEN

KAYLA WALKED BACK into the Rath'Varein family quarters with Alec and Seara. Carl had gone off to retrieve the rest of the crew.

"I'm going to go make sure the rooms are set up for our guests. I'll be back in a few minutes. Please make yourself at home."

After Seara disappeared, Alec walked over to the bar area and poured himself a drink. He turned to Kayla. "Would you like something?"

"Sure, I guess."

He poured her a glass and brought it over to her. Taking a sip, she said, "So I didn't get a chance to ask you about that girl."

"Who?"

Kayla made another bad attempt at fluttering her eyelashes. "You know, the tall, leggy blonde hanging all over you earlier?"

Alec chuckled. "You must mean Celeste."

"Right. Her." She swirled the drink around her glass. It probably wasn't any of her business, but she couldn't help being curious. "Who is she anyway? Do you two go to dinner together a lot?"

Alec considered the question for a moment before responding. "Yes, we go to dinner together every now and then."

Kayla nodded. "It seemed like you two are pretty close."

Alec raised an eyebrow. "We've spent time together and enjoyed one another's company."

She bit her lip and peered up at him. "You can connect with her the same way you do with me?"

"She's part of the Inner Circle," he said with a chuckle. "Everyone with our backgrounds has the ability to link with someone. Some people are more desirable based on the amount of energy they can channel. We're naturally drawn to those who are either close to or exceed our same level of power."

"Have you done that? With her, I mean?"

Alec stepped closer and said disapprovingly, "I don't ask you what goes on between you and Carl."

"Point taken," Kayla muttered and looked away. She deserved the verbal slap. It wasn't logical, but she didn't like the thought of Celeste sharing the same sort of connection she'd had with Alec. She wasn't sure if she was ready to examine the reasons though.

"When you're ready to get rid of your distractions, I'll get rid of mine," he challenged.

She gave him a sharp look, putting her glass down a little harder than she intended. "Carl is not a distraction. I was just curious about how this works."

"So you say," he replied, calling her bluff. He took another sip of his drink. "Is there anything else you'd like to know?"

Damn him. He's got that whole mysterious and sexy thing going on.

Alec chuckled. "Thank you."

Kayla scowled. "Get out of my head."

"You still have a small connection with me. You never removed it."

She sat on the couch with a sigh. Sure, she could remove the connection, but the thought of separating herself from him was upsetting. Alec walked over and sat next to her. Draping his arm over the back of the couch, he said, "I don't mind. I rather enjoy it. But then again, I don't have any problem admitting I'm incredibly attracted to you."

Kayla frowned. "You make my life confusing."

He leaned closer to her. "I know you're attracted to Carl and have feelings for him, but I also know you're attracted to me and have feelings for me." He reached up and lightly caressed her face, sending chills through her. "The difference is," he said softly, running his thumb over her bottom lip, "I can touch you in ways he never can."

Kayla closed her eyes when he sent a trickle of energy through her. She shook her head and jumped up. "Okay, you need to keep your distance. You're confusing as hell. I don't need any more confusion in my life."

"Very well." He chuckled. "Would you like to learn how to defend yourself?"

Her eyes narrowed, and she crossed her arms over her chest. "Yeah, I could handle kicking your ass right now."

Alec smiled and stood, his eyes twinkling in amusement. "Go ahead and try it, dear."

Kayla concentrated and threw a large amount of energy at him. She felt him grab it and twist it back around toward her almost immediately. He wrapped her in it, and her eyes narrowed.

"Break my hold if you can," he taunted her.

She pushed more energy toward him, and he wrapped that around her too. She felt stifled but could also feel his exertion as he continued to suppress her.

"You have two choices," Alec instructed. *"You can either keep pushing more energy toward me until it possibly breaks, or you can study your prison and look for a weakness."*

Kayla paused, realizing the wisdom of his words. She took a moment to study the way he wrapped energy around her. He had somehow used his own threads to create a tight barrier around her. It was her own energy imprisoning her and not the other way around.

"It's a reverse shielding technique," he explained when he felt her examining the energy threads. *"It's purely defensive. Pull back your energy and you'll see what I mean."*

Kayla withdrew her assault and frowned. She wasn't truly imprisoned. She sent out a tiny burst of energy, and it bounced off the shield before wrapping back around her.

Alec nodded encouragingly. *"Do you want to try it?"*

"Wait. I want to try something."

He kept his shield in place while she took her time exploring it. Some areas appeared weaker than others, but for the most part, it appeared extremely well-crafted.

"If I sent a hard burst toward one of your weaker areas, would that break through your wall?"

"Yes, if it was strong enough and precise enough. But if someone senses your exploration of their shield, they can reinforce the areas you've discovered."

She nodded and said aloud, "Okay. I want to build my own shield now."

He walked her through the steps of weaving a tightly-knit group of energy threads together and then showed her how to surround him. When Kayla finally had the shield in place, she let him know she was ready.

Alec sent out a strong pulse of energy, and she felt it bounce off her shield. She could see it wrap around him, and he quickly withdrew his energy. Her eyes danced in excitement when she realized it worked. "This is awesome!"

He chuckled at her enthusiasm. "Do you want me to try it again?"

"Yeah. Send more." She gave an eager nod.

Alec sent out a larger and more powerful burst of energy. Kayla felt her shield ripple slightly, but it remained intact.

"Good," he encouraged. "But you need to concentrate to maintain your shield. If someone is truly attacking you, they won't hold back. It takes years of training to be able to craft a strong shield. This will require a great deal of concentration on your part until you've mastered it."

Seara came back into the room and looked back and forth between them. "You're teaching her how to shield?"

"As a precaution, yes."

"That's probably wise," Seara admitted. "It can't hurt anyway."

Kayla looked at Seara. "From what I've seen, everyone seems to have specific talents. What's yours?"

Seara smiled and walked across the room to stand next to one of the plants. She held out her hand toward the plant. Nothing happened right away. After a moment, the plant began to grow and blossom. "I can connect with plant energy. It's one of my passions. We have a garden room, if you'd like to see it sometime."

Kayla's jaw dropped. The implications of such an ability were extraordinary. No wonder they were able to grow their own food to feed all of OmniLab. "That's freaking amazing. How did you do that?"

"I'll show you," Seara offered and took Kayla's hand. "You'll need to go ahead and create a small connection with me."

Kayla used one of her threads to create a small connection with Seara and was surprised at the feeling. The connection between Seara felt distinctly different than the one she shared with Alec. A flash of a memory crept into Kayla's mind and she gasped, remembering a large room filled with plants and Seara's smiling face.

Seara looked hopeful. "You remembered something, didn't you?"

"I think so," Kayla whispered. "The garden room, I think. Did you take me there when I was little?"

Seara nodded. "You used to play in there while I was gardening."

More memories and faces flooded Kayla's mind. The suddenness of the images was disorienting. She dropped Seara's hand and stepped back. "Are you doing that?"

Seara shook her head. "No. It might be the connection."

Kayla frowned. Alec walked over to her, a look of concern on his face. "Are you all right?"

She was quiet for a moment. "Yeah, I think I started remembering little flashes." She looked up at him and cocked her head. "Did I... push you into a fountain?"

Seara burst into laughter. Alec gave a wry smile and nodded. "Yes. You were a rather precocious nuisance even at five years old."

"Actually, it was well-deserved if I recall correctly," Seara added. "You were teasing her."

Alec chuckled. "Yes, well, I was apparently a rather precocious nuisance too."

The door beeped, and Seara headed to the door. Alec looked down at Kayla. "I expect those are your friends. I doubt they'll appreciate my presence. I should probably take my leave, but I'll be back in the morning."

He took Kayla's hand and kissed the top of it gently. She felt him send a slight trickle of energy over her. She raised an eyebrow. "Not that I'm complaining, but what was that for?"

"So when you're with Carl, you'll remember what I can offer you," he said in a low voice.

Oh crap. He's doing it again. He's too damn sexy for his own good.

Alec smiled at her knowingly and Kayla muttered, "I don't know why I even bother thinking anymore. Go. Get out of here. You're nothing but trouble."

Seara led Veridian and Carl into the room, followed by Cruncher and Xantham. Cruncher let out a low whistle. "Damn, Kayla, you've got a nice place here."

Alec turned to look at the newcomers. "You'll be expected to take your leave the day after tomorrow. Your entrance to this area will only be authorized until then." He turned to Kayla and said more warmly, "If you need me for anything, please call. I'm right down the hall."

With a brief nod at Carl's crew, Alec bowed to Seara and left their quarters.

————

Crossing his arms, Carl was glad to see him go. It hadn't escaped his attention that Alec seemed to take every opportunity to touch Kayla in some way. He didn't consider himself to be a jealous man, but there were limits. He just wished he could get a read on Kayla's feelings.

Xantham leaned toward Carl. "I don't like that guy."

Carl nodded and muttered, "You're not the only one."

"Let me show you to your rooms," Seara offered.

They followed her down the hallway, and she showed them to each of the prepared rooms. After putting their things down, Seara opened up the safe room for them. "I know you have things you want to do so I'll get out of your way. I'll have some food out in the living area whenever you get hungry."

Kayla set up one of the computer terminals and glanced over at them. "How far did you guys get with the program?"

Cruncher linked his terminal connection with hers and said, "We were able to get into the system easily enough with

Alec's access codes, but their monitoring system is pretty complex. There are a few loopholes we discovered, though, and I started coding a few things. We could definitely use your help in exploiting them."

Once their systems were up and running, Kayla set to work reading Cruncher's code and making modifications. Carl watched as Cruncher began debating back and forth with her about possible changes. Her adeptness with technology continued to impress him, especially given her camp's limited resources. Xantham occasionally threw in a few comments but primarily amused himself by reading through OmniLab's sensitive data with Alec's passcodes.

Once he was confident they were engrossed in their project, Carl headed back into the living room with Veridian. Seara looked up from placing a tray of food on a table and smiled at them. "Please help yourself. If Kayla's anything like her father, she'll end up immersed in whatever she's doing and forget to eat."

Veridian laughed and reached for a plate. "Yep, that's her. Kayla forgets everything when she gets started on a project."

Carl looked at the expanse of food. "I'll take something to her."

"Thank you, Carl," Seara said, handing him an empty plate. She looked at him, her gaze hesitant. "I know it's none of my business, but most people wouldn't have gone to the lengths you have for my daughter. You jeopardized your entire future. You care about her, don't you?"

Carl paused, assessing Seara carefully to gauge her reaction to his words. He was well aware that many Inner Circle members didn't care much for outsiders. He wasn't sure if she was one of those who harbored conventional views but decided it best to keep his answer conservative. "Your daughter is an incredible woman. I've never met anyone like her."

Seemingly unaware of his concerns, Seara smiled happily. "She is, isn't she? The more time I spend with her the more she reminds me of her father. I wish she'd been able to get to know him."

Relaxing somewhat, Carl began making up a plate of food. "I can't help but wonder how different her life would have been if she had grown up here instead. But I'm glad I've had the opportunity to get to know her."

Seara studied him thoughtfully for a long moment, but she didn't say anything more. Instead, she handed Carl a fork and napkin to take to Kayla. Armed with a plate of food, Carl carried it to the safe room while Veridian stayed behind with Seara.

Xantham's eyes widened when he saw the plate. "Real food? I'll be back." He jumped up and ran out of the room.

Carl chuckled and put the plate down next to Kayla. "You need to eat something."

Kayla nodded absently and took a bite without bothering to look away from the screen. She continued working, and Carl waited patiently for her to resume eating. When she continued to ignore him, he cleared his throat to get her attention. "One bite isn't going to cut it, Kayla. Have you eaten anything today?"

"Huh? What?" Kayla blinked at him, her confusion evident.

"You need to eat something," he reminded her.

"Oh, right." She glanced down at the plate as though seeing it for the first time. She dutifully took another bite before turning back to the computer.

Carl stopped her. "If I have to physically remove you from the computer, I will. Take a short break, Kayla."

She scowled. "You're a pain in the ass."

"So you've said," he agreed. "Repeatedly."

Cruncher looked up, pretending to be affronted. "What? You didn't bring me a plate?"

Carl raised an eyebrow. "Next time you're locked up against your will, I'll consider it. In the meantime, though, you can get off your ass and get yourself something."

Cruncher chuckled, stood, and headed out of the room. Kayla ate a few more bites before pushing the plate away. She looked at Carl expectantly, and he sighed in resignation. He took her plate while she turned back to the computer. Within a few minutes, she was back to being totally engrossed in her computer.

He shook his head, heading back into the common area.

"Well, she ate a few bites," Carl informed Seara. The woman took the plate from Carl and gestured to the table. "Why don't you have a seat and fix yourself something?"

He obliged and sat with the rest of his crew. When they finished eating, Cruncher and Xantham headed back to the safe room while Carl, Veridian, and Seara remained behind, talking. After several hours, Veridian and Seara headed to their respective rooms to get some rest.

Carl walked back into the safe room. It appeared Cruncher and Xantham had already gone to bed. Kayla was still sitting at the computer, reading intently.

"Still working on it?"

Kayla jumped at the sound of his voice. She turned to look at him and relaxed slightly. "No, it's finished. I wanted to take another look to make sure we didn't miss anything. It looks like it'll work."

Carl walked up behind her, resting his hands on her shoulders. He started massaging her tired muscles, and she lowered her head, making a small noise of contentment.

"You have no idea how wonderful that feels."

He continued rubbing her shoulders. Leaning down close

to her ear, he said, "Everyone else has gone to bed. Why don't you turn this off? You can finish looking at it in the morning."

"Mmm," she murmured and turned off the monitor. Standing up, she turned around to wrap her arms around his neck and purred, "Was that an invitation?"

"It could be, if you're interested."

Kayla ran her fingers lightly across his chest. "I'm definitely interested."

He smiled at her and tilted her head back to kiss her. "Then let's go to bed."

CHAPTER NINETEEN

KAYLA WOKE up the next morning curled up next to Carl. Surrounded by pillows softer than anything she'd ever touched and lying next to a sexy, naked man, she was feeling pretty content. She'd been even better the night before, though, when Carl had managed to entice her away from the computer.

With a lazy smile, she stretched and climbed out of bed. She slipped into the bathroom and went through her morning routine before pulling on the clothes Seara had provided the night before. Careful not to disturb Carl, she crept out of the room. Heading down the hall toward the safe room, Kayla paused when she saw Alec and Seara sitting together talking in the living room.

Alec turned to look at her, giving her a warm smile.

"Good morning, Kayla," Seara said cheerfully. "We were just having breakfast. Would you like to join us?"

"Sure," she replied and sat down just as Seara placed a plate in front of her. It was some sort of scrambled egg mixture with seasoned vegetables. She took a bite, continuing to be amazed at how incredible the food tasted.

Alec smiled at her reaction. "Did you get any rest last night?"

Kayla nearly choked on her food as she remembered the surveillance system and her extracurricular activities with Carl the night before. She nodded and managed to swallow. Taking a hasty sip of water, she decided she'd have to figure out how to circumvent the cameras and do it soon. "Yeah, thanks."

Now she just had to keep Alec out of her head. She forced herself to think about her food and only her food. Alec raised an eyebrow at her questioningly, but Kayla ignored his look. "This is great, Seara. Thanks."

"I'm glad you like it. Everyone else is still asleep. I'm surprised you're awake so early. You were still up when I headed to bed."

Kayla nodded. "Yeah, I was up late working on stuff. Everyone else will probably be trickling out soon."

Alec reached out and placed his hand over hers. *"Were you able to finish the program?"*

"Yes. I want one more look at it, but it's finished. We can upload it to the system whenever you want."

She pulled her hand away and finished eating. "Thanks again for the food. I'm going to go check on something really quick."

Seara nodded and cleared away the plates while Kayla headed to the safe room, Alec trailing behind her. He looked around curiously. "Impressive. No one knew this existed."

Kayla activated the terminal and sat in the chair. Alec leaned over her to get a better look at the screen.

Wow, he smells good, she thought to herself and then sighed when she realized he probably heard her.

Alec leaned close to her ear and said softly, "I was thinking the exact same thing about you."

"Okay then." Determined to focus on the computer,

Kayla pulled up the program she had finished the night before and scrolled through it.

Alec looked at it in surprise. "You did this?"

She nodded. "Cruncher and Xantham started it, but I finished it."

"Carl had written in your bio that you could code, but I didn't realize you could do this sort of work."

"He wrote about me?"

"Yes," Alec replied. "It's standard practice when anyone signs an OmniLab contract. He had to submit an assessment of your skills. When I realized who you were, I took a much closer look at it."

Kayla wasn't thrilled about the existence of a dossier floating around with her name on it. She also wondered what Carl specifically had said about her. "I want to see this bio."

Alec chuckled. "I'll send you a copy. He had his eye on you for a while, according to the notes. I can't say I blame him."

"So I've heard," she replied dryly.

Alec gestured to the screen. "How does this program of yours work?"

She turned back to the computer and explained, "It's a masking program. Once we upload it to the system, it'll show the energy levels as remaining stable. I went ahead and added a feature so there will be slight fluctuations to make it appear more realistic. I had to go through and analyze the fluctuations over the past several weeks to get an idea about typical usage."

Alec nodded. "That makes sense. Whenever you're ready to upload it, we can try to remove Seara's bracelet."

"Fantastic," Kayla said. "Let me go wake up Carl and Cruncher. I'm going to need them to keep an eye on the system to make sure it's working properly."

Alec smiled at her enthusiasm as she jumped up and ran

out of the room. She darted down the hallway to her bedroom. Carl was still sleeping, but that hardly deterred her.

He grunted and opened his eyes sleepily when she climbed on top of him. "What time is it?"

"Early," she replied and kissed him.

Carl wrapped his arms around her and pulled her to him. Hooking his leg over hers, he rolled over and pinned her down. Propping himself up, he looked down at her as she ran her fingers through his loose, dark hair. "I like it when your hair is down."

"You do, do you?"

"Mmmhmm." The texture was softer than it looked. The fact he rarely put it down, and she was the only one able to run her fingers through it, made it so much more intimate and special. "It's sexy."

He gave her a long, slow kiss, running his hand along her thigh and up under her dress, and nuzzled her neck. "You're wearing too many clothes. You've been up for a while, haven't you?"

"Not long," she admitted, arching her neck to give him better access. The man's lips and fingers were magical. "I came to wake you up because we're going to try deactivating Seara's bracelet. I need you and Cruncher to monitor the system."

His eyes widened. "Already?"

When she nodded, he sat up and looked at her in concern. "Are you sure this is safe for you to do? I admit I don't know much about this, but I know you have to connect with Alec. That worries me."

Kayla ran her fingers over Carl's bare chest. It was nice to have someone concerned about her well-being. He wasn't trying to make demands or force her into anything, but he simply shared his reservations and trusted her to make the right decision. It made her respect him even more. "That's why I want you there. I don't know much about this woo-woo stuff, either, but I think I can handle it. Alec's not a bad guy, he's just different."

And he gets in my head and gets me worked up. I probably shouldn't share that though.

Carl frowned. "He wants you to stay in the towers. I suspect he'll do almost anything to keep you here."

Kayla shrugged. "I don't care. I belong on the surface and down in the ruins. You know that."

Carl considered this for a moment and nodded. "Let me get dressed, and I'll grab Cruncher."

"Just a second." She pulled him back for another long, passionate kiss. "Thanks. I just needed something to hold me over until I get you alone later."

Carl raised an eyebrow. "You sure you don't want to wait to do this bracelet thing? I wouldn't mind taking you back to bed."

Kayla laughed in delight. "Go get dressed. We can pick up where we left off later. I need to do this for Seara."

With a nod, he stood and headed for the lavatory. Kayla watched him go, admiring the yummy view. Sighing wistfully, she climbed off the bed and headed back out to the living area, where Seara and Alec were sitting.

"Carl's awake," she announced and swiped a muffin off the table. Even though she'd already eaten, they were calling her name. "He's going to get Cruncher up in a minute. Can you let me know when they come out?"

Seara nodded, and Kayla headed back into the safe room. She sat in the chair and pulled up the code again, studying it line by line to make sure it would work flawlessly. Satisfied it was perfect, she turned on an adjacent terminal and connected her computer to the energy monitoring system.

Munching on her muffin, she wrote a quick script to inject the masking program into the energy monitoring system. Carl and Cruncher came into the room a short time later, followed by Seara and Alec.

"Morning, Kayla," Cruncher greeted her. "How does it look?"

"It's ready. It's a freaking brilliant piece of work. You just have to execute the script when we're ready. The bracelet will still appear to work. Only those of us in this room will know it's no longer working."

Seara looked apprehensive and admitted, "I'm a little nervous about this."

"It'll be fine, Seara," Alec said and pulled out a chair for her. She sat and put her hands in her lap, anxiously twisting the bracelet around her wrist. Alec turned and held out his hand to Kayla. Carl's jaw clenched as Kayla took Alec's hand, but he didn't say anything. Alec put his other hand on Seara's wrist. "Whenever you're ready, Kayla, go ahead and begin."

Kayla nodded and sent her energy threads in Alec's direction. She was becoming much more comfortable with this intimate connection with him. She wasn't sure if that was a good thing or a bad thing.

Alec turned to Cruncher. "Activate the program now."

Cruncher nodded, pressed a few keys, and announced, "It's online."

Alec gave Kayla an encouraging smile. "When you're ready, I need you to send me a steady stream of energy. That's all you need to do. I'll handle everything else. I'll let you know when to increase it."

Kayla concentrated and did what he asked. She felt his desire to match her energy with his own, but he struggled to keep his feelings in check. His self-control was admirable. She didn't think she would be capable of doing the same if their situations were reversed.

Alec took a deep breath and focused on the bracelet. He

located the two target areas and gently probed them with Kayla's energy. "Increase it now."

She willed herself to tap into her energy resources. Amazed at the way the energy seemed to flow around her, she gathered it close and directed it toward Alec. It seemed as though the more she sent to him, the more loose energy drifted toward her, eager for her to scoop it up. It seemed to be attracted to her. Delighted with the playful energy seeking her out, Kayla focused on the loose strands floating around her and channeled it toward him.

Completely immersed in the game she'd made up—gathering lost energy and giving it a home—Kayla closed her eyes to get a better sense of the energy around her. Fairly humming with the power flowing through her, she stopped paying attention to Alec's reaction to the increased energy she was feeding him. Instead, she became intrigued at the path of energy he was channeling through the bracelet.

Kayla followed its path and was surprised when she found herself in an enormous hub of energy. It pressed against her, swarming her senses and threatening to overwhelm her. She tried to pull back and was surprised when the pooled energy seemed to gather around her, not willing to let her leave.

Panic set in, and she reacted instinctively, trying to channel the entire flow of energy. It was too much. Nothing in her experience had prepared her to handle something of this magnitude. She screamed Alec's name in her head, desperate to find their shared connection amidst the onslaught of energy threatening to drown her.

———

THE INACTIVITY WAS DRIVING Carl crazy. His gaze kept shifting from the monitor Cruncher was watching to the three motionless individuals in front of him. He'd get a sense of something happening almost peripherally, but it wasn't anything tangible he could describe. His fingers flexed, and he had to keep resisting the urge to tap his foot.

Seara's sudden gasp brought him to full alertness. She stared in shock down at the bracelet and whispered, "It worked. It's been deactivated."

Cruncher looked up in alarm. "I think we've got a problem."

Carl jerked his head up to stare at the fluctuations on the screen. They were going haywire. "What the hell is going on?"

"The energy levels are still masked for now, but there's been a huge increase of energy in the pool. I don't know what this means."

Carl turned back to look at Kayla and Alec, still motionless. Seara's hands flew to her mouth, her gaze darting back and forth between them. Carl wasn't sure what she saw that he didn't, but he didn't care much for the growing sense of unease in the pit of his stomach. Something was wrong.

At Seara's panicked expression, Carl looked back at Alec and Kayla. They were both standing still with their eyes closed. Without taking his eyes away from them, he asked Seara, "What's going on?"

Seara shook her head, visibly shaken. "I think Kayla and Alec may have somehow tapped into the energy pool directly. I don't know what's happening."

That didn't sound good. "Kayla?"

Whether it was the sound of his voice or something else, he didn't know, but Kayla suddenly staggered. Alec's eyes flew open, and he caught her when she started to collapse. He lowered himself to the floor with Kayla still in his arms.

Seara stood, hovering over them, her voice filled with fear. "Alec, what's happening?"

He ignored her, continuing to focus on Kayla. He traced his fingers over her face and closed his eyes again.

"What the hell is he doing to her?" Carl demanded, stepping forward to intervene.

Seara held up her hand to stop him. "I don't know, but he won't hurt her. They're connected right now. He can feel everything she feels and vice versa. They're sharing thoughts, emotions, everything."

Carl reared back as though stung. "That's what it means when they're connected?"

Seara nodded. "It's similar to telepathy, but it goes much deeper."

He resisted the urge to tear Alec away from her. Until he learned more, Carl couldn't risk putting her in more danger. "You can't tell what's going on?"

Seara hesitated. "Not exactly, no. Now that the bracelet is deactivated, I can try to see. I can't connect with them, though, unless they agree to it."

She knelt and put one hand on Kayla and the other on Alec's arm. Closing her eyes, she remained quiet for what seemed an eternity to Carl. When her eyes flew open, she stared at Alec in horror. Shoving at him, she yelled, "Alec, stop! You can't do this."

Carl's gaze darted back and forth between them. "What is he doing?"

Alec looked up, suddenly aware of his surroundings. He shook Seara away. "Seara, I have to do this. She channeled too much. She somehow followed the energy through to the pool and tried to reverse the flow. When the bracelet deactivated, she lost control of the flow. I had no idea this could happen." He looked down at her and whispered, "I should have never let her do this."

"Then let me do it," Seara urged, reaching for Kayla again.

"She can't forge another connection," Alec argued, his voice tinged with frustration and desperation. "She knows what's going on, but she can't find her way out of there. If I

318 • JAMIE A. WATERS

don't do this, what happens to her then? Are you prepared to lose your daughter again?"

Seara blanched. Alarmed at Alec's words, Carl demanded, "What are you talking about?"

Alec ignored him, his gaze focused once more on Kayla. Seara looked up at Carl, her expression one of sympathy. "He wants to exchange energy. Her energy is chaotic, and she's only partially channeling it. If he reaches for her with his energy, he can stabilize her. The allure of sharing energy is strong enough that she should be able to find her way back."

Fury lit through Carl, and his insides churned like dark, angry skies ready to erupt. "Exchanging energy? As in claiming her? Isn't that what almost happened yesterday?"

Alec gritted his teeth. "I won't do it if I can help it. Seara, get them out of here for a few minutes."

"Like hell," Carl declared. "I'm *not* leaving, and you're *not* doing this to her."

Alec's eyes narrowed. "You don't have a choice. If I don't do this, there's a good chance she'll remain this way."

Seara put her hand on Carl's arm. "I don't like it, either, but he's right. We shouldn't have tried this without giving her more training. This is my fault as much as it is Alec's."

It wasn't what Carl wanted to hear. He might doubt Alec's intentions, but Seara's sincerity was indisputable. Seara's voice was soft as she added, "I know you care about her. This is necessary though. Do you want to wait outside?"

Carl shook his head. He might not be able to do anything to help her, but he wasn't going to leave the woman he'd grown to care so much about in the hands of someone like Alec.

Alec looked up at him, clearly irritated with his continued presence. "Fine. Stay if you want. Maybe a first-hand view of what you're dealing with will clear up some of your illusions."

Carl's jaw clenched in anger as Alec effectively dismissed

him, turning his attention back to Kayla while Carl was help-less except to watch.

————

KAYLA FLOUNDERED in the darkness and gasped as the life-line reached her. Alec's energy poured over her, and she felt the strong pull toward him. She instinctively channeled her energy back toward him. The moment it reached him, she felt herself once more become aware of her surroundings.

She opened her eyes to see his concerned face. Feeling as though she could get lost in the blue depths of his eyes, she reached up to touch his face tenderly. His energy ran through her, and she sent her own flow of energy back to him. Alec gave her an encouraging smile as he felt her energy become less chaotic and more purposeful.

"It's working," Seara whispered.

Kayla leaned forward and put her arms around Alec, wanting to be closer to him. The energy flow increased, and she washed her energy over him. He pulled back slightly and withdrew some of his energy. Alarmed, she increased her energy and felt him hesitate with longing for her.

"*I don't understand. I know you want me,*" she thought toward him in confusion.

"*I do,*" he admitted regretfully. "*I want to complete the connection with you more than anything else. But not like this. As it is, I believe we've already formed a small permanent bond.*"

She smiled at the thought. "*Then we should complete it.*"

He shook his head. "*Kayla, you have no idea how hard this is for me. I want you, but we can't do this under these conditions. I want you to be fully aware and willing when we finally claim one another.*"

Alec took a deep breath and withdrew the last of his energy from her. She whimpered at the lapse. He pulled her onto his lap and held her tightly.

Kayla continued channeling energy over him. He struggled against the nearly irresistible desire to return her energy. He thought toward her, *"Kayla, you need to pull back on your energy."*

"No," she refused, her eyes pleading with him. *"I know you want me as much as I want you. I'm aware and willing. I don't understand why you won't join with me."*

Kayla recognized Seara's voice in the background but ignored it, intent on convincing Alec to join with her.

"Kayla won't break the connection. I don't know how much longer Alec can resist."

Carl frowned. "Why won't she break it?"

"It's instinctual," Seara explained in a hushed voice. "She hasn't grown up learning our ways, so she hasn't learned temperance. Alec is able to harness her energy. I suspect he's one of the few people who can. If he weren't as talented, she wouldn't have any hesitation in breaking the connection. But the fact he can match her strength is appealing to her."

"Is there anything I can do to help?"

"You could try talking to her," Seara suggested. "I don't know if she'll even be aware of you, but it's worth a try. Just don't touch her. I'm not sure how that will affect their connection."

Kayla was dimly aware of movement off to her side, but she wasn't willing to look away from Alec.

"Kayla, sweetheart, you need to break the connection. You don't want to do this."

Carl? At the sound of his voice, Kayla turned to look at him. The concern and longing in his gaze surprised her, and she started to reach out to him. Her energy flow faltered, and she felt Alec wince from the lapse. Her eyes immediately flew back to Alec. She realized she was hurting him from the withdrawal and started to increase the energy again.

Alec shook his head. *"No, Kayla, you have to stop. It's just like before. It'll hurt for a few minutes but it'll be okay. I'll still be here for you. One day, we will complete the connection, but the time isn't now."*

He leaned toward her and pressed his lips against hers in a promise. When he pulled away, she withdrew her energy from him. She felt his agony and yearning. It hurt her almost as much as it hurt him. He held her for a long moment, simply stroking her hair. Alec's voice was gentle when he said, "Break the connection now, Kayla."

Kayla nodded and pulled the threads of energy away from him, gasping at the sharp stab of emptiness where she had once felt completely connected. It seemed even more painful this time than it had been the previous day.

"It's because we have a more permanent bond now. Too much energy was exchanged. If we were fully bonded to one another, you wouldn't feel that pain."

She nodded and then looked over at Carl. His expression was full of agony. "I'm okay, Carl."

Holding out his hand to her, Carl helped her up. He yanked her to him and held her tightly as though he was afraid to let her go. Kayla wrapped her arms around him, resting her head against his chest. She'd scared him. Hell, she'd scared herself. She needed to try to make sense of her chaotic emotions, but she felt too raw.

Seara looked at Alec in concern. "Are you all right, Alec? I didn't think what you did was possible."

He stood and looked at Kayla and Carl in each other's arms. "I'm fine."

Kayla turned to look at Alec, feeling torn between the two men. She couldn't deny her feelings for both of them. They each represented something distinctly different. Carl was part of the world she had grown up knowing, whereas Alec touched her on a primal level she was strangely drawn to but didn't understand.

Alec gave her an understanding look. His thoughts touched her mind. "*I know you're torn, Kayla. I can be as patient as you need me to be.*"

Kayla swallowed and didn't answer. She turned to Seara. "Did it work? Is the bracelet deactivated?"

"Yes," Seara admitted and jingled the inert piece of jewelry on her wrist. "It's an ordinary bracelet now. But you two can't do that again. It's far too dangerous until you've been trained."

Kayla was about to object, but Alec stepped forward. "She's right, Kayla. I don't think either one of us can go through this again. It'll continue to be more painful."

Carl lifted his head, his grip tightening on Kayla's waist possessively. "Painful? It looked as though you were enjoying it well enough a few minutes ago when you were kissing her."

Alec regarded Carl with a look that would have sent most people running in fear. "You know absolutely nothing about us. Your ignorance is the only thing that makes your presence remotely tolerable."

Carl met Alec's look with one of his own. "And since you stepped in Kayla's life, you've done nothing but try to use her for your own means."

Alec's eyes narrowed, and he said in a dangerous voice, "You've crossed the line, Trader."

Carl released Kayla and took a step toward Alec. "So have you."

"Stop! Both of you," Kayla said in frustration. "Carl, Alec didn't do anything wrong." At Alec's smug expression, she added, "And Alec, stop baiting him." She looked back and forth between them. "We have enough to worry about without having to worry about your egos. If you two are determined to have this out and kick each other's asses, fine. But leave me out of it. I don't feel like dealing with this crap."

She gave them both an irritated look and stormed out of the room.

———

SEARA SMILED in amusement at the surprised looks on Carl and Alec's faces. "Excuse me. I'm going to join my daughter."

Carl and Alec turned to glare at each other once again. Cruncher cleared his throat. "Well, that was exciting. If I wasn't awake before, I am now. Anyone want some breakfast?"

Carl ignored him, focusing on Alec. "I don't know what sort of mind games you're playing with Kayla, but this needs to end. She doesn't belong to you. If you hope to change that by creating some sort of mental connection with her, you're wrong. It won't happen."

Alec looked at Carl with contempt. "You are an outsider and oblivious to our ways. Let me be clear so you don't misunderstand. Kayla has always belonged to me and she always will. She may believe she cares for you, and on some level that might even be true, but don't delude yourself into thinking you'll ever be more than a distraction to her."

Carl's fists itched to wipe the smug expression off Alec's face. The only thing that stayed his hand was his knowledge Alec didn't truly understand Kayla. Trying to possess someone like her was like trapping sunlight in a jar. "Have you tried telling Kayla she belongs to you? I guarantee she'll set the record straight."

Alec looked amused. "I don't need to tell her. On some level, she already knows. The only reason we're not fully bonded at this moment is because I refused. One day soon she'll come to me again and ask me to claim her. I won't refuse again."

Reason left him. Carl leaped forward toward Alec. He'd

kill him if he touched Kayla again. Cruncher grabbed him, holding him back while Carl struggled against his grip.

"Boss, he's an Omni. Come on, man. Don't do this."

"At least your crew has some sense," Alec said coolly and walked out of the room.

Carl jerked away from Cruncher and punched the wall in frustration. He paced back and forth, furious for losing control and letting Alec get the upper hand. Cruncher rubbed his chin. "Look, the guy's an ass, but I'm not sure this is the best way to handle it."

"I'll tell you how I'd *like* to handle it," Carl fumed.

"I bet." Cruncher clapped his hand on Carl's shoulder. "A day or two more and we'll be out of here. I have a hunch Kayla's going to be coming with us regardless of what happens here. You have to keep it together until then."

Carl ran his hands over his face. He just hoped she was still willing to leave after everything that happened with Alec a few minutes ago. He couldn't get that damn kiss out of his head. "Yeah, that's what she said this morning."

"There you go then. He's not worth it, man. Taking him on will only end badly for us."

"Shit, Cruncher, what the hell is wrong with me?"

Cruncher chuckled. "My guess? You've got it bad for our little dark-haired firebrand."

Carl rested his hands on the table and sighed. When it came to Kayla, he seemed to lose all sense of reason, and logic flew out the window. "Yeah, I do. I don't know what the hell I'm doing anymore."

"My advice is to ignore him. Kayla's going to do what she's going to do. But she had a point. This guy is trying to bait you. Don't let him get to you."

Carl frowned. "You're right. Dammit, you're right."

"So how about that breakfast?" Cruncher grinned and lifted a brow.

"Yeah, sure. Why the hell not?" He didn't need to leave Alec alone with Kayla any longer than necessary.

———

KAYLA FELT Alec approach behind her, but she didn't turn. Wrapping her arms over her chest, she tried to rub away the chill. She should be glad about what they'd accomplished with Seara's bracelet, but she couldn't help but wonder at the cost. She'd spent so much of her life simply trying to survive; she'd never had to think about the consequences before.

Alec took her elbow and turned her toward him. She looked away, unwilling to meet his eyes.

"There's nothing to be ashamed of," he said in a low voice.

She didn't reply, pressing a finger to her lips, thinking about the kiss they shared. Was it shame? Maybe in part. After all, she'd practically thrown herself at Alec—again. It wasn't fair to either Alec or Carl. But she was more confused than anything else. It seemed the more confused she became, the more she wanted to retreat. Running off and forming her own camp was still looking like an attractive alternative.

Carl and Cruncher emerged from the safe room, the door sliding shut behind them. She didn't want to deal with another altercation. Looking up, her eyes locked with Carl's. He hesitated for a moment, and Kayla thought he'd come over to her as Alec had. Instead, he turned to the table and had a seat with the rest of the crew. Her mouth curved in a small smile. They may not share a connection, but he always seemed to know what she needed, and she loved him for it.

Love? She paused, testing the word out in her head and it felt... right. She didn't need an energy bond with him to know how she felt about him. She loved him.

Before Kayla could assess her feelings further, the door

chimed, silencing all conversations in the room. Seara looked at Alec in alarm.

He shook his head. "I don't know, Seara. My guess is my father."

Alec reached out to Kayla with his thoughts. "*I'll protect you as best I can.*"

Kayla nodded at him. Seara went to the door, nervously twisting the bracelet around her wrist. She reappeared a moment later with Edwin, Director Borshin, and Cessel.

Edwin looked around at Carl's crew with disapproval. "Seara, your choice of company is proving rather questionable."

Seara lifted her chin and gestured to the crew with a regal sweep of her hand. "These are my daughter's friends, Edwin. They are welcome here as long as they'd like. That is, unless the High Council plans on interfering in more of my personal matters."

Edwin's mouth twitched slightly. "I understand your daughter has agreed to cooperate with us. I've brought Cessel to administer a blood test to determine if she's stable enough to have the bracelet equipped."

Cessel stepped forward, his movements stiff and wary. "My apologies, Mistress Rath'Varein. This will only take a moment."

"*Go ahead,*" Alec instructed her. "*Whatever happens, follow my lead. If we're lucky, your system won't be stable enough for the bracelet yet. Otherwise, I'll need you to play along with me.*"

Kayla stepped forward, masking her apprehension, and pressed her thumb against the testing device. A moment later, the monitor beeped. Cessel looked down at the display. "She's stable. We can fit her for the bracelet now."

"Excellent," Edwin declared, rubbing his hands together. "Kayla, go with Cessel and Director Borshin. It shouldn't take more than an hour."

Kayla's gaze darted to Alec, seeking guidance. He didn't look at her, his focus on his father. "I demand my right to appeal this decision before the High Council."

Edwin looked mildly surprised at his son's objection. "On what grounds?"

"It's my intent to claim this woman," he declared in a formal voice. "I have been given an exemption from wearing the bracelet due to the nature of my talents. Any claim on her could be compromised if she wears the device."

Seara muffled a gasp at the announcement.

Edwin's eyes narrowed, and he demanded, "Just what sort of game are you playing, Alec?"

Alec regarded his father and moved to stand beside Kayla. He linked his arm with hers, a show of solidarity. "There is no game. She has asked me to claim her twice now. The claim has not yet been completed, but it is my intention to do so."

Edwin perused Kayla slowly as though assessing the validity of Alec's words. She leaned closer to Alec, hoping he knew what he was doing. "Very well. The High Council is meeting in an hour to discuss the final trader bid this evening. You may present your argument then."

Kayla felt Alec tense beside her, and he shook his head. "That is insufficient. I require additional time to properly prepare for an appeal."

Edwin regarded his son in annoyance, his patience clearly at an end. "Your request is denied. You have one hour. If the High Council does not grant your appeal, I will see her outfitted with the bracelet by the end of the day."

Edwin motioned for Director Borshin and Cessel to follow him and headed for the door. When they had left, Kayla turned back to Alec. "What's this about an appeal?"

Alec sighed and took Kayla's hand. He led her back to the safe room so he could explain without worrying about their conversation being monitored. Seara, Carl, and Veridian followed them.

When the safe room door closed and security had been enabled, he said, "I was trying to buy us some time. We aren't in a position where we can directly challenge the High Council. There's no way we can safely deactivate the rest of the bracelets."

"Okay, so I just go in there, tell them I want you to claim me, and they drop this crazy bracelet nonsense? That sounds easy enough."

"I'm afraid not. They'll ask several questions, and you won't be able to lie to them. They have security features set up in the room that can detect if you're lying. The safest approach is to give them as little information as possible while remaining honest."

Seara looked at Kayla and added, "That's not all. By doing this, you're formally announcing your intention to allow Alec to claim you. It's essentially like an engagement, only more intricate."

The testosterone level in the room shot up. The look in Carl's eyes was murderous. "Engaged? Why not help us get her out of the towers?"

"I know my father. He'll throw every last resource into hunting her down. He got a taste of what Kayla is capable of doing, and he wants it for himself. I'll do whatever is necessary to keep Kayla from wearing the bracelet."

Seara frowned. "As much as I hate to admit it, Alec is right. Edwin's fixated on Kayla. He's not going to let up. As it is, there's a good chance he'll push for this appeal to be denied."

"Well, shit," Kayla muttered. This whole situation kept getting better and better.

Alec turned to look at her and said quietly, "Kayla, I'm

not trying to force you into anything. If there were another option, I would do it, but we're running out of time."

Kayla nodded, her gaze falling on Carl. The hurt and frustration in his eyes wounded her, but she didn't see any alternatives. Even if she ran, the backlash could affect Carl and everyone in his camp. She couldn't let that happen. They'd put everything on the line for her, risking themselves and their livelihood, to rescue her from the towers. At least if she did this, she could protect them from that.

"Do you mind if I have a minute alone with Carl?"

Alec inclined his head. "Very well. I'll be in the living area. We'll need to leave soon if we're going to do this though."

When they were gone, Kayla turned to face Carl. He put his arms around her and drew her close, pressing his forehead against hers. She clung to him, relishing in the security his arms offered. "This doesn't change the way I feel about you, Carl. I'm just doing this to save my ass."

"I know." His voice was hoarse as though the words pained him.

"I told you before that I never told Pretz I loved him," she admitted, touching Carl's face with her fingertips. She wished she could stay in his arms forever. "I don't want to make the same mistake again."

"What are you saying?"

Her eyes softened as she looked up at him. It was time to let go of the past and consciously reach toward a future. No matter what happened, she wanted that future to be with Carl. He'd been her anchor, grounding her when she needed a reality check, protecting her when her impulsiveness got her into trouble, and forcing her to consider possibilities she'd tried to ignore.

He wasn't perfect. Far from it. He was cocky, arrogant, and probably one of the most devious people she'd ever met. But he'd also touched her in a way she never thought possible. She might go through with this plan of Alec's, but she wouldn't do it without telling Carl how much he meant to her. Gathering her courage, Kayla poured everything she felt into three little words.

"I love you."

Carl froze, and then his arms tightened around her. "I love you too, Kayla."

Her heart fluttered, and he lowered his head, capturing her lips with his. She felt herself get lost in his kiss and the tenderness of his touch. On some level, she recognized she wouldn't be able to share the same sort of connection with him that she did with Alec, but she didn't care. Right now, this is what she wanted, and the energy stuff could go to hell.

He ended the kiss with a look of regret. "You should probably go. You need to arrive with Alec. I'll bring Veridian, Xantham, and Cruncher with me to the meeting. We can talk more when we get back."

Kayla ran her fingers lightly across his chest. "I'll hold you to that."

He let her go, and they went back into the living area. Alec looked up when they entered. "You're ready?"

When Kayla nodded, Seara stood up. "I'm going with you too. As your mother, it's my right to be present during the appeal."

"All right," Kayla agreed.

She gave Carl one last look before Alec led her to the door. Once they were outside, Alec took her hand in his while Seara followed behind them. She could sense Alec's irritation and realized he knew what had happened in the safe room. He was trying to dampen his emotions so she wouldn't pick up on them. She bit her lip, wishing there was a way to ease his hurt.

Alec squeezed her hand and thought toward her, *"It's all right, Kayla. I understand."*

He led her toward the priority elevator and they stepped inside. Alec keyed in the code to give them access to the top of the towers and explained, "The High Council meeting hall is on one of the top levels. It's above where we had dinner when you first arrived."

Kayla took a deep breath when the elevator door slid open. Several people stood in the hall watching their approach with interest. Alec ignored them and led her to the double doors of the meeting hall.

It was a large room with a broad, semicircle-shaped table serving as the main focal point at the head of the room. Numerous rows of seating were set up facing the table. Several seats were already occupied.

Alec walked down the aisle with Kayla on his arm and turned down the row closest to the front of the room. This area was roped off, and he pressed his thumb against a small panel. The rope retracted, and the three of them stepped through and took their seats.

"The hall is open to the public and broadcast to everyone during trader bids. The High Council will listen to the trader bids first, and then we'll be called up to appeal. Be honest, say as little as possible, and we'll get through this. I won't leave your side."

Kayla nodded, resisting the urge to squirm in her seat. A chime sounded, and people began filing inside the room. She glanced around, realizing she was sitting in some sort of priority area. The general population and many other Inner Circle members sat behind her. Her back straightened, and she shifted a bit closer to Alec, feeling the weight of several curious stares on her.

After several minutes, the High Council entered the room and took their seats at the table in the front. A handful of the chairs remained empty, and she silently asked Alec about it.

"The High Council hasn't been full in years. Only certain lineages

are permitted a place in the High Council. They accept one person from each family and it's usually a lifetime commitment."

Kayla studied the members of the Council. Each one carried himself with an air of authority, but most were much older than Alec and closer to Edwin's age. It was difficult to imagine him sitting up there. *"Carl said you're next in line for the High Council. How is that possible if your father is already on the Council?"*

"My mother was the last of her family's line. She was killed in the ruins with your father. With the shortage of High Council members, they're planning on appointing me to the Council as a representative of her family's line within a few weeks."

Kayla was distracted when Edwin stood to address the room. He welcomed everyone, introduced each of the High Council members, and explained the final trader bidding process. The two traders would receive fifteen minutes to state their case and qualifications before engaging in a brief question-and-answer session. Based on their responses, the High Council would make a determination and announce their final decision that evening.

"This is just a formality," Alec explained. *"They've already made their decisions."*

Milo stepped up to the podium first. Kayla resisted rolling her eyes as he detailed his qualifications and expertise. There was no question about his intelligence, she just doubted he possessed the skills to handle living on the surface.

When the question-and-answer session began, Kayla sighed when he stumbled awkwardly through the questions. Based on the reactions of the other council members, Kayla figured it was pretty safe to guess Rand had this nailed.

After Milo stepped off the platform, Rand took his place. Kayla leaned forward intently, curious to hear what he had to say. He rattled off his qualifications and experience, and then the High Council began interviewing him.

Kayla recognized Keith from dinner the night before as one of the High Council members conducting the questions. "There's been a question recently introduced about whether formal training in our pre-war history is relevant to the trader position. What are your thoughts on this matter?"

Rand paused for a moment before answering. "It is, but only to a degree. Studying history gives us a strong foundation regarding our past, but more importantly, it gives us a better understanding of human nature. I recently had the honor of meeting someone who used to live in one of the surface camps. She shared some of her experiences with me. It quickly became apparent that some skill in social engineering, diplomacy as well as formal training in core subjects, is necessary to succeed in this appointment. Only with these skills will we be able to bridge the rift between the traders and the surface camps so everyone benefits."

"And do you believe you have these skills?"

Rand smiled and winked at Kayla in the audience. "I do. Otherwise, I wouldn't be standing here before you at this moment."

Kayla bit back a smile. One of the other council members asked a general question, and Rand neatly responded. He handled himself better than she'd expected, replying confidently to each of the remaining questions before finally stepping off the platform.

Edwin announced, "Thank you for your responses. We'll confer with one another, and the official announcement of the trader appointment will be made this evening."

He paused, his eyes resting on Alec and Kayla as he said in a loud voice, "The next order of business involves an appeal of the issuance of a security bracelet to an Inner Circle member. Will the appellants please step forward?"

Kayla's heart pounded. Alec held out his arm for her, and they walked to the front of the room. She noticed the whispers and shocked looks when the audience recognized them. They stepped up on the podium, and Kayla felt a trickle of energy around them. She realized this was what Alec meant by not being able to lie—they had somehow erected some sort of truth barrier.

Edwin leaned forward. "Please go ahead with your argument when you're ready."

Alec's gaze swept the room before formally addressing the High Council. "My name is Master Alec Tal'Vayr, member of the Inner Circle and applicant to the High Council. The woman beside me is Mistress Kayla Rath'Varein, member of the Inner Circle and daughter of Andrei Rath'Varein, former leader of the High Council."

He paused for a moment, and Kayla was acutely aware he commanded the attention of everyone in the room. "In support of our endeavors to acquire additional resources, many Inner Circle members are wearing bracelets to pool their combined energy. Due to the nature of my talents, it was previously determined by the High Council that I should be exempt from participation in this energy pool."

Many members of the High Council nodded in agreement. Alec continued, "I formally declare it is my intention to claim Mistress Kayla Rath'Varein as my wife and partner. As such, I ask that she also be exempt from this request."

Many people in the audience gasped at this news. Kayla could see the shocked expressions of many of the High Council members. *Wife? Oh, shit. Seara wasn't kidding.*

The reality of the words made her want to bolt. As though sensing her panic, Alec gave her hand a reassuring squeeze.

Keith rapped the desk to bring everyone's attention back to him. "She didn't grow up learning our ways. Does she even understand what this means?"

"She does," Alec replied confidently. "I have explained it

to her. Her mother, Mistress Seara Rath'Varein, has also explained it to her."

"You haven't known her more than a few days," someone else argued. Kayla recognized him as Marcus, one of the dinner companions from the previous night. " How can you be sure you're compatible?"

Alec smiled at the question. "When Kayla was born, it was our parents' intention we eventually marry and the Rath'-Varein and Tal'Vayr families merge together. As far as compatibility is concerned, we have already determined our energy levels are highly compatible. A bond has already been formed, it just has not yet been completed."

Several of the council members looked shocked by this news, and Edwin leaned forward and demanded, "Calson, verify this so-called bond."

Kayla could sense Alec's annoyance when a middle-aged man with dark hair stood. He left the council table and walked toward Kayla and Alec, holding out his hands to each of them.

Kayla looked at Alec questioningly, and he nodded. They each placed one of their hands in Calson's, and the man closed his eyes for a moment. Kayla felt his energy float around her and Alec. She didn't like it but resisted the urge to pull her hand away.

After a few moments, he opened his eyes and turned to Edwin. "There is definitely a bond. As Alec indicated, the bond is not complete, but it is there. Even now, there's an energy connection established between them."

Edwin frowned at the news and studied the two of them. "Kayla, you've been silent during this appeal. I can't help but wonder if this is an elaborate ruse to get out of your duty as an Inner Circle member?"

Kayla hesitated, cognizant of the lie detector field pulsing around them. She may not be able to lie, but misdirection was

336 • JAMIE A. WATERS

part of the life of a ruin rat. She lifted her chin to meet Edwin's gaze, refusing to let him intimidate her. The man was nothing but a bully and had been using his position to take advantage of innocent people just like Ramiro. "Elaborate ruse? I've been in these towers for less than two days. During that time, I've been attacked, imprisoned, and hunted down."

Alec shot her a warning look, but she ignored him, focusing solely on Edwin. "Alec, with the exception of my mother, is the only member of the Inner Circle who's tried to do what's in my best interest. If you're asking if this is a ruse, I'll tell you this much: I don't want that damn bracelet on me. You use those things to imprison the Inner Circle and force them to your will without regard for anyone else."

Several members of the High Council looked nervously at Edwin. His eyes narrowed, and he warned, "Those are dangerous accusations to be making."

He was probably right, but after everything she'd been through over the last few days, Kayla wasn't going to stand by and let some big shot Omni dictate to her. Someone needed to stand up to him. If this meeting was being broadcast throughout the towers, all the better. "Don't piss me off, Edwin. I'm running out of places to put the bodies."

"So this entire charade has been nothing more than an elaborate attempt to avoid doing your duty for the people of these towers? You don't intend to allow Alec to claim you?"

Kayla glared at him. As far as she was concerned, it wasn't any of his or the Council's business who she slept with. Unfortunately, telling them that wouldn't help get her out of the current situation.

"I've asked Alec to claim me twice, and he's refused twice because he wants to make sure I fully understand what I'm asking." There. That was honest and yet, in true ruin rat fashion, she'd dodged the question. Kayla tossed her hair back, not finished making her point.

"As far as the people in these towers are concerned, and for all the people who live outside of these towers, I've always been willing to help." On her terms, but he didn't need to know that. "I'll do whatever is necessary to protect these people. But your methods suck ass, and forcing people to wear those stupid bracelets so you can get your little power trip is out of line."

"Enough," Edwin hissed, and the vein in his temple throbbed. "This is a public forum. Your accusations have no basis in fact."

Seara stood, holding up her wrist to display the bracelet to the entire forum. She moved toward the front of the room and announced, "My name is Mistress Seara Rath'Varein, and my daughter is correct. For the past nine months, the Inner Circle has been imprisoned. What started as an attempt to locate resources for the people of this tower has turned into a power play by some of the members of the High Council, namely Edwin Tal'Vayr."

The audience gasped in shock. Edwin reached into his pocket, fumbling for something. His head jerked when Seara didn't react. "What's wrong, Edwin? Your leash isn't working?"

She turned back to the audience, gesturing to Kayla. "My daughter has discovered a way to remove these bracelets. Earlier today, my bracelet was deactivated. To my fellow Inner Circle members, if you stand with us now, your bracelets can also be removed. It's time we returned to our old ways and use our skills collaboratively to locate new resources."

Several members of the Inner Circle stood. A man called out, "Is it true, Seara? She can remove them?"

Seara nodded. "Yes, Fredo. Edwin Tal'Vayr no longer has the power to control me."

As the din of voices in the audience grew louder and more

agitated, Alec's shoulders tensed, and he shot Kayla a worried look. *"Connect with me now. This may get ugly."*

Kayla did as he asked and connected all of her threads of energy to Alec. He asked her to send a large stream of energy to him. She watched in amazement as he forged a powerful shield around them.

Edwin looked at Kayla in shock. "You deactivated the bracelet?"

"Yes, and I intend to deactivate *all* of the bracelets. No one should have that sort of power over another person. If the Inner Circle wants to use their talents to help the towers, they should be given the option. You have no right to make the decision for them."

"I have every right as the leader of the High Council," Edwin sneered. "And as for you, your appeal is denied. Take her into custody and have her equipped with a bracelet."

Some of the other council members looked alarmed, shifting in their seats uncomfortably. Keith pushed up from his seat and held up his hand to stop the security officers from approaching. "Edwin, our laws clearly state we have to vote on whether or not the appeal is denied."

"Forget it," Edwin declared, banging his fist on the table. He turned to the rest of the Council members, some nodding at Keith's objections while a few others seemed to support Edwin's ruling. The remaining few looked apprehensive about the entire discussion but not willing to take a side yet. "This woman is a nuisance and threatens the towers. The bracelets were implemented to discover untapped resources. She's threatening our existence with her claims and causing dissention amongst our people."

Kayla blinked. She'd been blamed for a lot in her life, but this was a little much. Before she could formulate a reply, Seara spoke up on her behalf. "You're wrong, Edwin. Your intentions may have been honorable in the beginning, but you've taken away our people's free will. We should be given a choice about how our abilities are used. Kayla can help us correct the mistake."

Edwin glanced at Kayla, and she felt a suffocating pulse of energy press against the wall of the shield. Her eyes widened. She'd known he might try something, but she never dreamed he'd attack her in front of the entire room.

Alec squeezed her hand, reminding her she wasn't alone. *"Keep the flow constant, if you can. We'll need to maintain the shields. If he takes you out of the equation, he can bring the room back under his control."*

When the shield didn't crumble, Edwin's focus turned to Alec. Kayla had a sinking feeling in her stomach. Awareness and betrayal flickered in his eyes as his nostrils flared. He'd realized Alec was shielding her, and it only seemed to ignite his fury. Kayla flinched as another attack pulsed against the shield, stronger than the last. She gripped Alec's hand tighter, increasing the energy flow she was sending him to reinforce the weaker areas of the shield.

Some of the other council members stood in concern, realizing what was transpiring. Keith turned to the Council leader. "Edwin, what are you doing? This isn't how we handle things."

Enraged, Edwin ignored him and reached into his pocket. Kayla looked at Alec, and he warned her, *"He's tapping into the pooled energy now."*

Kayla closed her eyes, gathering up the loose energy around her. She channeled it toward Alec and reached for more. Loose energy floated throughout the room. Kayla grabbed at it and pushed it toward Alec.

Someone cried out in the audience, but Kayla couldn't stop to look behind her to see what was happening. Two of the Council members—a sharp-eyed, middle-aged woman and a younger man with a sculpted face—moved to stand next to Edwin and linked arms. The woman's face was blank and emotionless as she whispered something and then placed her hand on Edwin's shoulder.

The push on the shield became even more powerful, and Kayla felt Alec falter trying to maintain the defense even with the additional energy she supplied. Someone moved next to her, and she heard Seara's soft voice telling her to take what she needed. A warm hand slipped into hers as a rush of cool energy passed through her.

Understanding what she offered, Kayla reached out and threaded Seara's energy through to Alec. He wove it into the shield, struggling to keep it up against Edwin's continued assault. It still wasn't enough. Thinking quickly, Kayla moved her hand to Seara's bracelet. Even though it was deactivated, it could still act as a link to the energy pool. If Edwin was going to use it against them, she might as well try to even the playing field.

Alec realized what she was doing. *"Kayla, don't. It's too dangerous."*

"I can do this," she replied, trying to project a confidence she didn't quite feel. Edwin was too strong, and Alec couldn't keep up his shield forever. She had to do something.

She followed the energy patterns back through the bracelet until she reached the energy pool. Energy swirled around her, and she felt the link to dozens of people who wore the bracelets. Edwin was burning through their energy at an alarming rate, and she had to act quickly.

Kayla followed the energy channels and found Edwin's source. She gathered all the loose energy within the pool and directed it to the source. A brilliant white light flashed in her mind, and there was a deafening cracking noise.

Kayla staggered as Edwin's source burst apart. Loose energy floated around her chaotically as her world turned dark.

CHAPTER TWENTY

THE ENTIRE FORUM was in an uproar. Alec caught Kayla as she started to collapse. He looked up and saw Carl pushing through the throng of people to get to them. Alec pushed her toward him. "Stay with her. This isn't finished yet."

Alec stood as chaos erupted around them. Someone from the audience shouted, "The bracelets have been broken!"

Edwin staggered and leaned against the table for support, squinting and rubbing his temples. A mixture of shock and rage was plastered on his face as he realized he no longer had the ability to tap into the energy pool.

Alec scanned the room. Something needed to be done to take control of the situation or people might break out into a riot. Most of the Council members still seemed dazed by the energy feedback from the destruction of the bracelets. Seara met his gaze and seemed to come to the same conclusion. She stepped up on the platform, raising her hands for attention. Her voice cut across the room as she announced, "As the head of House Rath'Varein, I claim my right to a seat on the High Council."

342 · JAMIE A. WATERS

The announcement was enough to quiet down most of the audience.

"You?" Edwin mocked, recovering from the blast. "You know nothing about the politics in this tower, Seara. You're nothing but arm candy for those who actually get things done."

His words didn't seem to faze her. "That's where you're wrong, Edwin. I admit I've been blinded by grief, allowing you to lead the High Council and watching while you ran these towers nearly into the ground. For that, I appeal to the people of the tower for forgiveness. But my passivity is at an end. I will not watch you abuse and manipulate these people any longer."

Keith hesitated and rubbed his temples, looking at the angry faces in the audience. "Edwin, if she claims it, it's her family's right."

Alec couldn't resist a smug smile when several of the other council members nodded in agreement. With the volatile Inner Circle members in the room no longer being controlled by the bracelets, the High Council was backpedaling fast.

Edwin glared at Keith. "Absolutely not. As the leader of the High Council, I reject her claim."

"You have no right to reject my claim, Edwin. You are merely a facilitator. The rules and the laws have always been clear. There is a seat for each of the families who founded these towers."

Marcus stood and gestured to an empty chair. "Your acceptance is enough, Seara. Your position on the High Council is acknowledged."

She inclined her head. "As the newest member of the High Council, my first request is that a formal inquiry be made into Master Edwin Tal'Vayr's activities. It is my belief he is no longer fit to lead the High Council."

Edwin's face lit with fury. Alec had seen that expression

before and it boded nothing good. He quickly reinforced the shield to include Seara too. Without Kayla's energy, he was uncertain how long it would hold. Edwin sent another large burst of energy toward the shield, and Alec winced. In a voice low enough only Seara could hear, he said, "Seara, I don't know how long I can maintain the shield. I'm using what energy I can to keep my connection with Kayla active, but she's slipping even further away."

Seara nodded in acknowledgment and whispered, "Break the shield and go to Kayla. I'll handle Edwin."

Alec stepped off the platform and knelt beside Carl, who was unsuccessfully trying to revive Kayla. Edwin sent another assault toward Alec's shield, and Alec felt it weaken even more.

As his shield fell away, Seara quickly wove a wall of energy around Edwin. Even from several feet away, Alec could sense Edwin's energy pummel against hers. Seara wasn't as skilled in defensive maneuvers, and he cursed the fact she'd always preferred the more nurturing aspects of energy channeling.

Another large burst of energy erupted from Edwin and hit one of the weaker areas of Seara's shield. It tore through her defenses, and she cried out as pain lanced through her.

Keith jumped to his feet, rushing forward to intervene. "Edwin, stop! We do *not* attack other High Council members. You're behaving irrationally. Seara has the right to a formal inquiry."

Edwin grabbed the man, unleashing a powerful blast of energy that sent residual waves throughout the room. Keith's eyes widened in horror, his hesitation and shock at Edwin's attack delaying his reaction. The full force of the impact hit him, and he was helpless to defend against it. With a stran-gled gasp, he collapsed in Edwin's grip.

Like a connoisseur appreciating a fine wine, Edwin inhaled deeply as Keith's lingering energy flowed into himself.

Once he'd finished savoring the effects, he released the man, letting his lifeless body slump to the ground.

"I will not tolerate my orders being countermanded. This woman—this entire family—has done nothing but hold us back." Edwin raised his head and snapped his fingers at the security officials standing around the room. Up to this point, they'd been focused on keeping the audience in their seats. "Security! Take Seara and Kayla into custody immediately."

Alec knew his father was power-hungry and irrational at times, but he'd never before seen the madness in his eyes. The other High Council members gasped and looked at each other uneasily, sensing the same thing. No one seemed willing to step up after seeing what happened to Keith.

Alec glanced down at Kayla, feeling humbled for the first time in his life. Not only had she sacrificed escaping the towers to try to break the shackles binding the Inner Circle, but she'd stood before the entire room and faced his father head-on. He'd felt her fear, but she'd pushed it aside and focused on accomplishing her goals with unrelenting determination.

She didn't know any of them nor did she owe them any loyalty. They'd assumed she'd perished in the ruins with everyone else and written her off. He'd seen Carl's reports and the interviews with Ramiro's crew. He knew what she'd suffered at the hands of OmniLab her entire life, yet she was able to put all of that aside and try to protect them.

Alec looked up at each of the High Council members. Shame filled him. They were all cowards, even him. Each one of them could have taken a stand a long time ago, but they'd all stood back, smug in their own superiority and egocentricities. Alec's jaw clenched in determination, and he turned to face the approaching security officials.

With a sharp energy blast designed to stun, he knocked

them away from Kayla's unconscious form. "If you lay a hand on her, I'll kill each and every one of you."

Turning to face his father, his eyes narrowed. "You've gone too far. Seara and Kayla have done nothing wrong. Kayla had the opportunity to leave the towers but remained here to free the Inner Circle. She didn't grow up knowing any of us, but her bloodline is true. She risked everything to reverse the prison you've created. You're the one holding us back, not the Rath'Varein family."

"So you intend to betray your own father?" Edwin roared, knocking a pitcher of water off the desk. "I should have let you go down into those ruins with your mother and Andrei Rath'Varein. We were well rid of those easily manipulated fools when the ruins collapsed."

Seara's hand flew to her heart, and she stared at him in horror. "You had them killed, didn't you? My husband? Your wife?"

Edwin's eyes turned hard and his words were clipped, edged with bitterness. "You were supposed to have gone with them to the ruins that day with Andrei, not Catherine. Your husband was destroying these towers with his passivity. He knew our time was running out, and we needed to employ drastic measures to keep OmniLab viable. When he refused to listen to reason and step aside, I did what was necessary to ensure our survival."

Tears streaked down Seara's face. "He was your *friend*, Edwin. Some of the greatest minds and powers our kind has ever seen were in those ruins."

Several of the other Inner Circle members who had been previously imprisoned by the bracelets pushed forward to the front of the room. An elderly woman stepped forward and motioned for the other Inner Circle members to join hands.

The woman turned to Alec, her face wrinkled with age,

and offered her hand. "My son was in those ruins along with your mother. Our energy is yours."

He took her hand, accepting the weight of her pronouncement. Seara joined hands with the other Inner Circle members and gave him an encouraging nod. A few of the High Council members also moved away from Edwin and went to stand beside Seara.

"Stand down," Alec ordered Edwin. "The Inner Circle is united."

"You're a fool," Edwin sneered.

Alec felt his father gathering energy, and he felt his hopes for a peaceful resolution fade. Strengthened by the support of the people standing beside him, he channeled the Inner Circle's energy in response and crafted a reverse shield around Edwin. Edwin's eyes narrowed as the shield tightened around him. The shield might stop mental attacks, but not physical ones. Edwin stepped forward toward his son.

"You dare," he hissed, raising his hand as though to strike.

Before he could make contact, Alec grabbed his arm with his free hand. "I'm sorry, Father, but those people, including my mother, deserved to live."

Alec channeled an enormous burst of energy toward his father. Edwin's eyes widened in shock and he staggered. Alec gripped him tighter, forcing the energy into him. Edwin clutched his chest and fell backward. Alec didn't relent and kept channeling the energy long after his father was still.

"Alec..." Seara's voice broke through, and he pulled back. He stared down at his trembling hands, the reality of what he'd done crashing over him. He'd acted as the hand of justice, judging and executing without even a hearing. A hush fell over the room when they realized the High Council leader had been killed.

He looked up, afraid of what he would find on the faces

surrounding him. He expected to see recrimination, but most were full of understanding, support, and even gratitude.

Seara put her arm around him, offering him a comfort he wasn't sure he deserved. "You did the right thing, Alec. But please, Kayla needs you."

Alec immediately reached for the connection he shared with Kayla. It was even weaker now. His hands shook as he went back to Kayla and knelt beside her. He may have taken a life today, but he could save another. He wouldn't let her die.

———

MARCUS SHOOED everyone away to clear a space around Kayla. "Security! Clear the room immediately."

While the security officers scrambled to enforce his command, Carl relinquished his hold on Kayla. It pained him to let her go, but Alec had the best hope of reaching her. She'd been unresponsive since she collapsed, her breathing growing more and more shallow. Worry gripped him as he moved aside so Alec could assess her.

Seara hovered over them. "Is she all right?"

Alec shook his head, taking Kayla's hand in his. "She went into the energy pool and deactivated my father's source from there. I can still feel her, but it's faint. If she hears me at all, she isn't responding."

Carl frowned, reaching down to brush Kayla's hair away from her face. Her skin was cool and clammy to the touch. "Can you pull her out again like you did earlier?"

There was a long pause before Alec answered. "Yes, but the amount of energy required will most likely forge a complete bond with her."

Carl nodded. He'd expected no less. "But you'll be able to bring her back?"

"For what it's worth, I know she loves you."

Carl closed his eyes, lowering his chin to his chest in resignation. He'd rather see her with Alec than lose her forever. She deserved a chance to explore the possibilities life had to offer. He bent down, brushing his lips against hers. His voice was hoarse as he whispered, "Do whatever you have to do if it will bring her back."

———

KAYLA WAS FLOATING IN A NICE, fluffy cloud of nothingness. Time seemed suspended as she drifted in this spatial existence. She was dimly aware her physical form existed outside of the nothingness, but the link no longer seemed as important. It was becoming more difficult to tell where she began and ended. In all honesty, she wasn't sure she cared all that much.

A pleasant warmth teased the edge of her consciousness, bringing her back to a state of semi-awareness.

"That's nice. I didn't realize I was cold."

"Kayla, you need to come back now. Follow the stream back."

She recognized Alec's demanding voice, but wasn't sure she wanted to bother. Obeying his request seemed like more trouble than it was worth. She started to dismiss him, but a stronger pulse of energy washed over her, teasing and tempting as it flooded her senses.

Intrigued, Kayla basked in the promising flow of warm energy streaming over her. Wanting more, she instinctively returned a stream of energy in response.

"That's right," Alec encouraged gently.

She could feel him now, his thoughts and emotions growing more entwined with hers, but he was still too far away. Her stream of energy was clumsy and chaotic next to his, and she pulled back in frustration. She could sense him and wanted to merge their energies, but it was impossible to focus.

Kayla faltered, not knowing how to reach him. As though he sensed her despair, Alec's energy magnified until it became a brilliant display, penetrating and filling her with light. The beguiling warmth of his energy evoked a longing within her, demanding a response.

Captivated by the raw display of power, Kayla's stream of energy became more purposeful and she matched his intensity. She gathered all of the energy she was capable of holding and sent it toward him. When the two complete and intense energy forces collided, they blended and merged with one another.

Kayla watched in amazement as the darkness fell away. She was lost in a world of color and thought. She floated along Alec's stream of energy and felt the love and desire emanating from him. For the first time in her life, she felt complete and total acceptance.

She mirrored his thoughts and feelings. Opening her eyes, Kayla looked up into his brilliant blue ones. The tenderness in his gaze wrapped around her like a cocoon, offering comfort and understanding. Alec stroked her face, and she leaned into him, inhaling his rich, seductive scent. She reached for him, needing his touch as if it were an anchor.

"Welcome back, my love."

Kayla smiled up at him, tracing the contours of his face. The slight stubble of his jaw was rough against her fingers, and she marveled at the contrast of the softness of his mouth. She wanted to nibble along his jawline, tasting him until she reached his lips. Sensing her thoughts, his eyes dropped to her mouth, and she felt a sudden rush of desire from him.

"This is what it feels like to have a complete connection?"

"Yes. It takes harnessing all of our energy to form the complete bond."

Her fingers clutched his shirt, and she pulled him closer, wanting to feel the press of his skin against hers. *"I want you to touch me."*

A look of regret crossed his face. *"As do I, but our timing is bad. We're in a room full of people. But as soon as we're alone, you can explore all of these new feelings."*

"Make everyone go away."

He raised an eyebrow. *"We're in the High Council room, dear. Do you remember what happened?"*

Kayla frowned and looked around in confusion, trying to get a grip on her surroundings. Carl and Seara were both watching her anxiously. The room had mostly cleared out with only the remaining High Council and Inner Circle members who had been in attendance.

"I broke the bracelets," she whispered and sat up.

"Yes," Alec confirmed.

The security officials were removing Edwin and Keith's bodies from the room, and her eyes widened. "What happened?"

Alec stood and helped her up. "My father killed Keith. He was also responsible for the deaths of several others, including your father and my mother."

Kayla felt his agony as though it were her own and reached for him again. His hand threaded in her hair, and she felt his breath hitch. He pulled her close, wrapping his arms around her as she laid her head against his chest, offering solace.

There was a note of pity in Seara's voice as she said, "I'm sorry, Carl."

"I'm just glad she's okay."

Kayla turned at the sound of Carl's voice. Her heart lurched at the defeated look on his face. She looked back and forth between the two men, feeling torn. She recognized she still had intense feelings for Carl, but the allure and power pulling her toward Alec was strangely irresistible.

"A claim doesn't negate your feelings, Kayla," Alec explained softly.

Marcus stepped over to them, clearing his throat to get their attention. "I'm sorry to interrupt, but we're going to need all of you. We have quite a bit of damage control that needs to be done."

Alec nodded, taking Kayla's hand and leading the group back toward the platform where the High Council members were discussing how best to address the public. Kayla took a peek at Carl, wanting to go to him but not able to bear the thought of leaving Alec's side while he needed her.

Marcus turned to Alec. "We've all spoken and come to a decision. You were to be appointed to the High Council within the next few weeks based on your mother's family name. However, in the absence of a Tal'Vayr on the High Council, we offer you that position now."

Alec nodded. "I accept."

Marcus hesitated, glancing at some of the other members. "We no longer have a High Council leader. This position has always been held by either a Rath'Varein or a Tal'Vayr. Your families were the original founding members of OmniLab. It's only suitable for one of you to accept this responsibility."

Seara was quiet for a moment. "I have a suggestion."

Marcus and the other High Council members looked at her expectantly. "The position should be divided. No one person should have that sort of control over us again. Instead, I suggest both Alec and myself share the position of High Council leader. When the time comes for me to step down, I will turn my position over to my daughter. They will lead jointly."

Marcus looked at the other council members, who

nodded in agreement. He turned to Alec. "Is this agreeable to you?"

Alec looked down at Kayla and raised an eyebrow questioningly. Her eyes were wide, and she thought toward him, *"Oh, hell no. I'm still a ruin rat. I don't have any desire to lead this group of numbnuts."*

"You saved this group of 'numbnuts' by deactivating those bracelets. But don't worry. Your mother will lead until you're ready."

Giving her a reassuring squeeze, Alec turned back to Marcus. "Yes, I agree."

Marcus looked relieved and announced loudly, "It's official. Master Alec Tal'Vayr and Mistress Seara Rath'Varein will act as joint co-leaders of the High Council."

Muted applause erupted throughout the room, and several people offered their thanks and congratulations to them. Alec plastered on a smile, but Kayla knew it was a façade. She'd worn one long enough to recognize it even without his emotions filtering through her. The whole ordeal was bittersweet.

Marcus said, "Unfortunately, we still have the trader announcement this evening. You'll both be needed to make the announcement."

Seara inclined her head. "We'll be there."

Alec indicated his agreement before adding, "If you'll excuse me, though, I need to make arrangements for my father."

Marcus looked at him with sympathy. "I know it was difficult, Alec, but you did the right thing."

Alec managed a nod and then averted his gaze. He leaned close to Kayla. "Do you mind if we leave?"

She shook her head, putting her other hand on his arm. There weren't enough prototypes in the world to tempt her into staying. "I've wanted to leave this place since the moment you brought me here."

CHAPTER TWENTY-ONE

THEY WALKED BACK to the Rath'Varein quarters. After everyone had filed inside, Alec stopped Kayla at the entrance. "I need to make arrangements for my father. I'll be back in an hour or so."

Kayla looked up at him. "Do you want me to go with you?"

He gave her an appreciative smile. "Thank you, but you've done a great deal today. Why don't you relax for a bit before this evening? I know Carl wants to speak with you about what happened. It would probably be better to give you two some privacy."

Her throat went dry, her eyes darting nervously to the door. Once she went inside, everything would change. "I don't know what to say to him. I don't know what happened myself."

Alec's touch was a soothing balm as he caressed her face. "I know. He'll need to understand this is confusing for you." When she frowned, he added, "Kayla, you know how I feel about you. You've seen it for yourself. I can't say your relationship with Carl doesn't bother me, but I understand. You might be interested to know he was the one who told me to go ahead and complete the bond with you."

The news surprised her, and Kayla looked to the door again, wishing she could see inside his head. Why would he have done such a thing? There had been nothing but contention between him and Alec since the beginning.

Alec turned her back to face him. "He loves you, Kayla. He was willing to risk losing you to make sure you were going to be all right."

She inhaled sharply. The selflessness of Carl's actions floored her. He'd done nothing but protect her since the moment they met.

She looked up at Alec, trying to discern his motivation. "Why are you telling me this?"

He was quiet for a long moment. "I told you about Carl because I want you to resolve your feelings for him before you come to me. If you need more time, I understand. I'll support you no matter what you decide to do."

"Why are you being so understanding about this?"

He gave her a small smile, and she saw a glimpse of the familiar cockiness in his eyes. "Because, at the end of the day, I know you'll always come back to me. The bond between us is too strong and neither one of us will be able to resist it. Even if you decide to run off and leave the towers with him, you'll find dozens of excuses to come back."

The idea made her frown. Her first instinct was to pull back and deny it. She wouldn't allow herself to be ruled by some metaphysical bond. "Is that what it's going to be like?"

Alec ran his fingers along the side of her face. "When I touch you, you feel complete, don't you?"

She shivered and gave him a small nod, not comfortable with how much she enjoyed his touch. "That's because of the shared energy. The farther away you go, the more you'll feel its loss. That's not to say it's impossible to be apart, but you'll find yourself longing to be with me again."

Kayla hesitated, but she needed to be honest with him. "Alec, I don't know if I want to stay in the towers. My life and everything I've ever known is outside these walls. I don't want to give that up. When I'm in the ruins, it's like nothing I've ever felt before. I feel alive down there."

His look was one of infinite patience, and he gave her an understanding smile. "That's because you were using your energy without realizing it, Kayla. Do you feel alive when you're with me?"

"Well..." She considered the question, not sure if it was the same thing. She'd only known Alec for a handful of days, regardless of the intimacy they'd shared through their bond. When she was in the glow of an energy exchange with him, she felt more alive than she ever had. Each small touch from him evoked a promise of that powerful connection. "I don't know. Yeah, I guess. You're making my life more complicated. I don't know what's real anymore, but I know what I feel for Carl is real."

"You don't have to make a decision about anything right now, Kayla." Alec glanced up as a few people wandered down the hall, giving them curious looks. With a reluctant sigh, he pulled away from her. "I should go, but I'll be back soon."

Kayla nodded, not trusting herself to speak, and watched him walk away. Once he was gone, she let out a long exhale and went back inside her mother's quarters.

Everyone looked up when she entered. Uncomfortable with the stares, she managed a weak smile. "Quite a show, huh?"

Veridian frowned at her. "Are you really thinking about marrying him, Kayla?"

Panic, sharp and biting, flooded through her. She shook

her head. "Marriage? Me? Hell no. I'm not marrying anyone. I was just trying to keep that damn bracelet off me."

Veridian stood and gave her a hug. "I'm glad you're okay."

She hugged him back and then turned to Carl. Her palms were damp, and she rubbed them nervously on her dress. "Carl? Could I talk to you for a few minutes?"

He nodded and stood. Kayla felt everyone's gaze on them as they made their way toward her room. She heard Cruncher mutter, "She's either going to break his heart or make him incredibly happy."

Kayla stepped inside her bedroom and closed the door behind Carl. He remained silent and just watched her. She bit her lip and looked up into his brown eyes. A million things to say came into her mind, but nothing seemed appropriate, so she fell back on what worked.

She stepped close, putting her arms around him. Carl hesitated for a moment before resting his hands on her waist, keeping her in place. He shook his head, his movements stiff, and didn't make any other moves toward her. "Kayla, I don't understand what's going on with this whole energy thing."

"I don't either." The distance between them hurt, and she wanted to bridge the gulf. "Alec seems to be the only one who does."

At the mention of his name, Carl's face darkened. Kayla could see the turmoil in his expression as he asked, "So he's 'claimed' you now? What does that even mean?"

She wished she knew. As hard as it was for her, it had to be worse for him. She, at least, was a participant in the bond and could see the energy between them. Carl was trapped on the sidelines without any idea about what was going on. "I don't understand it. He said we're permanently linked now. I can leave the towers, but I'll always end up returning here because of him. I won't ever feel complete unless I'm with him."

"Is that true?"

She hoped not, but she didn't feel confident about it. "I don't know. I think so. Even now, I feel strange when he's not nearby. I don't understand it. I can still feel him, but it's just... not right. I don't know how else to describe it."

Carl released her. "So what happens now?"

Kayla shook her head and threw up her hands in frustration. "Carl, you know I suck at talking about this kind of thing." She dropped her hands, her shoulders slumping. She wished he could just look inside her and know. "My feelings for you haven't changed. I love you."

He hesitated, his fingers flexing as though he ached to touch her. The small action gave her hope. She didn't want to lose him. But then he asked, "How do you feel about Alec?"

"I don't know!" Frustration bubbled to the surface, and she paced around the room, stopping to kick the footboard of the bed. "I want to scream! Or hit something! Or break something!"

———

CARL GRABBED HER ARM, keeping his grip firm but gentle enough not to hurt her. "I don't think your mother will appreciate you breaking anything."

Kayla turned to look at him, her eyes filled with tears. The raw vulnerability staggered him, forcing his protective nature to the surface. She looked so lost, and he was helpless to resist her. He pulled her into his arms and kissed her hair. She clung to him tightly, burying her face in his chest. "I don't want to lose you, Carl."

"I know." And he did. He didn't understand what was between her and Alec, but there was no doubt in his mind about what he shared with her.

Kayla looked up at him, her cheeks flushed, and her lower

lip quivered. He wiped one errant tear away, wishing he could wipe away all her hurt so easily. He bent down and kissed her, tasting the salt of her tears mixed with the natural sweet and spicy taste that was all Kayla. She deepened the kiss, her fingers trembling as she tugged at his shirt with an almost desperate urgency.

Helping her along, Carl removed his shirt and tossed it aside. His willingness seemed to embolden her, and she pushed him toward the bed. He took a step back, bumping against the footboard, and landed on the soft mattress. With a single-minded determination, Kayla climbed on top of him, straddling him as she pulled her dress over her head. She shook out her hair, and he felt the blood from his head rush south at her impassioned boldness.

She reached for his belt buckle, and he inhaled sharply when her clever fingers yanked it off him. Aware she wasn't feeling particularly patient and at this point—neither was he —he shifted her, tumbling her back onto the bed. He unhooked his pants, pulling them off and then crawled upward over her lithe body. Entangling his hands in her hair, he devoured her mouth. His tongue slipped inside her willing lips, mating with hers in a fervent dance.

"I need you, Carl. I can't wait."

Kayla's desperate plea touched him, and he reached down, finding her hot and ready for him. With a groan, he slid inside her welcoming heat. She trembled at his invasion and clung to him, wrapping her legs around him and urging him to move faster. His pace was relentless, and she whimpered, her nails scoring down his back, begging him not to stop. When she finally cried out, shuddering in release, he exploded inside her.

Carl collapsed on top of Kayla, struggling to catch his breath. Aware he was probably crushing her, he shifted his weight. She made a small noise of discontent at his movement, and her arms tightened around him. He smiled at her reluctance to release him.

Her dark hair was splayed out on the pillow and her eyes were closed. He lightly ran a finger over her lips and then brushed his mouth against hers. She opened her eyes and looked at him tenderly.

"I'm going back with you when you go," she whispered.

Carl just looked at her for a moment, letting her words register. He rolled over to stare up at the ceiling, trying to decide how best to respond. Kayla propped herself up on one arm to look down at him.

She lightly traced her finger over his chest. "I thought you'd be happy. Don't you want me to go back with you?"

Alec's words echoed in his mind, and he knew there would likely be consequences for what he was about to say. He had already come close to losing her once today, and he wasn't willing to do it again without a fight. Carl felt a slight twinge of guilt as he said, "Kayla, I'm crazy about you. Of course I want you to come back with me, but I also know this is temporary. Alec made that clear to me. He told me yesterday that you 'belong' to him and you've always 'belonged' to him. What you told me a little while ago reinforced that."

His words had the desired effect. She sat up, her eyes narrowing. He could almost see the heat of her emotions as her temper flared. "He told you I 'belong' to him? Screw that. I don't belong to anyone. I'm not going to have my life controlled. If I want to be with you, I'm going to be with you. It doesn't have to be temporary unless we make that decision."

Carl watched her throw her legs off the side of the bed. She stood and snatched her clothes off the floor. He raised an eyebrow as she dressed, her movements clipped and abrupt. "I'm going back with you and that's final. I don't give a rat's ass what anyone else says about it either. My home is on the surface and that's where I belong."

Carl bit back a smile. He knew he was riling her up even more, but he couldn't resist. "You're incredibly beautiful when you're angry."

Kayla scowled at him, her lips turning downward into an adorable pout. "I'm not angry. I'm freaking pissed off. I'm sick and tired of everyone trying to control me. To hell with them!"

She turned and stormed out of the room. With a curse, Carl scrambled to locate his discarded clothing so he could go after her. It looked like he'd pushed her a little too far.

———

ALEC LOOKED up to see Kayla emerge from her bedroom. He didn't miss her mussed hair or disheveled appearance. He felt a rush of anger at the thought of a simple trader touching what was *his*, but he kept his face an expressionless mask.

Kayla's gaze locked on him. Her shoulders straightened, and her fists clenched as she marched toward him like a soldier prepared for battle. He could feel the fury rippling off her in waves. Before he had a chance to wonder at the cause, she swung her fist at him. His eyes widened, but he caught her hand before she could make contact.

"Damned mind reader." She jerked her hand away from him and hissed, "I don't belong to you. Just because we may have shared energy and there's some sort of bond between us doesn't mean I belong to you. How *dare* you say that."

Alec looked into her furious green eyes and reached for her hand, wanting to soothe her. She pulled away, denying both him and their connection. "Forget it. Don't you dare put your hands on me."

Carl entered the room, and although he hid it well, there

was a smugness in his demeanor. Alec glared at him, wanting to punish him for his insolence, but his hands were tied unless he wanted to further alienate Kayla. "I'm assuming you're responsible for this?"

Carl didn't reply.

"Carl's not responsible for anything," Kayla retorted and poked her finger against his chest. "I want to know who the hell gave you the right to say I belong to you. I'll be damned if I 'belong' to anyone."

Alec looked down at her, gauging her emotions and deciding how best to proceed. He wasn't used to dealing with enraged females. Most women in the Inner Circle would simply treat him with cool disdain if he ruffled their feathers.

Sensing arguing with her would only inflame her further, he lowered his head and held up his hands in a contrite gesture. "You're right. It was a poor choice of words."

Kayla's eyes narrowed, but she wasn't pacified. "I'm going back to the surface with Carl tomorrow. Whatever happens with this whole connection thing happens, but I'm going to live my life the way I want to live it." She crossed her arms over her chest, as though daring him to countermand her declaration.

Alec schooled his features, ignoring the sharp pain in his gut at the thought of her leaving. He'd thought they'd come to an understanding, and she'd even seemed receptive to exploring their bond. He reached below the surface to read her emotions and what he found surprised him. Behind her false bravado and anger, she was terrified.

He pulled back, not wanting to upset or push her further away. She needed time, and that was one thing he could give her. "If that's truly what you want, I won't try to stop you, Kayla."

"Good, because I'd kick your ass if you tried." She spun on

362 • JAMIE A. WATERS

her heels and headed back toward her room. The door slammed behind her, and Seara stood in concern.

Veridian gave an apologetic shake of his head. "Give her a few minutes. She'll calm down soon enough."

Alec gave Carl a harsh look. It took all of his restraint not to lash out at Kayla's lover. "I'd like to speak with you privately."

"I bet," Carl replied and followed him to the safe room. When the door closed behind them, Alec turned to Carl. He decided not to mince words. "So you decided to play on Kayla's emotions to get her to do what you want?"

Carl folded his arms over his chest and returned his gaze evenly. "I happened to mention your comment from yesterday. That's all."

Alec was quiet for a moment. "Kayla and I are bonded. That bond cannot be broken or altered. Because of that connection, I know she loves you. I also know if I were to raise a hand against you in any way right now, she would resist me and our bond even more."

At Carl's silence, Alec continued, "Since this is what she believes she wants, go ahead and take her with you tomorrow when you leave. But I want you to keep in mind that the day will come when she returns to me. There isn't anything you can do to stop that. When that happens, I promise you I won't forget your indiscretion, Trader Carl Grayson."

Carl's eyes hardened, and Alec knew this wasn't a man who would easily relinquish his hold on her. He felt a modicum of respect for his determination, but Carl's next words left him feeling cold.

"Then I'll face whatever comes. I don't know what's going to happen tomorrow or the next day, but as long as Kayla's with me, I'll gladly meet it head-on."

Without waiting for Alec to reply, Carl turned and left the room.

ACKNOWLEDGMENTS

I've heard that writing can be a solitary pastime, but I've found that to be largely untrue. There are so many people who have helped make this book and series possible. It's impossible to list all of you individually, but I want you to know that each of you have my heartfelt gratitude.

The love and support of my family has been invaluable. Thank you so much for your encouragement and for kicking me in the butt when I needed it. I'd especially like to thank Scherry and Tracy for reading all the different versions of this series and offering their suggestions. I can't believe you both put up with my countless phone calls and emails asking you to look at "just one more thing." You guys have been my cheering squad and my reality check, and I couldn't have done this without you. Thank you from the bottom of my heart.

I'd also like to thank my son and his band of merry men for all the helpful comments on speculative weaponry, military/police procedures and/or terminology, negotiation tactics, torture (ewww), and critiquing all the artwork I threw at them. If I ever needed to ask someone questions about ammunition or weapon casings at 2am, I knew I could count on you. I'm a little disturbed by some of your knowledge and depravity, but I've come to realize this is why text-only browsers were invented. I'm sorry for subjecting you to the ding-dong music over and over again, but I still won't get on the headset. :P

A very special thank you goes to Andrea for holding my hand through one of the darkest periods of my life. Your understanding, compassion, and strength inspired me in so many ways. You're the ultimate badass! Thank you for sharing your knife-throwing and martial arts experiences with me and for all the wonderful discussions—especially when I was tripping over plot bunnies and evil villains left and right. (By the way, your card made me cry. Thank you.)

Thank you to Adam, who read various raw and unedited versions of this series. You helped give me a different perspective, and your suggestions made these books and the characters stronger. I'd also like to thank Greta for her patience and assistance with the translations. You went above and beyond in reviewing the various scenes to try to understand the relationships between characters and my intentions. Any errors on this part are solely mine for not explaining things well enough.

The entire group of amazing ladies at Sigma Omega in the Florida Keys deserve their very own thank you, especially Jane. I loved meeting all of you and talking about books all night. Jane, thank you so much for your suggestions and for your remarkable patience. I hope I was able to redeem myself since I'm not leaving you hanging anymore!

I can't express enough gratitude to the amazing and talented editors over at Team Beyond DEF. Tiffany and Cristina, you have helped me grow so much as a writer. Thank you for all your wonderful advice and feedback. You're fantastic!

Thank you also to the incredibly talented cover designers over at Deranged Doctor Designs. You've all been so accommodating and helpful with bringing these books and characters to life. From the covers to the promo materials... you guys are amazing. I can't wait to see what you come up with next!

Thank you to all my other amazing alpha and beta readers who read various incarnations of this book and/or series. Your comments, suggestions, and feedback have been tremendously helpful.

And finally, a very special and heartfelt thank you needs to go out to all my amazing readers. I've met so many amazing people who have reached out to me via Facebook or through my website. I love hearing from you! You've been my inspiration and motivation in so many ways. You rock!

ABOUT THE AUTHOR

Jamie A. Waters is an award-winning science fiction and paranormal romance author. Her first novel, Beneath the Fallen City (previously titled as The Two Towers), was a winner of the Readers' Favorite Award in Science-Fiction Romance and the CIPA EVVY Award in Science-Fiction.

Jamie currently resides in Florida with her two neurotic dogs who enjoy stealing socks and chasing lizards. When she's not pursuing her passion of writing, she's usually trying to learn new and interesting random things (like how to pick locks or use the self-cleaning feature of the oven without setting off the fire alarm). In her downtime, she enjoys reading, playing computer games, painting, or acting as a referee between the dragons and fairies currently at war inside her closet.

You can learn more by visiting: www.jamieawaters.com

DEC 0 5 2019

CPSIA information can be obtained
at www.ICGtesting.com
Printed in the USA
LVHW021708260819
628958LV00002B/90/P

9 780999 664704